MINDING
BEN

MINDING
BEN

Victoria Brown

voice

Hyperion • *New York*

Excerpt from PISH, POSH SAID HIERONYMOUS BOSCH, copyright © 1991 by Nancy Willard, reprinted by permission of Houghton Mifflin Harcourt Publishing Company.

Library of Congress Cataloging-in-Publication Data

Brown, Victoria (Victoria Grace)
    Minding Ben / Victoria Brown.
        p.   cm.
    ISBN 978-1-4013-4151-0
    1. West Indians—United States—Fiction.
    2. Babysitting—Fiction.   I. Title.
    PS3602.R724M56 2010
    813'.6—dc22

                        2010018569

Hyperion books are available for special promotions, premiums, or corporate training. For details contact the HarperCollins Special Markets Department in the New York office at 212-207-7528, fax 212-207-7222, or email spsales@ harpercollins.com.

Design by Nicola Ferguson

FIRST EDITION

10 9 8 7 6 5 4 3 2 1

SUSTAINABLE FORESTRY INITIATIVE — Certified Fiber Sourcing — www.sfiprogram.org

THIS LABEL APPLIES TO TEXT STOCK

We try to produce the most beautiful books possible, and we are also extremely concerned about the impact of our manufacturing process on the forests of the world and the environment as a whole. Accordingly, we've made sure that all of the paper we use has been certified as coming from forests that are managed, to ensure the protection of the people and wildlife dependent upon them.

For my mother, Agatha Ule Brown, who let me go.

And in memory of Carolyn Helen Brown, and Daddy.

MINDING
BEN

Prologue

T he whole thing, from start to finish, from first talk to walk off the plane, took about ten weeks total. That was it. Ten weeks and I went from a small village on a small island to the middle of New York City. Well, to Brooklyn, but still, can you imagine?

On the morning I left, my mother came into the room I shared with my sister, Helen, and placed her hand on my shoulder. I didn't move, I just lay there feeling her cold fingers through the thin fabric of my nightie, thinking how this would be the last time my mother would come into my room and wake me with her touch.

Helen sat up in bed next to me. "Wake up, Grace," she said. "Time to go America."

I rolled over. "What time it is, Mammy?"

"What you asking what time it is for? If I come to wake you up, then it must be time, right? Come on, quick." She left the room, and I understood that, even on this morning of so many lasts, much would remain as it had always been.

Helen fell back against her pillow and cracked up. "You and your mother, boy."

I hugged her tight around her fatty waist. "Don't laugh too hard. I'm about to get on a plane and go." And so I was.

The wooden floorboards creaked in each familiar spot, and I could hear Daddy snoring in the front room. His watch on the dining table said one-thirty. My mother waited in the kitchen for me, her back against the counter. "The water in the blue bucket on the back steps already," she told me. I went outside and looked around. Buttery yellow moonlight lit the night, and everything was at once familiar and strange. I could see the sheeny outlines of trees I had climbed forever, the rose mango and the big guava on the hill with our old tire swing, the long trunks of coconuts and papayas. The back wall of the Baptist church on the hill, flat and triangular, and the big white cross that shone against the bright, dark night. Our garden spread off into the distance and then disappeared at the tree line marking the end of our property. My world for sixteen years.

I stepped down the uneven stairs to the bucket, glad my mother had at least decided I could bathe here. The backyard bathroom was bound to have at least two sleeping cane toads at this hour. I threw my towel over the half door and hung my nightie on one of the nails pounded into the wall.

"Wait," my mother said.

I covered myself. "What?"

She came to stand on the narrow step next to me and reached into the bucket.

"What are you doing?" I asked, stepping away. "I can bathe myself."

"Come back here." She was mashing something in the calabash dipper. I looked and saw wild licorice, lemon slices, whole green limes, and yellow stinking suzies. A bush bath.

"No way," I said, "uh-uh." I was not going to America smelling like the bush I had come from.

"Gracie, come here. Time wasting," my mother told me. She continued to mash around in the calabash.

"You must be joking. I'm not bathing in that, and I'm not letting you bathe me, Mammy. You know what?" I moved up another step. "I'm clean. Let Helen use it in the morning."

My mother sighed the sigh of martyrs, stretched one hand over the bucket and the other out stop-sign in my direction. She closed her eyes and began to pray. Helen swung back and forth on the squeaky half door and grinned. I flashed her a breast. "Rub your body hard with all the bush," my mother said when she had finished her prayers. "Your arms and legs, use the lemon on your face. Everywhere." She pantomimed a vague distance from her privates. "You hear me?"

She and Helen left me alone, under my banner of silver stars. I scooped out every leaf, every piece of lemon and lime, and every last stinking suzie petal I could find. With a washcloth I scrubbed my face, under my arms, and between my legs. Then, as I always did after bathing, I hand-washed my panties and hung them up to dry in the morning sun I wouldn't see.

We were dressed and ready to go by 2:15. My suitcase of unsuitable clothes was packed and by the front door. My flight was at 6:30, and it would take little more than an hour to get to Piarco, but my mother, quoting the parable of the ten virgins, insisted Mr. Herman leave with plenty time to spare.

By now my father had awakened and come out to sit on the couch. To ford the short distance from bedroom to living room, he had hopped awkwardly, holding on first to the bed's headboard, then the doorjamb, and finally the back of the couch before lowering himself, breathing hard, onto the tattered cushion. Helen perched on the edge of a dining chair, and my mother stood next to the door glancing through the curtain. I sat next to Daddy. This was the last time we were all going to be together for I didn't know how long. Soon, we heard Mr. Herman's quick footsteps, then his little knock knock on the gate. "All right, girl," he called and then clapped. "You looking ready to go in the cold."

I tugged on the neck of my uncomfortable sweater. "Mornin', Crane," he said to my father and reached for my suitcase.

"Watch you back, Herman. It heavy heavy."

Herman bent his knees deep, minding what my father said.

Then Daddy said to my mother, "Why you don't move from by the door and give the man some room? Watch the door there, Herman."

My mother pursed her lips and stepped out into the gallery. She stuck her head back through the curtains. "You coming or you staying?"

Hel got up and fake clouted my father's head as her good-bye. He and I were left alone. "Well, Daddy, I gone."

He pulled out a nip of *babash* from the side of the couch. "Here, take a drink with me before you go."

"Crane—" My mother would give him silent hell for the rest of the day if she saw this, but I took a quick swallow of the bush rum and passed it back to him.

He drank and tucked the small bottle away. "When you see you reach America and you sleep and wake up in the morning, don't wash your face with cold cold water, you hear me?"

"Yes," I said, as if this was the most important piece of advice I had ever been given. Mr. Herman's horn honked, and I jumped. "Go, go," my father said, "before she come back to get you." I laughed, and he laughed a little too. "You still have the parcel I give you yesterday?"

I patted the purse on my lap. Inside, wrapped in newspaper and then a piece of cellophane, was a pinch of dirt from our backyard.

"Good. Don't forget to do with it like I say."

"I won't forget."

The horn tooted again, and I got up, sure it was my mother who had told Mr. Herman to honk for me.

"You coming down?" I asked.

He nodded. "Go and bring the crutch for me."

I gave them to him, noticing that the padding meant to cushion his armpits was torn. "That comfortable, Daddy?"

"You mother taking them by Radix later today," he said, and I helped him up to standing. "You go. I coming."

I went out to the gallery, and my mother, sitting up front with Mr. Herman, beckoned me down. I ignored her and waited for Daddy. "Go down, go down," he said when he had cleared the curtains. "I coming." I ran down the steps and stopped at the bottom. Moonlight or not, my father couldn't come down in the dark. He could barely make it down during the day. Taking the steps two by two, I ran back up and hugged his still skinny belly. Since the big operation last year, his massive body had withered. His nickname was now more suited to the lanky water bird than to the heavy lifting equipment he used to be. "Okay, Crane. I gone, okay."

I felt his ribs expand and, without giving him a chance to say anything, ran down the steps and into the car. From the front my mother said without turning around, "I say like you did change your mind." And when I said, "Actually . . . ," Helen rammed me so hard in the side that I couldn't say anything else for a while.

Hel fell asleep against me before the junction marking the end of our village. I realized that I had dozed off too when the car jerked hard and Mr. Herman shouted "Whoa!" He pulled off to the side, and we all got out. My mother looked up to the sky: "But Lord Jesus father what kind of sign is this?"

I walked to the back, seeing the flattened tire and the greedy edge of the pothole even in the darkness. "You don't worry about a thing, girl. Ten minutes and we gone," Mr. Herman assured me. He got to work, and I went to stand with Hel. There was no one to help and no one to call. In the milky moonlight, Morne Diable was deserted. The few who worked outside the village would be in the deepest sleep until the four o'clock cock crowed. We were stranded at the edge of the world.

Mr. Herman's ten-minute estimate stretched to forty-five. I thought that my father would be done by now, and then I felt ungrateful. My mother hummed tuneless hymns that reached under my skin and to my fingertips. I wished we were little girls still and could play clapping games to drown her out. I hugged Hel when Mr. Herman said we were on our way, and she laughed and hugged me back. Soft enough so that my mother wouldn't hear, she whispered, "You going America today even if I have to fly you on my back."

IT WAS JUST OVER two months ago that my aunt in the Virgin Islands had included her telephone number in one of her infrequent letters to my father. The next week Hel and I had walked a mile down the Quarry Road to the lady on the hill and rung. My aunt's voice sounded just like my father's, and she told us to call collect the next time. Hel and I called the next week and the week after that. Pretty soon we were talking every Friday about what a great idea it would be for me to go to America to live with her oldest daughter.

My mother was not pleased with this communication. When I told her that I could not remember who first brought up the idea, she pursed her lips, unsure of whom to blame. She didn't put it past me to have told my aunt that I was miserable, that I wanted a big life and not a small island. Or it very well could have been meddlesome Velma trying to get my mother's children away from her. But my mother couldn't bring herself to actually talk to my aunt, and Daddy couldn't make it up the grassy hill on crutches. So, Aunt Velma and I came up with a plan for me to move to Brooklyn to live with her daughter and her six-year-old son. I'd go to high school during the day, and, instead of her daughter having to hire a sitter to watch her son in the evenings, I'd take care of him. She'd sponsor me to get my papers. It was a good plan.

I woke up to the sound of the trunk slamming shut. Helen peeled away from my torso, leaving a dark, wet stain on my sweater. Full of sleep, she asked, "We reach?"

I looked out the window, past the brightly lit car park, past the buildings' low, peaked roofs, and saw the painted tails of all the planes lined up ready to go. "We reach."

As soon as we walked through doors that slid open automatically, we heard over the PA system, "Passenger Grace Caton, please report to the check-in counter immediately. Passenger Grace Caton to check-in."

Mr. Herman looked at his watch, and I looked around for a clock. It was quarter past five, later than I'd thought we'd arrive but still with plenty time before I had to leave. My mother said, "But what is this?" and quickened her steps as we all did, heading over to the row of attendants waiting under the Pan Am sign. She stepped up to a lady with overblushed cheeks and a purple-smeared mouth. I stepped alongside her. "I'm Grace Caton."

"Your flight's already boarding, Miss Caton," she told me, and I wondered if she didn't feel clammy wearing all that makeup so early in the morning.

"But my flight not supposed to leave until six-thirty."

My mother didn't like this kind of boldness from me, but the attendant agreed. "Yes, but everyone's already checked in, and the captain can get an earlier push-off."

"But this is real stupidness, in truth," Mr. Herman said. "A time is a time." My mother looked around in her bag for my passport and ticket. When the attendant asked how many bags I was checking and my mother said one, I said, "Mammy, please," and she stepped back half a pace from the counter. I got my boarding pass, and we all rushed to the gate. "You see, is a good thing I say to come so early," my mother said. "The Lord works in mysterious ways."

She and I had never been big huggers and kissers, and now, when I needed to go quickly, it was Mr. Herman who came forward to squeeze me farewell. Standing a foot away from my mother, I said, "Bye, Mammy," and to Helen, "Your turn next."

Mr. Herman looked from me to my mother with disbelief. "Girl, you crazy or what?" he said. "Come over here and give your mammy a hug up." I stepped back, hugging Helen first, feeling her so familiar and warm. We had shared a bed since she was born. And then I hugged my mother, towering over her wrapped head and feeling her body, bony just like my own, beneath her light cotton dress. She didn't hug me back, only stood still to receive my affection. Then I let her go and walked through the gate.

I WAS ON AN aeroplane! I was on an aeroplane!

And since no one sat next to me, I bounced up and down, and opened and closed the window shade and lowered the food tray, and checked to see how far back the seat could recline, and pressed on and off the overhead light, and turned a ridged knob and felt a stream of cold air blast my forehead. We left exactly at 6:00 A.M., and as the plane rose, shuddering and pinging before whirling away, I was scared breathless remembering the news of that other Pan Am flight from a year ago. Beyond the patches of thick greenery and brown fields, I saw the island's curves and contours, familiar only from geography class maps, and the land's sudden drop into the lapping gray sea. Off on the horizon, a cap of blazing sun was beginning to spread sparkling light on what was no doubt going to be one more hot, dry day in Trinidad.

We stopped in Barbados and Jamaica for passengers who had come from the small islands scattered across the Caribbean Sea. They came aboard already wearing the woolen coats they wouldn't need for hours yet and sat still, looking serious and straight ahead. In Jamaica an old woman with heavy gold earrings in stretched-out lobes stood for a long time before taking the seat next to mine. She kept her straw bag on her shoulder and fumbled with the seat belt. Without her asking, I clicked the buckle around her waist. Then, we took off for good. The crew served white-bread triangle sandwiches with pink finger sausages that tasted like Christmas morning. The old woman refused everything and instead pulled out a brown bag from her purse and ate what smelled like a saltfish sandwich. After a half an hour she leaned over and said something I couldn't make out. "What?" I asked her.

"Mih wan pas whatah," she said again, and I understood.

"The toilet's in the back." She glanced over her shoulder but didn't move. Half an hour later she still hadn't gone, and I asked her if she wanted me to get one of the flight attendants. She couldn't answer out loud and, with her lips pinched in, nodded. I pressed the light, and when the flight attendant came, I explained what the woman needed.

The first noticeable shudder came while she was gone. A gasp sounded throughout the cabin. The second shake was harder, almost as if someone had grabbed the plane from the outside. Our cries on the inside were louder too. After a piercing ping, a flight attendant said that the captain had turned on the seat belt sign and that we were to stay in our seats. Another led the old lady back and buckled her in. With every roll and drop of the plane, we screamed, all of us terrified together. The pilot came on and said that this was perfectly normal, but we weren't buying it. The attendants walked the aisles trying to calm us, but we knew better. We were going to fall out of the sky and die. Feeling like a true hypocrite, I said some Our Fathers and threw in some Catholic Hail Marys, and promised God that if I lived I'd consider getting baptized in New York. After about half an hour, it was over. The captain apologized and offered a complimentary rum punch for anyone who needed it. I needed it, and so had my second drink of the morning.

Finally, we arrived in New York. Relieved people met their families, hugged and talked about the cold and how we almost died, and went off, and all I could think was *Oh, my God, I am here. I am presently standing in the United States of America.*

I searched through all the waiting faces and tried to find my cousin, but as far as I could tell she wasn't there yet. I didn't know what she looked like, but I figured she'd have one of those signs with my name on it or something, or that she'd just look like family. People thinned out and I still didn't see her, and after a while, except for a man against the wall in a trench coat, I was the last person standing in arrivals with my suitcase. Another flight came in, and they too left, and it was just me and the man again. By then more than an hour and a half had passed since we landed, and I thought *Okay, she's stuck in traffic, or maybe she had to go to her son's school, and it's a good thing I'm here to help her out.* But another hour later she still hadn't arrived. I waited and waited. She never came.

Chapter 1

Slivers of light slanted past the cracked molding and threw licks of pale, late-winter sunshine on the dingy walls. Tongues of old paint hung like cane trash right before the fields were burnt to chase away vermin. I'd been looking for work for seven weeks straight, and each Tuesday morning I'd been going out earlier and earlier for *The Irish Echo*. I layered up in the room's semidarkness, trying not to trip over balled up diapers, traps of unwashed clothes, and Uncle Bo folded tight in his corner on the floor.

"Grace, is you who there?"

I breathed out breath I didn't realize I was holding in. "Yes, Sylvia, is me."

"But is where you going this hour of the morning?"

"Today is Tuesday, Sylvia. The *Echo* coming out today, remember. I want to see if I can't find anything." All this Sylvia knew.

"Well, go quick." I started to the door. "And bring a pack of More for me when you come back. Menthol." She farted long and low, and her mattress, zipped in plastic, deflated as her bulk resettled to carve a new dent. Throughout the apartment, similar depressions marked the furniture Sylvia liked best: the raffia bottom of her kitchen chair hung loose and broken, like a tropical basketball hoop. Her cushion on the sofa was a trap to the unsuspecting.

I knew Sylvia wouldn't be giving me the $2.50 I spent for her cigarettes. For weeks now, I'd bought her a pack of More menthols every time she caught me going out. Two fifty every time and never once had she paid me back. I was down to my last twenty dollars. I needed money. I needed work.

Only one newsstand in the whole of Crown Heights, the one on President and Nostrand, sold the *Echo*. It was a small stand framed by pornographic magazines and black hair magazines, where jars of lollipops, sour candies, and jelly worms were displayed alongside boxes of wrapping paper, hairpins, and ginseng jelly. Tucked into the seams of the glass case, partially barring the condoms, were photos of smiling, dark-haired boys holding very big guns. Here, every Tuesday morning, the West Indian domestics competed for the nanny paper like marketwomen for fresh fish. I had my very own challenger, a short, thick woman who was usually walking away from the stand just as I got there. The week before last, she'd actually beaten me to the last paper, leaving me with nothing as she swished away in her nylon tracksuit.

I had never been this early before. I wasn't taking any chances.

"The *Echo* and a pack of More, please," I said to the Arab behind the kiosk. Everyone called him Ali. I didn't call him anything. Now, instead of taking my money, he took my hand and held it. "Pritty girl." His rusty mustache drooped around discolored teeth, and he tilted his balding head toward the back. "You come behind. I give you peppir and cigrette free."

I wrenched away, slamming my fingers hard against the counter. "Just give me the cigarettes and my change, okay."

"You no want come behind?" He dropped my change on the counter. "You look for job? I give you job."

I walked away fast, nursing my bruised fingers and holding back tears. I walked past the closed Chinese restaurant, the Korean greengrocer always open for business, the permanently shuttered soul food joint, and the twenty-four-hour "We Buy Gold" shop where Bo bought weed. Far enough away, now, I sat on one of the new benches lining the parkway and watched the morning traffic through hot, salty tears. Cars roared up and down the six-lane highway. People scurried past, heads tucked into turned-up collars and furry hoods, bounding like giant rabbits down the steps of the station. Hasidic men clutched black coats and hurried in the opposite direction, deeper into Crown Heights. All this rushing around me and my life stood still.

I unfolded the paper to scan the help wanted section. I'd almost stopped believing anyone ever got a job from *The Irish Echo*. Week after week I had scrolled up and down these columns, circling the jobs I could apply for. The ones that said "must be legal" I crossed out. The live-out ones, the ones requiring a driver's license, the ability to swim, five years' minimum experience, two years' minimum experience, knowledge of infant CPR, I crossed them all out. My friend Kathy said it was all luck and chance, and that I should put my own ad in the paper, make them call me. So I did:

FULL-TIME BABYSITTER, LIVE IN.
EXCELLENT REFERENCE AVAILABLE.
GRACE: 718-555-7263

Still, just in case it was my turn to be lucky, I scrolled through the "Domestic Help Wanted" section and circled an ad placed by a Mrs. Bruckner.

Passing winter days inside Sylvia's apartment was killing me. It had been over a year since I came to America, over a year since my cousin hadn't picked me up at the airport, and over a year since I got the job with Mora. But that had ended nearly two months ago, and I hadn't worked since. Well, not for money anyway. I didn't know what to do. A van zoomed by, and the huge picture of a gray-bearded face with kind eyes stared at me. MOSHIACH IS ON THE WAY. I wondered who he was and if he could bring me a job.

SYLVIA OPENED THE DOOR before I could touch it. Upright, she was huge. Five feet eleven and maybe three hundred pounds and change. She used to be pretty, but now her high cheekbones fought to stay above the fat crawling up her face. Her perfectly straight, bright white teeth were now her best feature, the only part of her able to withstand her slow corpulence. "So long you gone outside for a papers, Miss Grace, and you now come back." She gave me no chance to respond. "You bring my cigarette?" She stared at me as I handed over the pack, daring me to ask for the two dollars and fifty cents.

Micky, Sylvia's oldest, was waiting for me to do her hair. "You have the comb?" I asked her.

She shook her head. "Mick." I dropped onto the red sofa and pointed to the breakfront. "Did you check in there?" To questions about the location of anything, the answer was always to look in, on, under, or behind the breakfront. It leaned against the wall and held a few decorative plates, loose change, petroleum jelly, ribbons and clips, a half-empty bottle of body lotion, combs, remote controls that didn't work anything, spare ties for Derek's uniform, maxi pads, Vicks, and a stereo system.

Micky got the comb and knelt between my legs, gripping my thighs with her elbows. She was ten and still sucked her fingers.

Sylvia came and stood on the once red carpet, now the color of warm ground beef. "Grace, you not done with that child head yet?"

The extra flesh around her throat strangled her words on their way out. Even if she wanted to speak softly, she could not. "Grace, plait that child hair in two cane rows now for me please." This was not a question, and the *please* was not courtesy. She walked on, and Micky hung her head.

"You want that style, Mick, two cane rows top to bottom?" I asked.

Sylvia shouted at her so much that Micky spoke with a slight stutter whenever her mother was around. "I w-w-want two cane rows please, Grace."

"Two cane rows coming right up, then." I tickled her where her armpits, too moist for a ten-year-old's, tightly clamped my legs.

"Grace? Grace, you see my other shoe?" Derek was seven and wild. He never walked but sprinted across the short spaces inside the apartment and was forever hurting himself, running into walls and people and table edges. Now, wearing one shoe, he hopped in from the hall to the living room.

Micky giggled and clamped her fingers over her mouth. Derek's hair was uncombed, his light yellow shirt untucked, and his blue, checked tie tied in a knot around his neck.

"Derek"—I pointed the comb to the bulging fabric—"who did your tie?"

"Uncle Bo. He tied it sleeping, Grace. Grace, you could tie it again?"

I nodded. "First find your shoe."

"I lookeded . . ." He spun his head around the room.

"Looked."

"I looked for it, Grace, I did. I look under the bed and under the chessadrawers, and it nowhere."

My fingers were buried midway down the length of Micky's cane row, and I tilted my head to the seat. "You look under here?"

He slipped half his skinny body under the scrolled lip of the couch and slithered out with the shoe.

"Sit on the floor and put it on."

"And my tie, Grace?"

"In a second."

We all paused as Sylvia came down the corridor. "Hurry up, hurry up," she said and continued to the bathroom.

"Mammy smelling like pee-pee," Derek whispered, and Micky laughed.

"Don't say that, Derek. That's not very nice."

"Sorry, Grace."

I patted Micky's shoulder with the comb. "Go brush your teeth."

Derek scampered up. I slid the tie under his collar and handed him the two ends.

Over, under, and over again.
Up and straight through.
What a gentleman.

My mother's rhyme, taught to Helen and me to help the decent church-men we would someday marry. Derek said the words with me as I guided his twitchy hands slowly through the motions, but even after almost two months, I did the actual tying.

"You want me to comb your hair?"

He ran a small hand over his head. "I comb my hair already, Grace."

I snapped the comb against my leg.

"Okay," he said, "if you want me to comb it again, I'll comb it again."

I left Derek pulling the snags out of his hair and went back to the bedroom, where Uncle Bo was now unfurled and sprawled X-shaped and snoring. He slept in grimy jeans, his sweater flung over a broken dining chair. Bo breathed heavily. His hairy chest rose and fell with every grinding inhale. The stink of rum and weed hovered around his body, mingling with the general dank of the room. I walked over him and reached for my soap and towel. Little Damien was still on the bed, nestled in the scoop Sylvia had left. As much as Derek was rambunctious, Dame was quiet. Too quiet for an almost three-year-old.

"Dame-Dame," I called, and he smiled up at me. "Stay there, all right,

I'll come back for you." He kept on smiling, and I didn't know whether he understood me or not.

Derek fidgeted, and Micky stood silent in the corridor, ready to go. Sylvia was giving them a once-over.

"Derek, zip up your pants."

"The zip break, Mammy."

Sylvia raised her palms in supplication. "Lord Father Jesus, I begging you to give me patience." Unfastening a jumbo safety pin from her hem, she skewered shut Derek's fly, the pin on the outside and Derek's yellow shirttail visible through the gape in his crotch.

"Grace, give them children a dollar each for me please. I will pay you back later. They have some sale to raise funds. Always raising funds."

I reached into my pocket and peeled away two singles. I had fourteen dollars left.

"All right"—Sylvia shooed after I gave them the money—"go quick and reach before breakfast finish." Out in the hall, Derek must have sped ahead of his sister because I and everybody else in the building heard Sylvia's voice as she shouted for him to come back and hold his sister's hand.

Of course, she beat me to the bathroom. While she ran the water, I cleaned up the flotsam left in the morning's wake, starting from the closet in the corridor and moving down toward the living room. Sylvia used her front closet for broken baby strollers and a barrel bought to send clothes and food to relatives on the island. It never managed to get full. Also crammed in were two nonworking televisions, a vacuum, an old ironing board patterned with chocolate triangles, and a collapsible drying rack. A puddle of shoes for every season flooded the floor.

Perched at the very top of the spectacular mountain was the pair of shiny costume wings I wore to last year's Labor Day carnival. Mora didn't pay me for holidays, so on Labor Day I went to the West Indian Day parade in Brooklyn. Before I left, her daughter Hannah ran to the playroom and came back with her fairy wings. "Here, Grace," she said, slipping the wings over my arms. "You can't go to a carnival without a costume." And because they didn't look ridiculous, I wore them all day long.

The last time I had seen this many West Indians was on the plane ride to America. Trinidadians, Jamaicans, Bajans, Haitians, Guyanese, we were all there. For the first time since leaving home, I ate roti and doubles and curry everything. I couldn't tell who was having more fun, the revelers in costume jumping up behind the ten-foot trucks with twenty-foot speakers or the throngs of spectators eating, drinking, feting, and having a good time. My mother would have had a heart attack.

On a stretch of the parkway just past Nostrand Avenue, people paused to watch a huge woman shake a tree. I stopped too, and there was a woman holding a small boy in one arm and shaking the tree trunk with the other. "You playing monkey," she shouted up to the branches, "just wait till you come down from this tree."

An older boy's face looked down from the dark green leaves. "But Mammy, I couldn't see nothing from the pavement. Everybody taller than me, Mammy."

The woman looked around and passed me the boy she was holding. "Here, take this child for me."

I took the sleepy child and watched as she gave the trunk a violent shake. The kid held on tight and grinned. "Okay, okay, Mammy. I coming." He backed down and jumped the final three or so feet to the ground. His mother swiped the back of his head hard.

"Derek, why it is you trying to make me sin my soul on a day of fun?" She took the baby from my arms. "Thanks, Miss Lady. You see how children nowadays harden."

This was the first time I had ever been called Miss Lady. "What part of Trinidad you from?" I asked her.

"Down south, in Penal."

I looked at her again, trying to see if she resembled anyone I knew. "I'm from Morne Diable."

"You see how the world small. I bet we know plenty same people."

A little girl I hadn't noticed before said, "Miss Lady, I could try on your wings?"

Before I could shrug them off, the woman said, "Micky, what it is I tell you about talking to strangers. Lord help me."

I laughed and put Hannah's wings on the girl's slender shoulders. She twirled and took off after her brother. "Just don't go past Nostrand, you hear me." The woman and I chatted, and we figured out the people we both knew from home, and pretty soon I had told her my whole story about coming to America and my cousin not meeting me at the airport and working in New Jersey and being on my own. And when we were done, she told me her name was Sylvia and gave me her number.

"Here." She passed me her telephone bill. "Tear off the number on the top. Whenever you see you want to come Brooklyn to lime, or if you need a place to stay, give me a call."

I phoned Sylvia in January, and she welcomed me then, laughing when she saw the wings she remembered from Labor Day. Since then, she has repeatedly asked me to throw out the wings. To make space, she says. But I will not.

Now, almost two months later, here I was on hands and knees, reaching under her couch to find whatever else Derek might have misplaced, when Sylvia walked out of the bathroom. She stopped and looked down at me half buried under the couch. I turned and looked at her massive feet, ankles, calves. Then, drawing out too fast, I slammed the back of my head against the base of the stupid sofa.

I rubbed the sore spot, then looked over at Sylvia and froze. She was naked. At least I thought she was naked. She was definitely topless. Her huge breasts weighed down like two freshly slaughtered baby seals, dark noses still wet, that had been flung over her shoulders. A towel, hopelessly small, hung limp in her hand. She had no navel I could see.

"Wait till you make children and see what happen to you," Sylvia said, trying to dry her back with that scrap of towel. "I used to be *maga* too." She held out a breast and stropped the underside dry. "I going to see if my agency don't have any old people for me to mind. Watch Dame till I come back. You going anywhere?"

She knew full well I had noplace to go.

"Where it is you have to go, Grace?" she asked, voice rising, misunderstanding my nod.

"No, Sylvia. Yes, I'll watch him. I have to make calls this morning and wait to see if anybody call for me."

"Just try not to tie up my phone for too long, Miss Grace. I might try and call you from outside."

She walked off to the bedroom, and, still on my haunches, I stared in amazement at the flat, broad canvas, rippled at the edges and slit at the base, that was her back to her low-slung bottom.

AT TEN THE PHONE rang.

"You placed the ad in *The Irish Echo*?"

"Yes, that was me. You looking for a babysitter?"

"How old are you?"

"Twenty-one," I lied.

"How tall are you?"

"Five nine."

"And how much do you weigh?"

"Pardon me?"

"My boy is big," the man said a little breathlessly. "How much do you weigh?"

"About a hundred and twenty-five pounds."

"You're twenty-one, five nine, and a hundred and twenty-five pounds?"

"Yes. How old is your son, sir?"

"And what size are your tits?" he asked, his breath coming faster.

I hung up the phone, not knowing if what had just happened was funny.

WITH BO STILL ASLEEP, and Dame napping, I had some quiet time to make my calls. Ah, the fine balance of calling. First, not too too early to wake them; if you called them around eight, you could expect "Oh, could you please call back later, we're just heading out." Later, the phone was busy. Busy. Busy. Or "Sorry, the answering system is full. Please try your call again later." Sometimes, though, the phone rang and my heart leapt as I tried to compose myself. Usually the phone kept ringing. So I called later. Just not at five or at six. That's when they were coming in, making dinner, eating dinner, cleaning up after dinner. Finally! Finally I got through. "Oh, sorry, the position's been filled already."

"When?" I always wanted to ask. "When between six o'clock this morning and now was the position filled? When did you take calls, set up interviews, interview, call references, debate with your husband the merits of the old sitter versus the younger, the Bajan over the Trinidadian, choose and call back?" How did I miss this every week?

The phone rang again at 11:45.

"Hi," said a high-pitched voice, "may I please speak with Grace?"

"This is she." I tried to match the beat of my voice to hers.

I told her about myself, lying about my age and trying to sound more experienced than I was. In truth, I had mostly played with Mora's children in New Jersey and by the end felt more like their older sister.

"You sound wonderful," she said after I was done reminiscing about building forts and baking cookies and bedtime stories.

"Thank you, Mrs.—"

"Moira," she said, "like your Mora, but with an *i* in the middle. Let me tell you what we're looking for." The job she described sounded easy enough, and although I had never even held a newborn, I didn't think it could be all that hard.

Moira laughed like a little girl. "Silly me, I forgot to tell you the most important thing. We're paying three hundred dollars a week."

I smiled because three hundred dollars was exactly one hundred and thirty-five dollars more than Mora had paid me.

"You're from the Caribbean, Grace?"

"Yes."

"You're so articulate. And you have a green card?"

The End.

Every time.

However they phrased it—"Are you legal?" or "Can you work on the books?" or "So, you're authorized to work, right?" or "And, you have a green card?"—the question was always the end of my interview.

I took a breath. "Actually, no. I don't have my papers yet."

"Do you have a social security number?"

I still wasn't sure what exactly that was. "No."

"Oh, Grace, you sounded so perfect for baby Ezra. But Peter and I are both lawyers, and, ethically, you'd be a conundrum. We have to hire someone on the books. Oh."

I felt the room shrink around me; the walls came in closer, and the old shag of the carpet grew like rainy-season mildew. I wanted more than anything to be back home on the island.

Dame sat on the couch, smiling at the TV. I felt bad making him watch with the sound off.

"Get me a job, Dame. Any job," I said.

Bo came out of the bedroom, scratching his chest with both hands like a silverback gorilla.

He changed the TV from thirteen to eleven.

"Come on, Bo. Dame watching that." I looked at my watch. "Wait ten more minutes, please."

Without looking at Dame or me, he dropped heavily to the floor and rested his bare back against the couch's torn plastic. "Dame tell you he know what going on? I done tell Sylvia he retarded. Anything make him smile." He turned up the volume.

The phone rang again at one. Dame was down for another nap and Bo for the count on the carpet.

"Hello?"

"Hello" came back a faint woman's voice. "Did you place the ad?"

"Yes, I'm Grace."

She giggled. "I need a nanny after work, Gracie."

I didn't understand. "So I work an evening shift then?"

"When I come home at five-thirty, I need you to undress me and give me my bubbly bath and help me into my jammies. I like my curls brushed for a long time and for you to sing to me and then feed me my bottle."

I could not bring myself to end the call.

"Sometimes, like if I've had a really hard day, I might want to breast-feed—"

Horrified, I hung up the phone and laughed so hard I crashed against Sylvia's kitchen table.

"Grace, girl," Bo yelled from his spot on the living room floor. "Stop making so much fucking noise in my head."

BY FOUR DEREK AND Micky were home and Dame was up. "And how was school today?" I asked, rooting around the fridge to find them a snack.

"Fine," they answered together.

"What do you mean by *fine*? Tell me about your day. What'd you do who'd you see what'd you read who'd you play with? Details, please."

Micky grinned. She had twined a pastel strand of sour candies around her wrist and cracked them loudly off the string. Derek got up from the table and went to his bag, coming back full speed with a painting. "Look, Grace, I draw home."

I had to concede, it looked exactly like the island. A turquoise rectangle of seawater in the background, and a bright yellow sun in the clear sky, two tall coconut trees with spiky green fronds, and a little wooden shack with a smoking chimney. I could almost see my father sitting on the front steps.

"Who's that?" I pointed to the three stick figures holding hands in the foreground.

"Me, Micky, and Dame," he answered.

"Micky, Damien, and *me*. So I'm not in your picture? I like home too." And I missed home.

"Derek, I could see your picture?" Micky asked.

"I think we have to put this masterpiece on the fridge for everyone to see. Micky, go in the breakfront and bring the Scotch tape, please. Derek, pick a spot," I said.

After, we lolled about in the living room, not an entirely unpleasant space when Sylvia was not around. I read on the couch. Micky did her homework, screwing up her face with every bite of sour candy. Derek practiced the running man in place. And Dame knelt on the warm radiator box, gazing through the childproofing bars on the window, picking at the flecks of paint and putting the salty scraps in his mouth.

By nine Derek and Micky were in bed. Sylvia snored on the couch as she watched her shows. I was half asleep in the old armchair that Derek told me used to be his father's favorite, going through *The Irish Echo*. I figured I might as well read about New York City's Irish. The Ancient Order of Hibernians was threatening to cancel this year's St. Patrick's Day parade if the homosexuals were allowed to march, the Irish homosexuals were planning a protest march this coming weekend, and the city was stockpiling dye to make the rivers run green. The phone rang. Sylvia twitched to. "Somebody answer that."

I picked up.

"Sorry to be calling this late, but can I speak with Grace?"

"Who is that on the phone?" Sylvia demanded.

"For me, Sylvia." To the woman on the phone I said, "This is Grace."

"You placed the ad in the *Echo*?" She sounded like she had a cold.

"Yes, that was me. Are you looking for a sitter?"

She laughed. "I'm looking for more than that."

"Okay." I couldn't find any enthusiasm. This day had drained me.

"Before I waste your time and mine, I should tell you we can only pay two hundred dollars, and it's nonnegotiable."

It was so much more money than I'd had in a long time. "Where do you live?"

"Near Union Square, in the city."

Two hundred dollars for Manhattan? I'd heard that women working in the city came home with $450 to $500 a week.

"Are you interested?" She sounded wheezy.

"Yes. I'm sorry."

"Good. My name is Mrs. Bruckner. I have a four-year-old son. Well, he's almost four, and we need someone to live in and take care of him full-time, Monday to Friday. Give him his meals, his baths, take him to the park and his activities and playdates. You have to come in on Sunday nights because my husband and I both work. You get off at seven on Fridays. One Friday a month you'll have to work late. You get paid extra for this, of course; five dollars an hour, but no cab fare. If it's too late for you to take the train, you can spend the night and go home on Saturday morning."

She paused.

And then went on.

"And there's housework. I need someone to do laundry and keep the apartment clean. You'll have to mop the floors and keep on top of the dust and do the bathrooms. And we need someone to cook and to clean up after we finish eating. My husband gets in from work late some nights, so you have to make a plate and leave it in the microwave for him. I'd prefer for you to wash up after him before you go to bed. Our son wakes up about eight. You can either get up before he does, take your shower, and be ready for him, or, if you want, you can shower after you put him down for his afternoon nap. There's ironing, mostly my husband's shirts, but sometimes I might want you to iron a shirt or a pair of shorts for me. Does this sound like something you're interested in?"

No.

Sylvia shouted, "Grace, I find you staying too long on my fucking phone you know."

"Yes," I said to Mrs. Bruckner, who either did not or pretended not to hear Sylvia.

"Good. Do you have references? How old are you?"

"Twenty-one, and yes I have a reference. I worked in New Jersey for one year."

"Only one year's experience?"

"It's not a long time, but when you talk to Mora I'm sure she'll have plenty good to say about me."

Mrs. Bruckner interrupted me. "What's your accent?"

"Caribbean."

"Very articulate. And can you read?"

"Yes."

"Can you work on the books?"

I slumped against the wall, careful to avoid the smudged cockroach streaks. "No."

"Well, that's okay. We're looking for someone to be part of the family, someone we can sponsor maybe. So shall we set up an interview?"

"You're willing to do a sponsorship?"

"For the right person. You want to come in for an interview?"

"Yes."

"Okay, good. We're interviewing this Thursday, on Purim. Can you come in at ten?"

"Ten is fine."

She gave me directions and said, "Please be on time. We have a few interviews already set up, and if everyone comes when they're supposed to, we can move along."

"Of course. Thank you for calling."

Sylvia was upright on the couch when I walked back into the living room. "Who was on the phone?"

"A lady from the city," I said with a big grin. "I have an interview Thursday morning."

"Which Thursday? This Thursday here coming?"

"Yeah, day after tomorrow. Ten o'clock."

She pivoted in the seat and pinned me against the breakfront. "So who watching Damien on Thursday morning, Grace? And these children don't have no school on Thursday, to boot. You should of come and ask me if I have anything for you to do on Thursday before you make your interview. That is the proper way to do things." Sylvia looked around the living room and told her furniture, "You see how nigger people ungrateful? That is why the good Lord say you not suppose to take strangers in your house." Turning back to me, she asked, "And what time you think you coming home after this interview?"

I'd only ever been to Manhattan once before. I wanted to take the rest of the day to walk around and see that place. Eastern Parkway from Nostrand to Brooklyn Avenue had become my new world. Sometimes a bus ride with Sylvia and the children to Pitkin Avenue, and, even more rarely, the subway to Conway downtown on Fulton. Whenever I told Sylvia I wanted to see the city, she started muttering about young girls and men, and wanted to know what in the city was calling my name.

I stepped away from the breakfront. "Late," I told her. "The lady living near where Kathy working, and I thought I'd go and see her."

She didn't give in. "So you have to go and see Kathy Thursday?"

The relief from Mrs. Bruckner's call made me bold. "I don't have to, but I'd like to go say hello. We did A-levels together."

"And watch where you is now," Sylvia said, sneering, "going to wipe white people children ass. I bet you didn't think that is what you was going to end up doing when you was writing A-levels. Go ahead and see your friend, Miss Grace. Just make sure and come back in my house before dark for me please. I don't like people going in and out of my house at all hours. I have a girl child to set example for."

"All right," I said. "Leave Dame by Dodo for me to pick up."

"And what about Monday?"

"What about Monday?"

"You don't have nothing plan for Monday?"

Not unless I got a job. "No, I'm here. Somebody coming?" Apart from Bo and Dodo, hardly anyone ever came to the apartment.

"Yeah, the landlord. I finally get him to give me a paint job. Make sure if he ask to tell him you is my cousin from Flatbush come to watch Dame and let him in, you hear?"

"Okay. What is his name?"

"Jacob. One of them Jew man and them with the hat and suit from down the road."

Sylvia—one, two, three—heaved off the couch to take Dame to bed. I sat on the couch, but rose again immediately as a rancid smell steamed up from the upholstery and through the sweaty plastic. I sat on the tatty red carpet with the radiator warm behind my back and my legs stretched out, and tried to think of the better days ahead.

Chapter 2

Sylvia was up early, watching me get ready.

"So what time you say you coming home today, Grace?"

I hadn't said.

"I don't know. I'm meeting Kathy for lunch after the interview."

"So why you can't come home and eat lunch? Look how much turkey wing I cook last night still in the fridge. You have too much money to waste to go and buy them white people food."

I just shrugged.

"Grace, before you start to dress, make a quick bottle for Dame. Look it on the floor."

"You want anything else from the kitchen?" I asked, knowing that, as soon as I returned with the formula, she would think of some reason to send me back. Dame was cuddling in his mother's lap. Derek lay on the top bunk in a restless sleep. Micky was awake, propped up on her pillow watching everything. I brought the bottle in and started to get dressed.

I didn't exactly have interview clothes, just jeans and sweaters and sneakers. Clothes easy to take care of children in. The night before I had laid out a black turtleneck and a pair of nice black pants I'd bought at Conway and never had a chance to wear.

"Makeup?" I asked Sylvia. Cosmetics were a vanity forbidden in my mother's house, but I had come to love the way my eyes looked when I lined them with black pencil.

"Nah, them white people and them funny. They don't like you to wear too much makeup when you taking care of they children. How much years this child have?"

from her hi̇
most ashan
straight teet
SONALLY. Tl
coat.

"Oh, I'm
tiful, long l
I didn't s
coat and he
trils flare, n
I felt asham

The nur
Mrs. Bruck
could not n
park was a
ready filled
pushed sm
ger childre
their muffl
one eye tra
tions and tl

Actuall
tries in a st
still thougl
ners of Nc
down on a
planted in
sentry.

"Good
name is G
The co
down at n
said, "The
in a small-
Pause.
Laugh.

"The mother say three—nearly four."

"Well, maybe you could get away with some eye makeup, but you don't want to go in the people house looking too pretty pretty. Especially you. White woman funny with they husband, yes."

I walked over to my drawer. "Grace, what stupidness you doing?"

"What?" I stopped. "Going for the pencil."

Sylvia laughed. "I could really see you come from the bush, girl. Put on your jersey first, then do your face."

That made sense. Sylvia could be so normal when she wanted to. I pulled the turtleneck over my head and lifted my hair out from behind.

"If is one thing you have, Grace, is nice hair."

"All hair is nice hair, Sylvia."

She pressed her fingertips to her chest to help release a burp. "How all hair is nice hair? You want to tell me picky head is the same thing as long, straight hair?"

"Is not the same thing, but that don't mean straight hair better." Micky lay on the bed listening to every word. She passed her hand over the rumpled cane rows I'd done for her day before yesterday. I looked sideways in the mirror, frowning at the absence of breasts in my profile.

"You is a real ass," Sylvia said. "Before these children spoil my figure, I used to look just like you. I see you want to laugh, but is truth. I was tall and slim, not thin thin like you, but slim-thick with nice big breasts. Now look at me."

I didn't need to look. Sylvia was soft and mushy. She spread out over the mattress like hot lava.

"I'm sure after I have children I'll flesh out too." I didn't want to spoil the good mood Sylvia was in this morning.

When I reached for my pants, she said, "Outside cold, Grace. Put some tights on under them pants."

"Nah, this is wool. I'll be all right."

"Every once in a while I know what I talking about. Is fifteen years now I living in this America. These people apartment could be far from the subway. Then too, today is a holiday. You know how long you might have to wait for a train?" Dame finished his bottle and grinned up at his mother. "Morning, Guy Smiley," she said.

I slipped my pants on when Sylvia turned to Dame. The truth was,

I didn't h
on my bo

"I look
Sylvia
"You l
you, Grac
Sylvia
hearing?
is Grace
I knew
and walk
via, but tl

I GRINN
nanny in
my boots
grin mus
and smil
tokens th
The r
standing
the overl
tions. Zi
gen Stree
morning
I looked
posed to
I cha
woman i
unbuttoi
diamonc
When sl
dust her
me, sitti
paper. Sl

"All right, sir, you just call down when you ready."

To me in a much sterner voice he said, "Go in there and sit down. Me call you when them ready. Grace you did say?"

I nodded.

"You can't talk now?"

My mother's child almost answered him politely, but I stopped her in time. "What did you say to me?"

He laughed. "This one here talk fancy. Just go have a seat through there and wait."

The lobby was grand. Giants could have played checkers on the tiled floor, could have rested on the plump velvet chairs and waltzed to the wordless music padding the still air. Chandeliers, beaded like jewelry, twinkled high above, while mirrored walls reflected everything, even the concierge looking back at me. I watched him watching me, and then the walls opened. I started because I hadn't realized I was standing in front of an elevator. A man stepped out leading a lion of a dog. No, not one . . . two. And the man wore shorts! I was cold in my new pants ($5.99, and they were not wool), but he was in shorts. I must have stared, because he smiled at me. I smiled back.

"What kind of dogs are they?" I asked.

"Chows. This is Brutus, and this bad boy is Cesar. Come on, boys, say hi to the lady with the nice eyes." He pull their lead around. "They're friendly."

I smiled again and, rubbing the springy fur on Cesar or Brutus, glanced back to see if the concierge was looking.

The dog man looked too. "Morning, Duke."

"Morning, sir. You taking them for a morning walk, I see?"

"Yeah, I'm gonna go get a paper."

Duke grinned. "Front desk provide that service, sir."

"Yeah"—he patted his trim waist—"but we need the exercise."

To me he said, "See you around," and left through doors held open by the braided doorman.

A crowd of women waited inside the back room. "Anadder one?" the woman closest to me said. "But 'ow much people so them call for this two-hundred-dollar work?" She was short and fat with a raisin mole under her eye sure to scare small children.

The women talked to each other, their voices bouncing off the walls

like the sounds of a village market turned down low. The one at the entrance was Jamaican. The two younger girls in the corner were from
home, and the women huddled together at the far end of the room
sounded like Sylvia's Haitian super.

One woman I recognized. She wasn't in the nylon tracksuit she wore
to get her *Irish Echo,* but I had no doubt who she was. She had dressed for
the interview like a bank teller, in a navy suit not unlike that of the woman
on the train, and sat reading a newspaper. I stared at her for a long time,
but she never lifted her eyes to meet mine.

The woman on my left leaned in and whispered, "Me don't really want
this job, you know." She looked hot, still zippered in her puffy coat, still
wearing her hat, scarf, and gloves. "Child, you mustn't come outside so in
this New York, you know." She inclined her head to the woman on our
right, who was in a lightweight summer dress, and not wearing tights either. She raised her eyebrows. "People does catch cold and drap dead from
pneumonia in this country, quick quick. Me"—she choked her neck with
one hand—"I don't ever take off my things until you see I reach inside."

I didn't mention that she was inside.

"Me don't really want this job," she repeated. "I like baby-nurse job. To
mind the little one and them just born. Them can't give you no lip. These
white children talk to you like them is man, and the parents don't tell
them no better. Calling you by your first name like them is you company.
I does want to wring they lips good."

I was wondering how long I'd have to wait until my turn when the
doltish concierge came to the door. "Mabel?" He looked over his half
glasses. "Who Mabel?"

Mole woman followed him. Another woman came to the door and
beckoned, "Allay, allay," and both Haitian women left. Feeling relieved
not everyone had come for the interview, I walked to where several dog-
eared magazines sat fanned out on a corner table and picked up an old
issue of *Mademoiselle* with a torn-off address label. The room fell quiet.

"Them didn't put that for we to touch, you know." It was the woman
who didn't really want the job.

I looked at her. "Is just to read." The remaining Jamaican laughed, and
I put the unopened magazine on my lap. The woman to my left nodded
in a satisfied way that reminded me of my mother.

In about seven minutes mole woman was back.

"What"—her friend looked at her watch—"is finish you finish already?"

She looked around, dusted her hands together, and said for all to hear, "She no want no babysitter, sah. Me din leave Jamaica fih be nobody slave in New York." She snorted, and her mole moved. "She coulda pay two thousan' dollar and me still don't want she work."

The concierge came to the door. "Grace?"

Surprised, I looked to see who else was named Grace. No one moved. He looked at me. "Grace?" And realizing he meant me, I got up, leaving the magazine on the couch.

"Is there where you find that?" He pointed to the seat.

"Oh." I turned and quickly moved to put the magazine back on the table. The young girls cackled.

"But they were here first," I said to him once we were out in the lobby. "You sure is my turn?"

He drew himself up. Shoulder to shoulder I was taller, but the top hat gave him an advantage. "What time your interview?"

"Ten."

"And what time it is now?"

I looked at my watch. "Just past ten."

"So what kind of stupid question you ask me?"

Then I got his accent. He sounded like the cabbie who drove me from the airport on my first day in America. Bajan.

Chapter 3

I counted the lit numbers up to twenty-two, checking to make sure there truly was no thirteenth floor. I still hadn't got accustomed to the idea of living in an apartment. How could you live without a yard to step out in any time you wanted? Without trees and dirt? At 22B, I took a breath and rang the bell.

A tall man opened the door. Tall and lean with green eyes, curly orangy brown hair, and a nice smile.

"You're Grace?" One orange eyebrow arched to an upside-down vee. His voice sounded like a Muppet's, coming from the very back of his throat.

Willing myself calm, I smiled back. "Yes."

"I'm Mr. Bruckner . . . Solomon." He stuck out his hand. "Come on in, Grace."

I stepped in and, dazzled by sunlight from the wall of windows, tripped into him.

"Are you all right?" He put a hand on my back.

"Fine, I'm fine. The light made me blind."

"Yeah, it's bright in here. Stand for a sec." He was still holding me.

I stepped out of his touch. "No, no, I'm good." My eyes adjusted, and I did a quick look around. A rug ran the length of the corridor, leading into a sunlit living room. It was a neat and cheery space, but the cushions on the couch were messy, as if someone had slept there. A dining table with four chairs was pushed against the wall under a sunflower clock, and a television, much bigger than Sylvia's, sat in an open cupboard with a VCR, a stereo system, and a cable box. Next to the TV was a set of shelves filled with glass and ceramic barnyard animals: scratching hens and puffed-up cocks cast midcrow, fat sows with suckling piglets, grazing cows and sheep, a horse with a cart. Someone had arranged clusters—still life on a busy farm. Take away the horse, jumble the livestock, and this could be my yard back home.

"Can I get you a drink?" Mr. Bruckner asked. "Some coffee?"

Coffee was the last thing I needed, but still I asked for a cup. It seemed like something I should do. "Yeah?" He seemed surprised. "How do you take it?"

"Milk and no sugar, please." He went off, and I looked around some more. I expected chandeliers like in the lobby, but the ceiling was bare and nubby, a texture that made my forearms itch.

"Grace, you're still standing?" Mr. Bruckner had returned with a big mug that said HUSBAND #1. "Take off your coat. Please, sit. Anywhere." He gestured around the room with the mug.

I sat in an easy chair and sank like Goldilocks into Mama Bear's soft cushions. "Whoops!" I said, struggling out of the folds and feeling like an idiot. "Anywhere but that one, right?" Mr. Bruckner laughed, and when he handed me the mug, I realized that I'd got the caption wrong and it actually read #1 HUSBAND.

"Miriam's coming out with Ben. In the middle of all this, we're getting ready for shul. Coffee okay?"

"It's fine, thanks." Somewhere between asking and telling I said, "You're interviewing a lot of women."

Mr. Bruckner sighed. "Tell me about it. Miriam wanted a range. Duke's rung up every fifteen minutes since eight-forty-five. I think we have more coming on Saturday."

That didn't please me at all, and I held the warm mug close to my lips without sipping. Down the hall I heard voices, a woman and a giggling child.

Mr. Bruckner crossed his legs and flashed his patterned socks. "Dreidels," I said, trying to flaunt what I had learned at Mora's. I didn't mention that dreidel season was long past. He twisted his ankle to look, but, before he answered, his wife and child came in. Wrapped and tied tight in a fluffy white robe, Mrs. Bruckner's body waged war between thick and slender. Blond with shoulder-length hair and eyelash-grazing bangs, she had the narrowest nose I had ever seen, dark brown eyes, and her face glistened. She was short, but the high heels of her pointy red shoes threw her forward and up. Hel and I called those kick-and-stab, and they were forbidden in our house.

I stood, but Mrs. Bruckner waved me down. "You can sit." In person she sounded even more stuffed up. She turned to her husband. "Sol, finish Ben up in a bit?" To me she said, "It's Purim, so we're going to shul."

Mr. Bruckner reached for the boy. He had freckles dotting his nose and his father's ginger hair. "Hey, buddy, this is Grace. Say hi to Grace."

"Hi to Grace." He hid his face but peeked at me from between spread fingers.

"So you're Grace," Mrs. Bruckner said. "You're not at all what I was expecting."

I wondered what she'd expected that I wasn't. "Yes, Mrs. Bruckner," I answered. "I'm Grace." I smiled, as if my name could give me an advantage.

"Okay," Mrs. Bruckner said, "so I'm Mrs. Bruckner, this is Ben, and you've already met Mr. Bruckner." Her thin lips parted only slightly when she spoke. "Before we start, I should tell you again we're paying two hundred dollars. After a year there's a twenty-five-dollar raise. You're okay with that?"

"Yes."

She leaned in, and I saw that she had applied a cosmetic masque to her face. It had begun to dry into tiny gills at the corners of her mouth. I wanted to ask her if she was comfortable, but instead I sat with my hands folded in my lap, waiting to hear her out. Ben knelt, squeezing his father's cheeks between his chubby fingers and kissing the pouty lips he made.

"This is a very demanding job," Mrs. Bruckner went on, and the masque around her lips whitened on *demanding*. "I'll go over what we're looking for." She read the list of duties from two handwritten sheets and included some she'd left out before. "Anything I'm forgetting, Sol?"

"I think you covered it, Mir."

"It's a lot of work, but you've got to factor in what free room and board in this city is worth." She lifted one shoulder and turned her head to the side. "On the phone you said you could read?"

"Yes, I can read."

"Hold on." She clicked off down the corridor.

"Hey, Ben"—I faced him and his father—"how old are you?"

"Three years old." He held up four fingers and slid down his father's legs. He reached for my hand, bent my thumb and forefinger, and said, "Three."

"You're good with numbers. Do you go to school?"

"When I'm four years old I get to go on the school bus."

Solomon started singing "The Wheels on the Bus." Ben balled his fists and made rollover motions. "Sing, Grace, sing."

Surprised he remembered my name, and knowing my rendition of "The Wheels on the Bus" could get me the job, I sang along, feeling foolish. Mrs. Bruckner came in on "All over the town."

"The last nanny said she could read"—she shook her head—"so don't think this has anything to do with you personally." She passed me a children's storybook. "This is one of Ben's favorites. Start from the title."

"*Pish, Posh, Said Hieronymus Bosch,* by Nancy Willard."

Ben laughed and said, "Pish, posh," in an English accent. I smiled and, trembling slightly, read, "Once upon a time there was an artist named Hieronymus Bosch who loved odd creatures. Not a day passed that the good woman who looked after his house didn't find a new creature lurking in a corner or sleeping in a cupboard. To her fell the job of feeding them"—Ben recited along with me—"weeding them, walking them, stalking them, calming them, combing them, scrubbing and tucking in all of them—until one day—"

"Uh-oh, she's gonna get mad," said Ben.

Mrs. Bruckner was nodding, Mr. Bruckner smiling, and Ben, bless his heart, said, "More, more. Read more, Grace."

I read on until Mrs. Bruckner turned to her husband. "Time to finish dressing him, Sol." He scooped Ben in his arms, and the two of them disappeared down the hall, Ben saying, "Pish, posh, pish, posh."

"You're an excellent reader"—she emphasized *excellent*—"but reading is only a small part of this job."

She looked at the sunflower clock. "Hold on," she said and went into the kitchen, where I overheard "Duke? Duke, it's Mrs. Bruckner. How many are still there?

"It's ten-fifteen now," she continued, "if anyone else comes, say the position's been filled." *Yes!* Mrs. Bruckner paused. "Yes, filled." She sounded annoyed, but then she said, "Okay, take the names and phone numbers. Tell the ten-fifteen a few minutes more. Actually, don't tell her anything." There was a click, and she came back into the living room. Her masque had turned opaque white, like the hardened flesh inside a dry coconut. "Here"—she passed me a pen and notebook—"write your name and address."

Mora had done this too, and later confessed it had been to see if I could write. Mrs. Bruckner looked at the page and said, "So, Grace, tell me what you think I need to know about you."

"I'm from Trinidad—"

"Amazing," she interrupted. "You read and speak so well for someone . . . from the islands." Mrs. Bruckner laughed and shook her head. "You know, the last nanny, Carmen, Jamaican, she said she could read, so I never bothered to test her. I just took it for granted she had some kind of education. Well, Sol and I figured something was wrong after we told her to keep a list of, you know, things we needed. Cheese." Mrs. Bruckner snorted. "Ben likes yellow American grilled cheese sandwiches. C-H-I-E-S, that's it. That's how she spelled *cheese*. Can you believe it? Now, everyone reads at the interview."

I half smiled and thought about the older woman downstairs, the one muttering about not really wanting this job. In spite of needing the job myself, I hoped Mrs. Bruckner would give her something other than *Hieronymus Bosch*. "I've been in New York for a year, and I live in Brooklyn—"

"With family?"

It was easier just to agree.

"I called Mora last night, and she gave you a very good reference."

I smiled. "I liked working for Mora."

"I also spoke to the oldest boy." Mrs. Bruckner said, "He's a Ben too."

"You talked to Ben?"

She nodded. "He answered the phone. You learn more talking to children than to parents. But not to worry, Ben gave you a laudatory recommendation. Talkative kid. And they're Jews?"

"Uh-huh, they kept kosher."

She leaned in. "So you know how to keep a kosher house?"

"I know you can't mix meat and dairy, and the silverware. Are you kosher?"

"No, no." She tucked her chin and shook her head briskly. "But Ben's grandparents will like that you know that stuff."

I smiled. *Thank you, Mora.*

Her next question surprised me. "Do you have a boyfriend in Brooklyn?"

"No."

"So there won't be any men coming to visit you during the day?"

"No, Mrs. Bruckner. There's no one to bring."

"Good. Sol!" she called down the hall, "come see if you have anything to tell Grace. I have to wash my face."

Ben ran down the hall. She bent to kiss him, and he reached up both hands to grab her face. She pulled away, shaking her head. "Mama's face is icky."

Mr. Bruckner came and leaned against the side of the couch. "So you want to work for us, Grace?"

More than anything. I wanted to say, Yes, please hire me, please. But the thing to do now was sit calmly and make a good impression, and so I said, "Yes, I'd very much like to work for you."

He gave me the same look as when I'd asked for coffee and asked what Mrs. Bruckner had not. "Any questions you have for us?"

I wanted to know about the illiterate babysitter who couldn't spell *cheese,* and about sponsorship. "Mrs. Bruckner said the last sitter couldn't read. Is that why she doesn't work for you anymore?" My question seemed to surprise him. "One of the reasons," he said more to himself than to me. He leaned his lanky torso toward me. "She took Ben on the subway. We warned her to never take him on the subway, and she did. To run her own errands."

"Ya-ya took me on the choo-choo train, Grace. Choo choo!"

"Mr. Bruckner—"

"Sol."

"Sol, do you know how soon you and Mrs. Bruckner will hire someone?"

"I think very soon."

"And when would work start?"

"Either this coming Monday or the Monday after."

"How many other women are you considering?"

He smiled at me then and jostled Ben a little more. "That, I'm not too sure of, but I get the feeling you're going to be very high on our list. You know, Grace, you remind me a lot of someone I used to know."

He was going to say more, but Mrs. Bruckner came out, still packaged in her robe, though now the masque was gone. Her face was pockmarked on the cheeks and reddish on the sides of her mouth. Crow's-feet fanned out from the corners of her eyes and disappeared under her blond hair.

I held out my hand. "Thank you both very much." She shook my hand, tighter now than before.

I turned to Ben. "Bye-bye, Mr. Pish-posh."

He held a fistful of his father's orange hair and with his other hand waved. "Bye-bye, Miss Pish-posh."

Chapter 4

Kathy laughed when she opened the door. "Are you crazy? You must think you still living on an island. Grace, you not cold?"

"I'm frigging freezing."

"I'll lend you a scarf when you leave." Then, with a grin that showed her wide-spaced, pointed teeth, she asked if I'd come to lime for the rest of the day.

"That was the plan, but Sylvia wants me to pick up Dame from by Dodo."

Kathy shook her head. She was one of those Trinidadians of indeterminate race, a real callaloo. Her *chabine* hair came almost to her waist and in a ponytail looked just like a real pony's tail. She was red-skinned, short, and plump—or as she liked to call herself, slim-thick—and her brown eyes drooped down. Once we'd tried to figure her out. Her father's parents were East Indian and black, making him a *dougla*. Her maternal grandfather had been pure indentured Chinese, and her long dead grandmother was said to be mulatto, half black woman and half Scottish priest. When I first saw a picture of Kathy and her two sisters, I told her that for sure her mother kept secrets from her dad.

Kathy had taken to Jamaicans. She left Trinidad exactly three months before I did and dropped her *h*'s as frequently as she remembered to pronounce them. Not only had she picked up the accent but she had picked up the style. Now she sported a purple sweater and tight blue jeans. Simple enough, but Kathy had only last Saturday gone to the Empire Boulevard post office to pick up her very own BeDazzler. Brooklyn Jamaicans were crazy about the potential for transformation locked away in every bite of the BeDazzler. Three bracelets of rhinestones sparkled on Kath's cuffs, and a line of jewels dotted up each arm. From the shoulders the stones ringed the neck of her sweater in three rows to mimic the cuff effect. Kathy had repeated the triple pattern on the hem of her jeans and had studded up its outer side seams to the front pockets. This dazzling effect was completed with purple, spiny stars on both back pockets and one final oversize rhinestone centered on her back loop. All in all, I estimated about two and a half pounds of gems.

"You look nice," I told her.

"Fuck off."

"No, for real, Kath. You're all a-glitter." We were not in sync about the beauty of the night sky imitated on clothes.

"Why you don't let me BeDazzle your turtleneck?"

"And go home naked?"

"No, stupid. The machine 'ere."

"You brought your BeDazzler to work?"

"It's portable." Kathy got serious. "Grace, why you take all this rubbish from Sylvia. She's not your mother, she's not your aunt, she's not even your frigging cousin. She work *obeah* on you, or what?"

"After everything when I first came here"—I shrugged—"if it wasn't for her, I could be floating in a river or living on the subway. Who knows?"

"*I* know," Kathy said. "I know if not her, you'd 'ave found somewhere else and you wouldn't be so miserable."

"Who says I'm miserable?" I faced her. "I feel sorry for Sylvia—"

"Sorry for she," Kathy interrupted, and the venom in her voice forced her Trinidadian vernacular. "Tell me again why you sorry for she. So much trouble this miserable woman make you see in New York."

I shrugged. "I just do, Kath. Sometimes she sits on that busted kitchen chair—don't laugh—not talking to anyone and, you know, she just looks pitiful. Plus," I went on, "her husband's crazy and locked up in the G Building." Sylvia had run out of dreams. She had her children, cheap rent, and bought groceries with special checks she got every month. "But come on"—I looked around—"I don't want to waste time talking about Sylvia. Check out this place."

This was by far the largest apartment I had ever been in. From the outside, the building looked like a warehouse. Inside, polished wooden planks stretched out like in a dance hall. Rough, bare beams crisscrossed the ceiling, and white columns, thicker than a full-grown teak, broke up the space. Large paintings of nothing I could identify hung on the unfinished brick walls. They looked strangely right in the vast emptiness of the place.

"What do they do, Kathy? How much money do you have to have to get a place like this?"

She pointed to the rough red bricks. "For all the money they have, can't they afford some cement?" Kath put her hands on her waist. "Money don't mean taste, Grace."

"I guess." But I loved this open space. "I'd grow trees in here if this was mine."

"And I'd hire a mason."

Someone was missing. "Where the baby, Kath?"

"Sleeping."

I looked around for a crib or a bassinet. Nothing in this space indicated a child. "Where?"

"Come." I followed her but stopped to stare through a glass wall broken up into big old-fashioned panes. The view was stunning. Off in the cold, clear distance, a river moved slowly. Barges floated motionless on its calm surface. "You coming or what?"

I followed Kathy through a door and into the nursery.

"The father build the crib and that rocking chair," she whispered.

"Really?" The crib was something. Dark slats of smooth-planed wood fitted together without a single nail. "He make that too?" I pointed to the mobile from which hung a T-square, a hammer, and carved miniatures of the same buildings that were on the posters in the Bruckners' lobby.

Kathy nodded, and I said, "Amazing."

"Yeah," she agreed, "but he could've at least painted it blue or something. Look how bare this room is. When I have a baby, I want an all pink nursery. Or all blue. Everything to match. The curtains. The carpets. Everything pink or blue."

I liked the natural wood, and the sheep's wool on the floor, but I didn't disagree out loud.

We went back out and sat on the leather sofa. "Wait," Kath said, "before we start to talk. I'm hungry. You want to order some food?"

I was hungry too, but dead broke. "What do they have here?"

"Yogurt, Grace. That's not food. Let's get Chinese."

I made a face. "I've told you Chinese poisons me." Ever since my first full day in America, even the smell of Chinese made my stomach upset.

"Pure mind over matter."

"Give me yogurt now and order when I'm gone."

She got us yogurt and licked clean the underside of her foil top. "Okay, so the interview. You think you get it?"

"I have no way of knowing." The yogurt tasted like ice cream. "The little boy liked me."

She twirled her tongue around her spoon. "The father good-looking?"

"Kath."

"What? It have more than one way to skin a cat, Grace. You have to consider all the possibilities."

"Whore," I said and changed the topic. "How Donovan?"

She didn't answer, and I hoped I hadn't pissed her off. Her Donovan was married and conducted most of his work out of a silver Maxima. She got up from the sofa, where her jeweled pockets had left two starry prints deep in the cushion. The leather was so soft I could see the fine lines pressed out from her ponytail in the broad indent her back had made. Kathy refused to go Jamaican on her hair. The stylists in Brooklyn tried to get her to spray-paint her hair gold, offered gun and star stencils, glitter, and tubs of gel, but Kathy was firm.

"Grace"—her top half was deep in the refrigerator—"your birthday soon come, right?"

"Next week Friday. And yours is April twenty-first."

She came back with two more containers of yogurt and passed me one. Strawberry.

"No thanks, Kath. No more yogurt for me."

She shrugged. "You still so young."

This was precious. "I beg your pardon?"

"You still so young."

I threw a cushion at her head. "I always knew you were crazy. You're a year older than me."

She carefully peeled the foil and went for the underside. "Donovan's throwing a bashment, and you have to come."

I hated the Brooklyn parties. The dark caverns with one exit and hundreds of people sweating to the loud music made me claustrophobic. I did not want to die in a basement in Brooklyn.

"Four words, Kath: Happy Land Social Club. How many dead?"

She ignored me. "It's at International."

"*If* I do come, I'm warning you from now, I'm not dressing up."

"Oh, Grace, you have to." She bounced on the sofa and sounded just like the rich girl she had been in high school. "It's my birthday, and all them Jamaican yardbirds going to be decked out. You have to dress up. Represent."

"I can't believe you buy into that rubbish. Represent my ass, Kath. Representation costs money."

"I'll pay"—Kathy smiled to herself—"I'll give you an outfit for your birthday. Don't think about it, just promise me you'll come. Promise please, Grace?" She sounded like my little sister. I softened.

"Okay, I'll come."

"You know who else coming?" She couldn't wait for my guess. "Brent."

Brent was a friend of Donovan's who was not a dealer. He swore he had a real job, but, the two short times I'd limed with him before, he wouldn't tell me what he did. "He asked Donovan about you, you know."

"Stop lying, Kath."

"I'm not lying. He told Donovan to make sure and bring the sexy darkie, the tall one with the cat-eye."

"Did he say that?" I eyed her. "Don't play games with a big woman."

Kath loved this. "Will you dress up?"

"Maybe." I felt warm. No one had called me darkie since I left Trinidad, and I had come to understand that in America the word had a completely different meaning from what the Rastas back home whispered.

"You really like him, don't you?" Kathy looked surprised.

"Oh yeah, but don't say anything. He has a woman." I stopped short, not wanting to hurt her feelings.

"No, you're right. You shouldn't get involved with him. I'm in with Donovan already." She brushed the tip of her ponytail against her cheek. "God, Grace, what are we doing here? This is what we come New York for?"

"Is only for a time, Kath. Once we get our papers, it won't be like this forever, right? A little bit of catch-ass and then we can work it out. Besides, you forgetting home?" But Kathy had not. Neither had I. Life back home was over and had been over even before we left. There was simply nothing to decide. Live at home, go to school, graduate. Still live at home while teaching primary school, be courted by and marry either Clint or Carl, build a concrete house with a flower garden in the front, have some babies, and go to the beach on Sundays after church. It was all planned out.

Kath's life was planned out too, but in a slightly different direction from mine. Her family was well known and rich. Her East Indian grandfather had been disowned for taking up with a Negro woman. He and his wife had worked hard, starting off with a vegetable stall in front of their mud shack. The stall turned into a little parlor, then into a shop on the first floor of their two-story concrete house, and then into a chain of supermarkets. Their one son had attended the island's best school, married the green-eyed daughter of a Chinese shopkeeper, and gone into politics. Long past dirt under their fingernails, Kath's parents had raised her to be a princess.

"You know something, Kath?"

"Umm?" She was studying her bare toes.

"I've been planning to leave home since I was ten. My neighbor spent six months in New York. She came back talking about the skyscrapers and the lights and the snow and the subway and people always in a hurry and the big park in the middle of the city and two juicy apples for twenty-five cents, a quarter she said. I remember watching her daughter massage her legs from this big bottle of Palmer's lotion. A whole bottle of lotion for ninety-nine cents. Man, I was so jealous. Right then I made up my mind I was going to New York."

"So, if I getting this right"—Kath looked up from her toes—"you come America for lotion? Your neighbor didn't tell you how cold it was and how hard it would be to get a job and you needed to have papers for everything."

I knew Kath was right, but she couldn't get me down. I'd left. I'd said I was going to leave and I did it. That had to count for something. I held her gaze. "Yeah, but guess what? The hardest part is over. We're here. What time is it?"

"Half past one."

I jumped up. "I've got to go. I'm supposed to pick Dame up at two."

"You didn't tell me about the interview."

"I don't know. They interviewed about ten women, and they're not done. The most important thing, though, Mrs. Bruckner told me they would consider sponsorship."

"Really?" We were walking to the door. "Grace, be careful with these people though, once they have that to hold over your head, they'll make you see hell before they sign anything. Who would *want* someone without papers? That's just asking for trouble. Here." She handed me a floaty yellow scarf.

"Mmm." The fabric felt like a cloud against my cheek. "You sure I can use this?"

"She has about ten. If she misses it, she'll think the cleaning lady took it."

I wrapped the scarf around my neck, and something fell. Kath tried to close the door on my hand as I bent to pick it up.

"Hey, what the? You almost broke . . . Kath, what is this?" Two twenties tightly folded together.

"Take it." She adjusted the scarf around my neck. "You can pay me back when you get the job."

"I want to say no, but I need it. Thanks so much."

"Just come to the fete. And promise me you'll dress up."

"Blackmail. This is dirty money."

She held out her palm. "Give it back, then."

I curled my lip at her. "I'll dress up."

"Thought so."

"But I will not be dazzled."

Chapter 5

Dame was gone when I went to pick him up. Dodo too. I had just returned to Eastern Parkway and could hear her through the door.

"If it was me, Sylvia, so help me God, she was on the street. Island people like to take too much advantage. After everything you do for that girl."

With Sylvia, you always knew where you stood. She screamed when she was mad and a minute later, having heaved her anger off, asked if you wanted rice and peas and turkey wings. Dodo was pure bitch.

Sylvia came to my defense. "Nah, Dodo, Grace okay, man. And them children like she. When Derek and Micky come with home lesson, she have patience to sit down with them and do it."

Dodo snorted. I jiggled my key in the lock for a few seconds before opening the door. "Afternoon, Sylvia. Dodo. Sylvia, I went down to Dodo's, but I guess you reach before me."

Dodo sat on the couch, her mantis thighs tightly crossed and smoking a cigarette. She was unmarried, bitter, and had a fierce relationship with the Lord. She and Jesus had a deal with her Marlboros: for one-fifth of her salary, he turned away when she smoked.

She jumped in before Sylvia could say a word. "If you had come for Dame when you said you was going to be there, you would have found him." Dodo laughed, and it turned into a phlegmy cough. She unfolded a crushed Marlboro Lights box and spat into it. "Must be some man she went and look for in the city. You don't know them young girls and them now-adays."

I'd stopped trying to be nice to her. "Am I supposed to be answering you?"

"Grace, just make sure Derek and Micky get their home lesson finish for me please."

At least Sylvia wasn't going to insult me in front of Dodo.

"When you finding out if you get the work?" Sylvia asked later that night.

"The man, Mr. Bruckner, say they looking to hire somebody soon, so if I don't hear anything by this weekend, I guess they hire somebody else." My taking the negative track threw Sylvia. I didn't want to seem too enthusiastic about getting out of her apartment.

"I sure you will get it. White people like smart people to mind they children, not any and anybody." She settled back into the sofa, and Dame, who was falling asleep in my lap, reached out and circled my waist.

The phone rang. Sylvia reached for the receiver on the floor next to her. I could tell by the way she spoke that the caller was white. Sylvia adjusted.

"Yes, she is right here, Miss Lady. Please hold on for a minute, please." She tossed me the phone. With Dame in my lap, I couldn't get up to take the call.

"Hello?"

"Is this Grace?" My heart exploded. It was Mrs. Bruckner.

"Yes. Mrs. Bruckner?"

"Mr. Bruckner and I were very pleased with you today, and Ben cannot stop talking about you. Yours is the only name he remembers. Of course, you read for him better than anyone else."

"Well, that's very good to hear," I said stupidly.

"Anyway," Mrs. Bruckner continued, "we want you to come in for a trial this weekend. Can you come at ten on Saturday, and work through Sunday morning? This way you'll get to spend a day with Ben and a night at the apartment to see if you're comfortable."

Yes! I smiled and tried to respond with calm. "Yes. Sure. That would be fine." But when I looked over, Sylvia glared at me. "Can you hold on a second?" I asked Mrs. Bruckner.

"Sylvia, is the lady from the interview. They want me to come Saturday for a tryout and stay till Sunday morning. You mind? I mean, you want me Saturday?"

"Even if I wanted you to do anything for me you would still go your own way. Go ahead and do your work, Miss Grace."

I unpaused the phone. "Mrs. Bruckner, Saturday is good. You said ten?"

Sylvia was off the couch and humming to herself. Her short nightie came only to the middle of her legs, and the extra flesh in her thighs squeezed together and spilled forward. "Well"—she folded over to pick Dame off my lap—"at least you could never say I make you call me Mrs. Anybody."

I HAD TOO MUCH on my mind to go to bed yet. From Dame's spot on the radiator, I looked out at the nighttime traffic going by on the parkway. I cracked the window two inches, and a strong draft picked up bits of paint from the sill and scattered them over the turtleneck I still wore from the morning. After a while the elevator door grated open, and I heard a soft slapping on the front door. I got up and let Bo in.

"What, Grace, like you was waiting for me?" He stank as usual of sweat and weed.

"Yes, Bo. I stay up till midnight waiting for you." I turned away. "Now you reach I can sleep in peace."

"Wait, Grace." He leaned against the front door.

I turned back to him. "What, Bo?"

"Lend me fifty dollars till two weeks from now, please?"

"Bo, where I suppose to find fifty dollars?" I whispered. "I haven't worked since January."

"So you don't have no money save?" He eyed me with his head slightly raised. His warmed breath smelled of rum.

I backed away. "No, I don't have no money save."

"You think about the thing?"

"Yes, I think about the thing, but I not working, Bo. You know how long I will have to work to save three thousand dollars?"

He put his face a little closer to mine. "For a girl with education you really stupid sometimes, you know. You don't have to give me all the money one time. We get the license, do it the next day, and after that you give me, say, seven fifty. I sign what you need me to sign and you file the papers, scene? Then bam"—he pounded a fist into an opened palm—"first interview. If we pass that, you give me fifteen hundred. That is how much? Let me see." Bo did the math mentally, and I was amazed. "Twenty-two fifty. After that you have a whole two years before you file for permanent. Things go good"—he slammed his fist again—"we done and you give me the last seven fifty. Divorce and talk done. Three thousand is a good good price, scene." He scratched the back of his head.

Money talk always sobered Bo up. Now, after his rant, a foamy ball of *wappia* pooled in each corner of his mouth, and his thick black beard was speckled with white bolts of more spit.

"But if I don't have money, Bo I don't have it. You willing to go downtown for free?"

He laughed. "You mad or you crazy?"

From the bedroom Sylvia called out, "Bo and Grace, stop taking advantage, man. Night is time for people to sleep. Talk you business in the morning."

"Grace, you mean to tell me you don't have a friend to lend you some money?" Bo asked. "What about that red girl you always on the phone with?"

"Now who crazy? Kathy in the same position like me."

"All right. All I telling you is time running out."

Chapter 6

A different concierge stood behind the desk in the Bruckners' lobby, a youngish white guy with crooked teeth, blond hair, and a head that came to a point at his nose and mouth, like the *manicou* rodent my father had hunted in Trinidad. A heel-kicking leprechaun was pinned on his lapel. The uniform that had made Duke look like a dictator hung on his skinny frame, and he resembled a tipsy toy soldier under the top hat.

"Let me guess, let me guess, let me guess." He looked me up and down. "You're Grace and you're going to the Bruckners'."

I nodded.

"Ahhhhhh"—he sounded like a cheering crowd—"ladies and gentlemen, Danny has done it again. How does Danny do it every time without fail? A round of applause, please, for Danny the Doorman."

I smiled up at him. "Nice alliteration, Danny the Doorman. How do you know who I am?"

"Rule number one, Grace: never underestimate the men at the front desk. You'll be amazed at what we know." He leaned over the desk and eyed the small nylon backpack Sylvia had lent me. "Hey," he whispered, "so are you the Bruckners' new nanny?"

I wanted to be that more than anything, but the word rankled me. "I'm just here for the weekend. Take care."

Upstairs, Mrs. Bruckner opened the front door. She wore skintight jeans tucked into cowboy boots and a yellow sweater with a deep V-neck. A knotted leather strap hung around her neck and rested on her cleavage.

"Hi, Grace. How are you? Is it very cold?"

"Morning, Mrs. Bruckner. It is freezing." The apartment looked the same from Thursday morning, the couch still disheveled and a large pair of dirty sneakers, one side knocked over, on the rug.

"Come," she said, and I followed her down the corridor, "let me show you where to put your things. Mr. Bruckner is getting Ben ready."

The room she took me to wasn't really a room at all, just a small space partitioned from the kitchen by a jalousied sliding door set on tracks. A clothes dryer was mounted on the wall with a washing machine on wheels pushed under. On the other side a single bed with hospital-tucked sheets butted against an old dresser with beautiful red glass knobs shaped like acorns. A large window like the ones that let in so much light in the living room looked out on the street below, and from the twenty-second floor I could see shelves of empty brown terraces with dead plants and turned-over lounge chairs.

"If this weekend goes well," Mrs. Bruckner said, "this will be your space. It's not big, but you'll spend most of your time in Ben's room or doing stuff around the apartment. You'll only be in here to sleep."

This box was a shrine compared to Sylvia's. Besides my drawer, I had no space of my own in that apartment and in desperation had once jumped over the back of the couch to sit in the little triangular nook for solitude. I followed Mrs. Bruckner back through the kitchen. "So, no shul this morning?" I asked her.

She stopped short, and I stumbled to avoid her back. "What did you say, Grace?"

I knew she had heard me, but I repeated, "Temple. Mora and her family went every Saturday."

Mrs. Bruckner stood in the middle of the kitchen and with one foot crossed behind the other rested her hand on the counter. "I think you'll find I'm a little different from your people in New Jersey. The Speisers."

Together the words sounded like *despisers*. Already she was pissed at me, and I saw my chances for getting this job drain away. I had to remember that I was a domestic and not Mrs. Bruckner's friend.

Mora had four children, and combined they didn't own as many toys as Ben had in his room. Two of the four walls were honeycombed with shelves built almost to the ceiling, and each square compartment held a toy or a box with a toy or stuffed animals or musical instruments. Mr. Bruckner, in brown corduroys and a plaid shirt, sprawled on the carpeted floor, a pileup of small cars crashed around his legs. Ben sat next to him holding a sippy cup in one hand and a worn plush frog in the other.

"Hey, buddy, look who's here. Do you know who this is?"

Ben looked over at me. "It's Grace. Hi, Grace. Can Grace read me a book when my tape is over?"

"She can read you any book you want, buddy. Grace is going to spend the whole day with you." To me he smiled and said, "Hi, Grace. I see you made the final cut."

"Morning, Mr. Bruckner. Hi, Ben. Who's that you're holding?"

"Rabbit."

"Rabbit? Rabbit's a frog." Miriam was watching us.

"I know he's a frog," Ben said, "but his name is Rabbit."

"That makes perfect sense to me. Hi, Rabbit the frog."

"He just likes to be called Rabbit."

Aware that I was exasperating the object of my employment, I tried again. "Okay. Hi, Rabbit. Hey, Ben, I think you and Rabbit have a very cool room." I looked at the boxes on the shelves. "Maybe we can play with some of your toys."

Mrs. Bruckner pressed the heel of her hand against the wood. "My dad built all the shelves in here, the ones in the hall too." She turned to her husband. "Sol, you were supposed to be getting him ready, not watching a tape. Grace said it's cold. Find his snowsuit for when they're ready to go out."

Go out?

She turned to me. "Okay, Grace, here's the plan. Mr. Bruckner and I are going out for the day and leaving you with Ben. While we're gone, straighten up our bedroom, Ben's room, and the kitchen, and just see what you can't do with the living room. Try and do that while Ben's finishing up the tape. After, take him to the playground for a bit."

I looked at Mrs. Bruckner to see if she was serious. It was only about twenty degrees outside, and I couldn't believe anyone was at the park. "Are you sure you want me to take Ben out?"

"Oh, I'm sure."

"Mir, if it's too cold—"

But she cut Mr. Bruckner off. "One thing I should tell you now. We like Ben to get fresh air every day, regardless of the weather. You can't keep him cooped up. There's a plastic cover to go over the carriage if it's raining or snowing, and he has boots and plenty of warm clothes.

Another thing we found out that the last nanny did was go to her friend's house and spend the whole afternoon watching soaps when she should have been taking him outside. I cannot begin to tell you all the problems we have, have had with Carmen."

Ben heard his mother say "Carmen." "Where's Ya-ya, Mommy? I want to see Ya-ya."

Mr. Bruckner glanced at his wife before reaching over and rubbing his son's hair. "You'll see Ya-ya soon. Maybe you'll have a new ya-ya, Ben. Do you want Grace to be your new ya-ya?"

"No, not Grace, Ya-ya."

I wondered how long ago Ya-ya was fired and who had been minding Ben in the meanwhile.

"Sol," Mrs. Bruckner said, "keep getting him ready and I'll finish showing Grace around. There'll be traffic on the Taconic."

"It's Saturday morning, Mir."

"Still." I followed her into their bedroom. Spread across her unmade white sheets was a glossy black fur coat, and the top of her vanity was covered with tubs and tubes of makeup and brushes. "He called Carmen his ya-ya. We don't know where he got the name. To tell you the truth, Grace, she isn't—*wasn't*—a bad woman. Just not too bright. And then there was the train situation."

"Mr. Bruckner told me about that."

"We have strict rules about Ben. One is that we don't want him to go on the subway. There's all kinds of fricking crazies down there, and the steps, him in the carriage. Ugh"—she held up a hand—"God forbid. If Ben has to go to a doctor's appointment—his pediatrician is on the Upper East Side—we leave cab money. Or sometimes it's nice for him to ride the city bus uptown."

In the kitchen, Mrs. Bruckner reached for a clear plastic cup on the counter. "This is the money cup. Every Monday morning Mr. Bruckner puts twenty dollars petty cash in here. Do you know what I mean by petty cash?"

"Yes."

"The only thing we want is for you to put all the receipts from the supermarket, the pizza place if you take Ben for pie, whatever, in here. At the end of the week before you get paid, Mr. Bruckner or I will tally them up. If the total is a few cents off, fine, but generally if it's more than a dollar you're responsible for making it up. I think because it's your first day you should take Ben to Gino's for a slice. It'll help you guys bond. Let's see, what else?"

She stood with one leg crossed behind the other thinking about anything she might have forgot. "Well, I guess that's enough for today. The keys are always on the hook next to the front door, and here"—she pointed to the refrigerator—"is a list of phone numbers to call in case of an emergency. My in-laws live uptown, and if you ever can't reach us you should call them. We'll take you to meet them this evening." Her fingernail tapped against another name on the list. "Nancy, Sol's sister, lives in the Village, and she's usually around. Any questions?"

I didn't know where to begin.

"No."

"Okay, start on the dishes. I'll finish getting ready, and then you and Ben will have some time to get to know each other."

She left, and I turned to face the sink. Something about the speed of the morning, that just an hour ago I was leaving Sylvia's apartment in Brooklyn and now here I was standing in this woman's kitchen about to wash her dirty dishes, struck me as absurd. I turned off the tap and walked out of the kitchen. But then I stood in the hall, not sure what to do. I could hear the TV and Ben's laughter, but Mr. Bruckner was still with his son. Miriam came out of her room and almost collided with me. "Everything okay, Grace?"

"Yes, Mrs. Bruckner. Only . . ."

"Yes?"

I decided to ask her about money. "Um, you know, we didn't talk about how much I'm getting for—"

She didn't let me finish. "Of course. Hold on." She clacked off to Ben's room, and I went back to kitchen. There wasn't a flypaper from the ceiling, like at Sylvia's. And the yellow bananas in the fruit bowl looked plastic. Just as I was about to pick one up to see if it was real, she and Mr. Bruckner walked into the kitchen, he towering over her.

"Thirty-five dollars, Grace," Mr. Bruckner said. "Is that good enough, you think?"

No. Of course it wasn't good enough. If they paid two hundred dollars a week usually, then they should at least be giving me forty dollars and train fare.

Mrs. Bruckner spoke up. "We figured that since you're starting at ten rather than at eight, which is when you would usually start, you shouldn't get the whole forty dollars, right? You're here till the morning, but you don't have to do any chores tomorrow. So thirty-five is more than fair. Don't you think?"

No. "I guess."

"Tell you what," Mr. Bruckner said, "you're taking Ben to Gino's, right? Get yourself a slice and a soda too. Our treat." His wife looked up at him but didn't say anything.

"Thank you, Mr. Bruckner."

Mrs. Bruckner turned and walked out of the room. He leaned like a coconut tree against the counter. "Here"—he handed me five dollars— "get whatever you want at Gino's, Grace. Ben'll only have a cheese slice, cut up, but you can get pasta or whatever else they have. My treat."

I put the money in my pocket and thanked him again.

"Grace"—he folded his arms and looked at me—"I wish you would stop calling me Mr. Bruckner. My name is Sol. If you keep calling me Mister, then I'm going to start calling you Ms."

I didn't say anything but wondered how come he never asked me to call him Sol in front of his wife.

I HAD MADE UP my mind to spend no more than ten minutes at the playground. Ben, bundled into a winter suit, hat, mittens, and scarf, could barely bend his limbs. I unbuckled him from the carriage, and he tumbled forward, unable to bring his arms close to his body.

He chipped around to face me. "I go in the sandbox, Grace?"

I laughed and loosened his scarf. "Okay. You want your dump truck?"

He took the truck and sat in the cold sand. The playground was deserted. In the open square below was some kind of market. The stalls, peaked white plastic tents, some with green pennants snapping in the brisk wind, were pitched in a neat cluster. After three minutes I stooped at the edge of the sandbox and asked Ben if he was cold. "No siree, Grace!" he said. He filled the bed of his truck, dumped his load, and filled her up again.

I looked around. The sky was gray, and all the trees seemed dead. I felt homesick and alone. I wanted to be on the beach. I wanted to sit on my front steps in the hot sun reading a book or watching people walk up the road. I wanted a real Saturday market, not this tented mall in the middle of a city.

I tried to think.

I was here, in New York, and this was what I'd wanted since I was ten years old. But now that I was here . . . what?

"Hallo, Ben." A West Indian voice interrupted my thoughts. The woman's hood came forward like a funnel and, except for her eyes and forehead with greasy bangs, completely obscured her face. She stopped her double-wide carriage with two unmoving, cocooned bundles. Ben looked up at her but didn't answer.

"Morning," I said to her.

She looked at her watch. "Me guess me should say afternoon, morning done past."

"You know Ben?"

"Of course me know Ben. Everybody know the little bad boy. Ain't you the little bad boy in the towers, Ben?" Her funnel swept me, and she asked, "You are his new babysitter?"

"I'm just working today." I didn't feel like telling her any of my business. Again I asked her, "You work in the towers?" Again she didn't answer.

Instead she asked Ben, "You have a new ya-ya today, Ben?"

Ben looked up from his dump truck. "She's not my ya-ya, she's my Grace."

She swung her funnel in my direction. "All me can tell you, child, is to watch out for your new boss lady. That woman is pure snake, and I wouldn't trust she if me was you."

I hated that kind of mysterious talk. I didn't know this woman's name, she wouldn't tell me if she worked in the towers or not, and she spoke to Ben like I wasn't there, but then she tells me to watch out for who I assume to be Mrs. Bruckner.

"You mean Mrs. Bruckner? Why?"

Standing motionless and pushing her carriage back and forth, she countered my question with a question of her own. "Where you from, Grace?"

For spite I answered, "Brooklyn," and Ben, with perfect timing, decided he was cold. "Grace, is it time to go have some pizza pie?" he asked.

I pulled out my best Brooklyn accent. "It sure is, buddy."

Chapter 7

While Ben napped, I straightened his parents' room, trying to match the right lids to the opened pots of foundation and tubes of lipstick. Mr. Bruckner's worn shorts were on one side of the bed and Mrs. Bruckner's panties, yucky side up, on the other. *White people,* I thought, and used a blush brush to balance the two pairs together at arm's length to the laundry basket. By three-thirty I was bored. I rang Kath but got only the intro to Bob Marley's "Jammin'" on her answering machine. I called Sylvia, and Micky picked up. "Hi, Grace, when you coming home? I want you to help me with my homework. Grace"—she didn't pause—"you living with them white people now?"

"No, Mick, I'm just doing some work today."

"But why don't you work for my mammy, Grace? My mammy could pay you and you could take care of us."

"Where is your mammy?"

"Laundromat. Grace, the little boy more cuter than Dame?"

"No baby in the world cuter than Dame, Mick. You know that."

"Yeah, but Dame don't talk, Grace. Mammy tell Tanty Dodo that I talk when I was one year old and Derek born talking and Dame not saying boo, only smiling like Guy Smiley."

"All babies different, Mick. I bet you Dame will start talking soon."

"You promise, Grace?"

I didn't know what to say. "How about when I come tomorrow we sit and teach Dame some words?"

"You coming home tomorrow, Grace?" Micky sounded so happy.

"Yep, in the morning."

"Grace, you promise?"

This time I could. "I promise."

I hung up. Without the sound of my own voice, the room was perfectly still. If I strained, I could hear the faint ticking of the sunflower clock, the hum of the refrigerator, and the whisper of air coming through the vent. It would be nice to live someplace like this, to sprawl on the couch in the afternoon sunlight and read for hours. Not just to be the help. The phone rang, and, startled, I knocked the lamp clean off the side table, shattering the bulb.

Shoot.

"Hello?"

"Hi, Grace." It was Mr. Bruckner. "Just checking in. Everything okay?"

"Oh, Mr. Bruckner . . . I'm so sorry. Everything's fine except the phone made me jump." I looked down at the clear pieces of glass scattered like thin ice across the wooden floor. "The lamp fell over and the bulb broke."

"Did the lamp break?"

I stooped to check. "No, just the bulb."

"Okay, so sweep up the glass. Look in the linen closet, the one before Ben's room, for new bulbs. Everything should be fine. What else is going on?"

"I finished straightening up, and now I'm waiting for Ben to finish napping."

"Good. Look, Grace, sorry about this morning."

I was curious what exactly he was sorry for—the little money they were giving me for the day, or that I had to take Ben to the playground in the freezing cold?

"Mir's been under the weather lately, but I know she likes you. And, as I told you before, you're very high on our list."

"Thanks, Mr. Bruckner."

"Sol," he corrected. "So, come down to the lobby at six."

"Sol?"

"Yes?"

"I have to change for dinner?"

He laughed. "No, Grace, we're just going up to my parents'. You look great the way you are." In the background, I could hear country and western, the only music that my mother liked besides hymns. Sometimes, on Saturday, Hel and I would slow-dance together doing twirls and dips, while she sang along in her high, unbalanced voice to "Mamas Don't Let Your Babies Grow Up to Be Cowboys" and "Patches." Of course we liked best the raunchy calypsos and American pop songs, but the violins just now on the phone made me realize how much of my mother was under my skin.

BEN AND I PLAYED crash with toy cars in the room off the lobby. It looked different without the crowd of waiting women. "Move your legs, Grace," he ordered and then vroomed a small truck on the carpet. "We're going to have an accident."

"Drive carefully, then," I warned him and skidded my car dangerously close. We crashed hard.

"See, Grace"—he sat back on his heels—"now we've had an accident."

"Oh, man." We were deciding whether or not we needed an ambulance when Mr. and Mrs. Bruckner walked in.

"Mommy. You're back. Daddy. Mommy and Daddy are back, Grace."

I stood. "Told you they were coming back."

Mrs. Bruckner held Ben awkwardly. Sol took him from her arms. "Okay, let's get going. Grace, do you need to get anything from upstairs?" He sat Ben high on his shoulders. "Mir, we're all set? You need to run up for anything?"

"I look okay?" she asked him, pressing the fur at her hips.

"You look great. Okay, buddy, ready to go see Nana and Big Ben?"

Ben tried to deepen his voice. "Big Ben, choo choo."

Mr. Bruckner stopped at the car. "How are we going to do this, Mir?" She stopped too. "Do what?"

"Fit. Ben's car seat is behind your seat, and I need legroom up front." He turned to me. "Look at Grace's long legs. There's no way she's fitting comfortably behind me."

Miriam came back to the pavement and faced her husband. I looked away. "So what do you want to do? Why don't you pull up your seat so Grace gets some room for her long legs?" The doorman and the concierge were both looking at us.

He was oblivious to her tone. "No, that won't work. I'll be too bunched up."

"I'll sit behind Mr. Bruckner," I said before he suggested something stupid like I sit up front with him. "I'll be fine."

"Are you sure?" He looked straight at my legs. Mrs. Bruckner got in the front passenger seat and closed the door hard.

She was silent for most of the drive, and so was I. Ben talked nonstop, giving his parents a minute-by-minute replay of our afternoon as we drove through sheer walls of skyscrapers. "I played in the sand, and then Grace pushed me on the swing, but the slide was too cold." I was amazed at how much detail he remembered. "And then we saw Evie."

Mr. and Mrs. Bruckner said, "You did?" at the same time.

"You met Evie, Grace?" Mrs. Bruckner asked.

"A woman with a big hood and a double carriage? She stopped and talked to us, but she didn't tell me her name."

Mr. Bruckner laughed a little. "Evie all right. I didn't know she worked on weekends."

"She works always," I heard Mrs. Bruckner say, and then she said something else under her breath that I didn't quite catch.

We drove alongside a never-ending park until Mr. Bruckner found an empty spot. I looked out the window. "Is this Central Park?"

"Yup."

"This is *the* Central Park?"

"The one and only, Grace. Hey, buddy, tell Grace what Nana and Big Ben take you to see in Central Park."

"The penguins," he answered and clapped his hands.

Mr. Bruckner unfastened Ben and carried him.

"There are penguins in Central Park?" I looked at them both, and Mrs. Bruckner laughed.

"There's a small zoo with penguins, a polar bear, and some other animals," she said. "Ben is crazy about the penguins."

I got out of the car and looked around. Lights twinkled through an unending bank of trees, their bare branches overlapping in the early winter dusk. I bet that, come summertime, the wall of leaves would be impenetrable, that inside there'd be lush lawns and secret gardens hidden from the busy city outside. At home I knew the names of all the trees and bushes, but these skeletons were unfamiliar. Were they oaks and elms and maples, like Mora had shown me in New Jersey? Would they bloom in the springtime and sprout tiny leaves in that almost fluorescent shade of green? I took a deep breath. I could feel at home here. Anyplace where there were trees and plants felt familiar to me, even if I didn't know their names.

Mr. and Mrs. Bruckner were looking at me, smiling. I couldn't believe it. I, Grace Caton, formerly of the seaside village of Morne Diable, Trinidad, was standing outside *the* Central Park, *the* enchanted forest in the middle of New York City. I didn't know what lay in front of me—I barely knew what lay behind me—but here, for this one moment, it was perfect. How I wished Hel was with me.

And there were penguins? I laughed aloud.

I couldn't wait.

"THEY ARE 'ERE." THE door was opened by an old woman in a white dress, a frilly little maid's cap, and crocheted booties. Her eyes widened when she saw me. "Hallo, Sol. Miriam." She reached for Ben. "Come and give old Jane her kiss."

Ben flew to Jane and kissed her brown cheek. Sol kissed her lips. She shot me a look. "Come in, come in." Both Mr. and Mrs. Bruckner eased out of their shoes, and I bent to undo my bootlaces.

"Come," Jane said, "in we go. You done braught in a draught with you."

The apartment was like a museum. Paintings of fruit spilling out of horns, lilac-y colored water lilies, people at parties, a woman either getting into or out of a bathtub, and a small bronze statue of a ballerina clasping her hands behind her back. The carpet under my feet was thick and deep, and I wanted to stop and pinch the fluffy pile with my toes. But I didn't, I just walked with Jane and Mrs. Bruckner deeper and deeper into the dimly lit apartment.

I saw the old man first. His face covered in either freckles or liver spots and his rheumy eyes the same bright green as his son's and grandson's. Even with him seated deep in the chair, I could tell that he was very tall. He wore a cardigan buttoned up to the middle over a gray sweater, gray trousers, and brown suede slippers.

"Hello there," he said in a strong voice. "I can't get up from this damn chair, but come shake my hand." I walked over and put my hand into his. "I'm Benjamin. I used to be a Mister and even a sir, but everyone calls me Big Ben now."

"It's very nice to meet you, sir."

"Ah"—he shook his head—"you weren't listening."

I smiled at him. "It's very nice to meet you, Big Ben. I'm Grace."

"That's better. Grace. Hello, Miriam. You're looking very well."

"You always say that, Big Ben." Miriam bent to hug him. "Where's Ettie?"

Mr. Bruckner had taken himself over to a large chair, right next to the lit fireplace. I didn't know apartments could have fireplaces.

"Hey, Janey, can I get a beer?"

His father wagged a finger. "Shame on you, asking old Jane to get you a beer. Get it yourself, and get me one too. Does Grace want a beer?"

"No, thank you."

"And none for you either," Ettie Bruckner said to her husband as she glided in. She fitted so right with the paintings and sculptures in her apartment mansion. Her silver hair was bobbed, and a looped double strand of black pearls hung around her long, ropy neck. She wore flowy black pants with a shiny black shirt opened to show her freckly chest. She was beautiful.

"Hi, Mom." Mr. Bruckner rose and kissed her cheek. "Don't you look fantastic for an old girl."

"Nana." Ben ran toward her. She caught him midstep and hoisted him high up on her hips. "Mmmm"—she posed with the two of them—"my beautiful boys."

"Hi, Ettie," Miriam said. I remembered Mrs. Bruckner asking her husband before we left the towers if she looked okay. The daughter-in-law in cowboy boots, tight jeans, and leather strap knotted around her neck looked tired and overblond. Wrong, somehow. "Hello, Miriam." Then she turned to me. "And who is this?"

Ben touched his grandmother's necklace. "Grace, Nana. Say hi, Grace."

"Hi, Grace," I said, and everyone except Miriam laughed.

"Well, Grace"—she stared at me—"you remind me of the village girls from Burkina Faso." Ettie raised her voice. "Big Ben, remember Burkina Faso? That plank mask is from there." She pointed to a wall of African masks staring unbelievingly at their surroundings. "Now, Grace, don't think I compare all black people to Africans. It's just that you are quite striking. Extraordinary eyes, don't you think, Miriam? Are you sure you want to be a nanny, Grace, and not a fashion model in New York City?"

Right then, between her husband and her mother-in-law, I knew Mrs. Bruckner wasn't going to hire me. I started thinking about next week's *Irish Echo.* I hadn't renewed my ad, but hopefully there'd be jobs to call. Or maybe I would make some signs, charm my striking, leggy way past liveried doormen, and post them in the laundry rooms of all the buildings we had just driven past.

"Thank you," I said and then paused. "Mrs. Bruckner?" I wasn't quite sure what I was thanking her for and then was unsure what to call her. If Miriam was Mrs. Bruckner, then was she Mrs. Bruckner too? Big Bruckner?

"Please call me Ettie, dear. That Mrs. Bruckner business makes me sound like a schoolteacher." She turned to Miriam. "Don't tell me you've got Grace calling you Mrs. Bruckner. But then you *are* a schoolteacher." She put her arms akimbo. "Grace, I give you permission to call her Miriam. Solomon, are you party to this?"

He was back with his beer. "I've told her to call me Sol since the interview, Mom." He walked over to his wife, grabbed her in a gentle chokehold, and kissed the top of her head.

Ben said to his grandfather, "The choo-choo train," and shot out of the room.

Big Ben looked after his grandson, and his green eyes brightened. To Sol he said, "Give me a hand, boy."

Sol hoisted his father gently, and Big Ben followed Ben out.

"Is Nancy coming tonight?" Miriam asked.

"She was." Ettie relaxed into her husband's chair. "But then she decided to march."

"March?" Sol took a long swallow. "March for what?"

"Don't you read the paper? The old Irish fools don't want gays and lesbians marching in their parade, and I guess they decided to hold their own?"

"Is she that desperate?" Sol asked. "Did you remind her she's a Jew?"

"Ah yes." Ettie leaned forward. "But you forget she's a lesbian Jew, and, regardless of what I say, *lesbian* is her chosen definitive adjective."

Sol yawned. "Nancy needs to get laid."

Miriam laughed. "Maybe that's why she went."

I focused on the plank mask.

"How are you feeling today, darling?" Ettie stretched a hand and gave Miriam the briefest touch on the knee. Her short nails were a polished cream. "Would you like a drink?"

"A cold zin spritzer would be divine, but I'll just have orange juice. Grace, ask Jane to please pour me a glass of juice." The *please* I noticed was for Jane.

In the kitchen I asked Jane how long she'd been working for the Bruckners.

"Too damn long. Every day me tell them I am ready to go back to Jamaica. One of these days I am just going to get on a plane and go."

"Well"—I took in the glass cabinets that reached to the ceiling and the double-door fridge—"I'm just arriving."

"Grace them call you? Grace, don't make the mistake you see I make in this America, you hear me." She placed a glass and a white cloth napkin on a small wicker tray. "I don't know you situation, child, but work for these people, let it be a stepping-stone and not the whole island, you hear me?" She put four ice cubes from an ice bucket into a separate glass and laid a pair of miniature tongs on the napkin. "Take my advice and try and get all this for yourself instead of stopping and wondering how the white people, the Jews, the Japanese—whoever—get what they have." She poured some foamy orange juice from a pitcher and handed me the tray. "Get it for yourself and don't never content yourself with no scraps."

I WAS UP AND lying in Ya-ya's bed. Maybe my bed. The room smelled like clean laundry, and I thought about home, helping my mother fold clothes fresh and crisp from drying on the lines strung between the papaya trees. This scent came from detergent, but it still smelled good.

There were two full bathrooms in the apartment, one opposite the kitchen and the other closer to the Bruckners' room. Just as I reached past the sea creature shower curtain to turn on the tap, someone went into the other bathroom. I heard throwing up. Retch after retch echoed through the partition. Sol's voice murmured through and then there was more retching.

By eight I was ready, but I didn't want to knock after what I'd heard, so I sat on the bed and waited, hearing the apartment's unobtrusive noises. At nine I went to the living room. Sol came out first, in a knee-length robe. His hair was flattened on one side and up in a slant on the other. "Morning, Grace. Are you ready to leave?"

"Morning, Sol. I have to be in Brooklyn by ten."

"And you live with your aunt, you said?"

I hadn't said that at all. "With cousins." He didn't ask any more, so I decided to ask a question. "Sol, the first time I talked to Miriam on the phone, she said you guys were willing to do a sponsorship?"

When he sat on the couch, the robe opened to his thighs. "It's not that Mir and I are looking for someone to sponsor, but if we find someone who works out, we'd want to help them."

Miriam came out of the bedroom. Her face was chalky and pale except for two red spots on the sides of her mouth.

"Morning, Mrs. Bruckner," I said to her.

"Oh, Grace, go ahead and call me Miriam." She leaned her head against the wall, and the motion arched her back and sent her belly forward. She was pregnant. Not that she had a big bump or anything, but I knew it. That's why everyone kept asking her how she felt. "So what do you think, Grace? Do you want to work for us?"

There was so much to say, but all I managed was "Yes."

She looked over to Sol on the couch, and I thought they were going to make a you've-got-it announcement. Instead Miriam said, "We'll let you know as soon as possible."

Just then the intercom buzzed. Miriam got it. "Hey, Danny." "Okay." "Thanks, Danny."

She came back holding the money cup from the counter and then screamed, scattering change over the floor. "Shit, shit, shit."

Sol jumped from the couch, and I saw a white flash of underwear. "Mir, are you all right?"

She bent to cradle her left foot. I knelt to pick up the fallen change and saw drops of blood on the wooden floor. "Oh, God, you're bleeding," Sol said.

"No, no." She placed a hand on her stomach. "It's my foot. I stepped on something, a piece of glass. Did you break a glass?" She asked Sol and not me. I looked up from the floor, and he caught my eye.

"I did break a glass." He stooped to press his thumb against her heel but kept his eyes on mine. "But that was a while ago. Maybe Carmen missed a bit on her last clean. Here." He got up. "Press the spot. Let me get you a Band-Aid."

I don't know if Sol had in fact broken a glass or if he was covering for me. I was grateful for whichever it was.

Miriam rested her injured foot on its toes. "That woman. Ben could have stepped on that." She looked down at me as I rose with a handful of change. "Grace, did you get the receipt from Gino's?"

Shoot. "No," I said, calculating that the added-up errors of this week-end totaled me not getting this job. "Oh, Mrs. Bruck— Miriam, I'm sorry. I forgot."

Miriam didn't say anything and passed me some folded bills.

IN THE LOBBY DANNY looked pointedly at me. He kept staring and lifted his chin toward the room off the lobby then looked away. I walked over. The woman from the newsstand sat on the couch, legs comfortably folded, flipping through a magazine. I guessed she had made the Bruckners' final cut too. Outside was still freezing, and I wondered if I was ever going to be warm again.

Chapter 8

"Okay, Dame, ready?" I lofted his ladybug ball low between us. "Buh, buh, ball. Can you say that for Gracie? Can you say *ball?*" Nothing.

"Baalluh?" I stretched the word as far as it could go, touching my lip with the tip of my tongue for the added emphasis. "Baallluh." Dame gave me his sweet smile but nothing more. Then there was a knock at the door.

"Who are you?" a man asked, before I had a chance to open the door all the way.

"I'm Sylvia's cousin. From Flatbush."

He leaned down and looked into my eyes. "How long has she had you living here?"

"I live in Flatbush. I'm only here to let you in. Sylvia had to go out."

"What's your address in Flatbush?"

"Why on earth would I tell a strange man my address?"

He chuckled. "You're a smart one, eh? What is your name?"

"Grace."

"I am Jacob, the landlord. Sylvia's not here, you say?"

"Do you pronounce your name Jacob or Yacob?"

"You know some Hebrew?"

I said no and moved toward the living room. Jacob followed me, seeing the flaking paint on the walls and ceiling, the permanent flecks ground into the carpet.

"One of my best apartments, and look how she keeps it."

I saw him better in the bright living room and stared straight into his clear blue eyes.

"What?" he asked. "You never see a Jew before? Don't you see them walking up and down Eastern Parkway?" He waved his hand like a conductor.

"Yeah, but never this close."

He stretched out his arms in a "tada," and we both laughed. But it was true. I had never seen a real Jew this close before. Mora kept kosher in the house and went to shul on some Saturdays, but the boys did not have sidelocks, and her husband, Abe, did not dress all in black like a warlock. Sylvia's landlord was in full regalia, including a long, wavy beard and a mustache with a few strands of gray. He wore a black coat that came to his knees, and under that a black suit jacket and a white shirt. From his waist I could see a bit of white fringe.

"This is Sylvia's youngest child?" he asked. "He and my second-to-last son were born in Tishri."

"September or October?"

"Aha, you do understand Hebrew."

"A few words are not a language."

He folded his arms. "So what other words do you know?"

"I can say grace, the prayer before you eat. The *Baruch ata adonai eloheinu* . . . prayer."

"Amazing." He lifted his eyebrows. "You know, I can find a nice Jewish man for you to marry. You have to convert and cut off all your hair, though. You know how to keep kosher?"

I had half a mind to ask if said Jewish man was an American citizen.

"You're funny," I said.

There was another knock at the door, and as I moved past Jacob, I thought to ask on Sylvia's behalf for a new doorbell. Bo breezed in wearing a nice puffy parka with a fur-trimmed hood.

"Where'd you get that coat?"

He was about to answer when he saw Jacob. "But what the ass this man doing here? Jacob, who tell you you could come in here?"

"You are a bum," Jacob answered. "Look at you. Where did you steal this coat?" I thought for sure Bo would hit this man hard right here in Sylvia's living room and I would have to call the police and then testify in court and get deported. But the two men laughed and shook hands. "Grace"—Bo draped his arm around Jacob's shoulder—"this man is my good good friend, you know."

"I wouldn't go so far," Jacob said, but he was grinning. "Your Sylvia is complaining about the paint. It looks good to me." He dug his hands deep in his pockets and looked up at the ceiling. "When was the last time we painted? Last year? Eighty-nine?"

"Jacob, you know you really full of shit. Is going on five years now this place paint. And is a real cheap job them Russian boys do." Bo's fingernail flicked a quarter-size piece of paint from the wall. "Why you don't spend some of that money you hiding and give the girl a real paint job?"

"You know how much rent she pays? You know how much I could get on the open market for this place? Your Sylvia is practically living for free."

I was glad Bo came, because he could haggle much better with this man than I could.

"You see that little boy sitting down there only smiling smiling?" Bo pointed to Dame. "Is the paint in here get that little boy sick. That is why he not talking."

"You are the one who is full of shit," Jacob said. "The child is fine. I was just telling Grace that he and my son are the same age. My child too is not a big talker. It's the way of boys."

"Your child don't talk because your wife is your first cousin. The two of we know this place full up with lead." Bo threw his coat on the couch. "Give me a cigarette," he said to Jacob. He took four. "Let me figure how much your Russian boys have to scrape and how much paint they need to bring, and then I will decide if I should tell Sylvia to sue your ass."

Was Bo right? Did Dame have lead in him? Dame was so slow I could imagine lead on the soles of his little feet, weighing him down. I sat next to him and cupped his small, warm face between my hands. "Say *b-a-all* for me, Dame." I dragged the word out, but he only swayed and smiled.

SYLVIA WAS RUNNING HOT water on some turkey wings when she called me into the kitchen. "What you think I should do with this meat tonight? Stew or curry?"

This was not why she'd called me from folding her laundry.

"When last you make curry?" I asked. She cocked her head and thought about this.

"Sit down, Grace. I want to talk to you."

I didn't know if to be nervous, or frightened, or how. For a second I wondered if she was going to tell me that I needed to leave, that Jacob had figured out I was living here and she would lose her place if I didn't go.

"You hear back from them people yet?"

She meant the Bruckners. "I still waiting."

Sylvia nodded. "How the weekend pass? The lady nice?"

I wiggled my hand. "Hot and cold."

Sylvia belched. "This gas on my chest from since last night. At least it coming out." She turned to look at me across the table. "Grace, hear this. I not putting no pressure on you and do what you want. Is not because I giving you a lodging mean you have to do what I say."

"What is it, Sylvia?"

"What if I give you fifty dollars a week to mind them children for me? You don't have to do nothing different from what you doing now. Get Micky and Derek ready in the morning, watch Dame in the day, and help them with the home lesson when they come from school."

Of course she would offer me this now. Had she thought about arrears for the past two months? Or giving me back the forty or so dollars I must have spent buying her packs of More menthols? She had to be scared that I would actually get the job.

She was watching me. "So what you think?"

"Sylvia, I already living here for free. I can't take money from you to watch them children."

"Is just so you could have a little change in your pocket when weekend come and you want to go down Fulton or Pitkin."

I knew how it would go. Sylvia would start with the best intentions and give me fifty dollars for the first two weeks. By the third week she'd tell me she had only twenty and could she make it up next weekend. Then we'd be back to me minding the children for free and using the money she'd given me to buy her cigarettes.

"Grace"—she leaned her full weight on the table—"I not telling you to make up your mind now for now, you know, is just something for you to think about. Them children like you, and I see you trying to teach Dame to talk. Sometime I think Micky like you more than she like me."

"Sylvia, please." I hadn't told her that for the last Parents' Day at

Micky's school she had asked me to come. "I know fifty is all you have, but I have to help my mother. And then this thing with Bo," I went on. "When will I save three thousand dollars from fifty dollars a week?"

Sylvia had done me a huge favor by taking me in, but the thought of staying in her apartment was unbearable. My life moved in slow motion, and I could feel myself turning drab to match the color of her curtains. I hadn't quite figured out what I wanted from America, but it wasn't on the fifth floor of 579 Eastern Parkway.

"Grace"—she got up to run some hot water on the turkey wings—"what if Bo do the thing for you for free?"

I rolled my eyes. "You really think Bo would go from three thousand dollars to for free?"

She laughed. "If I send Bo City Hall in the morning he will go."

We looked at each other. This *was* a good deal. Miriam and Sol were willing to help the right person. Maybe. But the money they were paying was nothing, and the work was hard. Plus, I didn't know Miriam Bruckner. I knew Sylvia and all her hot and cold parts. Sponsorship could take ten years. If I married Bo, I could be legal in two. "Sylvia, I don't know."

"So you saying no?"

"I not saying no, but I not saying yes either."

"Well"—she turned away from me—"I can't stop you from living your life, mama."

For a few days now, Sylvia hadn't been herself. She hadn't lost her temper at the kids or me; in fact, she had barely raised her voice. I wanted to ask her something, and now seemed a good time.

"Sylvia?"

"Umm."

"You know Bo run into Jacob this morning?"

She faced me again. "He tell me he give him a good piece of he mind. Before, Jacob use to give all them boys work. They use to come and paint, fix the shower or the toilet, the electrikcy. Bo, Nello, and Keatix use to work for him regular regular. Now is only Russians he using. Is because them Jew could pay them next to nothing. And everything break as fast as they fix it." She flicked the loose tap on the faucet. "Jacob is a real Jew."

"I hear Bo tell him something."

"What Bo tell him?"

"That is the old paint what causing Dame to take so long to talk." I didn't tell her about Bo asking Jacob for work.

"What stupidness Bo talking about? Some children does take time to talk. Micky and Derek talk fast fast, but Damien just slow."

"Yeah, but why?"

"And Bo say it might have something to do with the paint? What Jacob say?"

"That his son is three too, and he not talking either. But maybe you should take Dame for some tests."

"Tests for what, Grace?"

I didn't know.

She thought about this and then changed the subject. "You didn't meet Michael, them boy father, when you come?"

"Only once or twice, and then they took him to the G— to Kings County." I almost said the G Building, the mad-people's section at the hospital.

"He skizzophenric, you know." She drummed her fingers on the sink. "Every day I pray them boy don't take after him. You see how Derek hyper, and how Dame quiet. Is just so Michael use to get, quiet quiet before the madness take him. Maybe my boy children mad?" She looked in my eyes. "Watch how Micky different from the two of them. They don't have the same father, you know."

She seemed worried, and I didn't know what to say. "But you don't have it on your side. Even though I think Dodo might be crazy."

She considered this.

"But still carry Dame to the doctor. And tell Micky and Derek if they see him eating paint to make him stop."

Chapter 9

Tuesday was a gaping yawn that swallowed me whole. Micky and Derek went to school, Sylvia went on assignment from her agency, and it was just Dame and me alone to spend the day. Dame fell asleep, and I looked out the window for a while and then did some sit-ups on the carpet. I turned on the TV, but the screaming women on *The Price Is Right* just made my day more meaningless. I sang the Trinidadian national anthem and then tried to recite the pledge. I tried singing the American anthem but couldn't go any further than "by the dawn's early light." I recited multiplication tables. Finally I got my letters out and, despite myself, smiled at the familiar fountain pen strokes of my mother's handwriting. I reread the letter about Henry cutting down the coconut tree and I should come home, the one where she told me that Mr. Logan had died and I should come home, and the one where she just said I had to come home. That was the last letter that I had read. Three weeks had passed, and now I was to ready to face my mother again.

> Dear Gracie,
>
> Hoping these few words reach you by the Grace of God. I make up my mind when I sit down to write that I am not going to tell you to come back home. Even though you are not yet a woman, not till the end of this month, you was always biggish and I have no right to try and force you to do anything. All I could do is give you my blessings and wish you luck.

Something was wrong here. For the one year and two months I had lived in America, every last letter I received from my mother had begged, threatened, demanded, and cajoled me to come home. She had even promised to sell the piece of land she inherited from her own father to get some money to send me to the island university. Only come back home.

> Everything here going good. I don't know if you heard from Rhonda. She ask for your address and say she going to write. Na doing fine. I still going in the garden everyday, trying to see what I can't get from the Lord and the Land. The little change you send for Christmas was a good help, but you need to save your money to do your business. Helen doing very well without you. I know she still miss you, but I won't tell you that because I already say that this letter is not about getting you to come back. All I will say is that she studying hard for exams. Mr. Haggard expects that she will do very well. Maybe not as good as you did, but she is a hard worker and we expecting her to get some passes.

My mother wasn't even aware that she compared us so.

> On the daddy front, well he not doing too well.

There it was. "On the daddy front." "Come home" in code. My mother had a special gift for manipulation. I was mad, and I wanted to cry at the same time, because I missed him and because I knew when I left home that there was a good chance I would never see him again. But that she would use that against me?

> On the daddy front, well he not doing too well. He went clinic the other day and his pressure was up and the sugar sky high. I don't know what else to tell him. Is like since you gone he give up hope. I cook food without salt and he putting in he own salt. He know he not suppose to drink and he drinking the worse rum, that nasty *babash* Hamil make in the bush. Is only you who could get him to listen, Gracie. I don't know what to do. Helen don't know what to do. If we had a phone well then you could call and talk to him, but with the one

foot he can't even go by the lady on the hill. So I don't know. Okay, hoping these few words reach you in the best of health and strength. Try not to be too rude to Sylvia. I know you say she could be hard to take, but sometimes you are not the easiest person in the world to get along with either. Write soon or when you have some extra change give us a call. The lady on the hill will give us the message. I know you have it but I will put her phone number at the bottom.

May the good Lord bless and keep you and don't forget to pray.

Your Loving Mother,

Grace

I stretched out on the carpet and closed my eyes. My mother had never had any hopes for Helen and me, not that she'd told us about. One day when she was bent over the tub, I had asked her what, when Helen and I were babies, did she dream for us? What did she want for her two daughters in this world? My mother had stopped scrubbing. With her wet fingers she'd pinched my arm hard, wringing my flesh, and told me she wished that neither of us would have a child before we were married to bring shame on her house.

I was Daddy's girl. I visited him at hospital every day for the month he was there before the rot spread so far the doctors decided they had to cut. After the operation I refused to go back. Helen went and my mother went and all the neighbors in the village went, but I refused to go. Finally my mother said enough was enough. My father was looking out for me every day. So I went. I walked into the ward and thought for the first time the air smelled like the abattoir in Penal market. I couldn't look at the faces in the other beds. I looked straight ahead to my father's bed. He was propped up against the thin hospital pillows, and he followed me with his eyes as I walked toward him. I was crying by the time I got to him, and he was crying too. I couldn't look down. So what going to happen when I come home, he wanted to know. The foot not going to grow back, Grace. I said it might, and he laugh-cried a little but shook his head. It won't. So I looked. I got off the bed, turned around, and lifted the cheap white cotton sheets stamped PROPERTY OF GENERAL HOSPITAL—DO NOT REMOVE and saw bloody bandages crisscrossed around a swollen stump resting on a halo of bright red blood on the bedspread. The abattoir filled my nostrils again, and I fell to the white-tiled floor.

When the chance came for me to leave the village, our house was split down the middle with the logic of King Solomon: he wanted me to go and see the world, and she wanted me to stay. Helen said I'd be crazy to stay. And besides, if I went then I could send for her. I left. And for fourteen months my mother had been trying to get me to come back.

BY 6:00 P.M. I was frantic. The Bruckners hadn't called. They weren't going to call. They would have called already if I had got the job. I toyed with the idea of calling to confirm that I hadn't got the job but didn't because the possibility existed that maybe just maybe they were still going to call. This morning I had bought another *Irish Echo,* and there had been nothing. Not one single ad to fit my size. It was Sol who'd screwed up my chance. *Look at Grace's long legs.* How stupid could one man be? Especially if I was right and Miriam was pregnant. And Ettie too. *Are you sure you want to be a nanny, Grace, and not a fashion model in New York City?* The phone rang, and I screamed, making Micky jump and Derek snap his head and Dame smile. It rang again. "You answer it, Mick." Derek reached for the phone, and I grabbed the receiver before he could get it.

"Hello?"

It was Kathy. "Any news yet?"

I was relieved and disappointed. "Nope. I thought you might be them, actually." I felt I owed Micky and Derek an explanation. "Kathy. Keep working."

"Minding your stepchildren?"

"Uh-huh. Home lesson around the kitchen table. There wasn't anything in the *Echo* today."

"I saw. And you didn't renew your ad, right?"

"Righto. Anyhow. What you up to?"

Kath inhaled. "I'm actually calling to ask you for a favor next week." She wasn't talking like a Jamaican.

"Sure, Kath. What you need me to do?"

"Babysit."

"Babysit who?"

"This little boy here."

"All right, stop the shorthand. Tell me what's going on." I got up from the kitchen table and walked into the hallway.

"Okay, next Monday we going to City Hall to get the license, and I need someone to watch this child. It won't be for long. I'll pay you."

I stopped pacing. "Oh, my God. You and Donovan, Kath?"

"No, idiot. How it could be Donovan? Is the man he find for me."

"Oh." I did feel like an idiot. "Oh. You don't have to pay me, Kath. What time you planning on going?"

"Around nine-thirty."

"It doesn't sound like a problem to me."

"And Sylvia?"

"It should be okay. I can always bring Dame. But hey"—I expected her to be a little more excited—"you're well on your way, Kath."

"I guess so, but, Grace, this means for sure that Donovan not leaving his wife anytime soon. If I'm married to someone else, he has an excuse to stay married to her for years."

I didn't know that Donovan had promised Kathy to leave his wife.

"You think I should do it, Grace?"

"I can't tell you what to do, Kath. But what more important to you? To be Donovan's wife, or to get your papers and start living your life?" I didn't mean to rhyme.

She laughed a little. "Well, still tell Sylvia you need to come to the city Monday."

"Okay. The other night Bo and I were talking—"

"Grace, somebody coming. I have to go, bye."

In the kitchen, Derek and Micky were fighting over a pencil. "Give it back, stoopid. Is mines."

"Nuh-uh"—Micky yanked hard—"my mother buy this pencil for me on Pitkin Avenue."

"Nuh-uh, my father buy this pencil for me at the corner store," Derek said.

"You lie, Derek. Your father in the G Building."

"You lie, Micky. And you don't have no father."

"Grace."

I walked back into the kitchen and, in an act that would horrify King Solomon, snapped the pencil in two. "Happy now?"

. . .

SYLVIA DIDN'T COME IN alone that night. As if belatedly answering my wish for company, she came in around seven-thirty with Dodo, Bo, and Nello, Chinese food, two six-packs of Bud, and a bottle of red rum. Bo and Nello were already drunk, and Sylvia, after telling Nello to keep his hands in his pockets, went to the kitchen to dish out food. As soon as Dodo walked into the living room, she changed the channel.

"Come on, man," I said, "you can't just come and take over the TV."

"Watch me," she said and clicked around the stations.

I got off the couch and grabbed the remote.

"But what the ass is this? Child, give me back that remote. Well, I never see more. Sylvia!"

I changed back to our channel, and she tried to wrestle the remote from me. She laughed while she did it, and I laughed too, but I knew she was mad.

Nello clapped and did a James Brown dance. He was a little mouse man with big front teeth who swore his grandparents had been Grenadian. Sylvia said any West Indian he had in him had already washed away and that he was pure black American. But Nello claimed the Caribbean. Now, in early March, he wore a hibiscus-splashed shirt and baggy linen pants.

"Look fight, boy," he said to Bo. "Ain't nothing I like more than to see two woman fighting. Place your bet, man. I betting on Black Beauty."

"Dodo and Grace," Sylvia shouted from the kitchen. "Stop playing the ass in front my children."

Her children were loving it. Derek said, "Grace, Grace, throw it." And Micky, bug-eyed and dancing on tiptoes, sucked her two middle fingers and laughed.

Bo studied us from the entry. "You see Dodo looking *maga maga* like she don't have no strength, but don't trust skinny woman, boy. They have hidden depths."

Sylvia shouted again. "Dodo and Grace, don't make me have to come and slap the two of you. Stop it."

Dodo wouldn't let up. She dug her long, nasty nails into my ribs, and I whacked her head with the remote. Her hard face hardened. "Oh, you serious now? Is fight you want to fight?"

"You can't just come from where you come from and take over." I wanted to hit her again. "Bo, I wrong?"

Nello put both hands on his hips. "No, Black Beauty, you not wrong at all."

Dodo, breathing like a bull and pocketbook hanging from her side, faced me. Calmly, she said, "Grace, give me that fucking remote control right now."

"I didn't know church ladies could cuss."

Nello adjusted his balls. Bo said, "The two of you is real ass for two big woman. Dodo, I find you wrong, you know. You can't just waltz in and change channel."

She unstrung her pocketbook and, before I realized what she was doing, swung it hard at me.

"Bitch!" I dropped the remote and reached for her. Bo, sensing the joke was done, grabbed me from behind.

Nello didn't like that. "Leave them let them fight, man."

"Put me down!" I was kicking him. "Bo, put me down!"

Sylvia came in from the kitchen. "Grace, I expect better from you, man."

"What? Tell your ugly sister that. I thought she was a Christian."

Sylvia walked over to the couch and took the remote from Dodo. I laughed, "ha ha," thinking she was going to give it to me. Instead she aimed and turned off the TV. Then she walked over to the breakfront and switched on the radio, filling the room with loud calypso. She put both her hands in the air as if in surrender, turned her head Egyptian profile sharp, and swung her huge hips from side to side. "Okay, every-body win. We come up the road to party tonight, not for foolishness."

I was only a little satisfied. "She still start it."

"And I finish it. Go in the kitchen and take some Chinese food and a beer. Bo and Nello, come on, man, we say we having a nice lime tonight. Bring the rum. Grace, you not eating?"

"I can't eat Chinese, remember?"

"Oh shit, yes. I forget. Well, heat up some turkey curry in the michael-wave."

"Okay, Sylvia." I didn't want to spoil her good mood.

I decided to be magnanimous to Dodo. "Can I get you anything from the kitchen, Dodo?" You could see in her face she wanted to say something nasty, but instead she crossed her skinny legs, drew extra long on her cigarette, and said, "Thanks, I'll taste a little rum when them boys bring it."

She rattled some phlegm and got her spitbox. "It good for the cold on my chest."

By nine o'clock Derek and Micky were in bed and the little fete was going strong. Garçon, the super from Haiti, had banged on the ceiling twice with a broomstick, and each time Sylvia turned the music up a little louder. I had two beers and was dancing with Nello, who kept trying to pull me closer. Sylvia was doing her hands-up gyration, and Dodo, drunk on red rum, had restrung her pocketbook around her body and was trying to shake what she didn't have. Bo, the bottle of rum held steadily to his head, crashed around the living room singing along to every calypso whether he knew the lyrics or not. Once I thought I heard the phone ring. Two beers weren't enough to make me drunk, but my head was spinning. I only wanted to dance. " *'Cause, we havin' a par-tay, a par-tay.*"

This time I was sure I heard the phone and pulled away from clutching Nello to answer it in the kitchen. "Hello?"

"Grace? It's Miriam Bruckner. Sounds like someone's having a party."

"Mrs. Bruckner? Hi. Yes, it's my cousin's birthday and we're having a little lime . . . a party, for her." The lie came without thought.

"Miriam. We wanted to let you know that we've decided to offer you the job. Ben liked you best. Sol and I think you're good with him, and the grandparents were very impressed by you. So, if you're still interested the job is yours."

I squeezed the receiver so hard the veins in my wrist bulged and my palm hurt. I got the job. I got the job. They hired me over the newsstand woman, and the baby-nurse woman, and the mole woman. Over everybody. Me! Now I had my own reason to party. *"Judy, when you go in town, girl."*

"Yes, Mrs. Miriam. I'm still interested." I wasn't making any sense. The noise from the living room pounded in my head. I tried to be calm. "When do you want me to start?"

"Tonight."

I thought I hadn't heard her right. "I'm sorry?" I held my breath.

"We need you to come in tonight."

How could I go in tonight? Who would help Sylvia with the children in the morning? But if I told Miriam no, she would call the newsstand woman and offer her the job. "Miriam, it's after nine. I can't take the train alone this late. Maybe I could come early in the morning?"

"Grace, we need you tonight. This time only I'll pay for a cab, and you'd be doing us a huge favor. Now, can you do it?"

Music blasted from the living room.

Judith, when you go in town, girl
Judith, when you go in town, girl
Watch how you movin' around, child
'Cause on Tuesday night, when them men get tight
They don't care who get bite.

"Okay. I'll be there in about an hour."

"Thank you, Grace. Ben will be thrilled to see you in the morning."

She hung up, and I held the receiver in my hand. Sylvia was screaming, and Bo too. They were clapping and stomping, and I thought, *Yes, yes, yes. I got the job!* I walked down the hall to the living room. "I got the job," I said. No one heard, so I turned down the volume on the radio. "Sylvia, the woman call. I get the work."

Finally she heard. "You get it? They just call? I didn't even hear the phone. All right." She shrugged. "So something else to party about. When you starting?"

"Tonight."

"Tonight?" Sylvia, Bo, and Dodo answered together.

"What stupidness is this I hearing? They want you to come in tonight? And you going?" She turned the sound completely off. "Grace, don't let them white people take you and make you they ass. Who ever hear somebody getting call to go for a job in the middle of the night?"

Nello, red-eyed drunk, slurred, "All kind of people go to work in the middle of the night." Reeling, he ticked them off on his pencil-stub fingers. "Policeman, nurse woman, fireman. Welcome to America, coconuts, the city that never sleeps."

"Nello. Shut your ass, please." Sylvia turned back to me. "Grace, use your head. For a bright girl sometimes you very stupid, you know. Why them people call you to come in the middle of the night, and on a Tuesday night to boot? Look, call that woman and tell she you coming in the morning."

Sylvia and Bo and Dodo and Nello were looking at me. The radiator hissed, and I could feel the cool air from the window Bo had cracked to catch a breeze. The room was now very quiet.

"I already told her I'm coming."

Dodo laughed. "Sylvia, long time now I warn you about this girl."

"No, Dodo"—Sylvia sounded rational—"Grace have to live she life. I don't want she to stay for me." She turned to me. "Grace, use your head. Why they want you to come like a thief in the middle of the night?"

She was right, I knew, but I'd already made up my mind. "Sylvia, I don't know. But I'm going. I could use the little bag?"

Drunk as he was, Bo said, "Grace girl, listen to Sylvia. She living in America plenty longer than you."

"I know that, Bo. Sylvia, I could borrow the bag?"

"Take the bag, Grace. You is a big woman, and I can't stop you from doing what you want to do. Okay"—she dusted her palms—"that is it. Party done."

"No, don't stop." I reached to turn up the volume.

"Leave off that radio," Sylvia snapped. "And go if you going. It getting late."

Chapter 10

Sol opened the door in his robe, gave me a bear hug, and thanked me for coming. "Mir and Ben are sleeping, but you can watch the game with me. You like basketball?" He made a fake shot and his robe hung open.

I was tired to my bones. "Thanks, Sol. I need to go to sleep."

"Okay, I'll turn it down for you." He touched my shoulder. "It's good to see you again, Grace."

I didn't say it, but it felt good to be there.

By quarter past seven the next morning, I was up and in the shower to be ready for eight. Two minutes later, someone knocked on my bathroom door. "Yes?"

"Grace, it's Miriam. We need you out here."

"Okay." I grabbed for the towel.

"Quickly, please." She sounded annoyed, and I hurried, happy I had brought clothes into the bathroom to change.

"Here—" She stood over an ironing board, face pale and spots bright, her blond hair hanging loose and wet. "Sol needs this shirt. Try not to leave creases on the sleeves."

"Okay." On the sunflower clock it was 7:30. I wasn't supposed to start until eight, but because of the hurry of last night, I figured this morning was special.

Sol's shirttail went past my knees. I read the tag: "Warm iron on reverse while slightly damp." This shirt was bone dry. I checked the tag again. "100% cotton." I hung the shirt over the ironing board and got a glass of water from the kitchen, then I turned the sleeves inside out and selected Cotton on the iron. But I couldn't find an outlet. The sunflower clock said 7:37.

"Morning, Grace. Done with that shirt?"

"Morning, Sol. No, um, not yet. I couldn't see an outlet so—"

"Here." Sol hitched his pants at the knees and stooped down next to the wall. "See here, on the baseboard. There's a foot-long outlet."

I knelt next to where he squatted between the table and the wall. He didn't wear cologne, and his body smelled like soap and deodorant and his breath like minty toothpaste. My arm brushed against the hairs on his forearm.

"Oh. I've never seen an outlet like that."

"Yeah," he said, standing up and shaking his legs so his pants would fall straight. "They're hard to spot if you don't know what you're looking for."

I set to ironing the shirt. It was 7:45. Miriam came out of the bedroom. Her hair was dry now and her face caked with that heavy makeup she pasted on like putty.

"Are you done with that shirt, Grace?"

Sol answered for me. "She couldn't find the outlet."

"She found the glasses, I see."

"Not to drink," I said. "The shirt needs to be damp."

Sol and Miriam looked at each other.

"It's not a problem, Mir," he said. "I'll see what Carmen left in the closet."

"Okay, Grace," Miriam said, "I know this is your first morning. Sol and I appreciate you coming in last night. But you've got to be quick." She snapped her fingers three times. "You were here on Saturday, so you kinda know where things are, right? For today, I made a list. Did you see it on the dining table?"

I had not.

She clicked over to the table and wagged a sheet of paper. "Here's what needs to get done today. Follow me."

We walked into the kitchen, and Sol came in wearing a white shirt, identical to the one I was supposed to have ironed. "Mir, while you're at it, show Grace how to make the coffee. There's none this morning."

Miriam turned, and I was caught between them. "Maybe you can brew a pot, Sol? It's not exactly a regular morning, is it?"

"Whoa." Sol raised his palms. "Don't take it out on me, Mir. All I'm saying is that you should show her how to use the coffeemaker."

"You were showing her the wiring just now, why didn't you show her how to percolate your coffee the way you like it?"

They faced off, Miriam's breathing audible through her skinny nose. In her heels, she came to Sol's chest. From the back bedroom, Ben called out, "Ya-ya."

"Shit," Miriam said.

"I got him," Sol said. "Finish showing Grace the washer."

"Stay here," Miriam said to me as she wheeled the washer into the kitchen. "You have to do a few loads of laundry today." She removed an armload of sponge from the dryer. "If you don't do this"—she rammed the strips between the machine and the cupboards—"the washing machine will take a walk during the spin cycle, and you'll have a lot more work to do. Next, connect the water." She unhooked a hose from the machine. "Watch carefully." She pressed a piece of rubber at the mouth of the hose and slipped the nozzle onto the faucet. "You have to listen for that snap. If it doesn't snap, the water pressure forces the hose off and the machine doesn't fill up. None of our clothes go in the dryer."

"They get hung in the small bathroom, right?"

"Right. Sort whites, darks, and colors. And, oh, no bleach. Any questions?"

I wanted her to show me how to attach the hose again, but I didn't want to ask. Plus it was still in, so all I had to do was turn on the water. "No."

"Good." Miriam reached over and disconnected the hose. "Now I'll show you how to make the coffee."

Sol brought in a still sleepy Ben. "Mir, it's after eight, you should get going."

"Should I get going or should I show Grace how you like your coffee?"

Ben looked around. "Where Ya-ya, Daddy?"

"Guess what, buddy? Grace is going to be your ya-ya today."

This was not the news Ben wanted to hear. He kicked his legs like a little boy on a stubborn donkey. "I want my ya-ya." I reached over to help settle him, but he kicked again and got me in the corner of my mouth. I tasted blood. "Ow."

"Sol, I really have to go," Miriam said.

"Get going. I'll pick up coffee from McDonald's."

"I want to go to McDonald's. I have a toy and french fries," Ben said.

Miriam tickled him, then she pinched Sol's waist. "Daddy likes french fries too." She turned to me. "Okay, Grace, I have to run. My work number is on the fridge. Call if there's an emergency. Remember the list."

She left and Sol moved closer. "Let me see." He reached over and gently peeled back the corner of my lower lip. "Just suck on it and the bleeding should stop. Are you going to be a good boy today?" he asked Ben.

Ben nodded, but when I reached for him he still clung to his father.

—MIRIAM'S LIST—

1. Feed Ben breakfast: one whole-grain waffle with pure maple syrup, sliced bananas, and juice. (If you have waffles or pancakes, use the syrup in the plastic bottle in the fridge door.)

2. Give Ben bath or shower, whichever he prefers this morning.

3. Pick up our bedroom, Ben's room, living room (vacuum rugs), clean both bathrooms.

4. Laundry. Three loads, no bleach. HANG DRY EVERYTHING!!

5. Go to Union Square playground. Ben may take one toy but NEVER Rabbit.

6. Go to supermarket (money in money cup, RECEIPTS!!). See sublist, over.

7. Feed Ben lunch: Grilled cheese sandwich (Ben likes to choose his plate), steamed carrots (in microwave for 1.5 mins.), juice.

8. Put Ben down for nap.

9. Cook dinner. Please see cookbooks in 3rd cupboard, *The Joy of Cooking*, p. 597, "chicken cacciatore." Make Rice-A-Roni to go with.

10. While dinner is on and Ben is napping, look around for chores: Is the kitchen floor as clean as it could be? Do we have fresh towels in the bathroom? Did Ben's bath leave a ring around the tub? There's always LOTS of miscellany.

Cook chicken what?

First I screwed up the wash. I tried for half an hour to get that stupid piece of rubber to fit over the tap. Ben stood outside the kitchen, still in his Onesie, watching me. "What you doing, Grace?"

"I'm trying to do your laundry, but I can't. It's stuck." He seemed to like those words. "It's stuck, it's stuck," he repeated a few times. I thought I heard the rubber go *click* and turned on the tap. The water pressure flung the hose into the sink and splashed water over me, the floor, the machine.

"Jesus H. Christ!"

Ben laughed. "Grace, you're all wet."

"And you know what?" I faced him, dripping, and so glad I had made him laugh.

"What, Grace?"

"You're going to be all wet too." I ran to him. Sensing a chase, Ben squealed and pedaled his little legs out to the living room. I let him dodge me around the furniture but ultimately cornered him in his room.

"You're fast, Grace," he said, grinning.

I hammed it up, breathing hard. "Yeah, but you're a speedy guy too."

"I know," he said. "My daddy can't even catch me, and he's big."

I decided to forget about the laundry and let Ben show me around his room. After Sol left, Ben had howled for his ya-ya and brushed several of his mother's figurines off the shelves in a fit of tiny fist-clenching rage. I sat down on the floor and told him I was sad too. While I waited him out, I wondered if Sylvia had to go to her agency this morning, and if she'd explained to Micky and Derek that I had gone to work but that I would see them on Friday night, and who braided Micky's hair, and who tied Derek's tie, and who was watching Dame. The answer to the last two questions was probably Bo, who surely did not have the patience to sit with Dame and sound out words for him to pronounce.

Chapter 11

In my last year of high school, I had entered the carnival queen show. I
didn't really care to, but my friend Rhonda had dared me, and, since my
mother said the pageant was the work of the devil, how could I not? I
didn't think I would win. The girls chosen queen year after year looked like
Kathy, with light skin and long hair. And if your eyes were any color other
than brown, well, the joke was that the crown was ordered in your size.

The auditorium was packed. Everyone turned out for any special event
to numb the drudgery of washing clothes and minding goats and washing
and minding children. The local boys too cool to sit with the students and
old women were in the back, some of them on chairs and some in the rafters. I waited in the dressing room, Rhonda fussing and adding more rouge
than I thought necessary. Wave after wave of roars greeted each girl as she
stepped out of the wings and paraded down the path. And then my turn.
"Miss Grace Caton." Rhonda shooed me out, doing her last adjustments to
my hair and dress. When I stepped into the auditorium, the thousand-watt
spotlight blinded me, and for a second I couldn't see. I could hear, though,
and I heard nothing. No roaring. No clapping. No wolf whistling. Nothing.
I wanted to run, to hide behind the curtain, to jump up into the rafters, and
most of all to kill Rhonda. But then the boys in the back went mad, people
jumped up from their iron folding chairs and clapped, and the judges
started scribbling in their notebooks. That quiet, which had seemed to last
so long, had been mere moments.

Something like that stillness, which afterward Rhonda had assured
me I'd imagined, greeted me when I walked into the playground. From
the streets surrounding the park, I could hear the sounds of traffic, but as

I pushed Ben through the open gates, the chattering women stared from me to Ben to each other and back to me again. Elbows nudged sides, chins and eyebrows lifted, and mouths twisted. I gripped the curved carriage handles, ridged like horns, and wheeled Ben over to the sandbox. A tight knot of skinny white women stood off by themselves sipping coffee. I undid Ben's safety belt, and a woman let out a piercing bacchanal laugh like they did back home when news spread that someone's unmarried daughter was pregnant. Then as clear as the ruckus after the silence in the auditorium, a Barbadian voice said, "Is not the white people, you know, is nigger people self does take the bread from other nigger people mouth."

Half an hour later Kathy, her chubby cheeks bright red, came into the park. "Me can't believe your call. Me can't believe I get to see you every day now. Too too exciting." The rhinestones in the diamond angles of her jacket threw off lances of sunlight. Stuck above her ponytail was a large pair of white-framed, jeweled sunglasses.

"Diamante, Kath, that's the word for you today." I stood from the edge of the sandbox. "You actually wear those glasses?"

"Here"—she pulled off the shades—"try them."

"What do you think?" I asked Ben. "Should Grace put on the funky glasses?" I was so glad Kathy was here. The glares and murmurs and occasional bursts of laughter of the other women unnerved me. I wondered at their cruelty.

"Put them on, Grace." He shielded his eyes from the sun and maybe Kathy's shooting rays.

The world was deep green through the lenses, and the sight took me back to late afternoons at home, to that time of day when burning heat gave way to cooler evening and the sun began its speedy fall into the hills. "Cool, Grace," Ben said.

"Grace"—Kathy stepped back and took me in with the silly glasses— "you are the only person I know who could look stunning minding a child in jeans and sneakers."

I handed them back to her. "Just don't tell me I should be a model, okay."

Kathy exaggerated the jut of her full hip. "So this is the likkle man." She raised her chin at Ben. "Redhead tock-tock."

I pinched Ben's freckled nose. "Yup, my bread and butter. Kath, the strangest thing though," I whispered. "Look at the women. God!" I hit her arm. "Not so obvious. You had to see how they watched Ben and me coming in the park. I said morning to those two over there—Jesus Christ, don't watch so bold—and they didn't answer. What the fuck?"

"That's a bad word, Grace," Ben said without looking up.

"This little one going to be trouble." Kathy wagged her finger at Ben. "As for them bitches . . ." She swiveled her head to take in the women.

"Kathy, shush."

"Don't shush me, Grace." Her arms were akimbo again. "Is jealous the old bitches and them jealous. Watch you and watch them." She took in the group and in a low voice said to me, "You need to learn playground politics. I bet you half of them had somebody for your job."

To look at the women rolling carriages back and forth, or pushing swings, or lined up on either side of the monkey bars, you couldn't tell that they were marking us unless you knew what to listen for. I heard *"maga* bitch," "cat-eye bitch," "that big backside," and, over and over, "poor poor Carmen."

Kathy and I sat on the lip of the sandbox watching Ben, who knew several of the kids playing in the cold dirt, especially two children with round heads and wide-spaced eyes, who moved a little unsteadily and kept their hands in front of their bodies.

"This is frigging great, Kath, my first day on the job and I have enemies."

Ben came over and said, "Juice, Grace."

"Juice, please." It really was quite warm outside, and I sipped some of the juice before passing him the small yellow carton.

"You have time to worry about them, Grace?"

I wasn't worried, but I wondered why Miriam had called me after 9:00 P.M.

"Kath, why you think Miriam asked me to come in so late last night?"

Kathy steadied herself on the sandbox. "You have the job. That is all you should care about. Maybe that other woman couldn't read or maybe she was a thief, or maybe she was too old. Who know how white people mind does operate—"

A child screamed, and we whipped around. The round-headed girl had fallen over and couldn't quite brace herself to get up. The other one, her brother I presumed, cried out, "Evie, Sammy fell!" A short woman separated herself from the group and half jogged over.

Ben ran over to me. "Grace, Sammy fell."

"But she's okay, see? Someone's helping her." I stared at the woman while she dusted Sammy off. She looked right back at me and smiled. Not a friendly smile.

I turned to Kathy. "Anyway, you're right, forget them. Tell me about Monday. You excited yet?"

She shrugged. "Not really. Business or not, is still marriage, right? My father will die when he hears this; this is not how he imagined his baby daughter getting married."

I knew what she was talking about. City Hall on a Monday morning was not the place for a blessed union. Kathy brushed the side of her face with her ponytail. "And what about you? They mention anything about the sponsorship?"

They had not.

"The only thing I'll tell you is that you shouldn't wait too long before they begin," she went on. "I've heard that sponsorship through a job takes donkey years."

I'd heard that too. I thought of telling Kathy about Sylvia's proposal, that Bo would marry me for free if I worked for her, but I was confused enough. I didn't want another opinion just yet. Instead I told her about my mother's letter.

"She still trying to get you to come back?"

In the sand, Ben had linked arms with the twins and a little Asian boy in an unsteady ring around the rosy. "You don't know my mother. She'll try to get me to come back until the day I walk off the plane at Piarco. This is all about my hymen, you know. She wants to keep an eye on it."

Kathy laughed out loud. "Is it still there?"

"Actually, it is. I haven't had a serious contender since I came to America. I'll give it to a weak contender, Kath." I crossed myself quickly. "I can't believe I said that in the same conversation about my mother."

"What about Brent?"

"He's a contender."

"You're a whore, Grace."

"Only for him." I laughed. "How are your party plans coming along?"

"Donovan's taking care of everything. You know how it's going to be, right?"

"Apart from outrageous?" The first bash I went to with Kathy I left after an hour. Back then I didn't know that you had to be in costume to party. Kathy had worn a skintight, gold short pantsuit and her over-the-knee, come-fuck-me boots. I'd met her outside the club on Empire Boulevard amid a swirl of neon and flesh. She'd taken one look at me in my jeans and T-shirt and shaken her head. "Oh, Grace," she'd said, "I should have warned you."

Now she shaded her eyes. "What you doing for your birthday? Which day is it on again?"

"Nothing. Friday." My eighteenth birthday, and Kathy was the only person in America who knew.

"Okay, we'll go to Fourteenth Street and see what we can't find for you to wear."

It was nearing noon, and the sitters were making moves to leave. The group of white women at the fence end of the playground walked toward the exit. As they neared, one of them stopped and looked down at us. Her lips were a thin, brilliantly reddened slash. "*Where* did you get that jacket?" she asked Kathy. "It's fantastic."

Kathy grinned and slipped on her sunglasses. "Saks. Fourth floor."

"Fantastic," the woman repeated and stalked off to meet her friends.

Kathy turned to me. "Saks my ass. Try Janice on Fulton and half hour with the BeDazzler."

Chapter 12

My hours were a sham. Like yesterday, Miriam called me into the kitchen at seven-thirty. She showed me how Sol liked his coffee: mix grounds from two separate blends, use cold water from the filtered pitcher, and microwave a mug of water for a full minute to have hot and ready for when he came out. He took it black. I also had to make Miriam toast and jam and pack her a bag lunch. While Ben had his breakfast, I started the cleaning: their room, his room, the bathrooms. Then out for morning play. Back in for lunch. During Ben's afternoon nap I hung laundry, cleaned the living room, cooked dinner, and kept up with what Miriam referred to as "miscellany": figurine dusting or refrigerator organizing or closet sorting. After Ben's nap, we had errands. Miriam came in, and I served her and Ben dinner and made a plate for Sol. Folded and put away laundry. Packed up leftovers. By the time I put Ben to bed, it was already eight-thirty and I still had to load the dishwasher.

Today, when I put the coffee into the machine, Miriam covered her nose and ran to the bathroom, her high heels tacking on the floor. When she came out of the bathroom, lipstick gone and red spots bright in the corners of her mouth, I smiled and asked, "So how far along are you?"

Miriam looked at me with a blank face. Her eyes were red too. "Far along with what, Grace?"

"Aren't you . . . ?" I left the question hanging.

"Aren't I what?" she asked, steadying herself on the counter.

"Nothing," I said.

"Nothing?" she repeated. "It couldn't be less, could it?"

I wasn't sure what that meant, but it wasn't an invitation to chat. "I rode the elevator with Evie yesterday," I told her instead. "Ben plays with Sammy and"—I didn't know the other one's name—"on Fridays?"

Ben walked into the kitchen and stuck his head between his mother's legs. Back home, whenever children looked between their mothers' legs the women asked if they were looking for a brother or a sister. I chose not to share this with Miriam.

"Sammy and Caleb," she said.

Ben, hearing his friends' names, said, "Sammy fell in the sand yesterday and Evie picked her up, Mommy."

"Evie introduced herself?" Miriam asked.

"Not exactly. She said Ben and the twins play together?" I wondered if Miriam would tell me about Carmen now.

"That's all she said?" And for a few seconds she looked at me, expecting to hear more.

"That's it."

"Evie's the queen bee of the playground," Miriam said. "She's been with the Zollers since the twins were born. They hired her away from the hospital, actually." While she spoke, Ben danced the maypole through her legs.

Sol came out, dressed, and I passed him his coffee. "And what did the Lady Miss Evie have to say?"

I shrugged. "Just about the Friday playdate."

The silence hung for a few seconds. "Okay," Miriam said. "Grace, there's a list on the dining table. Big ironing day today! If you have questions, call me."

BEN AND RABBIT WERE settled with *The Little Mermaid*, so I took advantage of the quiet to call Sylvia. A groggy Bo picked up.

"Hi, Bo, is Grace. How you going?"

"Grace, what the ass you doing calling here so early in the morning? You know what time it is?"

It was exactly 10:00 A.M., and if Bo answered the phone, it meant that Sylvia had gone to work. "Bo, where Dame?"

"Me don't know," he said, and I could picture him scratching his hairy chest.

"He probably still in the crib, Bo. You have to make a bottle for him and then give him something to eat and bathe him." I knew Sylvia must have told him to do all this. "Bo, let me ask you something."

"Talk fast."

"Why you don't tell Sylvia the paint in the apartment making Dame sick?" I didn't understand how Bo and them operated, if he knew that something might be wrong with Dame, why would he not tell Sylvia?

"And when I tell Sylvia, what she could do about it?"

"Bo, don't be stupid. What you mean 'what she could do?' She could take him to the doctor or pressure Jacob."

He belched hard in my ear. "You don't know how them Jew and them does operate," he said almost to himself, and then louder, as if coming to, "Grace, why you calling me this hour of the morning to hurt my head? If you so concern about Sylvia children, why you leave to go and work for them white people? I find you could of stay here and help she out if you so concern."

He was right, of course, partially. "And where I would get money to pay you?"

That snapped his attention to. "So how much money them people paying you? Is a good little change you making?"

Normally, I wouldn't tell anyone how much I made, but the amount of money was so small, I wanted Bo's reaction. "Two hundred."

He whistled. "Girl, you selling yourself cheap. You better look around and see how to get a little lagniappe." Bo laughed. "Maybe from the husband on the side."

"Why I wasting my time talking to you? Sylvia gone to work?"

He ignored me, liking the slack talk he had brought up. "No, Grace, in truth. Them white man and them like black pussy—"

I hung up.

WE WERE PICKING OUT Ben's lunch plate when the front door opened.

Ben ran to the living room. "Daddy's home. Daddy's home, Grace."

Sol came into the kitchen carrying Ben on his shoulders.

"Hi, Sol. You forget something?"

"No, Grace, I came to have lunch with my boy."

"Okay," I said, and then added, "nice to see you," even though it wasn't. I held up one plate with Pooh and Piglet strolling through the Hundred

Acre Wood and another with Mickey holding a blushing Minnie's white-gloved hand. "Which one, Ben?"

"Winnie-the-Pooh plate, Grace."

"Hey, buddy," Sol said to Ben, "do you want to say the blessing with me?" Together they singsonged, *"Baruch ata Adonai, Eloheinu melech ha-olam, Ha-motzi lechem min ha-aretz."* "Did you go to the playground today?" Sol asked him when they were done.

Ben reached for his cup. "I played in the sand and the tire swing, and Grace put me on the monkey bars."

"Sounds like you had a great time." He took a carrot stick off Ben's plate. "So how's it going for you, Grace? Are you comfortable, do you have everything you need?"

He had asked me this just last night when I was loading the dishwasher. "Everything is fine," I told him.

He rapped his long fingers on the tabletop, and I saw that the hair on his knuckles was red too. "So, how about some lunch?"

"Thanks," I said, "but I'm not hungry yet."

One orange eyebrow raised. "I meant for me, Grace. How about some lunch for me?"

My face burned as I recognized my mistake. "Oh, I'm sorry, Mr. Bruckner, um, Sol." Ben had taken his sandwich apart and was pinking the edge of the cheese with his front teeth. "What would you like?" It hadn't occured to me to make him something.

"Don't worry about it," he said. "Maybe tuna on rye with lettuce and tomatoes. Do we have rye?"

I got up from the table to check. There was tuna and rye, and I put together a plate for him. When I brought his sandwich, he was sitting sideways, with his legs stretched out and crossed at the ankles. He didn't move, and I had to step over him to rest the plate on the table. "Thanks, Grace. Can I also have a glass of water with ice?"

I went back to the kitchen and poured the water, remembering Jane's production with Miriam's orange juice. As I placed the glass next to his plate, Sol held on to my wrist. I looked over at him. "Yes?"

He swallowed before letting me go. Tapping the corner of his mouth, he asked, "How's your lip from yesterday morning?" Ben watched us.

I touched the spot with the tip of my tongue. It wasn't even sore anymore. "It's fine," I said. "It was better by the time we got outside."

"Good." He picked up his sandwich, but before he bit into the bread he winked at Ben. "Hey, buddy, look," he said. "Mine is bigger than yours."

MIRIAM CALLED IN THE middle of the afternoon. I was up to my waist in ironing. "Hi, Grace." I could hear her drafty breathing through the phone. "How's Ben? What're you doing?"

"He's still napping. Because Sol was here, he went down a little later. I'm ironing."

There was a pause. "Sol was home?"

"He came around lunchtime, and I made him a sandwich. He and Ben played for a bit, and then he left." Miriam was silent for a while. So maybe he didn't come home all that often for lunch.

"Okay, Grace, listen. I have a meeting after school and then an appointment. Take Ben to the park around five for about an hour."

"No problem. I'm about to start dinner now, so as soon as I'm done."

"Good," she said. "I'll see you later."

AT FIVE DANNY WAS at the front desk. He jumped off the elevated platform and landed next to us. Ben put up his hand for a high five, and Danny slapped him one. He still wore the leprechaun lapel pin.

"Hello again, Grace," he said. "So you *are* the Bruckners' new nanny." He nodded. "I like their choice."

"Just do me a favor, okay? Don't ask Ben if I'm his new Y-A-Y-A."

Danny dropped into a crouch next to the carriage. I could see his hair thinning in the middle like a sprouting yarmulke. "Ben here," he said, "is my main man."

Ben reached for the leprechaun pin on his lapel. "Why you still wearing that? St. Patrick's is over."

"Hey"—Danny pointed at me—"for the true Irish every day is St. Paddy's." He moved closer to me at the back of the carriage and lifted his eyebrows a few times. "So, Grace, what's the word upstairs? Why'd they get rid of her? She steal money? I hear they had you come in in the middle of the night. What was that all about?"

How I wish I knew. Danny reminded me of the *comess* women on the island, the ones who lived for gossip and who, when they couldn't find any news, made up stories themselves.

The doorman held open the front door for a woman. Danny touched his red hat. "Good evening, Ms. Eastman." She cocked her head and gave him a smile that was more of a grimace. Even though I stood closer to the desk than the middle of the lobby, she made right for Ben and me. "Excuse me," she said and shook her head as she passed.

I looked at Danny. "Was I supposed to move? We weren't in her way even."

The elevator closed, and the numbers lit her ascent. "No, man," Danny said, "I don't think you were wrong at all." He dropped his voice. "All the same, though, you shouldn't stand around in the lobby, especially at this time of day. It gets busy, and not everyone's a breeder. You know what I mean?"

A FEW MOTHERS LINGERED in the park with their children. They looked out of place squatting near the sandbox in their wool coats and business clothes and pumps. I unbuckled Ben and asked him what he wanted to do.

"The sandbox, Grace."

I wasn't surprised. It was where he spent most of his time. The tire swing, the loopy plastic slide, the monkey bars, everything else in the playground was a distraction between trips to the sand. "Hey, Ben"—I dug into the netted pouch for his shovel—"how come you're such a sandman?"

He liked that. "I'm a sandman, Grace. A sandman."

I passed him the shovel, and he scooped up his first mound. "Grace, this is like the beach."

Kneeling next to him, I picked up a handful of the damp brown earth—nothing at all like the pinky white sand on the beach back home—and let it fall in dismal clumps through my fingers. My father's little parcel of dirt was still in my purse, but the boxed-in sand in Union Square, sat in and spat in, played in and maybe peed in sand, was not the mix I needed to settle my stomach.

"Hello, Benjamin." We both looked up. I recognized the woman from the group of sitters on the benches yesterday and this morning. She was older, in about her mid-fifties, and had a small-island accent. Ben, I had noticed, never answered when any of the sitters said hello.

"Ben," I said, "this nice lady just said hello. You're supposed to say hello back."

He didn't look again at her, but he did say hello. She bent over her carriage and took out a small baby wrapped in a thick layer of blankets.

"How old is that baby?" I asked her.

"Not more than four weeks."

"It's late to have a small baby outside, isn't it?" I didn't mean to criticize.

She lit up when I said that, boy. "Exactly," she crowed, "is the same thing me try and tell the mother, but she don't want listen. I tell her dew falling already and America dew is colder than in the West Indies. A likkle child so should be inside. But nobady listen. She want me to bring the child outside for air, so me bring him outside for air. As long as when you see he catch pneumonia and drap dead them nah say is my fault."

I didn't think she was right about the dew. My mother had been the same way, and Helen and I had a long list of things to not do to avoid catching cold. We couldn't iron and then bathe, or step out of bed in the morning and put our feet directly on the ground. We couldn't even think about opening the refrigerator if we came in during the heat of the day.

I got up to see the baby's face. She peeled back the blanket, and he looked like every other white baby, bald, wrinkly, and vaguely alien. "He's very cute," I said.

"You crazy, child? Cute? No sah, you must take anadder look. This is the ugliest likkle wretch me ever did see."

I touched the child's cheek. "Well, you don't want to say that about a baby."

"You must always speak you mind, child. Even if the truf does offend."

She was right, of course, but it wasn't nice to call people ugly. "My name is Grace," I said to her.

"Grace is a good name. I am Ule Brown. I see you this morning and before." She dropped her voice. "Is a nasty somefing that boy mother do Carmen."

Finally somebody was going to talk to me about Carmen. "I didn't know what was going on, you know."

"How you could of know, child? That woman"—she chucked her chin at Ben—"that woman is a snake. She used to spy on Carmen. Yes."

"Spy on her doing what?"

She ignored that question. "You best watch yourself, you hear me."

I didn't know what I had to watch myself for. I did the housework Miriam told me to do, and cooked what she told me to cook, and took care of Ben as best as I could. There was nothing for her to see if she spied.

"So what did Carmen do?" I asked again, feeling like a hypocrite. Half an hour ago I was comparing Danny to a *comess* woman, and now here I was trying to get gossip from Ule. "You know what, Ule? I don't want to know. That doesn't have anything to do with me." I reached for Ben in the sandbox. "Is time to take him in. Have a good night."

She looked as if she agreed with what I had said. "Okay, Grace. Tomorrow is anadder day. Bye, Benjamin."

He didn't look at her, but he did said bye.

We met Sol in the tower lobby, and he and I switched cargo. "So what time do you normally come in?" I asked, pushing his briefcase. "Yesterday you came in after eight and today it's barely six." He carried Ben high on his shoulders.

"Usually somewhere in the middle, around seven. I went uptown to see my parents yesterday."

"How's Big Ben?"

Ben stopped counting floors and said, "Big Ben, choo choo."

"He's good. He liked you."

The apartment lights were on, and I guessed that Miriam was home. Sol called out, but there was no answer. He walked in ahead of us and stopped when he came to the kitchen entrance. "Miriam, what the hell are you doing? Get down from there right now. Are you crazy?"

Miriam was standing on the top rung of a step stool. She held a spray bottle in one hand and a wad of paper towels in the other.

Sol held her around the waist as she backed down. "Sol," she said, "stop overreacting. I just climbed up to clean some grease off the glass. It was filthy." She showed him the blackened paper towels.

"Listen, Miriam, this is why we have a maid, okay. I don't want my wife climbing around like a monkey cleaning windows."

A maid?

"This is why we have Grace. Grace"—he turned back to me—"these are your chores, not Miriam's. You're getting paid to do this stuff so she doesn't have to do it. Do you understand?"

I ran through the list from this morning. I had forgotten nothing. Still, I nodded.

MIRIAM WASN'T DONE WITH me for the night. At 8:15, when I had dressed Ben for bed and loaded the dishwasher and cleaned the cabinet glass, and was finally ready to rest, she slid open the jalousied door to my space.

"Come to the supermarket with me," she said.

Sylvia or Kathy or any of the other women it seemed would be able to say "I'm off," or "I'm done for the evening," or "This is my time." But I could not.

Sol was watching TV. Ben lay with him. "Where are you guys going?" He barely lifted his head from the armrest. Ben chatted with Rabbit and paid us no mind.

"Quick run to the A & P."

"At this hour, Mir? Have Grace go tomorrow."

"Nah." She buttoned a coat around her shirt. "I have to get some heavier things."

He half sat up. "Do you want me to come with?"

She tossed and caught her keys. "We'll manage."

In the elevator she made small talk. "My kids drove me nuts today."

"Your kids?" I asked.

She turned to look at me. "Yeah, my students. You know I teach, right? Special ed. Not the easiest class. Mostly crack babies with zero attention span. You know what a crack baby is?"

I had an idea. Once, Micky and Derek had got into a fight with the kids from next door. Micky had stood with her hands on her waist, quite bold when her mother wasn't around, and told Sonique, her best friend two minutes before, that her mother was a crackhead and her grandma was a crackhead and she was a government-cheese-eating welfare crack baby.

Miriam didn't wait for me to answer. As we walked into the supermarket conveniently located on the building's ground floor, she went on about taking care of people's troubled children when she much preferred to stay home and take care of her own.

"So why not stay home?" Sol was a lawyer, and his parents looked like they had plenty of money. It didn't seem to me that Miriam had to work.

She pointed to the conga-lined shopping carts off to the side, and I grabbed one. "I'd love to quit my job and take care of Ben full-time," she said, "but in my own sweet time, thank you." She added, almost to herself, "I'm not on anybody's timetable."

I pushed the cart up and down the aisles, and Miriam picked out groceries. A gallon of milk, cans of whole and crushed tomatoes, tins of tuna, boxes of Rice-A-Roni, olive oil, jars of gefilte fish in that viscous gray jelly that made a sucking sound when you pulled out a lumpy piece, bottles of Diet Coke and water, chicken, meat, frozen vegetables. Eventually, I had to use my foot to turn the cart up and down the rows. "Any coupons?" the checkout girl asked.

Miriam reached into her brown pocketbook and pulled out a sheaf. She fanned through them and handed over two.

"Delivery?" the checkout girl asked.

"No," Miriam said. "We've got it."

There were seven packed bags in all, and I picked up four and waited. The checkout girl said good night and turned to the next customer. Miriam snapped shut her purse. "You left some bags, Grace."

The checkout girl turned back to us as I tried to pick up the other three bags. "You sure you don't want us to bring those up, ma'am? Delivery's free in the building, you know."

"I'm sure," Miriam said. "Do you have them, Grace?"

"I think so." I managed to pick up all seven bags—my arms felt as though they were coming apart at my inner elbows. Miriam walked out of the store, scanning her receipt. I turned to smile at the checkout girl, who looked at me and shrugged.

In the lobby, the dog man leaned against the concierge's desk, listening to an animated Danny. "Hey, Dave." Miriam stopped. "How are you?" He kissed her on the cheek, and they held their hug for a while.

"I'm good, Sister Maria. How you doin?"

"Smart-ass," she said playfully. "You coming up on Sunday, right?"

"Wouldn't miss your gnocchi for anything in the world." Dave looked over at me and at the bags blooming from my clenched fists. "And who have we here?"

"This is Grace."

I pivoted at the hips like Pinocchio. I wanted to rest the bags on the tiles so that I could shake hands with the dog man—Dave. Also, my arms were on fire.

"Um, sorry, Grace, you can't put those there, house rules," Danny said.

Miriam glared. I straightened and felt the burn race up to my shoulders.

"Uh-oh," Dave said. "I guess I should move Cesar and the Brute before I get in trouble then." Danny didn't say anything, but Dave gently yanked the leashes and said good night.

Inside the apartment, Miriam told me to put away the groceries. Sol had taken Ben to his room, and I could hear them laughing and the rise in Ben's voice when she walked in. I bent again and slowly uncurled my fists to release the bags. My fingertips were bone white, and tiny bright red welts ribboned diagonally across my palms. I couldn't bend my elbows or my wrists without pain searing my arms. Slowly, slowly, I put away the groceries, listening to voices down the hall. Then I heard just Miriam's nasal voice as she read: "Once upon a time there was an artist named Hieronymus Bosch who loved odd creatures. Not a day passed that the good woman who looked after his house didn't find a new creature lurking in a corner or sleeping in a cupboard. To her fell the job of"—Ben and Sol joined in—"feeding them, weeding them, walking them, stalking them, calming them, combing them, scrubbing and tucking in all of them—until one day . . . I'm quitting your service, I've had quite enough . . ."

Chapter 13

Ben and I stood outside apartment 15F. "You want to ring the bell?" I lifted his thirty pounds and immediately regretted it as pain lanced through my arms. He happily rang the buzzer four times. I could hear feet dragging across the floor inside and children's voices saying, "Ben's here, Ben's here."

Evie opened the door wearing a blue housedress with grubby bedroom slippers mashed at the heels. She had her bangs rolled in one pink sponge curler. "You think you ring the bell enough?" she greeted me.

"I rang the bell," Ben said and pushed past her into the apartment. The Zollers' place was much bigger than the Bruckners' and seemed given over to Sammy and Caleb. There were two of everything. Two small desks with paper and pencils and two play kitchens with pots and spoons, two big bouncy balls and two tricycles. The pour yellow walls were striped with colored crayons up to where the twins' awkward arms could reach and the ceiling painted a cloudless blue with a silver, sun-shaped chandelier hanging from its center.

Evie aimed the remote at the TV. "You should have come two minutes later, man, you make me miss the end of my story." She turned to Ben. "Hello, Mr. Redhead. You come to make some trouble for me?"

Ben ignored her, and I didn't tell him to answer. He and the twins were clustered around one of the desks and already held fat markers in their hands. I didn't know what to do, so I sat on the couch wishing I had brought a book or a magazine. I waited for Evie to take the lead. She sat next to me and crossed her legs. "I don't want you to think I

don't like you, child. This thing that this woman do have everybody so
upset."

"What?" I asked Evie. "What *thing* Miriam do?"

"So you want to tell me you don't know?" Evie was waiting for an answer, for me to explain myself.

"How come Sammy and Caleb's arms are like that?"

She didn't expect my question. "Is so they born. They used to hug up
each other in the mother womb." I looked at her to see if she was serious. "All the pictures the doctor take before them born, when they was
still in she belly, you could see the two of them hugging up." She was
serious.

"Oh, okay," I said and leaned back into the food-stained couch, wondering how long these playdates lasted. Ben and Caleb had left Sammy at the
desk and rode bouncing balls across the bright red carpet in cowboy hats.

"Which part in the Caribbean you from?" I asked Evie, even though
it was plain from her accent that she, like Duke the doorman, was
Bajan.

"Barbados, born and bred."

"I always wanted to go Barbados," I said, and it was the truth. "In all
the pictures you see the water always blue blue." I looked up. "Blue like
the ceiling."

"Is me self who pick out this color for them to paint," she said.

"It's pretty," I said. It was.

"Now I hear you talk good," she said to me. "I think you from
Trinidad."

"Yep. Born and bred."

Evie seemed to relax a bit. She unrolled her bangs, combed her fingers
through her hair, and then put the curler back in. I scooted off the couch
and moved over to Sammy, standing by herself next to the desk.

"Hey, Sammy, can I see your picture?"

"I'm vrawing a cow," she said, her tongue thick in her mouth. She
turned close to my face, said, "Moooo," and laughed.

"You have a very good moo."

"Here." She handed me a black marker. "You can vraw a cow too." I
took the marker from her and did my best cow. Ben and Caleb came to see
what we were doing, and we all took turns drawing animals on the white-

board. Evie chatted in a low voice on the phone by the window, glancing over at us. I didn't pay her any mind. If this was all I had to do, I'd be happy. I could play with toddlers all day long and get paid at the week's end. The kids were not the problem.

I WAS DONE WITH every chore on the list. I had cooked Ben's dinner and theirs, made a plate for Sol, and had mopped the kitchen floor without her asking. Miriam came in around five, said hi to Ben and me, and went to her room. For an hour. At six she came out with sleep marks pressed into the left side of her face, the fresh-lined indents and her own deep pockmarks set up for an *x*-less game of tic-tac-toe. She called me into the kitchen, where she picked up the plastic money cup. She counted the money and then tallied the receipts. I tried to remember if I had put in receipts every time I had gone to the store this week. Ben and I didn't go out for pizza, so I had receipts only from the A & P. Three trips to the A & P. Three receipts. I was nervous standing there in the kitchen, even though I had nothing to be anxious about. The house was clean and the money had to all be there. Miriam turned to me and smiled. In relief, I smiled too. I grinned in fact.

"Okay, Grace, that works out. Just a minute." She turned and walked out of the kitchen to her room, for my pay, I assumed. Instead Miriam came back out with an armful of clothes, which she dumped on the easy chair, on top of my bag and my coat. It was 6:19. "Iron these before you leave. It's stuff I might need this weekend."

While I got the iron out of the closet, Miriam dished out Rice-A-Roni and sliced the London broil I had cooked earlier in the day. She sat at the table with Ben, right where I had to plug in the iron. As I pressed her clothes, she ate and chatted with her son about his day and his trip to the Zollers' and their plans for the weekend. At one point she said, "A minute less on the steak next time, Grace." I finished ironing, hung the clothes in her closet, put away the board and the iron, and still she sat at the table, taxiing spoonfuls of cold Kraft macaroni and cheese into Ben's mouth. I sat on the soft chair with my bag. At 6:57, when I was sure that Kathy had grown tired waiting for me, Miriam got up, went to her brown purse on the floral couch, took out a wad of bills, and passed them to me.

"Grace"—she was smiling—"thank you so much for coming in this week. You saved us. We'll see you on Sunday night."

"Hey, Ben, can I get a hug?" I stooped to kiss his forehead. "Have a fun weekend, okay."

I rose to say bye to Miriam. "Hold on, Grace." She dashed into the kitchen and came back with the bag of trash from the bin. "Can you throw it down the chute on your way out?"

KATHY WAS SITTING AT a closed checkout counter in the A & P, reading a fashion magazine she had plucked from the rack. An old woman with a laden cart stopped at her register and placed her groceries on the unmoving conveyor. Kathy blew a bubble with her gum and snapped, "I'm on break."

"Kathy," I said to her, "what you doing? Get up from there." She dropped the magazine and swiveled on the high stool.

"Grace, Jesus. Me thought you say you soon come. I've been in this supermarket for an hour and a half." I could see a huge wad of gum lodged in the back of her mouth. "I can't tell you how many old ladies I turned away. I've been on break for the last hour. Daddy would never leave a register untended like this. What a take you so long, girl?"

"Kath, decide. Either Trini, Jamaican, or American, but not all three in one conversation. That woman found some last-minute chores for me, but I'm done and I'm here and most importantly, I have two hundred dollars in my pocket. Shall we go shopping, my dear?"

"Abso-frigging-loutely," she said and spat her gum into the bin set behind the register for abandoned receipts.

Fourteenth Street was a wind tunnel with breeze gusting up from the river, but the Friday night air was bracing and not unbearably cold. Kids on skateboards bounced off the railings and clattered down the concrete steps, high-fiving each other when they made it and ducking off to try again when they fell hard on their bottoms. Kath and I linked arms, me a good six inches taller than her; she glinting and sparkling from the headlights and streetlights and brightly lit storefronts. I loved New York right now. The towers were behind me, and I didn't look back.

"What is this place?" Her special shop was not at all what I'd expected.

Lean-waisted mannequins were roped into corsets, and headless torsos wore stockings of various degrees of sheer. There were bullet-shaped bras and bras that laced up in the front, and bras that plunged in the back—any kind of bra Madonna could possibly need.

Kathy pulled me all the way to the back of the shop.

"Kath, for real. Why did you come here?" I asked her.

She stopped. "Okay, choose one."

"One what? You mad or crazy? Kath, these are drawers."

"I know it's underwear, Grace. You won't wear it like this. Pick one, and I'll decorate it for you to wear at the bash."

"Nuh-uh," I said, using Micky's absolute negative. "This is meant to go *under* clothes, not be clothes." I backed away, and she rummaged through one of the middle boxes. "What size are you, Grace?"

"Extra-large."

"Oh shut up." She took stock of my body and went back to her digging. No one else came in the shop.

"Got it." She straightened up holding a bulky package.

"You dreaming if you think I'm spending my hard-earned money for underwear," I said.

Kathy started up to the register. "Don't worry, this is my birthday present to you, remember."

"You must be mad if you think you getting me to wear that thing." I stood away from her as if she and the stocking suit were both catching.

Kathy just laughed. "O ye of little faith."

"What?" That was one of my mother's lines.

"Trust me." She paid and took the thing she had bought. "You're going to beg me to sew all your clothes when I'm done."

Afterward, when Kathy wouldn't even let me touch the package, we sat for a while in McDonald's. "Here," I said, "before I forget." I pulled out two twenties. "The money you lent me last week. Thank you very much." It felt good to pay off the debt. To square myself down to what I actually owned so I could begin again.

But Kath turned away. "Why you have to go and embarrass me like that, Grace? I didn't ask you for any money." She ended the talk and moved on before I could insist. "So," Kath started on my french fries, "how was your first week?"

Good question. I rested my chin on my palm and thought about coming in so suddenly, about Miriam's demands, and about Sol's daytime visit.

"Well?" Kath interrupted my thoughts.

"First"—I took a chip away from her—"stop eating my fries. This is a strange place to work, Kath."

"All white people strange, Grace."

"I don't doubt you. The husband came home for lunch yesterday—I had to make it—and when I told Miriam, she was not pleased."

"Grace"—Kath reprimanded me with a chip—"you come to make trouble in the people happy home?"

But I had not. Three days ago I'd been so happy to get this job, to start planning my future. Now I didn't know already. We ate in silence for a while, and I thought no one seemed to like me at the towers except Sol, and I didn't think that was such a good thing. "Kath," I whispered, "I think my mother working *obeah* to get me to come home."

"Grace, stop talking stupidness," she said, but she saw that I was close to crying. "I bet you reading way too much into everything. Just do what Miriam tells you to do, and stay far from her husband. Wait"—she grinned—"I have something funny to tell you."

I needed a laugh. "What?"

"Remember that scarf I lent you last week?"

In my rush to come in on Tuesday night, I hadn't thought to pack the scarf. "Shoot, yes. It's in my drawer at Sylvia's. I'll bring it on Sunday night."

Kath laughed, and I leaned over the table, ready to hear. "No you won't. This morning I hear Madeline saying she knows that she had that scarf in yellow. And what I tell you," Kath crowed, "she thinks the cleaning lady took it."

I didn't think this funny at all. "Kath, I'll give it to you. I told you she'd miss it."

"No way are you bringing it back. Keep it. If you bring it back, I'll throw it out. Some people have too much. Anyway"—she checked her watch and rammed the last of her fries into her mouth—"I have to get to Brooklyn."

I had no taste for the balance of my meal. I had come out with her to feel better, and now I just felt worse. How many people had I screwed just by being around?

. . .

NOSTRAND WAS A DIRT track compared to Fourteenth. I walked a little up the road to the Korean greengrocers and picked up the goods Sylvia would need at the house. The Koreans sold every item you could find in Penal market. I got tinned dasheen bush, fresh okra, and salted pigtails for Sylvia's Sunday callaloo, ripe plantains and sweet potatoes for her side provisions, and a big block of waxy cheddar hoping I could get her to make one of her killer macaroni pies. I picked up an edible necklace and some sour sweets for Micky; a box of Corn Pops for Derek, who really didn't need any more sugar in his diet; and a packet of caps for him to burst in the hallway. For Dame I bought a fish-shaped water shooter.

At the register the Korean woman leaned over and looked down at me close. Her hair was cut with blunt bangs over her eyes; a big clip-on bow held a short ponytail off her neck. She pointed a bony finger at me. "Is you!" she said, and the few other people in the shop turned to see who it was.

"Me what?"

"Don't play you don't know. Don't play you don't know! Yessaday, you come in here and you take two bottle soap." The people in the shop murmured and shook their heads. "You come out my store right now. I call police."

What the . . . ? "You're making a mistake. I wasn't even in Brooklyn yesterday."

"Is you!" she shouted. "I not crazy. I see you yessaday you take two bottle soap. I remember you eyes like that." She winged her palms to the sides of her face and pulled up her eyes.

All the people were looking on, and a tall old man with a fedora and a basket of yellow Haitian mangoes said, "How dem dam Chinee people and dem so stupid. If de chile tief someting yesterday, she a dam ass to come back today to buy something. If she tief yesterday, why she wouldn't tief today? Me thought dem say Chinee smart."

The woman standing next to him measuring fillets of black smoked herrings said, "Maybe today is payday."

I stood at the counter still looking up at the woman. "I didn't take anything in your store. I wasn't here yesterday."

A voice behind me said, "If was me, mama, I never spend anadder penny in they damn store, plus they too tief. Look how much they charging for salt beef. They forget what happen to they partner and them down Flatbush side last year."

She was right, of course, but I wasn't leaving. I didn't want to go empty-handed to Sylvia's.

The Korean woman shouted something in her language, and a younger girl came out from the stockroom. Only when she had climbed up behind the register did she look down at me. Her face was expressionless, but she shook her head. The older one folded her skinny arms and moved to the side for her to ring up my groceries. No apology. Nothing.

"Fifteen dollar."

"So that's it," I said. "You're not going to say sorry?"

The woman with the smoked herrings had joined the line behind me and was impatient. "Look, you done get your grocery, just leave the people store and go."

I walked out to Nostrand. There was nothing I could do. If I didn't go back to the store, Sylvia would still go or Dodo would still go. It was all the same. At the newsstand, I bought a pack of More menthols for Sylvia and a pack of Marlboro reds for Bo. The Arab behind the counter, coffee cup in hand, said, "Long time no see, eh," and even though I had come by just three days ago for an *Echo,* it did feel like a long time. "You have new boyfriend?" he asked. I took my change, almost grateful he'd recognized me.

SYLVIA'S APARTMENT WAS A mess. In the three days I had been gone, more junk had been squeezed into the hall closet—no doubt as a result of Bo's housecleaning efforts—and now the door wouldn't close more than halfway. Dirty clothes and toys and what looked like crushed Frosted Flakes were scattered over the carpet. The breakfront looked more dilapidated than usual, and I swear the floorboards had listed, threatening to slide the whole busted-up wreck into the wall. Someone had torn off the maiden lamp's lace trim, and now she looked truly wretched, the little match girl at the very end. Even the mother duck and her mismatched brood were out of order; the last duckling lay wounded on its side.

"Evening, everybody," I said.

"Jesus H. Christ man, Derek!" Sylvia bellowed. "What time them people and them finish with you, Grace?"

"Seven," I said, putting the grocery bag on the carpet. Micky sat still on the floor, and she neither looked at nor spoke to me. "Hi, Mick, did you miss me?"

Before she could answer, Sylvia gargled, "So seven o'clock them people let you off and is now you reach home?" She looked at the clock, a Trinidad-shaped wooden plaque with Jesus's clasped hands and "Footprints." Its time was 3:10. She leaned forward and peered at the VCR. "Now is nine-thirty-five. You want to tell me it take you three hours and thirty-five minutes to reach here from Fourteenth Street?"

I didn't want to tell her that, but I didn't want to tell her that I had been out with Kathy either. "I pass by the market first, Sylvia."

Bo came out of the bedroom, dressed in jeans and a bulky gray fisherman's sweater. "Aye-aye, look the millionaire reach home, boy. Eh, Grace, let me hold a little change, nah?"

I rolled my eyes at him and looked again at Micky, who just stared at the TV. I went over to the radiator, moved Dame to the carpet, and gave him the water pistol. He stuck the tail end into his mouth. "Dame, no," I said, trying to take it back to rinse it first.

"Leave him," Sylvia said. "American children need germs in they system."

I gave the cereal and the caps to Derek. "Hey, Mick, look. Your favorite." She turned to look at me, and I could see she was upset. Her mouth was set in a frown and she crossed her arms over her still flat chest. "You don't want the sour sweets?" I asked her. She nodded but didn't get off the floor to take them, so I walked over, handed them to her, and barely heard her say thanks.

I gave Sylvia and Bo their cigarettes and said, "I buy some groceries from the market too."

Sylvia undid the plastic wrapper over the pack of Mores. She took one out, and I marveled at the incongruity of big brown Sylvia and the skinny brown cigarette.

"What you buy?" she asked.

"A block of cheese, some plantain and sweet potato, oh, and I get the stuff for you to make callaloo too. Them Korean and them—" I started to tell her about the woman accusing me of stealing soap yesterday, but she cut me off.

"Please, Grace. Self for you to bring some cook food for people to eat, you bring food for me to cook? Is just more work you making for me. You mean to say you couldn't pass by the Chinee man restaurant and pick up some ribs or some wing and fry rice for people to snack on, man? Is not just because you don't eat Chinee food to say nobody else does eat it."

"Is after nine, Sylvia." In truth, I hadn't thought to bring home food at all. If I had, that stupid Korean woman would not have accused me of stealing her soap.

"Of course is after nine." She trumped me. "If you had come home straight from them people place instead of galvanizing with God know who, you would of been here early enough to bring food."

I slid down the wall next to the breakfront to the carpet. Of course she wouldn't be happy with whatever I brought home. This I knew had nothing to do with the groceries. She was pissed at me for leaving her during the middle of the week, and I couldn't blame her. "Well, you want me to go back and pick up some food?"

"No. Is too late already."

Rescue of a sort came from where I least expected it. Bo, leaning against the entryway and smoking one of the Marlboros I'd bought him, said, "Sylvia, I find you wrong, you know. The girl come with good intentions, man. She bring cigarette and thing for them children. I don't think you should boof she up so. Grace girl, thanks for the cigarette. I didn't even have a zoot left."

Sylvia heaved off the couch and went to the kitchen. She came back a minute later and said, "Thanks for the plantains, Grace." To Micky and Derek she said, "Okay, everybody was waiting for Grace to come to see what Grace bringing. Time for bed."

Micky got up, and as she walked by me on the floor, I reached for her skinny wrist where she had twined the candy necklace in a multistrand bracelet. "Hey, Mick, you not talking to me?"

She jerked her hand out of mine. "Leave me alone, Grace."

Sylvia sprang to action and grabbed her other arm. "Grace is a big woman compare to you, Madam Micky. Not because you hear me talking to Grace so mean you could talk to she so. Mind your manners." Micky mumbled an apology and shuffled out of the room.

"She upset because I wasn't here. She'll talk to me tomorrow," I said to Sylvia.

Sylvia shook her head. "Children nowadays don't know how to act like children. You think when I was small I coulda do that in front my mother?"

She started to follow her children out of the living room and then stopped and turned around. "Grace, how much money you say them people and them paying you?"

I couldn't remember if I had told her before or not, but I knew I had told Bo a couple days ago. "Two hundred a week. Why?"

"You have to start giving something for your keep." She closed her eyes and raised her head to the ceiling, thinking. "So, two hundred," she said. "Okay, every Friday you will have to give me fifty dollars. That is for food, to sleep, and because you things here during the week. You good with that?"

Of course I wasn't good with that, but what could I say? The Bruckners hadn't given me the option of living in with them for seven days, and, in truth, I didn't think I wanted to. Two hundred dollars a week wasn't enough to get an apartment, and if I got a room it would cost more than fifty and I wouldn't be able to save any kind of money to send my father.

She looked set for me to argue. "Okay, Sylvia, no problems. But this mean my wings have permanent residency in the closet, right."

"Grace, you too stupid. I will throw them when you gone." But there was jest in her throaty voice. "Since this is your first pay," she said, "and you done spend some money already, only give me twenty. From next week give me the whole fifty."

I WAS UP EARLIER than anyone. I straightened the ducks, swept the carpet, and tried clearing out some debris from the breakfront. On the second shelf up, where Sylvia kept a crimson-edged set of ceramic plates out of Derek's reach, and under a beer can probably left from Tuesday night, I saw an unopened red-and-blue-trimmed envelope. A letter for me from my mother. I didn't wait to open it.

My mother's familiar handwriting on the envelope made me homesick. This early on a Saturday, Helen would still be asleep in the room we had shared. Mammy would be "up in the back," where she grew quick herbs and easy vegetables for home. And Daddy, always an early riser, would probably have eased himself down the front steps on his crutches to sit on the wooden bench in the yard. He liked to catch some morning sun before it got too hot and to wave hello to the neighbors going to Penal market.

> Dear Gracie,
>
> Hoping this letter reach you in health and strength by the Grace of God. I didn't hear back from you since I send the last letter, but I all right. I know you must be busy looking for a work still. Have faith in God and something will come your way. This is just a quick little note to let you know that Daddy gone back in Sando hospital. Now don't get upset. Is nothing big. He went to the Penal clinic and Dr. Beard find the pressure reading a little too high so he send him in for some test. Like I say, is nothing too serious. At least not yet, but we keeping we fingers cross and praying. What we going to do? Everything in the hands of the Lord. Me and Helen go and see him everyday, I go one day, she go the next. But is hard on her, you know, seeing how she studying for exams in June. You was lucky when you was here. Daddy was home already and you didn't have nothing to distract your mind. But you know is as they say, "Gopaul luck is not Seepaul luck." Okay, so don't worry yourself too much you hear. If you want any reassurance, give a little short call by the lady on the hill with the phone and she will get us a message. Na doing fine and send her love.
>
> All right that is all for now.
>
> May the good Lord bless and keep you and don't forget to pray.
>
> Your Mother,
>
> Grace

Back in the hospital. I couldn't believe it. I felt so selfish for how angry I had been at my mother's last letter, so sure she was just trying to get me to come home. I squeezed the paper in my hand, paper probably torn from Helen's notebook. Helen couldn't take the time to go to hospital every other day. My mother was right. During my exams I hadn't had time for anything else. There was night after night of sitting up to study, drinking the sludgy black coffee that my mother grew, roasted, and ground herself, and staggering to school drugged in the mornings. I could still draw perfect cross sections of the human heart, the alimentary canal, and the inner ear, with its intricate hammer, anvil, and stirrup. Someone was pounding an anvil in my head right now. My mother I knew would rise to this new challenge, getting to be the Christian Soldier marching off to her duty in life's war. I could hear her praying now, girding herself with righteousness to bear her burdens. Jesus does never give you more than you back could bear, she liked to say. My daddy in the hospital again and his girl all the way in Brooklyn. I didn't know if I could bear this. How did I get to be such a selfish selfish girl?

Sylvia came out to go to the toilet. "Grace, what you doing up this hour of the morning?" For all her faults, she had no malice; she forgot last night as soon as it happened and moved on to another day. She saw the folded letter in my fist. "Shit, I forget to give you that last night. It come Thursday. From your mother?"

"Yeah, is from Mammy." My voice caught, and I blinked a few times to hold back the tears.

Sylvia wasn't stupid. "Everything okay with them? How your father?"

I didn't think I could say out loud that Daddy was back in the hospital. "Yeah, yeah," I said, "they doing all right. Daddy pressure a little high, but is only because of the rum."

Sylvia looked at me still. Her red nightie was cut for a much smaller woman, but the rich crimson color looked fantastic against her black skin. "Sylvia, that red looks good on you."

"You talking shit," she said, pleased. She looked around the living room, at the piles I had made and the cleared-out breakfront. "Grace, what time it is?" She looked at the wall clock again and then the VCR. "Come back and sleep. Straighten up later." Instead, I catapulted over the couch and sat in the small triangular space. Here, the carpet was still piled and bright red and the couch, through the plastic covers, was a clean cream. I didn't have enough room to stretch out my legs, but I could curl up comfortably. I fell asleep and didn't get up until Derek came in to watch Saturday cartoons with the mixing bowl filled with his sugar cereal and cold milk.

Chapter 14

I rang the lady on the hill to get a message to my mother. I told her to say come for three, but knowing my mother, if I called any time after two, she'd be waiting. I hadn't spoken to my mother since I'd called to make sure she got the money I sent for Christmas. I was glad no one was around for that call, because we fought. Or rather she was judgmental about me sitting down in a stranger's house and I yelled into the phone that it was better than planting pigeon peas. Now Daddy was back in the hospital and I needed to find out what was going on.

At two Sylvia decided to go to the Korean market for the rest of goods she needed for Sunday lunch and then to spend the evening with Dodo.

"Grace," she asked, "you coming by Dodo with we?"

"I don't think Dodo want me in her house, Sylvia." I had cleaned the apartment all morning listening to WLIB alternate between calypso and reggae and the occasional Haitian zouk, and with home on my mind. For the first time since Tuesday, I felt as though I was resting, with nothing else to do but lie on Sylvia's couch. Bo had stayed out last night, and if she and the children went to Dodo's, I could have the apartment to myself for a few hours.

"Oh, Grace"—Sylvia was searching in the breakfront—"don't be stupid. You know how Dodo is. Come on, we making curry crab and dumpling. I stopping by the Chinee man store to pick up seasoning." Sylvia made no distinction between the Chinese man and the Korean man.

"Nah, I tired. Anyway, I have to call my mother today." I got off the couch and went to get my black and white purse. I gave Sylvia $30. Twenty for my keep and $10 in advance for the call. After the $15 I'd spent last night and the $10 Bo had managed to get from me before he left, I had $145 left. Still, it was more money than I'd had in a long time.

"What time you tell your mother to come?" Sylvia asked. She'd found her brassiere.

"Three. Why?"

"Okay, come as far as the Chinee man store and you could bring back what I buy. The salt butter need to keep cold."

I didn't want to go back to the Korean market after that woman last night. "Sylvia," I said, "why you don't just send Micky up the road with the stuff for me?"

"Grace"—her voice went up—"you mad or you stupid? You want me to make my child cross Eastern Parkway alone? Stop being lazy, man. And I did well want to bomb this place, you know. Them roach and them too terrible."

I carried Dame, and Micky, friendlier today, walked alongside me. Earlier, I had given her the Bruckners' phone number so she could call me up to talk. I put barrettes in her hair, and her plaits hung like flowers bent by the weight of their blooms. The weather was beautiful, and to my eyes the tiny buds on the trees were getting fatter, branches crossed like fingers promising spring. Knotted ribbons of white clouds were strung across the pale blue sky, and the light breeze was more refreshing than cold. As we walked the cobblestone path toward Nostrand, Hasidim walked in the opposite direction, deeper into Crown Heights, where they lived. Sylvia marched ahead, holding Derek's hand. She never buttoned her enormous red coat over her belly, and now both sides flapped open in the wind like oversize moth wings. She didn't move from the middle of the path, and Hasidim and anyone else coming toward her parted and flowed on by her sides. Without turning to look at me, she said, "Them Jew and them don't move for nobody and they don't say good morning or good evening, dog."

No one in New York greeted anyone else ever as far as I had seen.

Nostrand on a Saturday looked like High Street, Penal, on market day. Ken with the keloided chop scar the length of his face was out selling sugarcane and green coconuts from the back of his truck. Don, his dwarf sidekick, whose locks were as long as he was tall, sold bootleg cassettes and never-last, made-in-China batteries. Miss Norma sold tamarind balls and sugar cakes and, if you knew to ask, pig-foot souse and spicy blood pudding hidden on a warmer under her table. Rastamen with bloodshot eyes, dreads piled mile-high under red, gold, and green knit caps, listened to dub and fist-bounced each other with the greeting "morning, brethren."

When we reached the store, I waited outside, still vexed at the Korean woman for calling me a thief. But when Sylvia got to the register she called me. "Grace, come and bring some change for me. I don't want to break a next twenty."

I walked down the rows of waxy yellow and green plantains, white plastic buckets of salt beef and pig tails floating in brine and peppercorns, cans of ackee and pigeon peas, and ripe *zabocas,* bigger than anything our trees at home ever bore but inedible without salt. My stomach foamed, ready for the woman's accusations. I knew Sylvia would defend me loudly, but I wanted to avoid another confrontation. I wore my same coat with the hood down. As I reached into the pocket to grab a handful of change, the woman at the register, today with a polka-dotted bow clipping back her thinning hair, said, "Ohhhh, Sivia, that your big daughter? She so pretty."

I turned to face her full-on. "Looka that skin, Sivia. She look pretty just like you. I remember you long time. Long time you look just like this your daughter." She looked at me again and wagged that bony finger from last night. "Don't get fat like Mother, you hear. You eat good and do exercise"—she pumped her arms—"stay skinny like model."

Sylvia laughed and, taking the change, played along with the lie. "Yes, Sue," she rasped, "this one is my firstborn. I make she in my youthful days. She was living with my mother back home until I send for she."

Neither of them seemed to mind that the line had lengthened. Micky showed Dame the little dried herrings, and Derek tried to juggle mangoes. Sylvia paid and passed me the bags she wanted me to bring home. As I turned to walk out of the store, the woman picked up a pack of preserved cherries. "Here," she said, giving me the bag. "You eat this. Salty, not sweet. You not get fat you eat salty. Make sure you go to school, huh. Come doctor." I took the cherries and didn't thank her, figuring that, if she knew I was Sylvia's daughter, she would think I was boldface just like my fat mother.

AT EXACTLY THREE I rang the lady on the hill. My mother answered the phone. "Hello, good afternoon." The similarity of our voices always startled me a little; talking with my mother was like talking to myself.

"Hello, Mammy?"

"Gracie, is you? How you going, girl?"

"I good. Things going good." I told her right away, "I get a work this week."

"All praises due to Jesus. What I tell you in the last letter? Not to leave everything in Jesus hand?" She paused and sang, *"He never failed me yet, he never failed me yet, my Jesus never failed me yet."*

"Well," I countered, "Jesus and the ad I put in the paper."

"But if it wasn't for Jesus . . ."

"Okay, Mammy. So what going on? I get your letter when I come last night. How you? How Daddy? Helen? She come with you?"

"No." Her voice filled with sorrow, and my stomach tightened. "Poor thing. She had to run San Fernando to take some clean towels for Daddy. You know they never have anything in that half-pital."

"So tell me about Daddy, then. When he gone back in? Tell me everything, okay, from the beginning." I had to tell my mother to tell me everything or else she would spend the entire call telling me about the will of the Lord and punctuating the sermon with snatches of hymns.

"What I tell you in the letter? I tell you not to worry. Dr. Beard say the sugar a touch too high, just a touch, and he send him for some tests."

"In the letter you say the pressure high, not the sugar, Mammy."

"What is the difference? Pressure, sugar, groceries, everything high." This is what she did to torture me, to make me want to knock the telephone against my front teeth.

"Mammy"—I tried for some of the patience Sylvia always requested of the Lord—"just answer what I ask, okay. Since Daddy gone to the hospital, what the doctor in San Fernando say?"

"You don't have to talk to me so, Gracie."

I tried to unhinge my locked jaw. "You right, is just that I so far and I don't know what going on, Ma." I knew she was biting her tongue, dying to tell me come home then.

"I wish you was here," she said. "You remember Dr. Silverton from ward six? The cut-foot ward?"

"Yes. Why he in six if is just the pressure and the sugar? He should be in four." One for mad people; two, a.k.a. slip and slide, for green papaya abortions gone wrong and other woman troubles; three for cancer; four for pressure; five for children; six to cut; seven before the morgue. I was scared, and my left eye felt as though its icy blue humor was leaking into my skull.

"Give me a chance to talk," my mother said. "He not in six. Dr. Silverton went and look for him down in four. He self take the pressure and test the urine and say everything looking good. Your father just too harden, Gracie. All he have to do is to eat what I give him and stop drinking that *babash* and everything will maintain. But he too harden. No matter how I pray and ask Jesus to give him understanding, he not open to the will of the Lord. You really take on he side, in truth."

I chose to ignore that, wishing for one mouthful of Hamil's *babash*. "So when he coming home?"

"We not sure, but when I went yesterday the nurse say they could discharge him Monday coming."

At least that sounded promising. "How you doing for money?" I asked her.

"We managing. I sell a little ground provision from the big garden, and the government disability does help. But every time we take him clinic or hospital we have to hire a direct car. He can't travel from taxi to taxi, and forget about bus."

I knew passage back and forth would be hard on them, plus Helen traveling to school. The fares had been high when I was home and were probably higher now. "Okay, Mammy, before you go back home, go by the Western Union and collect some money. I get pay yesterday."

"Gracie, you don't have to do that. By the grace of God we will manage." I knew she would say that.

"Well, Ma, maybe Jesus working through me. Maybe I get this job just in time to send you a little change. The Lord works in mysterious ways, right?" She ate this stuff like *coo-coo* from a calabash, and I expected her to start singing *"I am delivered, praise the Lord."* Instead she thanked me and asked if Sylvia was there. "No, she and the children went by she sister. I here alone." I checked the time on the VCR; we'd been talking for fifteen minutes already. "So how Helen and Na going? Anybody in the village dead?"

"Everybody home doing just fine. When was the last time we talk? December?"

"Early January."

"You did hear Jango drown?" I hadn't. "Yes, he and Badis oldest son, the crazy one with the wild wild hair and he shirt always open—you know which one I talking about?" I did. "Well, the two of them went out overnight and a tanker or a cruise ship or something pass and mash up the pirogue. Jango wash up in Quinam, but Badis boy didn't come in. A few days later Rolly crew see the body far far out, near Venezuela, but they didn't want to put that in they boat. People would stop buying fish from them."

I knew she was right about that, but I started to think about Jango and Crazy Horse out in the middle of the sea holding on to splintered pieces of blue board, trying to stay afloat. Drifting apart from each other in the waves made rougher in the tanker's wake and then sinking. "Jesus Christ, Mammy. How Jango wife?"

"How she going to be?" My mother did not chide me for using the Lord's name in vain. "She holding on. She could only hold on." She changed the topic. "So how the new people and them you working for?"

I didn't need to give her any details about the Bruckners that would cause her to worry. "They okay so far. Is just the man, Solomon, and his wife, Miriam, and one son, Benjamin. I making thirty-five dollars more, though."

She didn't let me get away so easy. "Watch out for yourself and do what the lady tell you to do. Don't wear no short short pants and tight jersey, you hear."

I pressed my warm fingertips to my aching eye. I had never in my life worn hot pants or tight jerseys. "Is still cold outside, Mammy. Everybody wearing plenty clothes."

She paused, then said, "Huh, all of them have name from the Bible, what religion they is?" I'd wondered how long it would take her to ask.

"Jews, just like Mora them." When I'd first started working for Mora and I told my mother they were Jewish, she hadn't understood. She'd kept asking again and again if they were real Jews. She couldn't define what exactly she meant by "real Jews," but I think she, we really, had sort of understood Jews to be people in the Bible, not a family of six living in a four-bedroom colonial with an aboveground pool in Highland Park, New Jersey. She had been full of questions about what they wore—not robes and sandals—and what they ate—not manna and dates. I had told her that the Speisers looked like regular white people, except they didn't eat meat with milk or cheese, and they went to service on Saturdays. My mother had asked, almost afraid to hear the answer, if they really and truly did not believe that Jesus Christ was the Lord and Savior and no man went to the Father but through him. Nope, I had told her. They didn't believe a word of it. Mora told me the best they made of Christ was that he was a rogue Jew with a God complex.

"Why is it," Mammy asked me now, "that you have to end up working for these people? This set look willing to hear the Gospel?"

I tried to picture telling Sol and Miriam the good news about Jesus and his love. "Okay, Ma, time to come off Sylvia phone. I going to send the money now, so go straight Penal and pick it up. Give Hel twenty. You have a pen?"

"Right in my purse."

"Here, take my work number in case you need to call me during the week."

"What I would need to call during the week for that can't wait until weekend?"

"You never know, Mammy, just take it please." I gave her the Bruckners' number and had her repeat the digits back to me. "You going to see Daddy tomorrow?"

"Yes, tomorrow is my turn. Plenty people from the village does go and see him to keep he courage up, so is good for them to see somebody from the family there."

"Okay, so when you go, make sure and tell him I call and to behave and do what the doctor say. Tell him I get a work and I start saving for the thing again. Tell Helen don't study too hard. Tell everybody hello. Okay, Mammy. Take care of yourself. Bye."

"Gracie . . ."

"Yes, Ma?"

"Nothing. Bye."

I hung up and made to jump into the space behind the couch, then didn't. I should be home for this. Helen was sixteen and in the middle of exams, and my mother was getting old. How old was she now? Her hair was completely gray. I had no memory of her looking young. Before I came to America, I'd gone through some papers tucked far in the back of her wardrobe and found her birth certificate. I'd looked at the year and done the math. She was forty years old. Still young, but scared of the world beyond her village and the capricious vengeance of her Lord, who took away limbs and children and lives whenever his fancy struck.

Around six the phone rang, and I realized I had fallen asleep on the couch. I sat up, and the yellow receipt from Western Union slid from my belly onto the dead red floor.

"Hey, superstar, wha' a go on?"

"Not a thing in the world," I told Kath. "Talk Trini, please. I can't understand Jamaican right now. You not going to believe what happened."

"What happened?"

What had happened was that Sol and Miriam had paid me for only three days. All the time I had been thinking I had $200, they had given me only $120.

"What? Grace, call them one time."

"And say what, Kath? And say what? If they don't pay me the rest I not going to come back?" I'd only realized at Western Union. Over and over I did the math: $15 at the Korean's, $30 for Sylvia, and $10 for Bo. I should have had $145, left, and no matter how many times I counted the bills in my hand, they added up to $65. One twenty and nine fives. "Nine fives, Kath. Tell me she didn't do that on purpose. Nine fives in the middle."

"Well, of course she do it on purpose, Grace. But what are you going to do?"

I knew I was going to do nothing at all.

Kath breathed hard for me. "Well, take some advice from a shop-keeper daughter, okay. Next time, count your money before you leave.

"You want to go out tonight with me and Donovan and Brent?"

I had sent my mother fifty U.S. dollars. She'd get about three hundred TT for that. Not much, but enough to help out. After the fee the balance from my salary was five dollars and change. "Kath, I want to go, but I just send money for Mammy."

"How your mother?" she asked. Without waiting for my answer, she said, "Grace, we going out with two Jamaican man, at least one of them involved in illegal activities. You think you need to spend your own money? And don't worry, we not going to a club, just dinner at Yardies. You ever been there?"

I had not. "Mammy good. Please don't say 'illegal activities' when you on the phone with me. You never know who listening. I have to dress up?"

"No jeans and sneakers please. What is Sylvia address again?"

"God, I hope Sylvia doesn't make a fuss about me going out."

"What she have to fuss about? More food for her to eat tonight." Kathy laughed.

I cracked up too. "You are one mean red nigger, Kath."

"I know, but you love me anyway."

Chapter 15

Kathy stood outside the building. "You look amazing," she said as I pushed open the security door and stepped into the cold night. She pressed her palms to her hips. "I really need to stop eating so much."

"You think I look all right?" I was wearing the one fancy dress I owned. Mora and I had gone with the kids to a mall in New Jersey, and she had insisted I try it on. The original price was $149.99, and, even marked down 50 percent, the dress was still too expensive. Her oldest son, Ben, had tried to wolf-whistle when I put it on. Hannah had said I had to get it, and Mora had put in forty dollars since it was her idea. The black, clingy jersey came to the middle of my thighs, and the back was cut to drape very low. I felt half naked.

"Where did you get that dress?"

"Saks. Fourth floor," I said, and she cuffed my arm. "So, he in the car?"

"Waiting for you." I started to shrug into my coat, and Kath yanked down on the hood. "What on earth are you doing?"

I didn't think my action required an explanation.

"You're spoiling the effect with this thing." She flicked a finger against my coat. "Plus, we're going in a direct car. You could take a little bit of cold."

I thought briefly about the cost of curing pneumonia but took the coat off anyway. Kathy looked nice too. Not a hair strayed from her slick ponytail, and she had BeDazzled a black scrunchie with red rhinestones.

"Kath, I should have dress up more?"

"No, you look fine. Me and Donovan going to the Bronx after."

Donovan honked the horn, and we walked toward the car. Kathy and I got in the back. A blast of reggae hit us, and a cloud of sweet, grassy smoke billowed out. The vibrating bass tapped me forward with every beat, and my "Good evening" was lost in Wayne Wonder's melancholy melody for Jamaica-land. Donovan looked at us in the rearview and smiled. His gold tooth flashed in the mirror. Brent turned around, raised his chin, and winked. I grinned and hit Kathy a little too hard on her thigh. Both guys wore furry black Kangols angled to the left. I felt cool and New York sitting in the backseat with my girlfriend and our borrowed boys going out for a night on the town.

EVERYONE AT YARDIES KNEW Donovan. The owner, Barrington, greeted us at the door and walked us to our booth on an elevated platform. Donovan walked ahead, pounding raised fists and heads-upping the other diners. The restaurant was nice. A low dub bass pulsed out of big black speakers, and the walls were painted with lush ranges I thought to be Jamaica's blue mountains. I wondered if the vegetation was supposed to be coffee or the other green plant Jamaica was famous for. The painting behind our booth was different. There, the Jamaican pantheon beamed down on us: Bob Marley mid-scant and dreadlocks flailing; Haile Selassie, wearing a gold crown and petting a lion; Marcus Garvey, stuffed into a tight suit and wearing a plumed military hat; and a topless black woman with amulets around her neck, a machete in one hand, and a shotgun in the other. The caption under her bare, broad feet read NANNY. I laughed.

"Wha' so funny, darkie?" Brent asked.

He was good-looking. A little plump in his oversize Karl Kani denim outfit. His round brown eyes pulled down a touch at the corners and made him look sexy sad. A close-trimmed goatee framed his full lips. He had a nice smile and no gold teeth. I realized they were waiting for me to share my joke.

"The painting on the wall," I said.

"Wha' so funny so?" Donovan asked. "All ah them ah Jamaican 'eroes, you know." He went through the group, squinting one eye and pointing, trigger fingered. "Ah, my man Robert Nestor; the honorable Marcus Garvey; 'Aile Selassie I, Rastafari; and that woman so, that is Nanny, the mother of Jamaica."

I laughed again, and Kathy managed to smile and glare at me at the same time. "You never 'ear 'bout Nanny?" Donovan asked. He made the word sound like *nahnih*.

I had, and so had Kathy in Mr. Rajkumar's sixth-form Caribbean history, but we shook our heads. "Uh-uh. Who was she? A runaway slave?"

"No sah." Donovan leaned back and put his palms flat on the tablecloth. "Nanny was never nobody slave. Is plenty white man she kill, though. Ah not true, B-man?"

B-man agreed, and Donovan went on. "Nanny was a real Jamaican warrior woman, you know. Them bring she Jamaican to try and make she a slave, but Nanny say none of that for she." He aimed at the mountain mural, and I wondered if he carried a real gun. "For years and years them white man ah try and catch Nanny up in ah Cockpit Country. Scene?"

"After a time," Brent picked up, "them white man and them tired fight with Nanny crew. Them give them land up ina the 'ills and leave them alone. Up to now, it still have Nanny great, great, great, and more great grandchildren living up in them 'ill in a place name Nanny Town."

"Well," Kathy said, "if Nanny do so much for Jamaica, I find the least Barrington could do is paint her a shirt."

We all laughed, and the beautiful Jamaican waitress, with a spit curl on her forehead, an impossibly short black skirt, and a white shirt unbuttoned almost to her navel, brought two slim bottles of cold Canei with compliments from Barrington. As she turned to leave, Donovan reached over and held on to her hand. She stopped and backed up. He tucked a bill up under her hem and patted her bottom. Kathy pretended she didn't see anything.

After the first round of drinks, Brent excused himself. Donovan leaned back in his seat and looked over the table at me from under his Kangol. "If wasn't for me friend," he said, "tonight coulda be me lucky night, scene."

Kathy turned to look at him with weary eyes.

"How so?" I asked.

Donovan laughed. "One tall cat-eye darkie, one sexy-body browning, and one Donovan ina the middle. Wha' you think 'bout that arrangement?"

I wasn't sure if Donovan was joking or not, so I laughed. I wondered if I was meant to answer this proposition. If it was a proposition.

He snapped his fingers. "Darkie, don't take me for serious, you know.

Is a likkle joke talk me ah talk. B-man ah me best friend from say we born out we mother belly."

"Yeah, Grace," Kath said, "he just full of shit."

Donovan's beeper tweeted, and he went over to Barrington, who led him to the back room. "Was he serious just now?"

"He's a man, right?" Kathy sounded surly. "If opportunity presents itself, I'm sure he would take full advantage."

"Well," I said, "my name is not opportunity." I changed the subject. "You come here with him before?"

I was surprised by the challenge in her voice. "We don't just fuck, you know. We go out to eat, we go for drives. One time we even went to the Bronx Zoo. This is a real relationship, Grace."

I hadn't thought otherwise. "I know that, Kath. I can tell that just from how Donovan looks at you."

This brightened her. "Really?" she asked. "How does he look at me?"

"Like he really likes you," I told her, emphasizing the *you*. Then, fortunately, Brent came back to the table.

Later, after we'd eaten, Kathy molded herself to Donovan and brushed the side of his face with the tip of her ponytail. I turned to face Brent, wondering if he would try to kiss me. "So," he said, "Katty tell me you working in the middle of Babylon. You like it?"

"Is only babysitting, you know. Not a real job." I didn't think now was the time to discuss the housework I did for a living. "It's just a way to make some money." I still didn't know for sure what Brent did to make his money. About Donovan, Kathy had told me, but when I asked her what Brent did, she told me I needed to ask him that myself.

"Just don't waste up you youth on them white people and them. Them so will eat out your belly and then fire you when they done."

His words upset me, and I pulled away. What option did I have? The people in the restaurant were eating and talking and laughing and kissing and leaving and arriving. Having fun. I wanted to have fun too, and I turned to Brent full-on. His palm, hot and moist, cupped the inside of my thigh. The warmth burned, and, surprised at his touch, I slapped my legs together, trapping his hand. I slid closer to him, and he stroked my bare skin with his thumb. Streaks of heat radiated up my leg. I got a little scared and tried to slide away.

"You 'ave some real puss eye, you know." I could smell him, the cigarettes and the weed and his body. I wanted him to kiss me. His thumb continued to brush the inside of my leg, damp now. I leaned closer. His lips were so full, the bottom one pinker than the top, and his eyes were heavy looking at me.

Then stupid Donovan said, "B-man, time to take that darkie 'ome, man."

Brent gave my thigh one more squeeze and let go, making me cold where I had felt so hot. "Man, Donovan, you no see the time. Time to go, man, me 'ave to work early ina the morning." Suddenly we were bustling to leave. And, just like Kathy had said, Donovan paid with a fistful of cash. He waved away the yardbird waitress when she came back with change. "Buy yourself something sexy with that," he said, and Kathy frowned.

Chapter 16

Someone was shaking my shoulder. "Come on, get up. You have to go."

"What?" I was still more asleep than awake.

The voice came again, and I realized that I was on Sylvia's couch. "What time it is, Sylvia?" Last night, when I had lain on the couch, I could feel Brent's phantom touch, his thumb brushing the inside of my thigh. Sleep had not come for hours.

Sylvia pulled open the curtain, and early spring sunshine flooded into the living room. "Eh, you gone out last night, but you can't get up this morning. Tell me what kind of house I running here, Jesus. And my girl child to raise. Enough with you and Bo stupidness, coming in and out my house all hours. You have to go, Grace."

My head hurt from the movement and the light. This was it, I realized. She wanted me to leave her apartment. Payback for choosing to work for the Bruckners rather than staying in Brooklyn for fifty dollars a week.

"But, Sylvia, where I supposed to go this hour of the morning?"

"I really don't care, Grace," she said and started to walk away. "Is just for two hours. Jacob coming with some Russian this morning. He can't see you here."

Relief flooded through me.

While I waited for the elevator, Sylvia opened her front door. "Grace, you still there?"

"What?"

"Bring a pack of More for me when you come back. The Chinee man store does open early on Sunday."

. . .

BACK ON THE ISLAND, and only on very early January and February mornings, Helen and I would exhale the gentlest puffs of air through our mouths and see fragile white clouds. It was just a fraction of a second before the tropical heat consumed the cool air. Now, my own breath shrouded me as I decided to walk in the opposite direction on Eastern Parkway, deeper into Crown Heights, where the Hasidim went.

Toward New York Avenue, sitting between Sylvia's building and an unbroken row of brownstones, was a real mansion. The house was the most dilapidated on the block. Dead winter vines varicosed the windows, and squares of black plastic hung in place of glass. Missing tiles made the once proud turrets gap-toothed, and pigeons nested under the eaves. About a month ago, I had seen the old African-American woman who lived there— Miss Florence. Sylvia told me she had been a famous model, but the woman I saw was crazy. While I was bundled into a coat, Miss Florence wore a see-through duster over a gauzy nightgown. A lit cigarette between her lips, she tried fruitlessly to shoo away some pigeons. When she saw me watching her, Miss Florence leaned her broom against the wall and, gesticulating with her cigarette, asked, "Now what the fuck you looking at, coconut?" When I told Sylvia, she said black Americans were crazy.

Down Eastern Parkway, thick crowds of Hasidim gathered behind police barricades, and I wondered if there had been a shooting. On the other side of the parkway, police directed a flowing stream of pedestrians toward a church flying Caribbean flags. The made-up women were decked out in broad, bright hats. The men wore sharp suits and shiny shoes. This wasn't my mother's group, for sure.

I stopped on the corner of Kingston, where two men had set up what looked like old-fashioned typewriters without keys. Three police cars were parked nearby, and more officers sat watchful, staticky chatter from their radios occasionally rising above the low buzz of the crowd. Everyone seemed to be waiting, and I wanted to see what for.

The church bell tolled nine times. The men shifted their stools closer to their machines, and more police came out of the cars. The Hasidim on the path rolled toward an entrance on Eastern Parkway. A wave of people, happy and chatting, poured out of the building's side door. The men collected dollars, which they fed into the machines, and I looked on, amazed, as they came out encased in shiny, clear plastic. Washington's head was gone, and in his place was the face of the old "Moshiach is on the Way" man.

A dreadlocked man rocked up to me on crutches.

"Today is one of their holidays?" I asked him.

He hawked and spat on the pavement. "'Oliday, sistah?" His heavy accent was just like Brent's and his voice a shout. "Every Sunday mornin' is the same shit them ah do on Eastern Parkway. Come and block up the rahtid street, and Babylon dey out in force for them protection. You think them do this for we when Labor Day ah come?" He spat again. "Them Jew them ah just like a brain tumor benign. Suck up energy and ah give nothing back to anyone but them own. Scene?"

I walked away from him fast, crossing Eastern Parkway even though I was on Sylvia's side. The last few people waiting to enter the church were making their way up the broad steps, and I heard someone call my name. Surprised, I turned and saw Dodo standing with a thick, redskin woman, the two of them dressed up and sucking down cigarettes. Big sweaty patches stained Dodo's armpits.

"Mornin', Dodo."

"You come to go to church?" she asked and turned to the woman. "This is the one without family I was telling you my sister take in. Grace, you here already, why you don't come for the nine o'clock service?"

Apparently she was serious. I had no desire to go to church and spread my arms wide. "I'm not dressed for church, Dodo."

The red woman dropped her cigarette on the pavement and ground it out with the pointy toe of her shoe. "The Lord say to render your heart and not your garments, child. Come and make a joyful noise."

Clearly she had never heard me sing. "Some other time, Dodo. Sylvia waiting for me."

She twisted up her face and took a last drag. "Suit yourself. Tell Sylvia I will pass for lunch." She and her friend sprang up the few steps to join the rest of the congregation.

JACOB AND HIS RUSSIAN were walking out of Sylvia's when I got back. "Ah. Look who it is. Cousin Grace from Flatbush. But how come you are coming from this way when Flatbush is in the other direction?"

He had me, but he was smiling. "Morning, Yacob," I said, ignoring his question. "Today is the Sabbath. I'm taking Sylvia's children to Sunday school."

"Come, Grace you are almost a Jew. You know that true Shabbos ended yesterday. Today is just another workday, no?"

"If it's a workday, then how come all those Jews on the parkway by Kingston? Today special for some reason?"

"These people, Grace. I'll tell you why they stand on the street in the freezing cold on a Sunday morning. To see the messiah." Jacob laughed.

"What, the messiah down in the basement? But how come they didn't leave money at the shrine?" I asked Jacob. What I knew about religion was that you usually had to pay God for favors.

"Grace," Jacob said. "The messiah is in the basement handing out dollars."

"Who are you talking about, the man on the van?"

"The very one. Our messiah lives on Eastern Parkway, not too far from your cousin Sylvia. You didn't know how close you were to Hashem, eh?" He opened his wallet and passed me a laminated dollar bill.

"Moshiach is on the way?"

"Moshiach." Jacob gargled the word in the back of his throat.

"So Moshiach is not a first name? I thought somebody was coming from Israel."

"That's sacrilege. He's never even been to Israel."

Jacob talked about all of this in jest. Plus he was at Sylvia's on Sunday morning instead of waiting to see the messiah. "So what about you, then?" I asked. "Do you believe the old man is the messiah? Does he do miracles?"

"Is that what your messiah has to do, Grace, miracles?"

"Miracles I can see now," I said. "Not when I'm dead."

Jacob got serious. "Some Jews believe that the old man can do that and more. Me, I'm not so sure anymore." He stroked his beard. "But it's hard to stop believing in something you were brought up to believe. Don't you agree?"

I didn't know.

"Okay, Grace from Flatbush, go and take your cousins to church."

I handed him back the plastic bill. "No, keep it," he said. "You're my mitzvah today. I have to go visit this lady who lives next door, and I need some goodwill on my side."

Jacob walked over to Miss Florence's house. She was not happy to see him. "Jew, what the fuck are you doing on my motherfucking stoop? I done told you all to stop coming to my fucking front door. You and the fucking Witnesses."

Jacob laughed. "When are you going to sell me this house, Miss Florence? This house is too big for only you. I have eight children and a wife. We need your house."

Miss Florence was not laughing. "I don't care if you have eighteen fucking children. None of y'all is getting my house. I own this sucker free and clear."

Jacob looked over at me. "I will give you one hundred thousand dollars cash for this house, Miss Florence. Cash money. And a top-floor apartment rent-free right next door. Look at this place," he said, but Miss Florence only looked at him. "One day a brick will fall on your head and you will get hurt. You know how much you could do with that kind of money, Miss Florence? Cash."

"I got more money than that under my mattress. Have a nice fucking day."

SYLVIA STOOD IN FRONT of the shelf with her duck family. "How I looking, Grace?" she asked me.

It wasn't hard to answer her truthfully. "Nice," I said. She had loosened her plaits, and her hair curled naturally. Her swipe of rouge was a touch too bright on her dark skin, but the color matched her lipstick. "Blend in your blush a little more." She delicately stroked her face upward with her peace fingers and rubbed her lips together.

"Better?" she asked.

"Much."

She straightened the smallest duckling, and Bo, lying on the carpet, asked, "How you dress up so, girl? Like you planning on giving the man a piece in the hospital, or what?"

"You is a real ass, yes," she told him, but she was laughing. "Anyway, is not a congujal visit. Time for me to go. Grace, if I don't come back before you leave, do me a favor and cane-row Micky hair, wash up the few dishes, and just make this place decent, please. Oh, and bathe Dame too. What time you say you leaving by?"

"Seven-thirty."

"Okay. Bo, stay with them children if Grace have to go."

As she was leaving, Sylvia did one of those rare things that reminded me she was the woman who gave me a place to live without knowing anything about me. She asked Micky, a sprite in my wings, and sulky Derek for a kiss to take to their stepfather and father. And from Dame, who could not execute her command, she carefully bent over and took one.

"Why you don't try to get a work with Jacob to fix up this place?" I asked Bo when Sylvia had left. He ignored me, and I pressed. "You and Nello could fix up the place however you want." I kicked his bare back with my heel. "Bo?"

Without turning to look at me, he said, "Jacob tell you he hiring any nigger people to work for him? Please."

In the two months I had lived here, I'd seen Bo soften. He hadn't had more than a few days' work since late December, and he and Nello spent all their time drinking and smoking. I didn't know where he got money. The spread of his once muscular back reminded me of how Daddy's tree-trunk leg had gradually softened to bog after his amputation and the useless exercises Dr. Silverton had told him to do.

"Well, anything better than nothing."

He rolled over then, his body sloshing like Mora's water bed. "You really think so, Grace? You think a man should have to work like a jackass for little little money and be content?" Bo didn't wait for me to answer. "Not me, sistren. You just come America, so maybe you, but I living in this country for too long to take that kinda shit from anyone, and especially not from a Jew who younger than me."

Micky, still wearing my wings, had come to lean by the entryway and listened to her uncle.

"Mick, get the grease and the comb from the breakfront, please," I told her.

She grimaced and dragged her shoulder against the molding, snapping the frame of the left wing. "Shoot, Grace, it broke," she complained.

I had to laugh. I didn't break it, *it* broke.

Bo shook his head. "Sylvia children could break air, yes."

Micky reached her hand behind her to try to straighten the crooked wing.

"Don't bother, Mick," I told her. "The other one still good, right? Fairies can fly with only one wing, you know."

She didn't look like she believed me, and Bo said, "I don't know why you fulling up them children head with all that nansi-story shit." He attempted an otter roll, made it halfway, and said, "Me and you need to talk. I might be able to do this thing for you on a installment plan."

It was the first time he had brought up our pending deal all weekend, and I nodded to him, not wanting to discuss a marriage like this in front of Micky. "I'll call you from work during the week," I said.

He flopped back to the TV. "Just don't wait too long to call, you hear. I is a hot commodity on the market."

Chapter 17

When I got to the towers that night, Dave stood in the lobby talking to Danny. Brutus and Cesar were sprawled across the floor.

"Hey, Grace," Dave said. "How's it going? You in for the week?"

"Yep, my first full week. Do you know the time?" I asked them.

"You're in trouble," Danny said. "It's nine-fifteen."

I felt a heavy stone in the pit of my stomach. "Really? Okay, good night, let me—"

"Danny, you know that's not the time," Dave said. "Grace, it's not even nine yet. Danny's just being a potato bug."

Up on the platform, Danny laughed, throwing his head back so I could see his discolored teeth from the underside. "Don't sweat it, Gracie Mansion, it's only eight-thirty-five. You can stay with me for twenty-five minutes."

"You think that was funny?" I asked him, wondering how they both knew what time I had to be in.

"Well, it cracked me up."

"So," Dave asked. "Did you have a good weekend? Where do you go when you're not tending Ben?"

I didn't mind telling Dave about myself, some, but I didn't trust Danny at all. He watched us both from his perch, skinny hands clasped behind his back and that too big hat slipping down over his left eye. His whole body shook like a rutting mongrel hungry to know everything.

"My weekend was fine," I said to Dave, then asked him, "How come you're always wearing shorts? It's still so cold outside."

He put a hand to his forehead. "I dress in sympathy for Key West."

Seeing I had no idea what he meant, he explained. "I'm a young snow-bird, Grace. We're usually down in Florida. This year unfortunately I need to be here, but mentally the boys and I are in Old Town, and there I only wear shorts."

"I love the cold," Danny said. "Irishmen don't do well in the heat."

Dave didn't say what he needed to be here for, and I didn't ask him.

"Well," I said, "I've been cold since Labor Day."

"Yeah, your people don't do well in winter, right, Grace?"

I ignored Danny.

"You have to embrace it," Dave said. "Have you ever been skiing?"

I stopped myself from laughing out loud. The closest I had come to skiing was riding a fallen coconut branch down the grassy slope behind my house. "No, I've never been skiing. Not in snow, anyway."

"Well, we should definitely take you skiing sometime. I'm sure you'd love it; you look athletic."

"Do you ski in shorts too?" I wondered if Dave was flirting with me or if he was just being nice.

He laughed. "Hah! You got me. For skiing I wear long pants."

He wasn't handsome. He didn't look like Sol, with his green eyes and curly red hair, or like Brent, with his sexy stare and trim goatee. Really the only thing noticeable about Dave was the black afro, and, as Kathy would say, that was not necessarily a good thing.

"Okay, time for me to go up. I'll see you guys around. Good night."

"Hey, Grace," Dave said, "you should come up to the thirtieth floor sometime. Like when you get off from work. Sol and Miriam won't mind."

"No, but I might mind." I was surprised by my own boldness.

"Nah," he said, "trust me. You won't. And the view is the best in the towers. Anytime, just come on up. We're usually there."

"Grace, I've been up there, and the fricking view is amazing," Danny said. "You can probably see all the way back to Africa."

"Daaaaanny," Dave said. I ignored him again, said good night to Dave.

I WASN'T SURPRISED WHEN Sol opened the front door in his robe and folded over to give me a hug. I didn't put my arms around him, only stood there as he gave me a quick squeeze and told me that Miriam had gone to bed already.

The apartment was a wreck. The floral couch looked like a trampled garden, and Ben's toys were littered across rugs and under chairs. The dining table was covered with plates of half-eaten pasta, a slice of pie still in a foil dish, and melted ice cream. I thought I smelled weed.

Sol lay back on the couch to watch TV. "Miriam wants you to clean up tonight. You don't mind, do you?"

Yes, I minded. I didn't start work until Monday morning. It wasn't fair to come in and have to clean up their Sunday mess. I took a deep breath. "Sol, I don't think I should have to do any work on a Sunday night." There. I'd said it.

"Grace," he said, his eyes fixed on the TV, "that's between you and Miriam. She really wanted you to get this stuff into the dishwasher tonight."

I had always done everything Sylvia asked me to do, and all that got me was more chores. Standing in the living room, I knew that if I cleaned that table off tonight, next Sunday night it would be piled even higher. And last week they had paid me for only three days.

"I don't start work until Monday morning, Mr. Bruckner. Good night."

Now he looked at me. "Mir's going to be very upset in the morning, Grace."

I knew she would, and I also knew that this might make me even less likely to be the right person for them to sponsor.

"I know. Good night."

Early the next morning, so early that it was still dark, I crept into the living room to clear up the mess. Trying hard not to make any noise, I scraped pasta nuggets into the rubbish with my fingers and used both hands to slide the plates into the dishwasher. I was almost done when Miriam came and stood over me in the kitchen doorway. From where I knelt on the floor, she looked like the mythical *soucouyant* women my na told Helen and me stories about. Pale, evil women who shucked their skin at night to go flying through the villages looking for men and blood.

"Jesus Christ, Grace. What on earth are you doing this hour of the morning?"

I thought I should stand up, but all I did was say, "Morning," and, needlessly, "packing the dishwasher."

She crossed one leg behind the other and said, "Didn't Sol tell you to get those done last night?"

"He did, but it was nine o'clock already. I just thought I'd do them in the morning. Is that a problem?"

"Is that a prob-lem?" she taunted. "Yes, that's a problem. We're still asleep and you're making a racket. If you hadn't waited until exactly nine to come in, you could have cleaned up last night. Just stop, okay. When Sol and I leave, you can do the dishes by hand."

I stood up now, still holding the last plate. "Why by hand?"

"Dinner things go in the dishwasher, and breakfast things get done by hand. If you had done what you were told to do last night, the dishes would have been dinner dishes. Now, they're breakfast things."

She turned off the kitchen light and went back to her room. I wanted to drop the plate I was holding onto the kitchen floor. To raise it over my head, like a perfect full moon, and just let it slip through my fingers and crash into a million tiny splinters.

I WAS SITTING NEXT to Ule watching Ben play. "So what part of Trinidad you say you come from?" she asked me.

"The bush, Ule. A small village so far south you can see Venezuela from the beach." From any shore on three sides of the island, a small bolus in Venezuela's dragon mouth, you could see the mainland.

Evie was across the way, pushing Caleb and Sammy in the tire swing but paying more attention to us than to the children.

"And where your family?" Ule asked, gently pushing the newborn in the carriage back and forth. "Them here with you?"

"No, they're home. I'm in America alone."

Ben came over for me to take his jacket off. "I'm hot, Grace. Off, off, off," he demanded.

It wasn't too cold outside, and as I undid the zipper Ule said, "Child, you mad? You want this little boy to catch cold and drap dead right here? Police will lock you up if you make the white people children sick, yes."

I ignored her and took off the jacket anyway.

"Please your mind," Ule said, making me laugh. Evie didn't take her eyes off us.

So far I was pleased with the way spring was coming along. After cold mornings, the days warmed up, and then at night the temperature cooled again. If you sat very still in the sunshine with your coat zipped up, the heat managed to warm you slowly, all the way to your insides.

It was 10:30 by the time Kathy arrived. Presumably in honor of getting a marriage license, she was dressed in all white, but her eyes were red, as if she'd been crying.

"Well, this is it," she said, parking the carriage and sitting down on the bench. I wasn't sure if she meant the baby or her trip to City Hall.

"Where's the guy?"

"He's there already, holding a place so we don't have to wait too long."

"Makes sense. Kath, this is my friend Ule."

Ule said hello and Kathy barely answered, leaning her head back against the bench. Evie had moved from the tire swing to the sandbox, from where she watched us openly.

"You doing all right?" I asked.

Kathy shook her head, and I saw tears streak down the side of her face, cut a clean line through her blush, and fall in a small, pale pink splash on her fur-trimmed collar.

"Hey, Kath," I whispered so Ule wouldn't hear. "You don't have to do this, you know."

She turned her head to me and did not whisper. "What choice I have, Grace? I don't want to be doing this for the rest of my life." She pushed the carriage with the tip of her white boot.

Ben came over. "Where your cool sunglasses?" he asked Kathy. She pulled them out of her bag and put them on. "Cool," he said and ran back to the sandbox.

"Anyway, I shouldn't complain, right? At least it's happening for me." She took a deep breath and stood up. "I should be back by twelve, twelve-fifteen. Is just to sign some forms. You staying here?"

I was hurt by her words. *It* was happening for her. All around me, in the city, for the busy people walking to and fro with a sense of purpose, *it* seemed to be happening.

"He eat already," Kathy said, "but I bring an extra bottle. Thanks for doing this, Grace. Bye."

She walked out of the park, her black ponytail an exclamation point in sharp contrast against her coat. I pulled the carriage closer and looked at the baby asleep inside. Ule looked too. "Now that is a good-looking white child," she said.

Evie had been making her way toward us, and now she came and peeked into the carriage. On her forehead she had a patch of dried and fresh pimples I thought came from her greasy bangs.

"Who child that?"

Before I could answer, Ule said, "I doing a little half-day work for Grace friend. Is nobody you know."

"Huh." Evie put both hands on her hips and looked into the carriage again. "Me never see this one before."

By the sandbox, I saw Ben stand up and snatch his dump truck from a little blond boy. He held it aloft as if to bring it down on the child, and I ran over. "Ben, what are you doing?"

"He took my truck, Grace. It's mine."

No other sitter came over, and I figured the boy belonged to one of the skinny mothers standing in the corner.

I sat on the edge of the box. "Ben, you have to play nice. Don't you want to share your toy?"

"It's my truck, Grace," he said. I looked back to where Ule and Evie were with Kathy's baby. And then I saw Miriam Bruckner walking into the park with her black stirrup pants looping into her shoes.

Evie and Ule saw her too, and the other sitters who knew who she was nudged those who didn't. She came over and smiled down at Ben and me in the sandbox. "Surprise!"

Ben dropped his truck and ran to Miriam. "Hi, Grace," she said, still smiling. "I had a doctor's appointment this morning, and I thought I'd drop by to see you guys. How's it going?"

"Hey, Miriam. This is a surprise."

"Grace, Mommy's here," Ben told me.

"Yes, I see. How about that?"

Miriam held Ben's hand, and they walked over to Evie and Ule. "Hi, ladies. Mind if I sit between you for a bit?" she said to them.

I walked slowly to the bench, where Ben had draped himself between his mother's knees. He hung there, dump truck completely forgotten. Sitters glanced in our direction from every corner of the park. *Oh, dear God. Help me,* I prayed.

"So, how's it going?" Miriam asked Evie, and she called hello to Caleb and Sammy.

"Things good," Evie said with a smile. "Caleb and Sammy, don't you guys hear Miriam calling you? Come say hello like you have some manners."

"Ah, it's okay. They don't have to," Miriam told her.

Miriam turned to Ule. "You watching two babies, Ule? Linda Bloomberg's and who else's?"

Oh, God, I thought, here it comes. But Ule didn't flinch. "Is only Linda I working for, you know. I just watching this one for a friend with a deaf in the family. She had to run wire some money home."

Evie laughed—"Hey hey"—her fat breasts rising and falling. I wanted to slap her greasy face.

What if Kathy came back from downtown and Miriam was still in the park? What if Miriam told Linda Bloomberg that Ule was minding another child and Linda fired her? And I had made Ule tell a lie. *Dear God,* I prayed silently, *help.* I shook my head at my own hypocrisy.

"Miriam," Ule said, "when you making another one to give me the baby-nurse work?"

She hoisted Ben onto her knee. "You want a little brother or sister?" she asked him.

"I want a little penguin please, Mommy," he replied, and Ule laughed.

Miriam shielded her eyes and looked up at me. "So, Grace, how's the morning?"

The twins were trying without success to climb on Evie's knees.

"It's good," I answered. "I was just telling Ben that he should share his toys with the others."

Ben looked up at his mom. "Finnegan tried to take my dump truck, Mommy."

"He did?" Miriam hugged her son and looked at me. The spots on the sides of her mouth were faded, and the little craters on her cheeks were Spackled smooth with face clay. "Grace, Ben doesn't have to share his toys with anyone if he doesn't want to. It's totally up to him," she told me.

Ule pulled her mouth into a straight line. Evie said, "Well, Caleb and Sammy don't have a choice. Is the two of them together, so them have to learn to share."

Soon, the other sitters were packing up to go in. Evie, too, started gathering the twins' toys. I wondered how long Miriam would stay in the park. I walked over to the sandbox and asked Finnegan for Ben's dump truck, then picked up his jacket.

"No, Grace," Ben said, "Mommy do."

I handed her the jacket and looked again at the subway exit next to the park, expecting any minute to see Kathy's scrunchie ascending.

Evie, with the twins strapped in, turned to Ule. "You coming?"

"You go," Ule said, "me waiting till my friend come back."

I knelt to buckle Ben in. "Are you having lunch with us, Miriam?" I asked her.

"I've got to get back," she said, "but I'll sit with you for a while. Hey, Ben, guess what? Mommy's going to have pizza pie with you."

I pulled my head back just in time to avoid another busted lip from Ben as he kicked his legs.

Ule waved at me. "I'll see you when you bring him out later," she said.

This was crazy. I was leaving Kathy's kid with a strange woman in the park. I pushed the stroller while Miriam and Ben chattered. Luckily she didn't catch it when he said, "We're leaving the baby, Grace?"

Of course she took forever to leave. It was after one when I got back to the park, pushing Ben furiously across the street as the red sign flashed DON'T WALK. Ule and both carriages were gone, and I cursed myself for not going upstairs first and calling Kath on her job. We raced back, and Ben said, "Wheeeee! We're going fast, Grace," and then "Oh, fuck" when we hit a hole in the pavement.

I didn't know which apartment Ule worked in and I didn't want to ask Duke. I willed the glass elevator doors to open. "Say 'open sesame,' Ben," I told him. He did, and the doors opened and shut, then opened and shut again on the twenty-second floor. I fumbled with the keys, opened the apartment door, and called Kathy with Ben still strapped into the carriage. When she answered the phone and I started to cry, she laughed. "Me 'ave 'im, fool. Ule said you had left about ten minutes before with Miriam. Thanks."

Chapter 18

On Tuesday night the Bruckners ate dinner and I got a head start cleaning the kitchen, running into the dining room every so often to bring Ben juice or get fresh pepper for Sol's London broil. After a while, I heard Sol ask Miriam how she felt.

"Much better. Twelve weeks come Saturday, and after that hooray! Coffee."

"So, Mir," Sol asked, "what do you think? After this term full-time mama?"

A fork chinked against a plate. "I'm not sure, babe"—the raspiness of her voice clashed with the tender word—"maybe one more year."

"Mir, this is ridiculous. The firm is mine. You haven't needed to work since ever. Just quit already. We can still have help, you know."

I wiped the counter in slow circles, trying to hear everything. The worst possible job was with a stay-at-home mother whose main task quickly became managing you.

"Why don't you just quit?"

"Quit it, Mommy," Ben said, and Sol replied, "Thank you, buddy."

"I'll quit when I'm ready, okay." She lowered her voice, but I could still hear. "I don't want anyone to say I married you for your money. You know that's what they all say anyway."

"Who says that? Name one person."

"Please . . . let's not pretend. Ettie. And your sister. Your father is the only one who likes me, and even he doesn't think I'm good enough for you."

"Come on, Mir, be fair. Mom loves your spunk. She adores Ben. And Dad worships him."

"Of course they love Ben, Sol. Look at him. He's a Bruckner. I'm lucky he was born with red hair."

"You're talking nonsense. You don't have to show anyone anything. I can take care of you and Ben just fine. End of story. Your job's the only thing keeping us in the city."

The counter was spotless, and my fingers were irritated from the cleanser-soaked sponge. When Sol called my name, I jumped.

"Can you clear the table? We're done."

I moved around collecting their plates and glasses.

"So, Grace," Sol said. "We hear you're going up to Dave's?"

Danny, of course.

"Dave? Um, no . . . I'm not going up to Dave's," I said. "I saw him in the lobby Sunday night, and he told me to come up and see the view. I haven't gone."

"Dave's fantastic." Miriam propped her chin and smiled. "You can go up when you're done with your work here."

This was not what I had expected. "But . . . I don't even know him."

Sol laughed. "Don't worry. Dave's as harmless as a plant."

How did he know?

"Well," Miriam said, "you're safe up there. Plus, he does have the best view. Can you bring us the gelato?"

Okay, this was my chance. I'd been waiting for a week for the right time, and here they were, laughing and smiling and encouraging me to go up to some strange man's house. This had to be it. I placed the ice cream on the table. The label on which Miriam had written "don't touch!" curled on one side.

"Um, Miriam . . . Sol? I need to ask you a question, please." Ben ran down the hall to his room. I held the back of his empty high chair. "What about the sponsorship? When would you want to start that?" There. I'd said it.

Miriam licked the back of her spoon. "Grace, let's wait and see. You've been here a week. Who knows, maybe you won't want to come back next week."

I had to be persistent. "Wait for how long, exactly?"

"Mmmm . . . Let's wait one month," Sol said. "If in a month every-thing's working out, you're comfortable and Ben's doing well, we'll go ahead and start the filing. How does that sound to you?"

That wasn't unreasonable. "Okay, thanks. By the end of April, then," I said, with a longing glance at Ben's abandoned ice cream.

BEFORE SHE LEFT FOR work Wednesday morning, Miriam called me into Ben's room and closed the door. She placed a pair of denim overalls on the bed. "Dress Ben in these when he gets up from his nap," she told me. "Take cash from the money cup for a cab, and bring back receipts for both directions. Ettie's address is on the list."

"Okay. How long should we stay?"

She chewed the corner of her lip, eating a good third of her left red splotch. "Listen, Grace"—Miriam turned to see that the door was closed all the way—"don't tell Ettie anything, okay?"

"Anything about what?"

"Anything about anything. Whatever she asks about, you just smile and tell her you don't know anything."

I nodded.

"And make sure Ben wears the overalls, even if he doesn't want to."

"Sure, of course."

"Thanks, Grace," she said. "I mean it."

THIS TIME JANE SMILED when she saw me. She knelt and unbuckled Ben from the carriage and managed to get a quick kiss before he ran into the apartment calling, "Choo choo."

"Is amazing 'ow much 'im look like Sol when 'im was likkle," she said, showing me where to park the carriage.

"You have pictures of Sol as a baby?" I asked her.

Jane stopped and cocked her head. "Me not talking 'bout some pic-tures, you know. Is not me self who mind Solomon from 'im born out Ettie belly? I tell you last time I been working for this family for too damn long. I mind Solomon and the next one. But this is the end." She dusted her hands together. "Next year I am going back to sweet Jamaica. Old Jane tired stand on these two foot."

Jesus Christ in the wilderness. Forty years of domestic labor. I tried to imagine knowing Ben's wife and children and still working for Sol and Miriam at fifty-seven.

"Miss Ettie and Nancy gone to the stores, but them soon come." She paused outside the kitchen. "You and Ben done eat lunch already?" she asked. We had. "Okay, you can go in the back and see what Ben and the old man doing. Come to the kitchen if you want anything."

Ben knew the drill and had run straight into the room where his grandfather's model train was set up. I followed and was greeted by Big Ben, wearing saggy denim overalls, a bulky turtleneck, and a striped cap.

"Wow," I said, walking over, "this is amazing." And it was. Big Ben had a real setup. The tracks rested on a platform about the size of two pool tables, with rails that looped around glassy ponds and over a river with a fancy metal bridge. The tracks snaked up steep hills with orange and red fall foliage; miniature cows grazed in cool, green pastures. Tiny people in warm winter gear clustered in the waiting areas of the two stations, while porters permanently strained under the weight of their packed trunks.

"It's not bad, is it," said Big Ben. "Seems wrong for a grown man to be playing with toys, but I love it." He looked down at Ben. "Let's show Grace how she runs."

He eased the throttle, and the train slowly shunted into the station. On cue Ben called out, "All aboard!" The whistle screeched as the locomotive pulled out, leaving the people and porters on the platform despite Ben's warning. Even though Ben must have seen this circuit countless times, he leaned against the tabletop edge and followed the train's progress without missing a curve or a climb.

"I want to drive a big dump truck and a choo-choo train when I grow up. Choo choo," Ben said.

Big Ben laid his head against the chair and worked his fingers in Ben's red curls. "You can be anything you want if it makes you happy." And then to me, "What about you, Grace? What do you want to do?"

That question again, and I realized I still didn't have an answer. I had wanted to get away from the island and from my mother. I had wanted to come to New York. Now that I was here, I didn't know what to do, or how. I shrugged. "Go to school?"

"Grace, you have to get on the school bus," Ben said.

His grandfather agreed. "Look into the city schools, Grace. Hunter, City, Brooklyn's good too. I used to sit on their board a long time ago. Everything was a long time ago now. But school is the right place to start."

He closed his wet eyes, and Ben relaxed against his chest, the flame of the child's red hair burning bright against the dull gray of his grandfather's turtleneck.

LATER I MET NANCY, another tall, redheaded Bruckner. She looked normal. You couldn't tell she was a lesbian.

"Mom, you were right. She is just gorgeous. But, Grace," she said, "what are you doing working for Sol and Miriam? You should come down to Perry Street, to my studio. I could paint you all day long."

"Thank you," I said, waiting for one of them to ask me to sit down. "You are a painter?"

"Oh, and I love the way you speak." She singsonged, "You are a painter." Then "Yep, I'm the artist in this family."

I thought about that, being an artist, painting all day long. Walking around the city, looking for inspiration, and then coming home to put it all down on canvas. "What do you paint?"

"Oh, darling, do not get her started," Ettie said. "Sit down and talk to us. How're Sol and Miriam doing?"

"They're good," I managed.

Ettie snorted. "Good, is that all they are? How's Miriam feeling? Has she been shopping?"

"Mom, don't pick on Grace."

"Is that what I'm doing? Well, sorry, Grace. I don't want to pick on you." To Nancy, she said, "I bet you she's been buying more of those precious animal figurines. God, she must have about two hundred of those things."

Nancy laughed. "They mean something to her, Mother. And you know Sol buys them for her too, so it's not just Miriam to blame."

"Peasant roots."

"Grace, you will have to excuse my mother. She's quite a snob, really," Nancy told me.

Ettie turned to face her daughter. "Is that what you think, Nancy? That I'm a snob?"

Nancy didn't flinch, and she didn't change her tone. "You're so hard on Miriam, Mom. You won't give her a break. Not everyone comes from"— she cast one arm out at the room—"this."

Ettie sat up. "Precisely, Nancy. Not everyone comes from this, but certainly, certainly—and even Grace from Africa I'm sure will agree with me—even if you don't come from it, once you are exposed to *this,* as you call it"—and here she mimicked Nancy's sweeping arm—"shouldn't your instincts be able to . . . to appreciate, to *want,* okay, if not want then at least to *know.* One wants objects that please the eyes, not offend. Surely you of all people agree with me, Nancy."

Nancy eyed Ettie. "I'm not agreeing to anything, Mother. Maybe Miriam finds beauty in her figurines. Maybe it's as simple as that. Ask Grace." Nancy turned to me. "Grace, what do you think about Miriam's collection?"

I didn't think anything, except that they collected dust.

"Now you leave Grace out of this, darling," Ettie said, pressing her palms on the seat to push herself up. "I'll just go in and see what my boys are doing at the station."

NANCY SHARED OUR CAB downtown, Ben half asleep between us. She twisted in her seat, looking over at me as the car inched through heavy traffic. I glanced at her fingernails to see how long they were. At the convent where I had gone to school, the lore was that the girls with short nails were lesbians. Sure enough, Nancy's nails were cut to the quick and unpolished. I shifted a little closer to the door.

"So how long have you lived in New York?" she asked me.

"Just over a year," I said, and because I didn't want her to question me the entire ride home, I asked her, "Is Sol older or younger than you?"

She reached over to scratch Ben's head. "Solly is my baby brother. You know, Grace, I saw the other woman Sol and Miriam interviewed, and I liked her. She seemed very prim, you know, a proper nanny for Ben." She smiled at me. "But now I know why Mom and Dad preferred you, though."

"Why?"

"Are you kidding me?"

I shook my head.

"Look at you. You're perfect for Mom, and Mom gets what she wants, usually. She's probably the one paying your salary, for all I know."

I thought about this, and since Nancy seemed willing to talk, asked, "So what, Miriam didn't have a choice?"

"Of course she had a choice, darling." Nancy patted her nephew's head. "But even if you weren't the nanny she wanted, you're the nanny she's convinced she should have."

Chapter 19

Sylvia wasn't expecting me. I had called from the Bruckners' and told her Miriam needed me to work extra, that I might be in as late as midnight and she shouldn't wait up. As long as I didn't make too much noise when I came in, she said, I was to please my mind. For once I was going to do just that. The night was cold and fresh, and I felt full of energy and ready for anything.

I met Brent outside the Nostrand Avenue stop. He was sitting on a bench with his legs squared open and his arms spread wide across the back, watching traffic go by on the parkway. He had on jeans, work boots, and an enormous black coat that looked like a shiny quilt. "'Ello, darkie," he whispered as he kissed me. I closed my eyes and leaned all my weight into him, inhaling great gulps of his cigarette and cinnamon smell.

"Aye," he said, "you gone to sleep, or what?"

I rubbed my forehead against his chest, unwilling to move, then finally pulled away. And then I felt shy. He took my hand. "Come on."

We walked over to a small green car. "I didn't know you drove," I said. He held open the passenger door for me before getting in, then he leaned over the gears and kissed me properly.

"So where you want go?"

I wanted him to kiss me again. "Can we just drive around for while? You can drive and talk at the same time, right?"

"Yeah," he said, laughing, and I loved the deep sound, "me think me can manage that."

But we drove in silence, coasting down Eastern Parkway, down by the big museum and past the library and looping around the great arch at Grand Army Plaza, landmarks I knew only from underground. Brent hadn't turned on the music, but the silence in the car was comfortable. "So, what you want talk about?" he asked.

I wanted to talk about him. I wanted to ask what he did for work and if he had a girlfriend or any children and brothers and sisters and if his parents lived in America or if they were still back in Jamaica, and how had he and Donovan met, but instead I asked, "So, how was your week?"

" 'Ard work, you know? But Friday come and me dey here with you, so things good, right? Wha' 'bout you? You work 'ard for them white people them too?"

On Thursday morning before Miriam had left for work, she had pulled a stepladder from the hall closet and shown me some yellowish spots on the ceilings of both bathrooms she wanted me scrub out. I also had to move all the figurines off their shelves, wipe them with a soft cloth, and line them back up in order as best as I could remember. And just before I left, she had asked me to use the brush under the toilet rim, where bits of vomit had caked from her morning sickness.

"Not too hard," I said to Brent. "It's just work, you know."

"Trust me, me know. You want get something to eat?"

"Yes, please. I'm starving. Did you hear my belly just now?"

"You a funny woman. Nah, me didn't hear you belly. You want pick up some Chinee food?"

"I hate Chinese food."

"What? You the first person in America me ever hear what hate Chinee food. You want go Yardies?"

"No, not there. I'm not dressed up enough for Yardies."

"Ah, what you chat 'bout? Me bet say you look better than any woman what sit down in there right now."

I loved the way he talked, jutting his chin forward for emphasis. "Okay, so Yardies then."

Barrington greeted Brent just as warmly as he had Donovan. I willed myself not to worry about what he did for a living.

"You see," he said, "no woman in 'ere can touch you."

"Except that waitress," I muttered as the same gorgeous server from Saturday wended her way through the tables to give us menus. I understood only one word of the deep patois she spoke to Brent: "Donovan."

"Tell me what kind of work do you do," I asked.

"Mule work."

"What?"

"No, no"—he laughed—"not that kind of mule. All me mean is that me work 'ard. 'Ard work to break man back. Scene."

"Construction?"

"Nah, not no construction." He didn't say what but asked, "So where Mammy and Daddy?"

I thought this funny, a grown man asking about my mammy and daddy. "Trinidad. I have a younger sister too."

The waitress slunk over with our drinks, a frothy golden ginger beer for me and a Red Stripe for Brent.

"You know, me never ask you how much years you have."

I looked at my watch before answering, thinking Kathy must have forgot to tell him. "Today is my birthday. Eighteen."

"Whoa! For real? Today self is your birthday? 'Ow come you never did tell me, man? We'da gone and do something well special."

"This is special."

He flicked his wrist. "Now me 'ave to make this up to you. Don't worry."

I wasn't worried. My telling Brent about my birthday made him forget he'd asked about my family, and I was glad. How had I ended up in Babylon? Stubbornness, my mother would say. But even this, just being able to go out with a friend and have a meal on my eighteenth birthday, would have been unthinkable back under her roof in that village. I shook my head, ashamed. Had I come to America for a plate of oxtails and rice, for a glass of ginger beer?

"What happen?" Brent asked. "What you shake your head for?"

"I just can't believe I'm eighteen already, is all. I'm getting old."

"Wait till thirty."

I pounced on that. "Is that how old you are, then?"

He squinted at me. "Sometime you talk real stush, you know."

"Thanks, but answer the question."

"Thirty-one come August. That too old for you?"

"And no children?"

"Two daughters and a likkle man," he said without pause.

I reached for my drink. "Here or in Jamaica?"

"My big girl, she eleven already, she with her granny back Jamaica. The younger two—"

I didn't want to hear anymore. "Okay, okay. I don't want to know all your business." And I didn't. I just wanted to have my meal, to listen the music, and to talk about anything. How Kathy did it, I didn't know. If Brent had children, then he had a woman. Even if they were broken up, he was still tied to his children's mother, and I would always come after that. The ginger beer burned my throat going down, and I told myself that the wetness in my eyes came from its sharp sting.

"You coming to Kathy birthday bash next month?" I asked him.

"For sure, yeah."

"Are you coming alone?"

"You want me to come alone?" he asked, raising his eyebrows.

I smiled too, in spite of myself. The hussy waitress came over with our food, the stewed oxtails hot and curling steam. "Yes," I said, "I want you to come alone."

It was after midnight by the time Brent dropped me off. I hoped Sylvia would be in the bedroom, not wanting her to see my lips swollen from kissing Brent for half an hour in the car on the parkway. She was snoring hard on the couch but woke up as soon as I opened the front door.

"What time it is, Grace?"

The apartment was wrecked worse than usual. I could barely see carpet on the floor for all the clothes and toys scattered about.

"Just past twelve."

"Them white people and them give you cab fare, though?"

"Uh-huh."

"You take a cab, or you keep the money and take the train?"

"Cab. Miriam tell the doorman to hail a cab, so I had to take it." I hoped I didn't smell like Brent's cologne.

"You is a ass." Sylvia struggled up from the couch. "You should have tell the driver, Mister, take me right around the corner to the number four train."

"How come you still up?" I sat in the armchair, across from her.

"Is you I was waiting for," she told me. "You mother call."

The oxtails rose sour to my throat. "Oh, God, what happen? Daddy? Oh, God."

"Grace, stop playing the ass before you give yourself a heart attack and dead in my house. You mother call to tell you happy birthday. I didn't even know today was your birthday, self. And them white people them make you work. You tell them was your birthday?"

I was so relieved.

"Better to not tell them nothing, anyway. So yes, she call to say happy birthday and she say your father say happy birthday too. You mother sound like a nice nice lady."

The night's joy drained out of me. "Anything else about Daddy?"

"No. All she say is that she was coming home from hospital and she decide to stop and give you a little call. Oh, and she ask if you giving me any trouble."

But the news was there. Last week she had told me that my father was to be discharged on Monday. Five days later he was still in San Fernando General. I counted out two twenties and a ten for Sylvia, wondering again if a little bit of money and a restaurant meal was worth being away from home.

"What you have plan for tomorrow?" Sylvia asked.

"Nothing special. Why?"

"You see all this clothes on the ground here. I have to put all of this in garbage bags. The city sending somebody tomorrow to do some tesses—"

"What kind of tests?"

"Me don't know, mama. I carry Dame by HIP Wednesday, and Thursday they call to say the city coming to run some tesses and to take the clothes out the closets. I tell Bo clear the hall closet, but I still waiting. Tomorrow-please-God help me to bag up all this stuff, nah?"

"No problem."

"Anyhow," she said, bracing herself against the armrest, raising the other end of the couch off the floor, "is a good thing all this rubbish move. Jacob Russian and them coming from next week to start the paint job."

I stayed up to bag the clothes, and after about an hour Bo came in.

"So, was only a last week thing. You didn't bring no cigarettes this time?"

"I work late tonight. And anyhow, Bo, I not supporting you. I look like your wife?"

He dropped onto the springless couch behind me. "Speaking of which, we doing this thing or what?"

The fur edging Bo's parka was matted and dirty, like wet hair on a mangy pothound. "Don't you need to have a job before you could sponsor a wife? You need to show income, Bo."

"You don't worry about that," he said, reaching for the remote. "Just tell me when you have the money save and you ready to go downtown."

"And what if I tell you I have the money save now?"

He kept the TV on mute and leaned toward me on the floor. "You talking seriousness, Grace? You have it already? How much?"

In all, I had about $170. "I have five hundred to start."

"We could work with that. Remember Jacob?"

"Yes?"

"Well, the other day he promise me a few days' work. All I have to do is get a letter from him saying I is one of he regular guys and them and that good enough to put in the paper. Scene? You ready to do this thing?"

Slowly, I folded a purple winter coat of Micky's for the bag. She wouldn't need it again for nine months. In nine months, if I married Bo, I could have a green card. "Month end," I said. "Let's wait until the end of April, so I don't have to spend all my money. We'll get the license, and then we could have a June wedding. It'll be more convincing."

Bo leaned in closer. "Sylvia tell you what happen?"

I didn't know what he was talking about. "About the city coming tomorrow?"

He brushed imaginary flies from in front his face. "With she husband last week in the G Building."

She had not.

"She and he was sitting down in the visiting hall talking cool cool, when all of a sudden he grab she in a headlock and start to choke she." Bo was talking so softly I could barely hear him. "The guard and them had to rush to separate them and lock him up fast fast. Me don't think they letting him out of that madhouse anytime soon, mama."

Sylvia hadn't said a word, but then I hadn't called all week to find out what was going on either.

"Bo, what send him mad, so? Sylvia say he was good good, and then he start to go off. Something happen?"

He settled in the couch and aimed the remote. TV laughter filled the room. "Is this place, girl. Babylon does send man mad mad when you see they can't take care of they family. Back home he used to teach, you know, but here he papers didn't count. He not build for construction and sit down inside all day minding child like a woman. Is why you think I does go and walk about when you see morning come? Sitting down waiting for what break up he mind. Scene."

I continued to fold clothes and fill bags. The mound was almost cleared, and the dull carpet so matched the faded red of my Conway jeans that my legs and the floor seemed melded to one.

I WAS NOT EXPECTING a woman.

"I'm Cassandra Neil. Are you Mrs. John?" she asked, standing in the hallway.

"No, I'm Grace. Sylvia's not here. You're from the city, right? To do the tests?"

"Are you over eighteen and have permission to let me on the premises?"

"As of yesterday."

She said happy birthday and walked in. I was embarrassed. You could brush a pig only so much. The apartment was clean on the surface, but the decayed carpet, the smudged walls, and the listing breakfront could not be camouflaged. Micky sat curled in a corner of the couch watching TV with her thumb in her mouth.

"So, do you live here too?" she asked. She had taken a small meter from her bag and now unhooked an attachment from her belt. The pieces made a nice *click* as they fitted together.

"No," I said, "I'm only here to let you in. My cousin had to run some errands this morning."

She placed her meter flush against a wall where the peeled paint hung in tongues. "Man," she said, "this is bad."

"What?"

"The lead levels. This place is a death trap. Do you feel tired and sluggish when you wake up in the morning?"

"I don't live here, remember."

"That's right," she said, and I wondered if she had been trying to catch me in a lie. She continued around the apartment, and I followed her. "So you're eighteen," she said, opening the junk closet in the hall and confronting the pile. "Where do you go to school?"

Not *Do you go to school?* but *Where?* "I'm not in school right now."

She closed the door and wrote something in her notebook. "This closet should have been cleared. Where'd you go to high school then?"

She had no right to ask me these questions and I didn't have to answer her, but I wanted her to know. To know that I wasn't a dummy living like the Haitians in a dilapidated apartment with ten other people. "Back home. I did O-levels and A-levels. Do you know what those are?"

She adjusted a button on her meter. "Like in England, right?"

"That's right. I'm just waiting for a few documents to start college."

She didn't look up. "Which college?"

"Hunter." *Thank you, Big Ben.*

"Hunter's good," she said.

"Where did you go to school?" I asked her.

"Columbia."

"Columbia University?"

"Uh-huh," she said, shaking her head at what her meter told her about the windowsill.

"What did that cost you?"

She turned around and looked at me. "A lot, and I'm probably going to be paying it back for the next twenty years. Big deal, though. If you've got the grades or your A-levels whatever, don't worry about what school costs, just go."

She knelt in front of the radiator and angled her meter between the accordion grates. She whistled and asked Micky, "Are you the only kid living here?"

Without taking her thumb from her mouth, Mick said, "I've got two brothers. One fast one and one slow one."

Cassandra took her notebook out of her back pocket. "How old are your brothers?"

Micky glanced at me for permission to answer. "Derek's seven, and Dame's almost three. I'm ten."

"Thanks," Cassandra said, slapped closed her notebook, and unscrewed the meter attachment. To me she said, "Tell your cousin that she should hear from the city by Wednesday, and if she doesn't she should call this number." She gave me her card. "In the meanwhile, do me a favor? I know you said you don't live here, but when you're over could you make sure that the kids, especially the two-year-old, could you make sure he's not putting any paint in his mouth or licking the windowsill? This place is hazardous."

"That's all my baby brother do," Micky said. "Grace already told my mother to stop him eating the paint."

"Good." At the front door Cassandra Neil said, "Watch out for those kids. This place needs to be gutted. These landlords are the worst in the city."

"I'll tell my cousin."

"And don't wait too long before you go back to school."

Chapter 20

Miriam didn't really announce that she was expecting a baby, she just started talking about being pregnant. "Like clockwork, Grace," she said on Tuesday morning. "Twelve weeks and no more morning sickness, thank God. Same with Ben."

I didn't know how to answer her. "Good?" I offered.

"Uh-huh, very good." She stood in profile and pressed her shirt against her belly. "What do you think? Can you tell yet?"

Before I could answer, Sol walked down the hall and stood outside the kitchen, trapping me between them. He fiddled with his tie and wolf-whistled at her, and I swear she exaggerated the kick of her flat bottom. "Still feeling okay?"

She held up crossed fingers. "Can you tell, Sol? Am I showing yet?"

"Not that I can see." He slid past me into the kitchen. "You look as gorgeous as ever." He put his arms around Miriam and said into her hair, "Now, wouldn't you prefer to be off today? You could go shopping, you could go to a movie, go to the spa, house hunting."

I pretended not to listen, but I saw her jab him with her elbow. "Don't start" was all she said.

Later I told Kathy, "Well, she definitely pregnant." We were at McDonald's with the kids. Kathy paid for our food with money her boss had left her and, after asking the displeased and disturbingly acned cashier for duplicate receipts, gave me one for the money cup. We had a clear view to the park, and I could see the other sitters clustered around Evie. Before she responded, Kathy aimed her chin in Ben's direction and lifted her eyebrows. "It's okay," I said. He was taken with the little green monster toy that came with his meal and didn't seem to be paying us any attention.

"She tell you so?"

"Not plain plain, but she said that her morning sickness had ended just like it had with Ben, and then she turned and asked me if she was showing."

"Sounds pregnant to me," Kathy said with a heavy sigh. "Maybe she was just waiting for three months to pass. You not supposed to tell anyone before twelve weeks, bad luck. You ever hear that?"

I hadn't.

Kath put her chin in her hand. "Must be nice."

I offered Ben a drink of my chocolate milk shake, which he took without even looking away from his toy. "What must be nice?"

Kathy made a face. "God, Grace, look how you drinking after them dirty little white children."

I sucked on the straw. "American antibodies. Answer me, though, what must be nice?"

"You know, nice. Nice to have a husband and a child and to be expecting another one. It just sounds nice to be settled, is all."

Sure it would be nice, but not now. Getting married for real and settling down was the last thing on my mind. "Yeah, but we don't need to worry about that yet. Hey, Ben," I said as I stole one of his fries, "do you want a baby brother like Kathy's baby in the carriage?"

Still without looking up from his toy, he shook his head. "Baby duck," he said.

"Duckling. You know, he says a different baby animal every time."

Kathy got up and put on her sunglasses, showering the tabletop with dancing rainbow spots. "I have to go."

"Already? I thought you said you wanted to go by your shop on Fourteenth? I don't want to go back upstairs yet. And I sure don't want to go to the park," I said. But she didn't stop, just pushed the receipt my way.

THAT NIGHT MIRIAM CAME into my room. I put down the book I was reading, a thick romance I had pulled off her shelf, and sat up as she switched on the overhead light. She had a camera looped around her wrist.

"Grace, can you do me a favor?"

I had done everything including put Ben to bed, but I was already accustomed to the idea that I was on twenty-four-hour call. "Okay." To-morrow was Wednesday. I was sure Miriam was going to give me her don't-say-anything talk. Instead, she pulled the louvered doors shut and handed me the camera. Without saying a word, she wriggled her jersey over her head—she wasn't wearing a brassiere—then stepped out of her panties. Still without any explanation, though it was clear now what she wanted me to do, Miriam put both garments at the foot of my bed and stood in profile in front of the closed doors.

"Go ahead." She lifted her chin. "It's point and click."

Her body, unlike her craggy face, was smooth and plump, filled out so that she looked slightly inflated. A surprisingly black triangle of pubic hair curled out bushy from her crotch. I slid off the bed to stand in front of the bureau, as far as I could get from her in the small room. She posed with her thin nose tipped up, and her arms hanging straight down at her sides. With each hoarse rustle of her breath, her full, firm breasts heaved. When I snapped the picture, the flash caught her diamond ring. I wasn't sure if the shot was going to come out, but I didn't tell her that because I wanted her gone from my space. She turned around to face me full-on. "Take one from the front too," she said.

I snapped again, sure that the picture would be of the washer because I refused to look at her pale and uncooked nakedness. I had never even seen my own mother naked from the waist down, only the fried egg breasts she assured me would be mine after I was married and had nursed ungrateful children.

"You got it?" Miriam asked.

I gargled something, unable to speak.

"Good," she continued. "I've got a project in mind. I wanted to do it when I was having Ben, but then it was too late." She pulled on her clothes as she talked. "I'm going to try to take pictures of my belly every night and then have them animated, you know, like how cartoons are done. When you watch it, you'll be able to see my belly grow"—she moved her hand slowly up from her navel—"like you see flowers open on the nature shows."

Miriam reached for the camera, and I passed it to her, still unable to say anything. She checked the film count and said, "I'll keep the camera and just bring it in every night."

Every night? "Miriam, you want me to do this, to take the pictures of your belly every night?"

"Uh-huh, as often as I remember anyway. Sol was doing it before, but now that you know, you can do it."

This I wasn't comfortable with. I didn't want to see her naked in my space night after night for six months. I willed myself to have Kathy's boldness or Sylvia's tongue. If I didn't say anything tonight, tomorrow would be too late. Breathing deeply, I said, "Um, Miriam, how come Sol can't continue to take the pictures for you?"

She was dressed now and ready to leave. "Ugh, he's so not reliable for this stuff. It was hell getting him to do the past three months. The shots need to be consistent."

She spied the book I was reading. "Is that one of mine?"

"Yes. I got it off the shelf."

"You're not reading during the day, I hope?"

"No, no. Just at night when I'm done."

"Okay then," she said, "because we're not paying you to read."

And then she left. But I didn't get back into bed. I put on my clothes and walked out the door.

I DIDN'T HAVE TO worry about which apartment was Dave's because on the thirtieth floor there was only one door, a few steps up from the elevator. Brutus or Cesar barked when I rang the bell.

"Grace," he said, "so nice to see you. I was wondering if you were ever going to come up and visit." He was wearing a faded green jersey, khaki shorts covered in dirt, and an old pair of low-top Converse sneakers. There was a dried leaf in his bushy hair. "Sorry," he said, moving away from the door, "I'm very dirty. I was all the way in the back repotting, and I didn't even hear the bell. Thanks for the bark, Brute. Come on in."

It is impossible to tell from the streets that such places exist. Dave didn't live in a regular apartment with rooms and walls, and, unlike the open loft where Kathy worked, this apartment wasn't once part of an old factory. His place, apparently, was an entire floor of the tower. The walls on three sides were glass, and because the tower dome protected the ceiling, it too was made of glass, or some kind of see-through material. Dave had cultivated the wild, and, with the constant light, the greenery, at only the beginning of spring, was as lush and abundant as the island bush in October—the height of hurricane season.

"Give yourself the tour," Dave said. "Start here and walk around the apartment. Stay close to the walls."

I did as he said, first walking the length of the one plastered wall and then turning at the corner where brick met glass. Immediately, I felt dizzy. With only glass between the night and me, I felt weightless and hollow. Outside, the crisp city grid and then the black river and still beyond lay sprawled before me. The view to the south showed much more of the twin towers than I could see from downstairs, and Brooklyn was somewhere in that direction. But Sylvia and that world might as well have been in another galaxy.

"You live here? This is your house, your apartment? This is, my God, this is fantastic, Dave. Wow."

He scratched the back of his head. "Yeah, it's not bad, is it? Now you know what I do here all the time. The forest in the sky."

I wanted so much to ask him a money question, but of course I didn't.

"My father," he said, using a dented hand spade to loosen the soil around a flowering papaya. "When he had this place designed, he was the one who wanted a glass house above the city. The top floors in the other three towers have smaller versions of this apartment. This is the only one that takes up the whole floor."

"Is that a papaya?" I didn't have a response for what he had just said.

"It is, actually." He stopped digging and looked up. "How'd you know? It hasn't fruited yet."

"We have trees in my yard back home."

"Really? Then maybe you can tell me why the flowers on this one keep falling off without growing into fruit. It's healthy too. I changed the soil. I gave it more sun. It's been under lights since last October. Not a single papaya."

And there wasn't going to be one any time soon. The flowers on this tree hung from streaming stalks instead of coming directly out of the trunk, meaning only one thing. "This tree is male, Dave. My mother had a freak mango tree that did that." She had hung a blue milk of magnesia bottle from its branches to shield it from withering *mal jeux* and put up a chicken-wire fence to protect it from *mal élevé* children, but year after year that tree had flowered and not one single mango. Finally, my mother had taken her cutlass and, calling the tree an abomination in the eyes of the Lord, chopped it down.

"Male, huh." Dave put both hands on his waist, sizing up the mutant plant. "I hadn't thought about that. Figures I'd grow a male papaya."

"There's a way to fix it, you know."

"How d'you mean 'fix it'?"

"To get it to bear."

He looked up at the spiky crown of leaves. "How?"

"You've got to cut off the top, cover the stump with a pan or something so that it only takes water through the roots, and then it'll branch out with female flowers. My mother turned papayas all the time."

Dave was looking at me with his mouth open. "Ouch. You want me to castrate my tree? I got a papaya to grow in New York City, in the wintertime, from seed, Grace. No way I'm cutting it."

"Okay, but no way you're eating homegrown papaya either."

"You're funny," he said and pulled off his work gloves. "Come on, let me show you inside."

The apartment did in fact have an inside tucked away at its core. The open space all around was more of an aerial yard, and because of the dense growth of trees and bushes around the perimeter, the huge inner flat was almost invisible. We ended up in the kitchen. "What would you like to drink? I've got beer and red and white wine and all kinds of liquor for cocktails and Diet Coke."

"A beer, please," I said but then thought about going back downstairs reeking of alcohol. "Not a beer, I'll take some Diet Coke."

"Please, Grace. The last thing you need is diet anything. You worried about Sol and Miriam?" He took two bottles of beer out of the huge refrigerator.

"They don't even know that I came up here. I just walked out the door after Miriam had me take naked pictures of her belly."

Dave cracked up and passed me the beer. "She did what?" He put his finger to his lips, picked up a phone. "Hi, Miriam darling . . . Dave . . . Just wanted to let you know, Grace is up here . . . Don't worry, I won't keep her too late . . . Good . . . good . . . Ohhhhhh, congratulations. I feel demoted. I get told with hoi polloi now?" He rolled his eyes at me. "Okay, I'll tell her . . . uh-huh . . . Yep, see you later, good night." He made a kiss sound and rang off. "Drink up, Grace Jones, but you're not allowed to stay past midnight."

"Is that what she said?" We knocked cheers, but I took only a sip. "She didn't sound angry?"

He took a long draft of his and sat on the stool on the opposite side of the counter. "They won't be mad that you're here."

"How come?"

He lifted an eyebrow. "Trust me, they won't."

On the redbrick wall behind the stove, Dave had hung plant cuttings to dry. He had big bunches of bay leaves and lots of different peppers and plaited ropes of papery garlic. On a line like at the newsstand, he had tied smaller bunches of big- and small-leaf thyme, basil, chives, rosemary, every herb possible, within easy reach of a cooking pot. "Did you grow all of that stuff on the walls up here?"

"Everything except the bay leaves. I brought that up from Key West. Do you know a lot about plants, Grace?"

I guess I did, by osmosis almost. Between my mother's small backyard garden, as well as the bigger one where we grew vegetables to sell in Penal market, and the old people in the village who had a bush medicine for every ailment a sea bath wouldn't cure, you couldn't grow up on the Quarry Road and not know about plants. "I know about the plants we have at home."

Dave slid off his stool and walked over to the wall. "Come, let's test your knowledge. See how many you can name."

Standing in front of the wall with my nearly empty beer bottle, I reeled off first all the herbs and then the larger bunches suspended above. When I got to the benne, Dave said, "What?"

"Benne. Every year my mother hangs some to dry, and then she makes benne balls with them. It's benne for sure."

"What on earth is a benne ball, Grace?"

"It's a kind of sweetie, a candy, with benne and sugar, and it's crunchy." My mother was a pro at gauging the right temperature to roll the sticky mixture. Too hot scalded your palms and the balls softly collapsed. Too cool and it all hardened into a shapeless, inedible mess. "They're so good."

"You know what we call benne in America?" He drained his beer. "Sesame seeds."

"Are you serious? Is this what a sesame seed is? So why is *Sesame Street* called *Sesame Street*?" I snapped off a pod and, shaking it close to my ear, heard the dry seeds rattle around like mini maracas. I was happy I had come upstairs, and happy too to know that Miriam and Sol didn't seem to mind me leaving the apartment. We finished going through the plants, and then I thought it was time to go downstairs.

"You sure you don't want a quick cup of coffee before you head down, Grace?"

Caffeine was the last thing I needed when I had to be up by seven. I could easily hear Miriam telling me that my nights upstairs were wearing me out. Then I smiled because I had already thought about coming back to visit with Dave. "No, I should just go down, but I'll come and see you again. Maybe I can help you pot plants or something."

"You bet," Dave said. "You have to come back up again, and soon."

"I will, and thanks for the beer." I ran down the short flight of stairs to the elevator, then waited for its long ascent to the thirtieth floor. As it neared, I tried to time the door's opening and said, "Open sesame," at just the right moment.

Chapter 21

The market was in session. The white lady market, Ule called it. Once when she and I had taken a walk through its tented stalls, she had screwed up her face and put down a bunch of something called ramps. "But what is this? Ramp? Not food for goat and cattle this is? Tell me when you ever see them selling yam and cassava, food for black people to eat. No, mama, me say this is one market for white lady."

A lot of old white people were out taking the sun, some alone and some with their minders. A tall, seriously underweight woman with long platinum hair stalked by in five-inch heels, a tight jersey, and a short black skirt.

We all stared. Meena, the Indian sitter from Guyana whose wrong shade of foundation was an ill-applied death mask, and who always mentioned that her mother was a half-white woman, said to no one in particular: "Please. You think she looking good? When you see my lady dress to go out, nobady can't touch she, you know. Is head-to-toe name brand. I'm telling you. Is not me self who take the clothes to the cleaners? Is only Calvin Klein and Danna Karan and all kind of fancy thing, mama. I tell you, I never see that woman in anything but the very best. Down to she panty and all have name. Hanes Her Way."

I remembered Miriam's balled-up panties in her bed. Last week I'd told her it was hard to make the bed when she left clothes tucked into the sheets, expecting her to take some shame and drop her dirty underwear in the hamper. But all she said was "Don't just tug the duvet. Make sure to strip and shake the sheets before you make the bed, Grace."

Marva, whose dark skin was often covered with bruises, said, "My lady, she not cheap at all, at all like some of them other white woman and them. Is nine years now I working for Sally and not a Friday come and she didn't give me my pay envelope eight o'clock sharp. And every year is five days holidays I does get when you see summer come. With pay, to boot. That is why you see I not in no hurry to leave them and go to work for anybody else. You know what you have, my dear, but you don't know what you getting." She touched the swollen spot on the side of her eye and lowered her voice. "Is a lot of nasty and low-down white people out there. Trust me. Is thirteen years now I living in America, and I meet my share. And how, I does make my little extra change on the side too. Yes, you have to know how to profit yourself. When you see she leave the change for laundry, well, I take my little dollar here and there. Or the grocery money? Well, you not stupid enough to take the money, but is who self going to the grocery? Not Marva? I buy for she house and I buy for my house. Not big things, but little things like soap or peas and carrots in the tin. Things you could stick easy easy in your pocketbook. You have to know how to make your profit, yes."

"Well," Evie joined in, "I don't have to thief nothing from nobody. Not that I calling you a thief, Marva. Everybody have to do what it is they have to do. But my lady does give me plenty things. When you see she go away for two, three days and she stay in them big fancy hotel and them, well, she does bring back all them little soap and little shampoo. One time she went away for the whole weekend and I stay over with Caleb and Sammy, and to show she appreciation she bring me back a white towel set. Was two bath towel, two hand towel, and a washrag. I pack that in a barrel to send to my house in Barbados. No sah. Me don't need to take nothing from nobody. Again, Marva, I not calling you a thief, I just saying—"

Evie made a dash for the sandbox. Every once in a while she surprised us with a youthful burst of speed, usually in the direction of one of the twins. She grabbed Caleb, who had just opened a fistful of sand over the yellow hair of a little girl with a stay-at-home, spy-on-us mother. She brought him over to the bench. I swear she said to him:

"Whoy ooh dooah ting loike dat?"

"I'm sorry, Evie."

"Buh whuh dis likkle goil do ooh, Caleb?"

"Nothing. I said I was sorry."

"Oi shuh gi ooh ah pinch on ooh buhfum fuh dat. Goiver dere an tell ar ooh sorry."

He walked over to where the girl's mother exaggeratedly shook out her daughter's hair and, presumably, said he was sorry. Evie turned back to us. "That little wretch. You see what I have to deal with? You see how he bad? Caleb is one of the name for the devil self." Then she turned to me. "And you, Miss Prim and Proper, sitting down playing quiet quiet. How come you didn't tell we your lady making baby?"

How on earth did she know that?

"I can't tell anybody Miriam pregnant if she didn't tell me."

Evie looked at me through upraised arms as she tightened her curler. "But I right, though? Even though she didn't tell you. Come, child, you only working for these white people two weeks now and you keeping they secrets from you own people? Is who you trust more, them or we?"

I didn't trust her for sure.

"Ule could well do with the little baby nurse job," she said. "You know how to mind baby?"

Ule said, "Evie, I don't need you to be no solicitor for me, thank you very much."

A woman who I thought was one of the mothers came into the park and walked toward us on the bench. After Miriam's surprise visit last week, I wondered whose lady she was. Then Evie saw her. "Look who it is, my dear, the one and only Bridget."

Bridget was grinning as she came up to the bench, and the women scooched around to make space for her. "How are you bunch of slackers doing?" she asked. "Still minding the little buggers I see and having your lemons. Hiya, Evie, Ule, Marva, Petal. Guys, don't let me have to say hi to everyone. How's the craic?"

Her hoarse accent was Irish and heavy. As soon as she sat down, she took out a pack of cigarettes, offered them around to no takers, and lit up. She inhaled deeply and then blew out the smoke in a steam-kettle rush. When she did that, her top lip pruned and she looked older.

"Hello, Miss Bridget," Evie said. "A lime, we liming. We say since you gone you don't come to look for the old-timers no more."

Bridget laughed, her voice husky. "Not at all, me darlings. I've been to Ireland for over a month. Me ma was well sick over there, but she's doing better now, bless."

Petal raised both palms skyward. "Thanks to Jesus. The husband went with you?"

Bridget screwed up her face. She was pretty, in a way. Her hair was shiny black and cut with long bangs, setting off her freckled, white skin and wide, startled eyes. "He came for a week and then had to come back to New York, or so he said. What's been going on around here?" She leaned forward. "Hey, Ule, how are you doing? Got a new one, I see."

Ule gently jostled the baby. "Yes, my love. You remember the Bloomberg lady on the twentieth floor? She make another one, and she give me the work."

Bridget sucked her cigarette again. "That old cow still giving milk? Let me see him." Ule peeled back the blanket, and Bridget looked. "Bless, ugly as sin, in't he? But good for you. Don't take any shite from her now. You know how bossy these bitches can be."

I wondered who this woman was. The sitters were usually restrained, speaking good English and giving one-word answers and nods whenever one of the mothers came by and tried to pal around. They simply didn't trust these women, and I was fast realizing that the relationship I had had with Mora was very different from how most of the women in the towers got on with their help.

"Oi." Bridget reached into her really nice pocketbook and pulled out an envelope. "I almost forget, yeah. I brought yous something from Ireland." In it were several green, clover-shaped key chains, which she passed around. "That's so every time you open you doors, you can think about me sneaking in to take your menfolk."

All the women laughed, and Marva said, "Bridget, you done take one man already. You not going to leave we with what we have?"

"You can have yours," she said. "And what the fuck is that on the side of your face, Marva? That drunk's still coming at ya? I've already told you to pour some hot oil in that bastard's ear when he's asleep."

Marva pressed her finger to her lips, and Bridget wagged one of her own at her. "You have to stop taking his shite, Marv."

Ule passed me the envelope, but I didn't take a key chain. "Oi." Bridget turned to Evie. "You've done replaced me in the crew, then?" And to me, "Hello, luv, I'm Bridget, who are you?"

Evie said, "Who you see who missing?"

Bridget surveyed the group and called out names. "Petal, Marva, Meena,

Ule, you, them lot whose names I never knew." Then she got it. "Bloody hell, where the fuck, gosh, excuse me, kids around, I know. Where's sourpuss Carmen?" And she looked at me through her bangs with her chin drawn down.

Before Evie could fill her in, Ule said, "That woman, nah, what you expect? You know she is a nastiness. She fire Carmen on Tuesday night and Grace was with Benjamin on Wednesday morning. None of we didn't know what happen."

I looked from Ule to Evie and to all the other women. No wonder then. No wonder they had all hated me and Duke had stared, and even Dave must have known. How stupid had I been? I remembered Ben crying for his ya-ya that first morning. I had thought . . . What had I thought? Over and over Sylvia had said to me she could tell I was from the bush. I guessed she was right.

Bridget put her hands on her hips. Evie stared at Ule, pissed and pouting. No doubt she would have delivered the news differently.

"What a dirty, low-down thing to do to a hardworking woman," Bridget said. "I always told you guys that Miriam is the worst kind of Catholic ever. A Jewish one. Grace they say you are?"

She held the women enthralled as she drew hard on her cigarette and pushed a lock of hair repeatedly behind her ear.

"That's me," I replied.

"Well, Grace, just you watch yourself with that Miriam," she said and then smiled in a way that my mother would have said was wicked. "You need to pull a Bridget on that bitch. That'd teach her. Her Solomon's a looker, in't he?"

"Uh-uh, Miss Bridget," Ule said, "stop right there with your stupidness. What you telling this child?"

"Child? Oh, Ule, come on. Are you still blind? She's my age, practically." She turned back to me. "Have they told you about me?"

I liked her too. "No."

"Shame on you, ladies, letting me lore fade away. Grace, I used to be a nanny—"

"Another word, Bridget, use another word," Petal said.

Bridget laughed, her voice low and raspy from the cigarettes. "Oi, I forget it means pussy where you come from, Petal. But in my case it's not far off the mark, is it?" she said, still laughing. "Grace, I used to be a child minder, and then I fucked my lady's husband a couple of times, and the next thing you know, he's divorced her and I'm living on Fifth Avenue. Not shacked up either, 'cause I'm Catholic, you see, got the ring and all." She held out her left hand, and I saw the real BeDazzler, larger and throwing more light than anything Kathy ever tacked on to her clothes. "Not bad for a girl from County Kildare, innit?"

"Lord," Ule said, "deliver us from this lass," but she and the other women were laughing.

"Seriously though, Grace," Bridget went on, "you could come out of this on top. Ha-ha." She laughed at her own joke. "Serve Miriam right too. You, luv"—she snapped her fingers—"can get a husband like that."

I could see why the sitters loved her. Bridget said exactly what came to her mind and had the actions to back up her chat. She had crossed over from the park to Fifth but had not forgotten the women still pushing carriages in the playground. Bridget was living the American dream the rest of us had found ourselves on the other side of. And there in Union Square, with one eye watching Bridget tuck her hair behind her ear and the other on Ben in the sandbox, I had to wonder if I too wanted what this Irish girl had slept her way to.

Chapter 22

This year Easter would coincide with Passover, with the first night of the Jewish holiday falling on Good Friday. It was the Tuesday before the holidays, and spring rains had been forecast for most of the week. Except for our daily dose of fresh air, Ben and I spent most of the time indoors, watching Pooh videos and building castles.

"Grace, can you get the phone? I'm trying to rest," Miriam called out to me.

I hadn't even heard it ring.

"Hello, Grace. How are you, my darling? How's Ben? Big Ben misses him terribly."

"Hello, Ettie. I'm fine, thank you. Ben's good." I looked over to Ben. "Hey, buddy, Nana's on the phone. Come say hi."

"No, Grace." He wouldn't take his eyes off Pooh and Tigger. "Tell Nana I'm watching *Winnie the Pooh*."

"Hi, Ettie. I don't think he wants to stop watching his movie right now."

"That's okay, darling. Is Miriam home yet?"

"She's resting."

"Oh, she won't mind talking to me."

Miriam lay propped up in her darkened room reading the same romance novel I had started the other day.

"Ettie."

Miriam dog-eared her page and lifted the phone next to her bed. I turned to leave.

"Just a second, Ettie," Miriam said. "Grace, give me the other phone too. And close my door all the way."

I did as she said and went back into Ben's room.

"Grace, you missed the best part."

"I did? Tell me about it." I sat on the floor next to his little furry chair.

Ben shook his head. "Uh-uh. Shhh, Grace."

I shhhed and, restless, got up to stand by the window. The rain was steady and gray, but I could still see the bright new leaves on the trees in Union Square. Those vendors who had bothered to come to the market had already packed up, and the tops of umbrellas wove in and out. At home I loved the unexpected showers that came in the blazing dry season, sizzling the hot pitch and drumming the galvanized roofs. When we were younger, Helen and I had fled outside at the first few drops, shedding clothes and inhaling the burnt tar smell. We got soaked quickly, before our mother could start on number sixteen of her hundred and one ways to catch cold.

Miriam came in. "Grace, can I talk to you for a minute in my room?"

"Shhh, Mommy." Ben put his finger to his lips.

Miriam put up her hands. "Sorry, mister."

She sat on the bed. "I need you to work through Saturday night and take next Monday off instead."

I was about to agree but then remembered Sylvia. "I have to talk to my cousin first. She might need me."

"Can you call her now? I need to know as soon as possible."

I left the room, not wanting to talk in front of Miriam. When I made the call, Micky answered. "Ma! Grace on the phone."

"What?" Sylvia picked up in the middle of a coughing fit.

"You need to stop smoking them cigarettes, Sylvia. Them things going to kill you dead."

"Grace, shut your ass before you put goat mouth on me please. What going on?"

"Nothing much. The lady ask if I could work this Saturday and take off Monday instead. I calling to make sure you don't need me for anything Saturday."

Sylvia coughed again. "You see how them white people like to take advantage. She paying you extra to work on a Saturday?"

"Um, she didn't say anything about that."

"Grace, stop playing the ass. You have to learn how to operate in this country or else people will take you and make you they fool. You know

Saturday should pay more than a regular weekaday? People does get double money for working weekend."

I didn't know that. "Well, I will ask she and see what she say."

Sylvia inhaled deeply. "You not listening to me. Why nobody don't listen when Sylvia talk? Don't ask she, tell she you want extra money. I sure she want you to work for they holiday coming up. Tell she Saturday is not Monday and she should pay you extra. And too, you is a Christian, right? You must work on Good Friday for them and not get nothing extra? This is what Christ crucify for? Come on, Grace, you is a girl with brains."

"Okay, Sylvia. So you don't need me, right?"

"I know you, Miss Grace. You not going to tell that lady one thing I say. Go ahead, please your mind and play *bobolee*."

I needed to change the talk. "So, Sylvia, Jacob start the work yet?"

"Uh-uh." She gargled, and I could tell that she was struggling to sit up. "Is good you not coming. This place is a mess. Everything have to move for them to start proper. I think they say early next week."

"Make sure Dame not eating paint."

"I know. Is not my apartment alone they fixing, you know. After the city come, is plenty people in the building getting paint job."

"Good. Sylvia, I have to go. The lady waiting. I will see you on Saturday night, late."

"Okay. Grace, wait, a letter come from your mother."

I was staying too long on the phone. "Put it up for me. I'll see it when I come. Bye."

I went back to Miriam's room. "My cousin says it's okay."

"Good. Friday, we're going to visit my family in Brooklyn, and on Saturday, we're going up to Ettie and Big Ben's for Passover Seder."

Why was it so hard to tell her that she would need to pay me extra for Saturday, that my weekend was worth extra money? "Miriam, how much you paying me for Saturday?"

"Same as usual. Why?"

"Well, it's the weekend, so, um, you should pay me more."

She laid the book down and sat up on the rumpled sheets. "Why should I pay you more, Grace? You're getting Monday off."

I was going to start off with "my cousin said," but that sounded lame to me. "I think weekends are worth more than Monday to Friday." I couldn't look her in the eye.

Miriam let out a big breath. "Let me talk to Sol tonight and see what he says, Grace."

I felt like a fool.

"I'M LENDING GRACE TO Ettie for Passover," Miriam said between bites of chicken étouffée.

"Good. You told Mom already?" Sol answered.

"Not yet. She only asked to borrow her today." She lowered her voice, but I could still hear. "Grace wants more money for Saturday."

"Why? Didn't you offer to trade her a weekday?"

I didn't hear Miriam's response, but Sol said, "Then you should lend her to Mom on Friday. She could help Jane set up. You already own her Fridays."

"I can't spare her on Friday. We're going to Brooklyn, remember?"

"She doesn't need to come. Send her uptown."

"No. Ettie really wants her for the Seder. All your cousins are coming over. Jane's getting too old."

"Please don't make it sound as though my mother's the one who wants to show off the help. Give me one good reason Grace needs to come to Brooklyn on Friday. A bad reason, even."

"Hush, Sol." Miriam was laughing.

"So give her an extra twenty for Saturday, then."

"You think so?"

"Twenty bucks, sure."

DAVE FILLED ME IN. "Sol comes from lots of money. Miriam doesn't." We were pruning the hibiscus. "I think you're cutting back too much on that one."

"No, I'm not. The hedge around my mother's house is red hibiscus. Daddy used to cut it way back in the dry season, and as soon as the rains came, they grew like mad."

"Got it," he said.

"So, how do you know so much about Sol and Miriam?"

Dave made a sour face. "Sol and I went to school together."

"College?"

He rubbed under his chin with the back of a gloved hand. "Before that. Prep school. Uptown."

"You know, Dave, you shouldn't work with gloves on. You have to get a feel for the roots and the soil. You're doing old-lady gardening. My mother never wore gloves. Did you know Miriam too?"

"I got to know her later. This is America, Grace Jones. Gloves are a necessity. Who knows what's in this dirt."

"Do you know you can use hibiscus stalks as chew sticks—like a toothbrush." I took a finger-thick branch and peeled an inch of bark off the end. "See, you just chew on it for a while and it cleans your teeth. Whitens them too."

Dave faked brushing. "Why not use a toothbrush and toothpaste, Grace?"

"Ah. You don't get it. My sister and I used to feel so cool walking around the yard like men with sticks in our mouth. God, it used to drive my mother crazy. Everything did." I laughed. "My father used to cut hollow papaya branches for us to blow bubbles, and she couldn't stand for us to hang over the banister for more than fifteen minutes." I hadn't told Dave too much about home, only about plants.

"Sounds like you had a great childhood, Grace."

"I guess."

"You guess," he teased.

"So Sol and Miriam married. How come you're not married, Dave?"

"Married?" He laughed. "Are you kidding?"

When he saw that I wasn't, he put down the pruning shears and pulled off his gloves. "Sol and Miriam haven't told you?"

"Told me what?"

"Neither Danny? Duke?"

I wondered if his wife had died. "No, no one's told me anything."

"Grace, I'm gay."

"Really?" The surprise spilled out before I could stop it. "You're gay? Ah, that's why Miriam said you were safe. How come you don't have a . . . a friend?" The only gay man I knew, or at least the only man I thought was gay, was crazy Hen-man back in the village, who wore dresses and makeup and stole women's panties off their clotheslines.

"You mean a boyfriend?"

I guessed that's what they would call it. "Yes . . . a boyfriend."

"That's a long story, and I'll tell you about it some night, but not tonight, okay?"

"Okay."

Dave pulled his gloves back on and carried the pot he had been working on to another table. "Anyhow," he said when he came back, "that's one reason why your bosses don't mind that you're here. I'll tell you another reason if you come back next week. It's time to bring my gay papaya out into the sun."

ETTIE CALLED EARLY WEDNESDAY to say that it wasn't such a good idea for Ben to come uptown. Big Ben had a cold, and she wanted him to save his energy for the holiday. Because we were going to Brooklyn on Friday, Miriam decided that Ben should have his playdate with the Zoller twins early.

Petal opened the Zollers' door after I lifted Ben to lay into the bell.

"Hi, Petal, how you going?"

Ben barged in.

"I going good, Grace, thanks to God. How you?"

The babysitter lime had moved to the fifteenth floor of Tower One. Petal had come by, and so had Marva, Meena, and Ule. The Bloomberg baby was asleep in his carriage, and, perhaps subdued by the weather, all the children were seated around Caleb's and Sammy's worktables coloring, amazingly, quietly. The Zollers' place was wrecked as usual. Evie apparently, like Kathy, did no housework above anything required to take care of the twins. The house looked like the hideaway of a hoarding clown. Colorful bouncy balls, turned-over trucks, and discarded dolls were scattered all across the bright red carpet. Ben beelined to his coloring friends, chose a book from the pile, and found a nook next to Sammy. Marva, Meena, and Ule sat at the Zollers' dining table playing cards. Evie was nestled in a corner of the couch, feet tucked under her and curler against her forehead, watching her story and ignoring me completely. Petal went over to the couch, picked up her Bible, and sat down.

"Grace," Petal said, "you don't watch the stories?"

Back home *The Young and the Restless* was the craze. People were so tantalized by the show that all the restaurants and roti shops installed televisions so their lunchtime patrons could keep up. "I used to watch *The Young and the Restless,* but long time now I haven't seen it."

"Nah"—Petal shook her head—"me never did like that one. I like Channel Seven stories."

"Grace and Petal"—Evie never looked away from the screen—"wait for the advertisement to talk, please. Me can't hear one word them saying."

Petal rolled her eyes and went back to the show. I walked over to the dining table, where Ule held her cards against her chest.

"What you playing?" I asked as I pulled out a chair.

Meena, made up for the crypt, said, "A kind of all fours, but we a man short." She added, "You is Trinidadian, right?"

"Uh-huh."

"I hear your people does play all fours for tea, breakfast, and dinner."

Indeed they did, but not in our house.

Ule said, "You know how to play, Grace?"

"Nah, my mother didn't like cards."

Marva's bottom lip was cut and swollen, bright pink against her blackness, and I wondered what the woman she worked for thought about her battered babysitter. She rearranged her hand. "Well, your mother not here and we a man short. You want to learn?"

I sure did. For the next hour and a half, through the end of Evie's story, four o'clock snack, and four-thirty nap, I partnered with Marva and learned to beg and stand as we lost eight games in a row to Meena and Ule.

"You ever make bets?" I asked.

Holy roller Petal, too curious about the ways of the corrupt world to stay on the couch, had come to sit at the far end of the table, but only to watch. "But, Grace, I didn't know you is a gambler."

"No, Petal. I just asking."

Evie stood behind Ule, who promptly hid her cards. She trusted no one and, as far as I could see, found it hard to give the required winks and nods to Meena.

"We don't bet money," Evie said, "but we play for favors sometime."

Marva winked at me, and I didn't know if she was signaling a high card or seconding what Evie said.

"What kinds of favors?" I asked.

Meena said, "All kind of thing. Sometimes losers have to watch the children for winners to go and do their business. Or losers have to come over to the job and do some housework for winners."

Ule gave me a meaningful look that I couldn't read. "And what we playing for today?" I asked, thinking about me and Marva having lost eight games straight.

"Don't worry, Grace," Ule said, "today was just to teach you the rules. We didn't make no bet before you sit down."

Meena closed out the game, bringing our losses to nine. Evie sat down and picked up the pack to deal. "Don't worry, girl," she repeated, "if you ever want to go and do your business, just bring Ben for me to watch. Is not a problem at all. All of we in the same leaky-ass boat." She broke the pack in two and fanned the cards like a pro so the halves fit perfectly. "So, Grace how you secrety so? Nobody don't know nothing about you."

"What you want to know, Evie?"

She shrugged, and Ule shot me that look again. "You have a man?"

"Me don't know if she have a man," Meena said, "but I bet you anything she have Chinee in she."

Petal laughed. "Oh, God, Evie, you going to kill me here today. Why you want to know if the child have a man? She not married, but she to age for courtening."

"Well," Evie said, "we don't even know how much years she have. How you know she to age?"

"Me not too particular to hear nobody business," Ule said. "Time for me to take ugly man upstairs. Almost six weeks and he still ugly like sin."

She pushed back her chair, but Evie wasn't ready for the lime to be over. "So, Grace, tell we, nah. You have a man or no?"

I stared at the ripe pimples on her shining forehead. "No, Evie, I don't have a man. You have one for me?"

She laughed—"Hey hey"—and said, "But I hear every night you does go upstairs to that man apartment."

Ule frowned. "Come, Evie, now you talking stupidness for truth. Not you the same one who tell we that man is a buller-man?"

"I just telling what I hear, mama. Is not me who say, you know."

"Dave is my friend," I said.

"Child," Petal said, "you must stay away from them kind of people.

God don't like that kind of living, you know. The Bible say man like that is a bomination in the sight of the Lord. You never hear about Sadam and Gomorrah?"

Dave an abomination? He was the nicest person I had met the entire time I had lived in America. "He doesn't even have a boyfriend, Petal. I like to go upstairs to help him with his plants. Nothing wrong with that."

"Man with boyfriend?" Petal hugged herself. "But that alone crawling my blood."

"That is what you leave the West Indies to come and do?" Marva asked me. "To plant garden and lime with buller-man? Child, you must stay away from people like that."

"Who tell you he don't have a man?" Evie said.

"He did."

"And you believe him?" Meena asked.

"Why I wouldn't believe him?" I asked, looking around.

"Well, maybe he don't have a next man yet," Evie said, "but he used to have one."

"Not the good Lord self who strike him down with the plague he send for them?" Petal said. "God don't like to see ugly on this earth. The days of Sadam and Gomorrah shall return."

"I mean," Evie continued, "he is not the best-looking white man out there, but look how much money the father dead and leave him and them two nasty dog. Man like that could get any woman they want: black, white, or Chinee. I can't see why he have to go and put he self with another man. Is disgusting, man. I hear in Jamaica they does stone man like that to death."

The time had come for me to leave. Petal's boy came over, rubbing his eyes after his nap on the carpeted floor with the other children. He leaned his little body against her and said, "Nanny, I want to go home now, please."

And Petal, who seemed to be the calmest woman in the park, turned on Bruce in a rage. "What I tell you?" She seized his upper arm and shook him. "What it is I tell you? How much times me have to tell you, Bruce, don't call me nanny. You hear, don't call me nanny. A nanny is a she-goat, Bruce. My name is Petal. P.E.T.A.L. Say it." She squeezed his arm tight. "Say it."

Bruce started to cry and said, "Petal."

The other children looked on, and Ben crawled into my lap. The women too were silent. Ule turned down her mouth.

The lime was over. We said our good-byes, and filed out of the apartment.

I started to talk after the others rode down.

"Hush your mouth," Ule whispered, cutting her eyes at the Zollers' front door.

I understood and waited for the elevator to come. Ule rode up to the Bruckners' floor with me. Pushing the carriage with the ugly baby back and forth, she said, "Don't mind what you see today. Petal is a good woman, and she love that little boy like she own son."

"How you could say that, Ule? Bruce is not her son. She shouldn't talk to the people child like that. And she shake him so rough." Ben clung with all his limbs around me, and I held him tight.

"I know, I know. But what we going to do? Take bread out we own mouth? Sometimes, child, you just have to wait and see how things work out on they own."

I didn't agree with this at all. "And what about Evie? Why she minding my business so? How she know I went upstairs? She's not even at work at that hour."

"Child, all I could tell you is watch your self with Evie. That woman know everything that going on in these four towers. Sometimes is best to just sit down and listen and don't say a word. When name call later on, nobody can't say you say nothing. And remember too you didn't come America in no boat. Is fly you fly and come just like the rest of we. You not in no same boat with nobody."

Ben pulled on my arm again, and I stepped out of the elevator. After the doors closed, he asked, "Why she make Bruce cry, Grace? Bruce is my friend."

I didn't have an answer for him, so instead I flipped him squealing onto my back for a jockey ride down the length of the hall.

Chapter 23

Helen and I had a Good Friday tradition. At the stroke of noon we'd each crack a freshly laid egg and drain the white into a glass of pure rainwater, then watch as the swirling albumen shaped itself into a symbol of our future. The ghostly shapes were never quite clear, but we managed to see boats and books and planes and rings and steeples. Our mother warned us that looking for the future was risky, that we could just as easily see an omen of death instead of the adventures we craved, but we never paid her any attention, and we never saw anything suggesting misfortune.

On this Good Friday I was working.

"Don't you have a skirt?" Miriam asked.

"Sorry, um . . . no," I said. "I only have jeans here."

She came back a minute later with a black velvet skirt. "Here, see if this fits."

I took off my jeans and pulled on the skirt, wishing I had some privacy.

Miriam pinched the sides of the fabric. "Maybe if we pinned it," she murmured.

"I don't think so. . . . Miriam, why do you want me to wear a skirt?" I thought her parents might be really strict Jews, that a woman in pants might be too much for them.

"Oh, I don't care what you wear," Miriam said, "but my father is old-fashioned. Do you have anything black?"

My turtleneck and the pants I had worn to the interview. "This?" I held up the clothes.

"That's fine."

The trip to Miriam's parents' house took about twenty minutes. Driving over the bridge, I pointed out to Ben the twin towers of the World Trade Center, the Statue of Liberty, the other bridges spanning the river. But, truly, I was the one who was excited about New York. I had been in America for so long and had seen so little.

From the front seat Sol said, "Grace, you couldn't fit into Miriam's skirt?"

Not exactly. "No."

"I remember when you were as skinny as a strand of spaghetti, Mir."

I hoped he wouldn't start with that again, but Miriam didn't seem to mind. "Grace isn't expecting baby number two, Sol."

"My nickname was Bones," I said.

"When I was a child," Miriam countered, "my father used to call me Zippo the Human Zipper."

"Well." Sol chuckled. "You sure did light my fire."

"The fireman is my friend," Ben added.

"Would you like to be a fireman when you grow up, buddy?" I asked.

Ben made siren sounds. *"Whoooo whooooo."*

"I guess that's your answer, Grace," Sol said. "So, how's Dave doing? I haven't seen him since dinner a few weeks ago."

I'd seen him on Tuesday night for the grand relocation of the papaya. "He's fine."

"Do you have a good time up there?" he asked and glanced at me in the rearview mirror.

"I want a baby doggy," Ben said.

The three of us corrected him. "Puppy."

"So, Grace, do you have a good time up at Dave's?" It was Miriam's turn to ask.

"I do. We spend a lot of time working on the plants."

"That apartment," Sol said, "has been featured in every home magazine in circulation. They filmed something up there too, once. Has Dave said anything to you about Florida?"

"Not really," I said. "Just that he used to spend a lot of time down there."

Miriam pulled on dark sunglasses. "I think it's fabulous the two of you get along so well."

"Grace, I'm thirsty," Ben said.

But Sol had turned in to park.

"Just a minute, mister," Miriam told him. "We're at Nonna and Papa's house."

THE FIRST THING I noticed was the shrine. In the middle of the yard, in a concrete alcove painted sky blue and surrounded by blooming yellow daffodils, was the Blessed Virgin Mother. Mary's black hair was parted in the middle under a long white veil, and her hands were clasped in prayer as she looked piously at the ground before her. My mother, with her aversion for graven images, would not have approved. And it wasn't just this house. All up and down the block were different versions of Jesus's mother. In the yard on the right, she cradled her newborn son with the idiot Joseph standing nearby. On the left, she held her hands over her heart and gazed toward heaven. And directly across the street, Mary knelt at the foot of her crucified Christ.

Miriam opened the low iron gate. Sol followed with Ben and waited to latch the gate behind me. "Here we go, Grace. The in-laws."

The door opened before Miriam could knock.

"Ah, Maria, Maria. At last you here."

Maria?

The woman was tiny and round, her white hair half hidden under a black head scarf. She opened her arms and reached for Miriam, then clasped her own hands together much like the Virgin in her yard.

"Look at you. Look at you, Maria," she said. "So beautiful."

"Hi, Mama." Miriam leaned over to hug her mother. "How are you? How's Pop? Is everyone here already?"

Her mother held Sol's upper arms. "Hello, Solomon. How you doing?"

Sol bent deeply and kissed her fallen cheek. "Hello, Mrs. Forgione. Good, good. Good to see you."

Miriam gave her mother the small, wrapped package she carried. "I brought the nanny. I hope Pop won't mind?"

Her mother patted my forearm but didn't answer. Instead, blinking away tears, she reached for Ben. "Benjamin. Come to Nonna." She smacked her lips, making loud, kissing sounds. Ben buried his face in his father's neck.

"Don't you want to say hi to Nonna, buddy?" Sol asked.

He didn't.

The house was dark, but I could make out the pictures on the walls: formal family portraits that looked like they had been taken at an old-time photo studio; more recent pictures of children, posed in school uniforms; religious pictures of saints and the Virgin. Miriam walked through to the kitchen, where the rest of her family waited.

Besides Mrs. Forgione, there were three women in the kitchen. One could have been Miriam's twin but for her long black braid and manly nose. She even had the same pockmarks on her cheeks, the same healthy plumpness. The second woman looked nothing like the others. She had a dried out, slightly C-shaped body, and fine blond hair and blue eyes. The third woman was a nun.

Mrs. Forgione made a beeline for the stockpot. "Aye, Linda," she said, "look at that. I told you keep watch, else it boil down too much."

"Is it ruined, Mama?"

"No, is not ruined, but it could have ruined. You need to watch." She tapped the corner of her eye.

"Hey, Maria, you look fantastic. Come let me see you."

"Hi, Sophia. Hi, Irene. Linda, you still can't make *cioppino*?" Miriam laughed. Sophia was the nun. Irene was the look-alike. Linda was the other one.

Irene's voice was the echo of Miriam's. "Hi, Solomon," she said. "Hey, Benny. What's the matter? You don't want to say hello to Zia Irene?" She turned to Miriam. "Aren't you hot in that coat, Maria? It's so warm outside already."

"Irene," Sophia said.

"What, Sophia? Alls I'm saying is that it's hot already. Sam Champion said it was gonna go up to sixty today. It's a very nice coat."

"I wish I had a fur coat," Linda said. "You know how many years already I been asking your cheap brother to buy one for Christmas?"

"How are you, Maria?" Irene asked.

"I'm good, Irene, thanks. Hey, I brought Ben's nanny. I hope Pop won't mind."

The women turned toward me. Sophia said, "And does Ben's nanny have a name, or do you call her Ben's nanny?"

"Grace," I said.

"Hello, ladies," Sol said. "Where's Frank and Pino?"

"I don't think Peter's going to make it," Sophia said. "They're serving Good Friday lunch over at St. Mary's. Frankie's in the back helping Pop unwrap the fig."

"Can I leave this here?" Sol shrugged out of his coat.

"Grace," Miriam said, "hang Sol's coat on the hook behind the door. Ben's too."

"Do you want me to hang yours also, Miriam?" I asked her.

"Carefully," she said and passed me the soft fur hot from her body. "What can I do?" She took off her sunglasses and sat down at the table. "Grace, can you get me a glass of water with ice?"

The women looked at each other. Sophia said, "Grace, sit down. I'll get Maria some water. Do you want anything?"

"No, thank you."

"Grace, are you from Trinidad?" Sophia asked. Linda was watching the simmering pot, and Irene was tearing iceberg lettuce—the kind Miriam had warned me never to buy.

"One of the sisters at the convent is from Port of Spain. You sound exactly like her."

"Maria," Mrs. Forgione said, "help Irene with the salad."

"It's all right, Ma. I got it. Sit, Maria," Irene said.

Except for Mrs. Forgione, no one besides us wore black. Even Sophia's habit was gray with a white band around the neck.

"So I have some news," Miriam said.

Linda spun from the pot. Mrs. Forgione shook her head.

"Well . . . tell us," Sophia said. "What is it?"

"I'm three months pregnant. Fourteen weeks to be exact."

"Maria, that is truly wonderful news," Sophia said. "Did you have the bad morning sickness again? Do you know if it's a boy or a girl yet?" She laughed. "But you wouldn't know so soon yet, or would you?"

"When I was having Frankie junior, I was sick for nine months; every day I threw up," Linda said.

Mrs. Forgione left the pot and came over to Miriam. "Ah. Look at you. Another baby. Good, good, good." Then she crouched at her daughter's feet. "Maria, you know better than this. Why you wear the high heels when you're having a baby? No good." She tried to remove Miriam's shoes, and the other women laughed.

"Mama, stop fussing." Irene was squeezing lemons into the salad. "Women don't care anymore. I see them when I go to New York. High heels, tight clothes, the belly hanging out. It's all fashion now, Ma."

"When do you ever come to the city?" Miriam said.

"And when are you going to invite me to come to the city? Any of us?"

Sophia clapped her hands, and the heavy silver cross on her bosom jumped. "Jesus, Mary, and Joseph. You two are ridiculous. This is just as bad as when you were children. Grace, do you have any brothers or sisters?"

"A younger sister."

She was going to ask me something else, but Linda, who had been torn between watching the pot and watching her sisters-in-law, said, "I think it's ready, Mama."

Sophia went outside to get the men, Linda went upstairs to round up the children, and Miriam asked Irene and her mother in a low voice, "What about Grace? Should she eat in the kitchen?"

Irene untied her apron. "Oh, don't be stupid, Maria."

"Of course she sit at the table," Mrs. Forgione said, patting my back.

"And what about Pop?"

"It's Easter," Irene said. "Pop can deal."

In the dining room, I understood where Miriam's passion for figurines had come from. Mrs. Forgione didn't have just animals. Her collection included children at play and at rest, globes and trees and crosses, fruits and vegetables, little glass houses and big glass castles, glass hats. The centerpiece was a clear glass sacred heart, topped by a doubly dangerous glass crown of thorns. The new piece that Miriam had brought in the wrapped box, a crystal spray of roses, sat in the middle of the table between the pots of real Easter lilies.

The Forgione dining table was built to accommodate family feasts: Linda, Frankie, and their three children; Miriam, Sol, and Ben; Irene, Sophia, Mr. and Mrs. Forgione; and me. Before we sat, Miriam said, "Pop, this is Ben's nanny. Grace."

He grunted.

"Since Pino not here," Mrs. Forgione said, "Sophia, you bless the table."

She bowed her head and prayed, first thanking God for the sacrifice and resurrection of his son, Jesus. Next she thanked God for her mother and her father, and for the family together again at this table. She even thanked him for bringing me to break bread with them. She then inserted a special plea to God to watch over Frankie as he patrolled the streets of New York. She asked him to bless all the children, including the one Miriam carried. And then they all joined in for grace, the one we said at school. *"Bless us, our Lord, and these thy gifts, which we . . ."* The words came easily; I joined in too *". . . are about to receive . . ."* I opened my eyes a little. All their heads were bowed as Sophia went on, except for Ben, who looked at everyone, and Sol, who caught me looking around and winked. Miriam's head hung down, her slim nose slicing out from between a panel of dyed blond hair. *". . . through Christ our Lord. Amen."*

Mrs. Forgione grabbed my forearm. "Grace, you Catholic?"

"Anglican, but I went to Catholic school."

Mrs. Forgione squeezed my forearm tighter. "Never mind that. You teach this blessing to Benjamin, make him say before he eat breakfast, lunch, dinner."

From the other end of the table, Miriam said, "Mama."

Sophia, who I realized had the role of peacemaker, said, "Come on, these kids are starving. Let's eat already."

Miriam and her father sat side by side, and throughout lunch they talked mostly to each other, and to Frankie, the policeman. Toward the end of the meal, Mr. Forgione leaned over to Miriam and said something so funny that she spat out some food. She laughed and apologized, using an embroidered napkin to dab at her chin.

"Well"—Sophia looked at their end of the table—"are you going to tell the rest of us what was so funny?"

"What's the jokey, Mom?" Ben asked.

We waited, but Miriam said, "It's nothing. Finish up eating. I know Mama has ricotta cheesecake for dessert. Right, Mama?" She was still laughing.

"Come on," Linda said, "Pop. Tell us your joke already."

Mr. Forgione looked right at me. "It wasn't even that funny. Alls I said to Miriam was that I didn't like eggplant. Never liked it all my life."

Miriam laughed again, and so did Linda and Frankie. Sol let out a long sigh. Irene shook her head, and I didn't think that Mrs. Forgione even heard what her husband had said. The kids, not getting it, looked at everyone, and Ben asked, "What's eggplant, Mom?"

"Okay," Sophia said to the children, "you guys are excused. But no cheesecake if you don't play nice." Then she wagged her finger at her father. "And you, Pop. Be-have."

Chapter 24

Had my egg white in rainwater foretold my days in America, neither my mother nor I would have been able to decipher the signs. On the day of the Seder, I got off the subway one stop before Ettie's to see more of New York. The rains had washed the city clean of its winter stains. Daffodils and tulips bloomed where before had lain craggy formations of black snow and ice. The sun was warm, not hot yet, but I felt a deeper thaw in the chill that had been in my bones for ages.

I stopped to look in a shop window where mannequins were decked out in miniskirts and shorts and polo jerseys in pastel blues and pinks and greens. One wore an orange halter with white strings. I swear she called out to me by my name. I answered her and walked into the shop. Immediately a saleswoman approached. "How are you this morning?"

"Fine, thank you." This was not Conway. The clothes here were neatly folded and spaced on shelves mounted to the walls. The music here was soft, just a man singing in Spanish accompanied by a plucking guitar. The saleswoman, who looked like a fashion model, raised her perfect eyebrows and asked, "Is there anything special you're looking for?"

I was glad I'd taken care getting dressed, and had lined my eyes with the last nub of liner I had. "I'd like to see the top on the mannequin, please."

She pulled back. "You're a small, right?" She came back with two halters, the orange and white one I had seen in the window and a limey green one with orange strings.

"Let me take your bag."

I couldn't find a price tag. "If you need help tying the strings, let me know."

"I'm good, thanks." I reached around to make a bow, then looked in the mirror. It was beautiful, beautiful, beautiful.

"If you want to see the back, you can come out and use this mirror."

I stepped out to look. "This color was made for you," the sales assistant said. "The white and orange go perfectly with your tone. Don't even bother trying the green." She retied the strings so the bow sat lower on my back. "What a beautiful spine you have."

I didn't know a spine could be beautiful. I turned and looked again in the angled mirror, liking the halter even more from behind. The white stripes did look good against my black skin.

"What do you think?"

Before I could answer, an older woman stepped out of the next cubicle in her brassiere and Bermuda shorts the same orange as my top. She glanced at herself in the mirror and grimaced. "Look at how pale I am. But you," she said, "you should definitely get that. You can wear it to the beach or out to the country, or if you want to, you can dress it up with black pants for a more formal look. You'll get mileage out of it, for sure."

I liked the idea of mileage.

"Okay, I'll take it." At the register, the saleswoman folded my halter into the lightest tissue paper, peeled off a round sticker with the shop's logo, and sealed the package.

"Cash or American Express?"

"Cash."

The woman from the dressing room stood behind me holding a white linen shirt minus the shorts. She checked her watch and frowned. "Don't ever put off shopping until three hours before you fly to Mustique."

"That comes to a hundred and twenty-seven dollars and nineteen cents."

The Spanish man was singing more furiously now, strumming his guitar with force. I could see my halter in the shopping bag, the gentle pillow of its folded bulk, one white tendril curling out like a young vine. I had $220 in my pocket. Tonight I had to give Sylvia $50. One hundred and eighty dollars gone. I pulled out six bills from my wallet.

"Goodness," I said. "One-twenty-seven nineteen?"

The saleswoman smiled without parting her lips. "That's with tax."

"Is there a Citibank around here? I only have a hundred and ten dollars."

She bit her bottom lip and thought about bank locations. "And you don't want to put it on your AmEx?"

I didn't even know what an AmEx was.

"One ten. If you had ten dollars more, I could give it to you for one twenty." Not a speck of lipstick showed on her teeth.

I looked in my wallet again, seeing the thin accordion of remaining bills. I shook my head and patted my back pockets. "No. I'll just run to the nearest bank."

The woman with three hours to Mustique checked her watch. "The Citibank on Madison and Sixty-fifth has machines."

"Thank you." Turning back to the saleswoman, I asked, "May I have my bag, please?"

She gave her tight-as-a-ripe-grape smile. "Aren't you just running over to the bank now? I can hold it for you."

She slicked on her smile again, and the other woman, digging into her own bag, twice the size of mine, said, "It's literally right around the corner."

I smiled, also without teeth. "Thanks, but I'll take it."

She shrugged ever so slightly and dipped without bending her back to get Sylvia's old bag. She kept on her smile and said, "I hope you find the bank."

YESTERDAY MIRIAM HAD ASKED for black clothes. Today Jane wanted white.

"Sorry, Jane. I only brought blue jeans."

"You no can help me cook, clean, no serve in them fancy clothes you are wearing, missy." She hadn't let me in the apartment yet.

The last thing I wanted to do was upset Jane from jump. "Gosh. I wish I'd known. Miriam didn't tell me anything, you know."

She shook her head. "That woman, eh. Okay, come in, come in. You can tie one apron over yourself for now, and later you can wear one of my uniform."

Jane was five-three and round in the middle like a rum barrel. Surely she was joking.

Every year, Jane told me, Ettie and Big Ben kept Passover Seder. In the past she alone had done all the preparations, but now that she was old and gray and ready to retire to Jamaica, Miss Ettie catered most of the dishes from some fancy place, m'dear. Except for the brisket. Big Ben wouldn't have anybody else make his brisket.

"You ever get ready for a 'olyday before?" Jane asked me.

"Uh-huh," I said, putting on the apron she had given me. "Home, me and my sister used to help Mammy fix up the house for Christmas and Easter—mix the cakes, hang up the new curtains . . ." Those were the best times.

Jane turned to face me and, shaking her head, came around and knotted the apron way too tight. "Not Christmas and Easter, child. Jew 'olyday. Passover, Rashashannah."

"Oh," I said, feeling foolish.

Jane sighed, and I made up my mind to do anything she wanted. "I'm here to help you, Jane, so tell me where to start."

We worked without stopping from ten past twelve until three. Even though Ettie had earlier in the week hired two Polish women to do the heavier cleaning, Jane insisted we go over everything with dry cloths and feather dusters, then run the vacuum to make sure. For Passover, she explained, the house had to be spotless, and the only way to make sure it was, was to do the work yourself.

"Watch out for bread crumbs."

"What?" I asked, shining imaginary dust off the brass ballerina.

"The house can't have no bread in it for this 'olyday. *Hametz* it name." She stressed the *h* hard. "Last week Miss Ettie done sell the doorman all the big bread in the 'ouse, but them Polish woman she bring here, you can't trust them to do the work proper."

I had no idea what Jane was talking about, but I kept an eye out for pieces of bread. I wiped the masks and paintings and sculptures and sconces, while Jane used the feather duster to clean the tops of books on their shelves and behind picture frames propped on tabletops. She was a hard worker, pausing every once in a while to check on her brisket or to ask me if I wanted water, but never taking a break herself. Finally at three she said, "Okay, time for the dining room. We have to set up the tables."

"Tables? How much people coming?"

"Make me see." She gazed up to the ceiling and touched a finger to her chin for each name. "Miss Ettie and Big Ben; Nancy coming alone; Solomon, 'im madam, and little Ben; Susannah, Michael, and them two little girls; and Miss Elsie; that's it for this year. How much is that?" She counted off again silently. "Eight big people and three children. Eleven. The little ones get them own table."

I had never heard any mention of Susannah and Michael, or Miss Elsie, before, and I asked Jane who they were.

"Miss Elsie is Miss Ettie big sister. Never married. Susannah is Big Ben niece and Michael 'er husband. She grow up like sister to Solomon and Nancy. Spend more time here than with the own father. Mother dead when she born."

"And how old are the little girls?"

Jane opened a drawer from a glossy wooden armoire and removed a white tablecloth embroidered with waves of pale blue flowers. "How much years them have now?" she mused to herself as she gently unfolded the fabric. "Samantha going on five, and Bennie near same age as Solomon Ben."

She shook her head at the sharp creases checking big squares into the tablecloth. "This have to press," she declared.

"Let me do it for you," I offered, sure that Jane shared my mother's dread of ironing and catching cold. When she came back with the ironing board, I asked, "So Susannah's daughter's name is Bennie, like Ben?"

Jane set up the board, plugged in the iron, and passed me a can of spray starch. From the bottom drawer of the armoire she pulled out two purple velvet cases. "Lord, but you ask plenty question, child." But she didn't seem to mind. "Yes, m'dear. This is a house of Bens."

While I ironed, Jane polished the knives and forks and spoons she took from one case. After she had gone over each piece, she held it up to check for spots and then set it loosely back in its slot. Together we spread the freshly ironed cloth on the table, and then Jane began the setting. I stood off to the side as she placed plates and saucers and bowls, napkins and all the cutlery, wineglasses and water goblets, transforming the barren expanse of white into a four-star extravaganza. Done, she stepped back with hands on hips and cocked her head to check out her work.

"Jane, this looks like a fancy restaurant," I told her.

She beamed. "Is years now I doing this, child. I didn't grow up stupid, you know. I worked for the governor of Jamaica before you see I come to this country." Jamaica, like home, hadn't had a governor since 1962.

She went out and came back carrying a vase exploding with white, trumpet-shaped flowers on long green stems, which she placed on the table slightly off center. I reached to shift it, but Jane stopped me. "Wait and see."

In the kitchen she asked, "You can get that platter up there?"

I stood on a step stool and got down a big oval plate like the one my aunt Velma had sent my mother from the Virgin Islands. That platter, with its embossed race day scene, was a treasure we only ever used when my aunt came to visit. Last time, Auntie had got drunk on the Harveys Bristol Cream she had brought my mother, and she sent the platter and its little triangle sandwiches crashing to the floor. My mother had pretended not to mind, but she had Helen and me collect every piece of china, every broken horse and headless rider we could find. She tried for days to put it together again, but it was no use.

Jane set the platter on the kitchen table and opened the oven. With a pair of tongs, she removed a huge roasted bone with no meat. This she placed on the platter.

"What the heck is that, Jane?" It looked like a femur.

"Me sure your mother is a Christian woman and didn't teach you to swear," she responded. She went back to the oven with her tongs. This time she took out what looked like a stained brown egg and placed it next to the bone.

"That is an egg? What kind of animal lay that?"

She gave me a look like she was too tired of my questions. From a jar on the countertop, she took out a bunch of parsley, and, instead of chopping it for garnish like Miriam had me do on almost every dish they ate, she shook out the extra water and set about half of the stems on the platter.

I didn't ask.

Jane uncovered a bowl and, with a spoon from the top drawer, scooped out a mound of something dark brown. "Here, taste that," she said and offered me the chunky pyramid. I didn't want to, but I opened my mouth and was surprised by the sweetness of the mixture.

"Umm, good. What's in . . ." I let the question trail off.

"What you taste?"

"You know"—I smiled at the memory—"it tastes like my mother's soaked fruits for Christmas black cake." The cherries and currants were soaked from September in red wine, the only alcohol to enter our house with my mother's approval, the remainder of which Helen and I slowly depleted by the capful.

"Good, it supposed to taste like that."

She stooped in front of the opened refrigerator and took a small albino carrot out of the crisper.

"Wow, I've never see a white carrot before."

"No?" Jane quickly peeled the carrot and, with a hand grater, minced the whole root into a rough heap right onto the platter. She took a pinch and fed me a small bit. "Here, taste."

The pepper was intense, and I spat the hot carrot straight out at her.

Jane laughed and laughed, holding her middle and heh-hehing until tears ran from her eyes. "White carrot. Well, I never. Wait till me tell Miss Ettie this one. Whey! This 'orseradish, not no white carrot, but them call it *maror*." She laughed again, pleased to have an apprentice. "Parsley me sure you know, that is the *karpas;* it have salt water on it. The mix-up fruit is wine and nuts with a little honey, *charoset*. And this is a regular hen egg and a lamb bone from the butcher that been roasting since 'fore-day mornin'. All for the table. Bring it come."

Carefully, I picked up the plate and followed Jane back to the living room. She pointed to a spot on the table, and I set the platter down, trying my best not to tip anything off onto the white cloth. Jane adjusted my placement about a quarter inch to the right and then back to exactly where I'd had it before. She opened the other purple case and took out a candlestick. It didn't seem like anything special, it wasn't big and didn't shine or have ornate decorations carved into the metal, and Jane didn't seem to feel the need to pass the chamois she had used on the knives and forks over it. Small as it was, though, she held it up with both hands and placed it exactly at the center of the table, between the platter of everyday things transformed by their mystical new names and the hydra-splayed bouquet of long-stemmed lilies.

AT FIVE JANE POURED a small sherry. "How much years you have?"

"Twenty-one," I told her. I leaned against the counter and tried not to smile.

"If you have twenty-one years, then the mountains in Jamaica are really blue," she retorted, but she passed me the drink and poured herself another. "Come."

Her space was bigger than the room Kath rented. Besides a four-poster bed piled with fat pillows and lots of stuffed animals, there was a couch against one wall, a wide-screen TV, and a cushiony easy chair next to a real fireplace. On her bedside table were framed black and white snaps of little white children and a faded seaside postcard from Jamaica. A garment bag lay across her comforter.

Jane set her sherry on the bedside table and, after undoing the long zipper, took out a black maid's uniform and held it against her body. "This the one me think you can fit," she said to me. The skirt fell just beneath her knees. It had a high white collar and a pleated bib, tiny white bows at the elbows, and a long line of fabric-covered buttons down the back.

"Here"—she presented me with the dress—"put it on." She picked up her sherry and sat in her easy chair to watch, not seeming to think anything at all of me stripping down to my underwear in front of her. "Hold on," she said and came over and twisted the sleeves so the bows were on the outside, straightened the collar, and smoothed the pleats over my bosom. The buttons took forever.

She stepped back. "Little short, and . . ." Clearly for Jane it was a less than perfect fit. She fetched a small box off her dresser, undid all the buttons, and peeled the dress down to my hips. "But you need to eat some 'ome-cook food, child, you got no meat on these bones." She pinched the fabric at each side and, using a mouthful of safety pins, patiently took in an inch from the waist to the bustline. She redid the buttons and told me to look.

This was a dress my mother would approve of, fooled by the high collar and three-quarter sleeves and not seeing the way the bib emphasized my small breasts and the hem, hitting just above my knees, lengthened my legs.

"What shoes you have?"

"Only my boots."

She said what I thought she would. "You can't wear some boots with that dress. What size shoe you wear?"

"Nine and a half."

"You have some big elephant foot, like Miss Ettie. 'Old on."

She left the room, and I downed the whole shot of sherry she had poured for me, then took Jane's glass and drank that too. I picked up the postcard and read "Love, Miss Ettie and Mister Ben."

Jane came back carrying two-inch-heeled, black leather shoes with ankle straps and an unopened pair of sheer black stockings. I sat on her couch to put them on and saw her pick up her empty glass and set it down again with a frown.

"How do I look?" I stood and did a half turn.

She reached under her table for another bottle of sherry. "Fit to serve Princess Margaret afternoon tea."

JANE AND I WAITED in the entry while the family removed their shoes, putting on instead the soft booties Ettie kept in a basket next to the front door. They all came in together, laughing and talking, with the children running around and Big Ben's old cheeks bright red from the evening air. By their red hair you could tell the Bruckners by birth from the rest (except for Samantha, who had black, wavy hair like her father, Michael). Ettie and her sister, Elsie, wore calf-length fur coats and Susannah a short fur jacket like the stylish, stay-at-home mothers in the park. She was tall and very skinny, and her red hair, unlike Nancy's springy curls, was bone straight and parted on one side. Miriam did not have her fur today. She wore a black woolen coat.

Jane moved to ease Big Ben into his chair, but he waved her off. Ettie came to where we stood. "Good choice of uniform, Jane. Have Grace serve the sherry." Jane lifted her chin a little higher.

I walked with the tray of drinks, praying to avoid a mishap. Miriam took one and Susannah, sitting next to her, turned and said, "Surely you're not drinking alcohol, darling?"

"She's past her first trimester," Nancy said. "She can have a small drink."

Miriam sat between them without tasting her sherry. "For both of my pregnancies," Susannah said, "as soon as I knew, I didn't have a drop of alcohol. Not even while I nursed. Both girls, right, Michael? Didn't have a taste for it, really. Michael?"

He glanced in his wife's direction and nodded. "How are you, Grace?" Nancy asked me as she took her drink. "I'm still waiting for your call." She too had come in with a bit of fur thrown over her shoulder. Under it she wore a nubbly black shift with a deep V-neck. Her only jewelry was a gold ring with an enormous red stone on her right middle finger.

"Fine, thank you," I answered. I didn't feel I should say anymore. Nancy turned to Ettie. "Grace looks like a Vermeer, doesn't she, Mom? All she needs is a turban."

"There are no colored Vermeers, Nancy," Aunt Elsie said.

"Come, Aunt Elsie, you're a Vassar girl. Use your imagination."

"Vermeer would have had to use his as well," Aunt Elsie replied and drank the tiniest sip of sherry from the delicate tulip-shaped glass. "There were no Negroes in Europe during Vermeer's time."

Sol winked at me when he took his drink, and Michael said hello as he took his. On my way back to the kitchen, Miriam said, "Grace, can you get me a glass of water with ice?"

Jane looked up from assembling little plates of appetizers. "You done?" She passed me a bamboo tray with colorful vegetables cut only a little thicker than matchsticks. "Okay, this go out next."

"Wait, Jane. Miriam wants ice water."

Jane looked outraged. "Ice water? Now she want ice water to full up she belly before the meal serve?"

I shrugged, and Jane, muttering and shaking her head, filled a glass with ice and put scarcely any water in it. "'Ere, give her that."

Ettie came in. "How are we managing, Jane?" she asked. "Everything under control?"

"And tell me when it not."

Ettie took Miriam's ice water from me. "Bring the tray," she said. "I'll carry this."

I walked out in time to hear Miriam, her jeweled glass held up, ask, "So, does the aperitif count as one of the four glasses of wine, Big Ben?" She leaned forward while Nancy and Susannah talked behind her back. Aunt Elsie relaxed into her chair with her eyes closed. Big Ben, talking to Michael and Sol about the mayor's mistakes, paused and smiled over at Miriam. "Drink up, dear, four more to come with the meal."

Susannah snorted while Nancy smiled and shook her head. Miriam stared hard at Sol, who did not look over at her. Aunt Elsie had fallen asleep, and her sherry tilted at a steep gradient in her wrinkled fingers. I walked past her out of the sitting room, and she called out, "Young woman, you did not offer me the canapés." She had righted her sherry and was looking at the wall over my shoulder.

"I'm so sorry," I said, holding the tray out to her.

She glanced at the rainbow selection of vegetables and raised her left hand in refusal. "Thank you." She didn't take anything.

Jane was waiting for me in the kitchen. "I see that, you know."

"What, Jane?"

"I see you didn't offer Miss Elsie none of that something in the tray."

"Jane, she was sleeping."

The anger in her voice surprised me. "That don't matter," she snapped as she took the tray from me and held it by her side as if I no longer deserved to be its bearer. "Sleep, asleep, awake, drunk, it don't make no difference. Offer everybody some everything, you hear?"

"Sorry, Jane." I looked at the terra-cotta floor tiles, the same color as the clayey soil behind my house. "You got it. Just tell me what to do."

JANE SAW ME TO the front door, and I realized that, at some point during the evening, she'd found the time to come and straighten the jumble of shoes. The pile of high heels and men's dress shoes and children's shoes had been organized into two orderly rows, largest to smallest, toes all facing one direction. She handed me an envelope. "Here, Miss Ettie give you this."

Just then, looking tired and small, Jane reminded me of my na. I gave her a quick hug and a kiss. "Thanks, Jane."

"Is the other way round, child. Me should be the one who thank you. You was a big 'elp to me today. Remember what I tell you."

"You tell me so much today, Jane."

"No, what I did tell you the first time you come up here with Sol and 'im lady. I done make my bed already, and it is very comfortable. You have to get what you want in this America. Don't wait for nobody to give you nothing."

"I remember, Jane. Thanks, good night."

"Here"—she folded my fingers over warm paper—"take this." It was fifty dollars. In the elevator, I found a crisp hundred in the envelope from Ettie. Plus, I had got twenty extra from Miriam, twenty from Big Ben, and forty from Nancy. More than a whole week's salary for eight hours of work.

I walked down Park Avenue, looking at the lights. Then I cut across to the boutique with the halter. The same saleswoman stood outside now, snapping a huge lock on the grating she had let down to pen the mannequins in for the night.

She jumped and clicked the lock shut, then she recognized me. "Oh, hello. The orange and white halter, right?"

"Do you still have it?"

"Still wrapped and waiting for you. I thought you were just running to the bank."

"Can I get it now?"

"Well"—she thought for a while—"you can't try it on again, and you'll have to pay cash."

"I'll pay you cash."

"Okay," she said, "let's do this quickly."

She opened the long padlock and keyed some numbers into a security box inside the grate. Slowly, the links rattled up, and she used another key to open the door. The mannequins, called to duty on their off hours, struck their poses as the lights came up. She went behind the counter and pulled out my package, the white tie from this morning still peeking out. She lifted an edge of tissue, checked the size, and looked at the receipt. "One hundred and twenty-seven dollars and nineteen cents."

I reached for the money. "This morning you said you'd give it to me for a hundred and twenty cash."

Now her smile seemed genuine. "You have a good memory. I can still do that."

I passed her Ettie's hundred and Big Ben's twenty, and took the cute shopping bag and the receipt.

Of course Sylvia's elevator was broken, but the final walk up the steps cemented the exhaustion I felt. I knew I'd have a good night's sleep.

Chapter 25

I missed my mother.

I felt like a hypocrite, but that didn't stop me from wanting to be home. On Easter Sunday, the three of us went to church with her without much complaint, even though Helen and I refused to wrap our hair in the head ties the church women wore and my father sat us near the back to better slip down the hill soon after the last hymn was sung. I lay thinking that my mother was up now, moving about in our kitchen. Helen was still asleep in the bed we shared. And my father . . .

My father. I remembered I had a letter from home. In the breakfront the envelope was behind a red, white, and blue box of Brillo pads that perfectly complemented its patriotic airmail colors. According to the date stamp, the letter had taken only a few days to get to Brooklyn. I sat shrouded in Sylvia's thin sheet by the awakening radiator.

> Dear Gracie,
>
> Hoping this letter reach you in health and strength by the Grace of God. I didn't get to talk to you when I call for your birthday, but I have a belated present for you. Your daddy come home. Is only to-day (the 1st) he reach, but before you have to say I don't tell you anything, I sit down tonight self to write and let you know. I would have called, but I don't know when you at Sylvia and when you on the little work you doing, so I putting a express stamp on the letter. Mr. Assing in the post office tell me it should reach you in 3–4 days.
>
> Daddy looking good. It didn't have no *babash* for him to drink in hospital and he didn't have a choice but was to eat what they give him

so he even gain a little weight. He was too happy to come and sit down in he own gallery and he only waving right to every fool passing up and down the road. All who didn't come to see him in the hospital stop by already and everything going good, thanks to God. Okay, is not a long letter I writing. Helen going okay. She start to write you a letter two weeks now and she can't find the time to finish it.

By the time you get this it should be close to Easter. Maybe you could find a church to go to? It could be any church, even Catholic, just don't tie up yourself with no sign of the cross. Don't get vex, is just a suggestion. Okay, that is all for now. Tell Sylvia I say hello.

May the good Lord bless and keep you, and don't forget to pray.

Your Mother,

Grace

My tears wet the paper torn from Helen's notebook, and because my mother had used her old fountain pen, two big blue splotches smeared away the beginning words of her second paragraph. He was home. I knew he hadn't come home *on* Easter Sunday, but the timing seemed miraculous all the same.

I went back to the room and sat next to the sleeping Sylvia. For three or four seconds, with her body still comatose, only her eyeballs bounced around the room. When she realized it was me, she was relieved, and then furious. "Grace, but what the ass wrong with you in truth? Look how you nearly give me a heart attack this hour of the morning. I say is some crackhead come in my house and sit down on my bed. Is so you does creep round them white people house all hour of the morning? Jesus, Mary, and Joseph."

Bo said, "Man, what the ass wrong with you and Grace this hour of the morning, Sylvia? Sun not even up yet. I Tush your blasted mouth and go back to sleep, man."

"Nah, Bo. You worse than Grace. You forget who house this is. You forget is a lodging you begging here and is by mines and sweet Jesus tender mercies you have a roof over your nigger head. Is only the same father we mother have you know. Bo, I not even sure you is my cousin."

By now Sylvia had struggled up, and the sleep lines on the left side of her face slanted down like the grooves on a sheet of galvanize Micky watched her mother.

Bo tried to defend himself. "Man tired, Sylvia. You know what time I come in last night?"

"And that is the whole problem." Sylvia gargled. "I is actively aiding and betting your stupidness. Enough."

Sylvia turned her attention back to me. "Now, Miss Grace, tell me what the ass you doing coming and sitting down on my bed like the madman in the queen bedroom."

I almost smiled, and I wondered if Sylvia knew about that from the news or from the calypso:

There was a man in me bedroom,
He came on the bed doux-doux
And I thought he was you

"I was coming to ask if you want me to take them children to Dodo church since today is Easter Sunday."

Sylvia blanked, and really for the first time since I had come to live with her she had nothing to say. "Grace, is a good idea you have. That is it. All man, Jack and he brother, wake up. Everybody going to church with Dodo today. Grace, call Dodo and tell she wait for we, and get Dame ready. Mind yourself."

I moved out of her way. Sylvia went to Bo's corner by the dirty clothes. "And you, Mister Bo, if you ever want to eat so much as a turkey wing in this house again, you is the first man reach in that bathroom." She landed a real kick in Bo's ribs. "Up!"

IN CHURCH, DODO WAS in her element. I don't think that Sylvia or the children had ever gone with her before. In her new white Easter hat and her pocketbook hilted at her hip, she marched us like a misfit company of Christian soldiers straight down the aisle to the front pews.

Sylvia followed Dodo and obliterated her from my sight when we fell into single file. Derek and Micky walked behind their mother, and Micky kept her hands on her brother's shoulders to stay his course. I carried smiling Dame in my arms behind them, and Bo, who sulked and mumbled under his breath the whole time, closed out our ranks.

At her chosen pew, Dodo directed traffic. "Bo, go in first."

Sylvia snatched his ratty gray Kangol off his head as he walked by. When she saw what lay beneath, she passed the hat back to him. "Here, I don't know if you more dispectful with it on or off."

Dodo sighed. "Sylvia, behave yourself. Derek, go and sit by your uncle. Grace, you next."

When Dodo had answered the phone earlier and heard my voice, she'd said, "What you calling my house for this hour of the morning?"

Of course, she'd thought I was messing with her. "Miss Grace, I is not Sylvia to put up with your stupidness, you know. What it is you want?"

"No, Dodo, for real, we coming. Everybody. Sylvia say to wait ten minutes."

Dodo sucked on a cigarette. "Don't play games with a big woman."

"Dodo, just wait, okay."

The church was crowded but comfortable, and still many of the ladies, Dodo included, cooled themselves rapidly with paper fans that snapped open from lacquered frames. Up behind the pulpit, the choir gathered. There was an expectant murmur mixed with the sounds of rushing fans and scratchy children in new clothes. Bo, with his arms on the pew's backrest and his legs spread wide, leaned over Derek's head and said to me, "If you want, we could get married in a church like this, you know."

"Bo, what stupidness you talking about?"

"Nah, to make everything look more real. You could walk down the aisle. Dame could carry the ring. Sylvia could be your maid of honor, even though she maid gone long time."

Derek said, "You stupid, Uncle Bo. My mammy never had a maid."

Bo and I cracked up, and Dodo, whipping her fan under her bony nose, leaned back and glared down the pew. "Shh," she commanded.

The start didn't come from the front but rather from high up in the third tier. A woman Sylvia's size stood at the balcony and in a clear and strong voice, sang out, "Jee-eee-eee-eee-zus."

Everyone spun in their seats to look up at her purple-robed magnificence and teased halo of fake hair. Bo said, "Mama, that is woman," and Dodo snap-snapped her lacquered fan at him.

The song went on for ages, rising and falling according to the whims of the choirmaster. In my mother's church, there were no instruments other than their voices. Here, up on the stage, was a six-piece band with a bass, drums, a two-man brass section, and a steel pan. It was loud, but they all seemed to like it that way. I glanced down the pew at Dodo. She had her eyes closed and had put down her fan to better dust-clap her hands together.

Suddenly, the voices fell away, leaving only one section singing over the rising band. This was a signal for bacchanal to break loose. Sisters started making their way out of the pews and into the wide center aisle, doing intricate steps and dances. Dodo slipped out with the rest, and Bo poked me hard in the ribs as he tried not to laugh at her getting down on those *maga* legs. All around us women, and women only, were going crazy worshiping in the aisles. Derek tugged my sleeve. I bent down to hear him over the din, and all he could say was "Lookit, Grace. Lookit."

It died down, and, at last, only the drummer still pounded his kit, soothing the women and coaxing them into their seats. Dodo wandered back to our pew, wet and beaming. One by one the women sank to their pews, spent and ecstatic, and drew open their plastic fans to help ease the heat within their souls. We sat too, and Sylvia leaned over Micky to take Dame from my arms. As she did so she whispered, "Mama." I knew exactly what she meant.

After the first and second readings, the pastor came to the pulpit. Pastor Rome had to be younger than forty and, with his slicked, wavy hair, thick but trim mustache, and muscled arms visible under his three-piece suit, looked more like a shoe salesman at the Macy's than like a pastor.

Bo leaned to me over Derek's head. "I bet you anything he is a sweet man," he said. "How much of them woman in here you think he bull already?"

I shushed him, glad that Dodo hadn't heard, but this pastor didn't put me at ease. Pastor Rome said, "Now, you all know I used to be dead."

A ripple went through the congregation, and Micky leaned over. "Grace, that man is a ghost?" she asked me.

"No. I'll tell you after."

Again, louder, he asked his question, "I said, do you all know that I used to be dead?"

The church's answer rose to match his volume.

"When they locked me up in that cage, brothers and sisters, I used to be dead. When they violated me in that cage, I said I used to be dead. Oh, when they brutalized me in that cage, I was dead, dead, dead." The organist came in again on cue, and the ladies in the congregation, perhaps feeling a little relieved that, dead or alive, Pastor Rome had paid some price for his earlier sins, shook their heads and groaned deep ooohs and uhhhs. "But then, my brothers and my sisters, I saw the light. From the depths of that dark death, I said I saw the light. Shining all around me, light. Spreading all around me, light. That light touched my toes, and, oooh"—he took a high step back from the pulpit—"I was burned."

Dodo, keen, pinched her face at every emotion Pastor Rome recounted, feeling his pain. This was the longest I'd ever seen her go without a cigarette. Sylvia was nodding her head, and when I turned to Bo, at least Pastor Rome had his full attention. Derek and Dame were asleep, and Micky leaned against her mother and sucked her fingers.

Pastor Rome said, "I wonder if you're with me, brothers and sisters. I wonder if you know where I'm going this morning. If you're taking the journey with me, or if you're just along for the riiide."

He continued, "Jesus too was dead. He died, but then I say he was resurrected. He knew he still had work to do, and he was resurrected. He saw that light, and chose to be resurrected."

The band had kicked in now, and Pastor Rome was going on. I thought there was something wrong with the parallels in this sermon. Jesus hadn't been a career criminal before he died and was resurrected.

It was time to tie it all together. The band lowered their volume, and Pastor Rome said, "Are you living in the light, my brothers and sisters? I mean, have you been resurrected? Are you in the first life, the life of death, or have you been resurrected? The Lord said to me, 'Jerome, I want you to see the light, and be resurrected.' He's saying to you, 'Look at the light. Come to me. Forget the world. Leave it all behind. Take my hand. Walk with me. And be, resurrected.'"

The congregation combusted again, and everyone was on their feet, resurrected. Sylvia, lifted by the message, held Dame in the crook of one arm and waved the other. Bo had stood up and was grinning and clapping, nodding his head in agreement.

Micky looked scared, and I reached over to rub her arm. By now, *resurrected* had started to sound like a nonsense word that Pastor Rome had made up. But he had the congregation where he wanted them, and they were all chanting, "Lord, I want to be, resurrected."

He took his white handkerchief out and wiped the sweat pouring off his wavy hair. Then he beckoned. "Come to the Lord," he said. "Come up here and kneel and tell him for yourself that you want to be resurrected. If you're new and just heard the Word, the time is now, to be resurrected."

In all the madness, people began to make their way to the front, and I looked around to see who chose to be resurrected. The ladies with the hats and fans, those like Dodo, were presumably already living their second lives, and instead it was people like us, the ones who looked like they hadn't been in church in donkey years, who were going for life number two.

I felt Derek slump against me and turned to see Bo stand up. He eased past and made his way to beneath the pulpit. Dodo patted his back, and many of the church ladies reached out to touch his clothing as he walked up.

Dodo looked down the pew at me. "Grace, you want to go up?"

I shook my head. Pastor Rome's hard sell hadn't convinced me that I was a good candidate for a resurrection. Plus, I needed a green card to buy entrance to the wonders waiting in my second life.

Dodo tried to take Dame from Sylvia to get her to go up, but she wasn't ready either.

Pastor Rome didn't come down, but his deacons made their way around the hungry group, rubbing oil on their foreheads and giving them little shoves backward. Then, Pastor Rome blessed them all from on high and told them that this was the first day of the rest of their lives as the resurrected. He cued the choir, and they broke into "He Is Risen, Praise the Lord."

Dodo stayed for the second service but told Sylvia she would pass later for Easter dinner. After a quick smoke, and flush with the goodness of the Lord, she remembered to thank me for getting Sylvia and them to come, and introduced us to Sybil, her church-lady friend. Sybil was mainly interested in meeting Bo.

Walking home, Derek, taken by one of his fits, did a little chicken dance. Sylvia laughed. "Son, you mocking Tanty Dodo?"

Derek danced again, a dead mimic of Dodo's frontward march. "Sylvia, you see you encouraging the boy to do stupidness," Bo declared, but he was laughing too. "Let me show you how to do it, Derek," he said, and he took off, running circles around us in Dodo's fisted trot.

Sylvia and I were cracking up, and Micky said, "Wooooo," like Pastor Rome.

Getting into the fun, Sylvia and I pranced around on the pavement. From the stoop next door, Miss Florence, smoking a cigarette and wearing more clothes than I had ever seen her in, looked across at us and shook her head. We did look like a Labor Day band of fools coming down Eastern Parkway. But as we turned in to the building's entrance, Bo cut his capering short. There was Jacob's man, and two younger men with him. They were smoking and laughing, chatting in Russian. All three carried buckets, and all three had flesh colored somewhere between ashy gray and jaundiced yellow.

Bo stopped short. "What the fuck?"

Sylvia sensed something. "Bo, the children here. Don't start nothing, please. I begging you."

He didn't even glance at Sylvia. "Carry them children upstairs now."

Sylvia, in a tone I had never heard, said, "Bo, today is Easter. Wait till you see Jacob tomorrow. He coming tomorrow. Them man didn't do nothing, Bo. Is work them want work too."

Bo ignored her and planted himself dead in the way of the oldest man, the one who drove for Jacob. The van was parked in front of the building, but we hadn't noticed it because we were so busy mocking Dodo's performance.

"What you doing here?" Bo asked the wrinkled Russian. The younger workers stopped. Somehow crooked from shoes to cloth caps, they looked like a Baltic Mutt and Jeff.

"My friend—"

Bo cut him off. "Me and you is not no fucking friend."

The man put up his hand, but said again, "My friend, we are here to do job. Boss man he tell and we do. That is all, my friend."

Bo took two steps closer to the old Russian, and the younger two set down their buckets. "Which boss man send you here? Jacob?"

The Russian shrugged, and Bo shouted, only an inch or so away from the man's face. "Which fucking boss man send you here?"

Miss Florence cackled and blew some smoke out the corner of her mouth. "A monkey and Jew. I ain't seen this much action since I was in the game," she said.

Sylvia ignored her and said, "Bo—"

He spun around and shouted, "I tell you to take them fucking children and gone upstairs. You didn't fucking hear me?"

Miss Florence said, "Big, baaad nigger man."

Minding Bo, Sylvia hustled her children inside. We stood behind the glass doors burglarproofed with iron bars and peeked out. Bo was up in the old man's face, and the younger two men had come to stand on either side of him.

Derek punched air. "My uncle Bo could kick their ass."

The slap Sylvia dropped on his cheek echoed in the empty hall. Tears came to Derek's eyes. "You"—Sylvia pointed to trembling Micky—"take your two brother and go upstairs now."

Micky walked away, carrying Dame. "Mammy," she said as she turned by the steps, "look blood here." Sylvia, gripping the bars on the door, didn't hear her.

"Jesus Christ," Sylvia whispered, "I hope Bo don't go and start nothing with them man and them, you know. Police in my house on Easter Sunday."

"Nothing going to happen, Sylvia," I told her, but I wasn't sure. Bo was jabbing his finger in the old man's chest. The old man's callused hands were up, and Mutt and Jeff were getting agitated.

"Grace, I going out there."

"No, Sylvia, wait and see."

"Wait and see what? Murder happen right here in front my building? Grace"—she turned to me, a sheen of sweat glazing her forehead—"you don't know Bo, you know." She opened the front door, but Bo was done with the men. The three were nodding as they picked up their buckets and backed away from him. He stood like a big thundercloud over them, threatening as they made their way into the van. The old man got in on the driver's side, started the engine, and began to drive off slowly. Bo turned to walk into the building, so he didn't see Mutt in the middle lean forward and give him a jerky double middle finger and a ball of hawked-up phlegm that sailed clear over Jeff and landed on the sidewalk.

As he walked up the way, Miss Florence said, "Monkey, you need to come ring my bell in the nighttime."

Bo looked over at her and said without any real malice, "Miss Florence, why you don't take your old ass inside?"

We heard her cackling, and Sylvia kept the door opened for Bo. He walked inside but didn't say anything. The elevator was still broken, and Sylvia finally said, "Well, they didn't come to fix that."

At the base of the steps, she stopped. "Look, it have blood here, you know. Like somebody in the building get stab."

Bo smeared the red drops with the tip of his boot. "Is not blood, that is paint."

He sniffed the air, and we did too, inhaling the solvently ether that I associated with Christmas and home.

"Like they start to give people they paint jobs from today?" Sylvia's voice rose. "My walls done scrape already. Mines supposed to be the first apartment to get paint, you know."

Bo was furious again. "That mother-ass sonofabitch. He just tell me they didn't come to paint nobody place, and like a damn ass I believe him."

But the Russians hadn't lied to Bo. Two of the apartments on the second floor had daubs of fresh paint on their front doors. On the third floor, two more doors were marked, and three on the fourth. On Sylvia's floor, the fifth, hers was the only door marked with red paint. We stood on the threshold and stared at the still-wet smear sploshed above the peephole. Micky had left the door wide open, and the paint had trailed down its length and collected into a little puddle, bright crimson against the faded hue of Sylvia's trampled carpet. The children all stood on the other side. Micky, like a miniature mother, held Dame in one arm and had draped the other over Derek, still whimpering from his slap. Bo slowly cut his finger through the red streaks.

Sylvia breathed hard from walking up the steps. "Remember I did tell you was plenty people in the building getting paint jobs. Well, I see what they doing. Is mark they come to mark so when the real man and them come to do the job, they know which apartment is which. And, Bo, you see how you bawl up the man and them for nothing."

Bo wasn't as understanding. "You don't know Jacob like I know Jacob," he said. "That man care about one thing, he money, and that is all."

Bo was not ready to be consoled, and, still being mindful of him, Sylvia said, "Not to worry, boy. Tell me what you feel like eating and I will cook it for you."

But Bo shook his head and walked away from us, back toward the steps. "Is not me who need to worry. The only thing I feel like eating right now is a bottle of rum and some all fours."

Chapter 26

There was no Easter Monday holiday in New York. No early morning sports down in the junction by Deo's rum shop, with races for every age group, including pregnant women by belly size. No big lime on the beach for the whole village and Penal people if they behaved.

In New York, Easter Monday was just another day to get up and go. I had the day off, but Sylvia left for her agency at the same time Derek and Micky left for school. Dame was still asleep when Sylvia showed me the medicine he was to take as part of his treatment.

Jacob rang the doorbell at eleven. "Hello, Cousin Grace. Here again, I see."

There really wasn't any point in giving him an excuse.

"Did you have a good Pesach?" he asked, looking around as he made his way to the living room. Sylvia had pushed everything she could to the middle of the room so that the workmen could get to the walls. She had spread cut garbage bags over her furniture for protection.

"I worked for Pesach."

"A shame. Anyway, where is your cousin Bo?"

Bo was still asleep in his spot on the bedroom floor. "Watch the baby, and let me get him," I replied. When we came out, Jacob was stooped in front of Dame, his black coat fanned out behind him like a drab peacock's tail. In his hand he held the little bottle of medicine I had left on the coffee table.

Bo yawned. "You visiting your sins?"

Jacob rose. "We need to talk in private."

Bo rubbed the back of his neck and, yawning again, tilted his head toward the kitchen. I heard them as if they were still in the room.

"What did you say to my man Mikhail yesterday?"

"What he tell you I tell him?"

"Bo, you cannot fuck around with my workers when I send them to do a job. If you have some quarrel to make, then you come and see me like a man, not take it out on a poor immigrant."

Bo laughed. "I is a poor immigrant too, Jacob. Is only you who not poor."

"The point is that you can't terrorize my men."

"Your men," Bo mocked, "listen to you talking to me without shame. Jacob, is me and Nello and Keatix who used to be your men. Where the work you promise me? Have some shame at least, man."

"I have work for you, but it won't start for a few weeks yet."

"What kind of work we talking about and how much money? Pass me a cigarette." I heard a match strike.

"Gutting work." Another match. "I'm about to close on a building, and it will have to be gutted, but carefully, not a hack job. Three floors and a basement. Private house. Near here, actually."

"When this work starting?"

"Well, I haven't closed on it yet, but it's soon. I'll let you know by the end of the week." Jacob thought for a moment and then asked, "How much you think you will charge?"

"Jacob, you think because I black I stupid? How the ass I could give a estimate for a job I ain't see yet? Is long long time I in this business, you know."

"Approximately?" Jacob persisted.

But Bo was firm. "When I see the house we talking about, then we could start to talk about price."

"Okay. Okay."

"So what about the work you doing in this building? You know I is a boss scraper and painter. What happen to this?"

"It is too late for this. Mikhail and his boys already have this job. They don't work well with—"

Bo cut in. "With what? What it is they don't well with? Nigger people? But what the ass is this I hearing in truth? Them say that, or you saying that, Jacob?"

He didn't say which, only "Trust me, this gutting job is good for you. You will even be able to give those two bums you work with a couple days. Just make sure your Nello doesn't steal anything this time, okay? None of the fixtures or anything. You should see this building"—I heard the sound of a kiss—"beautiful, all original details, everything like when it was built. This is why I trust only you to do this job, but your two guys I'm not so sure about."

"You leave me to worry about Nello and Keatix," Bo said. "When you going to know for sure?"

"I should be able to tell you something by the end of this week, but it could take until the end of the month. No more fucking with my men, okay?"

I heard Sylvia's old chairs skid along the kitchen linoleum, then I heard the slapping of palms, then the front door open and close.

AS A PRIZE FOR not missing a single prenatal appointment when she was pregnant with Dame, Sylvia had been given a stroller. It was still in rolling condition, so I strapped Dame in to go for some fresh air. Bo lay on the couch, a plastic container of ice water within reach.

"So, this is the life of the resurrected?" I said to him.

He laughed. "I waiting until I go by Miss Sybil for lessons. Where you going?"

"Park. Dame need some fresh air."

"Grace, wait. Before you go"—he sat up and held his head—"you have twenty dollars you could lend me?"

I had twenty dollars, but the question was whether or not I wanted to lend it to him. "If I lend you twenty dollars, Bo, when I getting it back?"

"You didn't hear me and Jacob talking in the kitchen just now?"

"Yes?"

"Well, I think is serious thing he talking about, so I not going to lie and tell you next week. I will pay you when I get the little work from Jacob."

Bo seemed earnest, and I calculated that, if I never saw my twenty dollars again, it would be okay. I could afford to lose it. But I didn't want to dig through my wallet in front of him, so I went in the bedroom.

"Thanks, girl," Bo said when I came back, and he slipped the bill into the waist of his drawers. "And what about the other thing? You think about the other thing?"

Of course I had.

"You playing the ass with a big man."

"Okay"—I pushed Dame down the hall—"when I come back."

I took Dame for a long walk along the parkway, all the way up to the playground by the museum, trying not to think about what it was I was doing in New York, about my own second life. A horn honked, and Dame and I both turned around. It was Brent, and he was sitting in a green pickup truck with a white leaf outlined on the door, grinning and waving.

"You going up there?"

"Hey, yes."

"All right, let me find a park for this. Me soon come."

I couldn't believe my luck running into him. We kissed out in the open, and I realized that this was actually the first time I had been with him while the sun was shining.

"Hold on," I said. "Let me get Dame out."

"All the time me thought was a likkle white child you mind. And how you in Brooklyn?"

"I'm off today. This is Dame, the woman I live with son."

"And what wrong with him so?" Dame was unsure on his feet, waddling slowly along on the padded ground, clearly not the same as the other children.

I shrugged. "That's what they're trying to figure out."

Brent cocked his head, "Mongoloid that."

"What?" I said, even though I had heard him.

"Mongoloid. You no know what that is?"

I did, and I didn't think it was a very nice thing for him to say. "Come, let's take him over to the swings."

Brent checked his watch. "Okay, me have ten minutes."

I pushed Dame gently back and forth. Brent said, "Wait." He stopped the swing, undid the zipper from up under Dame's neck, and took off his little hat. "It not too too cold out here."

I looked around, not wanting to think about where Brent's parenting skills came from. Most of the black women here had black children. The few white women seemed to be minding their own babies. I wondered if the three of us looked like a family. When Brent started pushing Dame harder than I had dared, I thought for sure that we did. At McDonald's Kathy had said that it would be nice to have a family; I wasn't too sure about that.

Trouble must have crossed my face, because Brent said, "What wrong?"

"Nothing. What are you doing driving around here in the middle of the day?"

"Looking for you, darkie."

I laughed at that. "Seriously, Brent."

"Nah, for real. Me had a feeling that me would see you, and look at that. Me make you appear."

He wasn't going to tell me anything more. "I didn't know you had that kind of power," I told him.

"Plenty you don't know about me, girl," he replied. And I thought, *That's for sure.*

Two men wheeled up to the next swing, and one lifted a little Chinese girl wearing a princess dress and a glittering crown out of their stroller. They pushed her together in the swing, one in front and the other in back, and her shiny, black hair lifted and swirled in the light spring wind.

"You see that?" Brent let his gaze linger for a few seconds and said in deep patois, "Man like that haffl bun."

And for a second time I said, "What?" to something I perfectly understood.

"Buller-man, nah," he elucidated. "I and I don't stand for that, at all, at all, scene."

The men either did not understand what Brent was saying or chose to ignore him, laughing along with the little girl they called Chloe. "You really think so?"

"But 'ow you mean? Jah-Jah nah make man for man. A pure 'bomination that."

I wondered who would think that two men out pushing a princess in a swing should be put to death by fire.

"Anyhow, time for me to go, yeah." Brent gave Dame a final push and put his arm around my shoulders. "See you come Saturday night?" He kissed me again and left, smelling so good I kind of understood how Kathy put up with Donovan's bullshit.

I continued to push Dame, gently again. "You like this, Dame?" I asked him. "You like swinging?" He couldn't say yes, but he kicked his legs and wiggled his arms.

"Is this fun?" He kicked some more, and one of the men next to us said, "Isn't it amazing how fast they grow?"

Dame was having such a good time, being in the open air and flying in the swing. I remembered from primary school: *How do you like to go up in a swing, Up in the air so blue,* and spinning through the air on the tire swing my father had hung us from the guava tree behind our house. That was the closest I had come to flying before my trip to New York. The closest I had come to feeling free.

DANNY HAD DESK DUTY that night, and he stepped off the platform when I walked in.

"Hey, Gracie Mansion. Didn't see you last night. Thought you were"—he drew his finger across his chicken neck—"gone for good."

"You would think something like that," I retorted. Up close Danny was especially vile. The top hat kept slipping down his forehead, causing him to tip his wedge-of-cheese head back, exposing a bramble of unclipped nose hairs.

"So what," he wanted to know, "you had an extra day off or something?"

"Yes, Danny, I had today off."

"With pay?"

"*Manicou,*" I said under my breath. "Why are you asking me my business?"

"Huh." He sucked spit through his crooked teeth. "I never get a day off with pay, and I'm an American."

"Good night, Danny," I said and made my way around him. Two young girls, both lamppost lean with long, straight hair, walked into the building laughing and bumping into each other. Danny lifted his hat with exaggerated courtesy as they walked by. They ignored him and got on the elevator with me.

"Oh, my God," one said and fell against the wall of the elevator. "I can't believe we did that. Oh, my God. We're super seniors now."

The other one laughed even harder.

"Okay, come on," said the first one, "pull it together. My dad's at home."

But neither could pull anything, and the second one crashed against the elevator wall, making them both laugh even louder.

"Seriously," the second one said, anything but serious, "your doorman is such a dog. He's as ugly as butt."

"As ugly as butt," the first one repeated, holding her middle and whipping her hair about. "Oh, my God, he is so nasty. Did you check out his teeth? Dude, use your dental and get some braces. And that stupid-ass hat he has to wear."

They got off on the eighteenth floor, laughing just as hard as when they came on.

It was Miriam who opened the door. "Hey, Grace," she said, turning to check the time.

"Evening, Miriam."

She rubbed her belly. "I'll come in in a few minutes."

More than cleaning toilets or mopping floors or dusting figurines I hated taking photos of Miriam's growing belly. And more than all of that I hated that I hadn't told her. While I waited for Miriam, I unpacked the few lighter pieces of clothing I had brought back to the city, including my brand-new halter top. It wouldn't be halter weather for a while yet, but you never knew. Plus, I didn't want to leave something so expensive at Sylvia's. Miss Micky might get ideas.

Ten minutes later, after I had shot pictures of the washing machine and the wall, Sol came and stood behind Miriam. She dressed facing him, her naked bottom toward me, but then, instead of getting out of my space, she came and sat on the bed. Sol edged closer to my room, and I wondered what was going on.

"So, Grace, how long have you been here now?" she asked.

"Just about a month." It would be exactly a month come Wednesday.

Miriam nodded, and Sol watched me. "Sol brought these home today."

She slid the folder toward me. The low lamplight deepened the pockmarks on her face. Sol cast an ogre's shadow on my wall. "What is this?" I asked.

"Open it," Miriam said.

I had no idea.

Immigration forms. I grinned and thumbed through the pages, some of which were already filled out in Miriam's loopy, schoolteacher handwriting.

"Are these my sponsorship papers?"

Sol said, "Yup, we're keeping you, Grace."

The flimsy folder was so light, but the papers it held meant so much. The papers meant my freedom.

"We think you're working out. Ben adores you, you keep the place clean. Suzy told me she wanted to steal you for her girls." She turned quickly to Sol and then back to me. "After Pesach I told Sol we should get the forms today and surprise you. Didn't I, Sol?"

Miriam leaned closer to me. "We have to place an ad in the paper to make sure that no Americans want the job. You'll have to pay for that, and all the filing fees and postage."

"And what happens if an American answers the ad?" I asked Sol the lawyer my question.

Miriam answered, "We'll just say that the position is already filled." I wondered how many of the ads in the *Echo* were placed by women being sponsored.

"So okay," Miriam was saying, "read through them and fill out your parts. If you have any questions, you can ask Sol."

She reached over and hit him lightly, and he said, "Yup."

I needed to say something. "Thanks, Sol and Miriam. I had no idea you were going to do this. I'll give you back the forms tomorrow night."

"Well"—she slid off the bed—"wait until you have the money and give us everything together. You have to pay the fees, you know, and I think you need to have some photos."

"Oh . . . sure. Of course," I said, already thinking that I would use the money I had put aside for my father. I could make it up. And maybe, instead of going to Sylvia's and wasting Saturday and Sunday, I could find a weekend job.

Miriam and Sol walked through the kitchen and into the living room. I looked more closely at the forms in the folder. The INS wanted a lot of information. Everything about my mother and father, siblings, education, my height and eye color. Everything. I would tell them anything they wanted to know. I thought about calling Kathy, but with Sol and Miriam in the living room, I'd have to talk too carefully. I decided to go up to Dave's.

He didn't look very good. "You feeling okay?" I asked, following him straight out to the back patio. It was cold to be sitting outside thirty floors up.

Dave sat and passed me a beer. "I'm good, Grace. How are you?"

But I didn't believe him for a second. His hair looked as though it hadn't been combed in days, and his baggy old sweater hung to his knees, almost covering his shorts. The sleeping dogs pressed against his lounge chair, and four empty beer bottles were in easy reach. The twin towers gleamed, a sparkly number eleven in the not quite black night sky.

"So, what did you do for Passover?" I asked.

"Oh, the boys and I just got in the truck and drove up to the country."

"You have family in the country?"

"Uh-uh. I wanted to be alone, so I just went up to the house."

"You have a house in the country?"

"I do. Duck Hollow." He shifted to look at me, and the sweater gaped away from his neck. "Sol and Miriam haven't mentioned it?"

"Uh-uh."

He turned again. "They love Duck Hollow. When Vincent was alive, they'd come up almost every summer weekend. Miriam rode at the stables, and Ben learned to walk up there."

I'd never asked this question of a man before. "Vincent was your boyfriend?"

He looked at me with such sadness. "If I turn the garden this year, I'll take you for a weekend." He paused. "If you wanted to go, of course."

"Of course I want to go. What do you plant there?"

"It was mostly Vincent's garden," Dave said with a laugh. "Very practical Italian. He planted herbs and vegetables. Seasonally appropriate, zone six vegetables. I'm surprised Sol and Miriam haven't told you anything about the place. Even in the winter, when Vincent and I went to Key West, they'd go up without us." He balanced the beer bottle on the handrest. "You don't know, do you?"

"Know what?"

"Grace, Vincent was Miriam's brother. Haven't you heard Ben call me his *zio*?"

"Her brother?" I didn't try to hide my surprise. The wall in the Brooklyn house featured Pope, priest, and policeman, but no planter. Even when Sophia had said the blessing, she'd made no mention of a brother Vincent.

"Vincent liked to grow things too?" I asked. "Did he grow eggplants?"

"Some years. Why?"

"It's nothing. At Miriam's parents' house in Brooklyn on Good Friday her father said he didn't like eggplant."

"He said that? And you were at the table?"

"Uh-huh."

"Did anybody say anything?"

"Not really. Miriam laughed."

Dave shook his head. "Miriam can't help who she is. She tries, but Brooklyn gets the better of her sometimes. She was the only one in his family who talked to Vincent. When he got sick, even the priest and the nun, they never came to see him."

I tried to add this softer side to the Miriam I knew, but I just couldn't reconcile the images.

"Now I've gone and made you depressed."

"A little bit." I felt sad for Miriam's brother cut off from the big Forgione table, for Dave going up to the country alone, for Sylvia with her crazy husband in the G Building, and for my mother with one-quarter of her family stranded all the way in New York.

"Hey, listen," Dave said, sitting up, "you want to neuter my papaya?"

"What?"

"Neuter"—he ruffled Brutus or Cesar—"like boy pets. But I guess it wouldn't be neutering if your operation will make the tree fruit, right?"

"Dave, what are you talking about?"

"Remember you told me you knew how to make the papaya bear fruit?"

"Uh-huh."

"Okay, well, let's do it."

"Right now?"

"Why not?"

"Because you can't cut plants at nighttime."

"Really?" Dave asked. "Anything else I need to know?"

"Well, I've been meaning to tell you for a long time that it's not appropriate to wear shorts in February."

"Cheeky girl. Didn't your mother tell you to respect your elders?"

In fact she had. "Over and over."

"So tell me why we can't fix the tree tonight?"

"Okay, but don't laugh." I gave him my serious stare. "It shocks the tree."

"Grace."

"No, Dave, for real. If one of us was unwell in the evening and my mother needed to boil up some bush tea, she always woke up the plant first"—I slapped my hands together lightly like my mother had done—"and then she would tell the plant she was troubling its sleep to heal a sick child. She taught me to respect nature too. There's no way I can give a plant a sex change in the middle of the night."

"Sounds like superstition to me, but okay. The next time you come up early, snip snip."

IT WAS STILL TOO early to go to the park, so I took Ben with me up to the thirtieth floor. Dave opened the door after the first ring, Brutus and Cesar close to his bared legs. "What took you so long?" he asked.

"How do you mean?" Ben scooted past without greeting his *zio* and grabbed the dogs. "Gentle, Ben," I warned.

We headed out to the deck. "Let's just say, I had a feeling after last night you'd be coming back soon."

Outside, next to the papaya, Dave had opened a stepladder and laid out several pairs of cutting shears on the worktable. I laughed. "How did you know?"

He looked to see where Ben was. "Because no one can resist turning something gay straight."

He was joking, of course, but I didn't think it was funny. "That's not why I want to cut the tree, Dave."

"Of course it's not, Grace. I'm not talking about you, silly." He came and put his arm around my shoulder. "I'll tell you the truth. I do feel a little funny about doing this. It's the kind of thing my father and Mr. Forgione would have considered for me and Vincent if it was an option, you know. In reverse, of course." He shrugged. "But this is a tree, and I like papayas, so let's do it already, okay?"

"Okay."

It didn't take long at all. I climbed up the ladder, and Ben left the dogs to come over to see. "Pass me the medium shears, Dave," I said.

He did and then hoisted Ben onto his shoulders so he could have a better look at what I was about to do. The wood was soft and spongy, easy to cut through at the crown, where the male flowers hung down like useless tentacles. Near the end I told them to step back. "Hey, Ben, when I count to three, yell 'Timber!' okay? One, two, three." We all cried "Timber," and the leafy crown crashed to the floor, scaring Brutus and Cesar away from their spots. Ben clapped, and Dave tossed him in the air.

"Okay, now get me a container," I said.

Dave came back in a few minutes with what looked like a solid crystal vase. "Are you serious?" I asked him. "You don't have a plastic container, or an empty paint can?"

"But won't this work? It'll look nice in the sun."

I shook my head, feeling like my mother, and worked the glass onto the fresh stump. Down from the ladder, I took the pinch of dirt from my father and wedged it deep into the papaya's tub of soil.

"And what was that?" Dave wanted to know.

"That was the magic, my friend," I told him. And Ben opened his green eyes wide. "Magic, Grace?"

"Uh-huh. Now keep watering it as usual unless it rains, and let's see what happens."

LATER THAT MORNING, DUKE watched us from his platform. "Did you enjoy your day off, Caribbean Queen?" he asked. I didn't answer but wondered again if the doormen didn't have enough to do without marking the sitters in the building so closely.

Kathy and I sat in the park. Ule limed with us, not really chatting, just passing her blue-covered New Testament close to her eyes and rocking the Bloomberg baby whenever it fretted. From across the way, Evie scrutinized us openly.

"Grace, what that lady have with you?" Kathy was in an antsy mood, and she too rolled her baby's carriage back and forth, using the tip of one of her BeDazzled sneakers.

"Who knows? From the beginning her blood didn't take me. How'd you dazzle the sneakers, Kath?"

She looked at her feet, and Ule stopped reading to check them out too. "You wouldn't like to know the trouble I had to go through to fit these into the machine."

"You do a fine job, though," Ule said.

Evie's eyes were still fixed on us. "She needs to stop fucking staring before I go over there," Kath declared.

"Watch you language, child," Ule said.

Kath apologized and asked Ule if she had anything she wanted Be-Dazzled.

Ule laughed. "I have a mind to give you a jersey for you to do my name. But I gone from here just now."

I hadn't heard this before. "Where you going, Ule?"

"Wherever the next job is, my child. You must remember is only baby nurse work I does do. As soon as they hit six, seven weeks, I done, you know. Close your mouth."

I did, but I still stared at her. Ule was the only sitter in the park who I felt truly liked me. I had Kath, but Ule was different.

"And who knows"—Ule talked, keeping her eyes on her testament—"plenty woman in the tower making baby. Maybe is right here self I going to stay." But I felt that she was just saying this for me.

"Grace, I need to talk to you about something." Kath said it in a way that made Ule close her testament with a sharp *snap*. "I didn't mean for you to go, Ule," she said, but it didn't sound sincere to me.

"Is not a problem, my darling," Ule said, rolling off. "Time to get this little imp upstairs anyhow."

"Well, I have something to tell you too, Kath," I said.

"Yeah, what?"

"Last night when I came in, Miriam had the sponsorship papers."

"You lie." Kathy raised her voice, and Evie whipped her head in our direction. Kath flipped her off.

"Oh, my God, Kath, no," I said, but I was laughing.

"Bitch, serve she right. So tell me about this thing. What she say?"

"That I was working out and they want to keep me." I was so excited. "I have to pay for everything, of course, but, Kath, I'm doing it."

She reached for the tip of her ponytail. "And you prefer to do this than marry Sylvia cousin, Grace?"

Her tone irked me. "Kath, if you ever saw the piece of man I talking about, you'd feel the same way. I have to kiss Bo if I marry him."

"One kiss, Grace, and you don't even have to fuck him." I winced. "And, even if you had to, what is a fuck if you get your freedom for it? You talking as if is for real."

I didn't agree at all. "It is for real, Kath."

"You too stubborn. You know how long sponsorship will take? Daddy always say white people make his grandfather cut cane in Caroni for five years for one stinking acre of swampland."

Her reference to indentured laborers annoyed me. Her father owned three supermarkets. "And who running everything home now? Not the same people who start off in bound."

"True," Kath said, "but is not really them, is it? Is their children and grandchildren. I suppose you have to decide if you working for you now or for somebody else later."

She was pissing me off. Ben came over for a drink, and Kath stuck her tongue out playfully at him. "Look, I not trying to make you mad, Grace. I just want you to think about this before you jump into it all hotty and sweaty and then is too late to get out."

I didn't want to talk about this with her anymore. "Hey, you know what else happen last night?" I asked.

She shook her head. "What?"

"I found out Dave's boyfriend, the one who died, was Miriam's brother."

"You lie." Kath's downcast eyes widened as far as they would go.

"Nope. And he said that Miriam is the only one in her whole family who kept in touch with him. I think he died from AIDS, you know."

"Wow," Kath said, "white people have more *comess* than we, mama. And so what about Dave, he have AIDS too?"

"That's really shitty, Kath. What happen to you this morning? You and Donovan fight last night or something?"

She laughed. "You're the only person I know who would pick up with a buller-man, Grace. You can't even fuck him and get some money."

"Okay"—I started putting Ben's stuff together—"you need to be alone this morning. Call me when you ready to talk some sense."

"Don't stay mad for long," Kath said as I rolled away. "My party is Saturday and you coming."

MIRIAM DIDN'T HIDE HER surprise when I gave her the folder after dinner that night. The forms were filled out, I had two notarized passport pictures, and $150, cash. One twenty-five for the filing fee, $20 for the ad in *The Irish Echo,* and $5 to cover postage.

"Wow, Grace, you move fast." She passed the folder to Sol for his lawyerly inspection. He placed it unopened next to his dessert plate, picked Ben up, and took him to his room.

Miriam sat still, rubbing her growing belly while I cleaned up. She flipped through the forms. "When did you get a chance to get the pictures taken, Grace?"

"Today, after the park. There's a guy right next to the pizza place on Fourteenth."

"You really should run your personal errands on your own time," she said. And with that she picked the folder up off the table, then went down the hall to meet her husband and child.

Chapter 27

"**Y**ou must be mad if you think I wearing this." I held the catsuit Kath had BeDazzled between my thumb and finger. "This is pornographic."

"Oh, just hush and put it on, Grace."

"To go out in public?" She had snazzed a rhinestone bikini onto the black fabric. "This thing just missing a tail."

"Only because I couldn't find one. I pick up something else, but it's the final touch. Wait and see."

"What? A whip?"

We were in the small room Kath rented for ninety dollars a week. Monday through Friday she had the communal spaces to herself as the other women boarders lived in at their jobs out in Jersey and Long Island. Now, it was Saturday night and everyone was readying to go out. A smoky-sweet cloud from iron-roasted hair clotted the low ceiling, and every five minutes someone wanted to borrow a black brassiere or a dip of hair gel or a spritz of perfume. Getting ready to go to a house party or a basement lime or Club Calaloo or International or Empire or Tilden Hall—any place to get far away from the choking rooms and even farther from the thought of going back to the suburbs on Sunday night.

Even with the window hoisted wide open, Kath's room was still unbearably hot. It was a scratchy, unnatural heat that never managed to mimic the caressing warmth of home. She sat in her white, lacy underwear on a short red pouf in front of her formica dressing table. I leaned against the mattress edge of her tall iron bed. For the third time she tried to outline her thin lips, and for the third time she messed up.

"Shit." She grabbed a napkin and rubbed it over the crooked lines, which only spread the black around her mouth. She looked like a coal miner.

"Here." I laid the catsuit on the bed and reached to take the pencil from her. "Let me do it."

"Grace, please. What you know about putting on makeup?" she complained, but she passed me the liner.

I held her chin and cleaned off the sooty smear. "Kath, what you so nervous about?" I asked her. She pulled her mouth wide to smooth the edges. She turned back to the mirror and nodded quickly, pleased with my work. Then, reaching for her lipstick, she knocked over a bottle of perfume.

"This is crazy," I told her. "You need to relax. What is wrong?"

She spun the pouf, and her beautiful hair, down still, lifted like a black mantilla off her shoulders. When she was eleven she had taken a pair of scissors and cut off her plaits. Her mother, livid, kept her home from an outing to Tobago for which Kathy had canvassed her posh neighborhood and raised the most money. When she was a woman, her mother had told her, she could do what she wanted with her body, but not while she lived under her roof.

"What if she come, Grace?"

I had no idea who she was talking about. "Who she?"

"*She*. Donovan's . . ." She spun back. "The idiot woman he living with. I hear she planning to show up tonight."

Before I could answer, Shivani knocked and pushed her head in the room. She had been a nice Indian girl from Caroni but had run away after her old-fashioned Hindu parents found a man twice her age with twenty acres of cane for her to marry. "Kathy, you have Stayfree to lend me one, please?"

"Grace, look in the drawer," Kathy said.

Shivani took one pad.

"Take the whole set," Kathy said.

"No, I just want one. I will buy a pack when I go out tonight."

Kathy snapped, "Shivani, just take it, all right." And Shivani, too timid to refuse again, took the bag from my hands and pulled her head like a tortoise out of the room.

I turned back to Kathy. "Who you hear that stupidness from, that she coming tonight?" I wanted Kath to be happy on her birthday. "Please, Kath. You think Donovan would put up with that, and lose he big-man reputation? You know these Jamaicans."

She reached for her ponytail and instead flicked a finger full of loose hair against her cheek. "You think so, Grace?"

"I know so."

Kath sighed. "I think you right." She turned back to face her reflection. "Come on, Grace, we wasting time. Put on your clothes. The car coming for one."

The outfit was insane, the clingy jersey outlining my breasts, my bottom, and my crotch, where Kath had done her dazzling. The long sleeves and full-length pants provided no modesty. "Kath, you have a scarf or something I could tie around my waist? Look at this."

She turned to look and beamed. "Grace, perfect, perfect, perfect. Oh, my God, you look like a—"

"Kath, I swear to God, if you say I look like a model, I am not leaving this house tonight."

She grinned, showing her little teeth. "But you know is truth, right." Then she did a vulgar Jamaican winer dance and sang,

Girl, yuh body good
no 'oman caan touch yuh
'cause yuh body good, oh.

"This is crazy," I muttered and started pulling my hair back into a rubber band.

"What on earth you doing?" Kathy shrieked and snatched at my hair. "Give me that. You spoiling the whole look. Grace, tonight you are 'Cat Woman.' Fantasy, please. Sit down." She took an afro pick off her dresser and started digging into my hair and covering me with hair spray.

"What are you doing? Kath, ow! Stop, Jesus." I tried to get the comb from her, but she was too quick, using it instead to crack me across the knuckles.

"Behave and wait," she commanded. She swung the pouf around so I couldn't see what she was doing—the combing and fluffing and spritzing— all the while biting her bottom lip and angling her head as though she had any idea of what she was trying to create. "Close your eyes."

"For what?"

"You so harden. If I wanted you to know, for what you think I would tell you to close your eyes? Just close them please, Grace. The limo coming in fifteen minutes."

"Limo?" I asked. She changed cans, sprayed another few bursts of aerosol poison, and then stuck something sharp into my scalp just behind my ears. "Ow!"

"Christ, you tender-headed. Hold on," Kath chided. I opened my eyes, and she was so focused on fixing something into my head that I closed them again. "Okay," she said, "look."

I spun the pouf around and laughed. "Kath, you gone completely mad."

She grinned. "Yeah, but tell me it don't look good."

I looked frigging fantastic. She had picked out my straightened hair with some kind of gel and that superstrength spray, and now the whole thing sprang from my head bushy and flecked with gold. And the sharp pinch I had felt came from a tiny pair of silvery cat ears set on a bandeau Kath had used to pull back the wild mess. My eyebrows went up into my hairline. "Holy shit."

"Hypocrite. You like it, don't you?" She was so pleased with her work. "I love it."

Kath started jumping around the room like a true true *sketel*. "Grace, tonight we going to mash up the place!" she told me. And I, unsteady in my tall boots and crazy hair, jumped around and shouted with her too.

WE GOT TO THE club at 1:30 A.M. Kathy stepped out of the limo and into a crowd of yardbirds who were waiting to check her out. She looked beautiful in her all-white outfit: a leather bustier and matching *poom-poom* shorts, over-the-knee boots with fishnet stockings. Her hair was piled extra high, and she had woven white sequined ribbons into the length of her ponytail. She held on to Donovan's hand and posed for photos before turning back to me, still in the backseat. "Grace, grab my coat please."

I smiled, already holding the same white coat with the fur-trimmed collar she had worn to City Hall a few weeks earlier. "Got it, Kath. You look amazing." She smiled again at me before turning to preen some more in front of the yardbirds. Then Donovan, bumping like a pumping jack, escorted her through the crowd and into the underground belly of Club International.

I followed a few steps behind, feeling foolish in my getup but fast realizing that Kath had been right, I fit right in with the outrageousness of the night. The yardbirds had come out in true Jamaican style for the evening. Girls competed for the shortest pair of shorts and between them sported just-under-the-bottom *poom-pooms* like Kath's or the one-inch-shorter batty riders that exposed just a crescent of fatty backside, or the highest cut of all, the two-inch-up punanni printers that did just that.

Donovan hadn't really rented out the whole club for Kathy, but he had paid the promoters good money to dedicate the night to her. All the flyers that had gone up in the jerk joints and barbershops and had been handed out on the street corners to advertise the regular Saturday night party had "HAPPY BIRTHDAY KATHY" printed across the top. Everyone knew Donovan, so word had spread that this was to be in honor of his likkle matey. There was no doubt wifey knew about the party, but unless she was an acid thrower, she wasn't going to be here tonight.

Inside I checked in our coats, checked out where the exits were, and looked around for Brent. The reggae was loud, and the DJ kept up a non-stop chant over the bass beats that consisted mostly of the word *massive* said over and over. The crowd, thick and warm in the closed space, swayed slowly in time to the music. Unlike at a Trini fete, where man and woman gyrated backside to crotch, or everyone jumped together in mardi gras abandon, the mostly Jamaican crowd was segregated by sex. Men in over-size denim and corduroy outfits lined the perimeter of the room, while in the middle women, their downcast faces obscured by wigs and weaves, clutched beer bottles and moved their hips and bottoms in hypnotic rhythm to the dub play. I lost sight of Kath and Donovan, and, just as I decided to find the bar and get my own drink, Brent's hand curled around my waist and pulled me to him.

"Darkie," he whispered, "where you been 'iding from me?" And then, tightening his grip, he bent his head and pressed his lips onto mine.

He smelled so good, like soap and cinnamon and cloves and woodsmoke. I looked up at him and grinned, glad to see him and not wanting to pull away. But he stepped back and whistled. "Me see me going to have to fight some man in this place here tonight. Girl, you look good, like a real cat 'oman. No 'oman in this place can touch you."

"Are you serious? I feel completely overdone. Kath made this outfit for me."

"Well, Kath leave she self undone. Sexy-body girl."

I laughed; everything Brent said sounded like a lyric from a dance hall dub.

"You drink anything yet for the night?"

"No"—I shook my head—"we only just come."

"What you want then? Beer, whiskey, soda, juice? Call for what you want, princess."

I really liked this man, and right now I was loving Kathy for insisting I dress up. The loud music, the low lights, the swaying women and chilling men, everything was perfect and all right.

"A rum and Coke, please."

Brent laughed. "'Ow me know you was going say that? That's what all you Trini girls drink. Rum and Cokes." He steered me over to the wall, just to the side of the DJ booth. "Don't move, me soon come," he said as he left.

He was gone for a bit, and Kath floated over to me. "You having fun? You find Brent?"

"Yes to both. You know you're the belle of the ball, right. Kath, you look like a superstar."

"Thanks, Grace. Look, I meant to tell you sorry for what I said in the park about your friend Dave earlier this week. I wasn't feeling too good."

"Don't worry about it, Kath."

"You glad you come?"

I hugged her. "Yeah, I'm glad. Happy birthday."

She wandered off right as Brent made his way back with the drinks. The DJ lowered the volume to just below deafening and bellowed into the mike, "Easy, easy, crowd a' panty. Settle, settle crowd a' bra."

I laughed, and Brent grinned as he passed me the plastic cup. Over the humming boom of the bass, the DJ chanted, "We calling one Kyatty to come pon the stage and do a likkle ting fe we. We have a song requested 'ere by none other than the world-famous superstar Mister Donovan

Manchester, and 'im say 'im want we fe play this tune and none other for 'im Kyatty to come up and dance."

Kath was standing on the other side of the DJ's platform, shaking her head vigorously, her ponytail sequins flashing shards of light around her face. The yardbirds were clapping and urging her up the steps. Donovan took a swig from his bottle, patted Kath's bottom, then leaned in deeper to whisper something. I saw her frown, but she stretched out her hand toward the DJ and mounted the steps. The crowd roared, and Kath stood like Wonder Woman in white, her hands on her chubby waist, and waited.

"Massive and crew, stir it up," the DJ shouted, ratcheting up the volume. It was a song I had heard before on the West Indian radio station:

Mih love mih car,
Mih love mih bike,
Mih love mih money and ting,
But most of all, mih love mih browning.

The yardbirds screamed in appreciation, Kath's light skin the perfect embodiment of the song's brown beauty.

"Come on, Kyatty," the DJ was chanting, "show we your motion, show we your motion, show we your motion. There's a brown girl in the ring, tra la la la la," as the song looped over and over and over again. The yardbirds were going wild, gyrating in front of the stand, and Donovan watched them rather than stubborn Kath standing with arms akimbo onstage. The men around the edges of the room paid full attention to the fury in short shorts, slowly easing forward toward the mass of writhing women. And still Kathy stood looking down at the party held in her honor.

The DJ laughed, a hoary, deep rumble. "There's a brown girl in the ring . . . wait, wait, wait, massive and crew. Me have another one, massive, hah hah hah." Quickly, he changed the music from the dub play to a tinny-sounding steel pan rhythm, then mimicking the folksy, old-time calypsos, sang, *"Brown skin girl, stay home and mind baby . . ."*

The crowd roared at him, not liking that one at all. And Kath, liking it less than the rest, shot Donovan a murderous look. With black lights turned on and her white leather outfit glowing, Kath held her hands in the air and

pirouetted slow, grinding her hips in a serious challenge to even the most
lithe yardbird on the floor. The crowd went crazy, and the DJ, feeding off
the energy on the floor, chanted, "Yes! Yes! Yes!" in time with every shift of
Kath's waist.

Hours later, after I had danced to every song except the ones calling
for bullets, hellfire, and acid baths for gay men, Brent asked if I wanted to
go outside. We slipped out along the edges of the dance floor, skirting the
den of male and female bodies that had finally come together in a baccha-
nalian orgy.

Even pressed tight to Brent, I was freezing by the time we got to his
car, parked two blocks away. He turned on the engine, and a loud dub
blasted from the speakers.

"Sorry," he said and turned it down low, then reached over and
switched the heat way up. "It soon get warm; meanwhile, let me see what
me can do for you."

It was awkward over the gearshift, but we kissed for long time. I liked
the way he did it, letting go my tongue to gently pull on my lower lip. My
bodysuit, too flimsy for outside, was just right for the heat of his hands to
penetrate. He warmed my shoulders, my ribs, my breasts, my belly. My
head knocked his Kangol off, and we banged foreheads reaching for it.
Then he checked his watch.

"You have to be somewhere else?" I asked.

"Not now, but me 'ave work seven in the morning."

"Is Sunday tomorrow, though. I thought we liming tonight." I heard
myself and cringed. I sounded like a child. "But if you have to work you
have to go, so no problems."

"You want me go or you want me stay?"

"I want you to do what you have to do. What time is it anyway?"

"You got to be someplace?" And even though the windows had fogged
up, I could see him smile.

"Nope. My only plan is to be with you tonight."

"You want to sit in the backseat?"

In the back we could just about manage to lie halfway. He kissed my
neck, and I felt him slide open my zipper. He peeled the bodysuit down
and buried his face between my breasts, his breath warm against my
skin. He reached his arms around me and asked, "I could do this?"

I nodded, unable to say anything as he unhooked the clasp and, with just thumbs, lifted my brassiere away. He groaned and swirled his tongue around my right nipple and then the left. I couldn't breathe—I mean I could not get breath—and gulped out loud.

He stopped and looked up. "You all right?"

I nodded quickly.

"You want me to stop?"

I found breath and voice. "No, no."

"You sure?"

I pressed his face back to my breasts and slid down farther in the seat, reaching up to cup his backside and pull him onto me. The windows were completely sealed, and the amber streetlight filtered in all soft and fuzzy. Brent kissed his way down my belly, stopping where I still had my bodysuit on.

"You have rubbers?" I asked.

He stretched past me. "In ah the glove."

I unbuttoned his shirt, wanting to make him feel good too. I straddled him on the backseat, our bare chests rubbing together. His hard nipples tasted salty, and I could feel him huge and hard beneath me.

"This is the first time I'm doing this, you know."

He stopped. "Ah what you ah say?"

"This is my first time."

"You serious, darkie?"

"Uh-huh."

"Ras, and why you didn't say so?"

"I'm saying it now."

He held me away from him by my bare shoulders. "You telling me you never been with no man before?"

"I'm telling you. I kissed boys at home—a boy—but I've never done this."

Brent said "Ras" again, and then he started pulling up my clothes.

"No, no. What you doing?" I protested. "I want to do this." He was dressing me now the way I dressed Ben in his onesies for bed, bending my arms at the elbow to get my sleeves on. "Brent, what you doing?"

"This nah right, darkie. You not suppose to have your first time in the backseat ah no man car. First you nah tell me about your birthday, and now you wait until nearly too late to tell me this."

"Well, let's go to your apartment then."

He inhaled for a long time. "You know we can't do that."

Actually, I didn't know shit. Brent buttoned up his shirt. "Ah, little girl. Me wish me did meet up with you sooner."

"Don't do that, okay. Don't call me little girl. You don't know the first thing about me."

"Now you gone all stush on me again."

For some reason, him saying that made me really mad. "Ah, fuck you, Brent."

He laughed. "You cussing me? Me didn't know you even know how to use them kinda words. Don't cuss me, darkie. Is 'cause me like you so much me don't want take advantage of you, you know. You gone remember this all you life, and you don't want remember that you first time was in the backseat of a car park up on the corner of President and Rogers. Trust me, yeah."

"You telling me to trust you, and I don't know anything about you. I don't even know your last name."

"Nettleford."

I laughed. "Are you serious?"

"Winston Brently Nettleford. Junior."

"Jesus Christ. And what do you do for a living?"

"Nothing illegal. You have to take me word on that one. Donovan ah me friend from we grow up together in St. Catherine, but me not running the same racket as 'im."

"Do you have a gun?"

"What?"

"A gun. Do you have a gun?"

"Yes, darkie, me have a gun."

"Is it here?"

"Next question."

"And you live with a woman?"

"Yes, darkie, me live with a woman."

There, he had said it. I had known all along, but hearing him admit it still distressed me. This was to be nothing then. I wanted to feel relieved now that I knew for sure, but instead I was crushed. My nose pinched, and I felt the stupid tears prick my eyes. I moved off him and slumped in the seat. "Can you take me home?"

"You don't want go back to Kathy party?"

I shook my head. The night was over for me. Brent nodded, and we moved back to the front. He drove in silence down past the club, where some of the yardbirds had come out for fresh air. They looked cold and ridiculous in their fantastic outfits and mops of fake hair.

In front of Sylvia's building, I reached to open the car door, and Brent said, "Wait." He fumbled around under his seat and took out a small, un-wrapped box. "Here."

"What's this?"

"Open it and see."

Inside was an inky blue glass flowerpot, just the right size to plant one bulb. "Kathy tell me you like flowers, but me didn't know which kind, so me just get you the pot. Happy birthday, darkie."

My nose pinched again, and I knew that if I tried to speak, to say thank you, I would cry. He seemed to understand. At the elevator, I kissed him. I held his body and tried to draw life out of him. In my ear, Brent said, "Plant something nice to remember me, hear?"

SUNDAY AFTERNOON I MET Kath downtown. For the first time in months she was sparkle free. "I can't believe this," I said, sizing her up as we trolled the aisles at Conway, "not a rhinestone in sight. Kath, you feeling okay?"

She turned and made a face at me. She looked tired, and her eyes pulled down even more at the corners. "I dazzled enough last night to last for days."

It was she who had called at Sylvia's this morning and asked if I wanted to meet for something to eat and to talk about her party. So far, though, she hadn't said much. I didn't want to push her.

Conway sold everything. The clothing department was upstairs, but the basement housed linens, pots, toiletries, toilet seats, toilets, cosmetics, cribs. Everything cheap and ready to fall apart after two uses. I had picked up a small red penknife. "I'm not even asking why you're getting a weapon, Grace," Kath said.

"It's not a weapon, idiot. Dave's always complaining he needs a Swiss Army knife in his pocket, so there, Conway army knife."

Kath smiled, but she was restless. She walked up and down the aisles, taking up bottles and jars, putting them back down, opening them to sniff, chattering on about nothing and especially not about the party. Finally we paid and stepped out into the warm, bright sunshine. Spring, at least during the daytime, was in full season.

We sat down on one of the benches lining Fulton Street. "So how everything wind up last night?"

"Well, nobody get shot."

"Was that a real possibility?"

"Oh, Grace, you know how them Jamaican have no behavior. But no, everything went good. What about you? Don't think I didn't see you and Brent leave and not come back."

"You were spying on me?"

"Of course." She grinned.

"Well, nothing happened."

"Bullshit, Grace, I can't believe that. Not after how I do you up. Talk truth, man."

Fulton was busy this afternoon, guys on the street selling watches and tapes, women getting their shopping done. "I am talking truth. We went to his car, started to fool around, I told him I was a virgin, and he stopped."

"Ras," Kath exclaimed, "you shitting me? For real?"

"For real. He said I wouldn't want to remember that I lost my virginity in the back of a car. Not that anything seemed wrong to me. And then he brought me home and gave me an empty flowerpot."

Kath said "Ras" again. I didn't tell her the bit about Brent confessing he lived with a woman. I supposed she knew that already. She turned from me, and I heard her say, "Donovan wouldn't have cared one fuck."

"That's not true, Kath. Please, I saw the way he was with you last night."

She turned back to me. "Oh yeah, then why does that fucker want me to have an abortion?"

I stared at her and stared, and she looked right back at me without blinking. "Oh, my God. Kath, you're pregnant? How far? What are we going to do?"

"See, Grace, see how much you better than Donovan? First thing you ask: what we going to do? We. You could think about people other than yourself. Not that"—she kicked the Conway bag so hard the pink plastic split—"motherfucker." The word was a hiss.

"He told me he was going to leave her, you know. I wasn't going on empty promises. He told me that they were having serious problems and that he was as good as gone from that house. Then talk change. God, Grace"—Kath was crying openly now—"I so fucking stupid. God, I'm stupid."

I edged closer, and she sobbed on my shoulder. She mumbled something into my shirt.

"What?"

"I have to throw it away."

"Don't think about that now, Kath."

"Is almost nine weeks already, Grace. When else am I going to think about it? You will come with me?"

Oh, I didn't want to do this, to have any part of this at all. "Of course I will come with you, Kath."

We sat holding hands, watching the people walk by. "Oh, my God, Kathy, look who it is." I hadn't expected to see Brent this soon after last night. He was across the road from us, wearing a bright green uniform under a vest with orange hazard bars. He was pushing a broom in the crevice between the sidewalk and the road. Behind him was a huge rubbish bin on wheels. "Let me go and say hi."

Kathy squeezed my hand hard. "No, Grace."

"You mad or what. Why?"

"Grace, trust me, okay? Leave him alone."

"I just saw Brent last night, Kath. You must be crazy if you think I going to see him across the road from me and not go and say hi." I made to get up again, but Kath yanked me back.

"Why you always so harden?" She reminded me of my mother. "How long you know Brent? He ever tell you what he do for work?"

She had a point.

Kath was looking at me. "If you go over there now, you will shame him."

"What? That is so ridiculous, Kath. I don't care what Brent does." I almost added "as long as he doesn't deal drugs."

"Yes, but he care. You have to let them be men, Grace. If he never tell you where he working, then is because he didn't want you to know. If you go over there now, the two of you will feel shame."

I looked at Brent again. After every few strokes of the broom, he scooped up a big pile of Brooklyn rubbish and dumped it in his bin. No one paid any attention to him. I kind of understood what Kathy was saying, but I didn't understand being ashamed of making an honest living. Brent kept his eyes on the ground while he swept, seeing no one. Still Kath said, "Let's go before he sees us, yeah?"

"Yeah," I said. "Let's go."

Chapter 28

It was still too early for the park, so I dressed Ben to go down to Ule's floor to ask if she would mind him for a few hours on Thursday morning.

"Okay." I lifted Ben to the bell. "But only one ring. We like Ule."

He pushed the black button once and I kissed his neck before setting him down. The woman from the newsstand answered the door.

"Is Ule here?"

"Ule does not work here anymore. I am the new babysitter for this family."

"Since when?"

"Since today on a full-time basis." She looked me up and down. "I am Margaret."

Oh, I didn't like her at all. The way she spoke in that phony accent, putting a full stop at the end of every word like the bitchy girl behind the bulletproof glass at the Chinese restaurant on Nostrand. I couldn't believe that Ule would leave without saying good-bye to me.

"Is there something perchance I can help you with?"

Perchance? Who talked like that? "No. I was just looking for Ule."

At the Zollers', Ben rang the bell for ten seconds until Evie opened the door.

"Jesus Christ, me don't know why you always have to put on such a racket. Come quick, me getting ready for the park."

Ben ran ahead, and I followed Evie. She was in her housecoat and slippers with her bangs still rolled in her greasy sponge curler. As usual, the apartment was a mess. Sammy was dressed and waiting, and Evie crouched in front of the half-naked Caleb. "So what it is you want this hour of the morning?" she asked me.

"I need to ask you a favor."

"Fa-vah"—she bent the word into its two syllables—"what favor you come say you want from me, mama?"

I told her, watching how gently she coaxed Caleb's stiff arm into his sweater, and how she kissed his forehead when it peeked through. Done, she pivoted to me. "And why it is you don't go ask your best friend Ule to watch him?"

So she didn't know Ule had left either. I gave her the news. "Ule's gone, Evie. The Bloomberg lady has a new sitter."

Evie smiled. "You don't say. Ule did tell you she was leaving?"

I shook my head. "She said that the time for her to move on was near, but she didn't say last week was to be her last."

Evie rose and put her hand on my folded arms. "Is so black people stop, me child. You think you can trust somebody, and then them turn round and ram one knife straight in the middle of your back. Bring the likkle bad boy on Thursday. Me will watch him for free." She turned her back to me and fiddled with her curler. "What it is you have to do so important?"

"Something in Brooklyn" was all I said, and she shrugged her shoulders as if she couldn't care less.

IT WAS THE WRONG kind of morning for an abortion, too bright and too warm.

Kath learned against the dirty red brick of the family planning center. She wore a black tracksuit that made her look bigger than she was, and she cradled an enormous handbag in the crook of her elbow. She waved, and as I walked over I saw that she had been crying. "Hey, Kath," I said. "Are you okay?"

"Not even close, but my mind is made up. No drama, Grace. Let's just go and get this over with."

As I took Kath's hand, a woman trotted up holding a placard over one shoulder and two brochures veeing out like tickets. She blocked our path and whispered, "Please don't kill your baby."

We both stopped. The picture on her placard looked like chunks of pork, fresh and bloody from the abattoir.

I blinked at her. "What did you say?"

"Jesus loves your baby."

Kath started to cry.

The woman smiled.

"Get the fuck away from us," I said.

She didn't move and started singing, *"In the name of Jesus, In the name of Jesus, we shall have a victory."* I heard Kath's snotty inhale, and the woman tilted her head, pretending to understand everything. People on the street walked by, minding their own business.

"You need to back the fuck up," I told her. Seeing that woman in front of us, having no idea who we were or what we were about, made me want to hit her so hard. I reached back and grabbed Kath's hand, dragging her straight into the building and the empty elevator.

"Okay, now you're really upset. Shit," I said to her.

"Grace." Kath used the heel of her fist to wipe her nose and laughed-cried. "I never hear you cuss so much."

"That woman made me so vex." I was looking at the numbers light up over the elevator door, no unlucky thirteen. "But what do you want to do?"

Kath found a fresh white tissue from deep within her bag and blew her stuffed-up nose. "I said no drama, right?"

"Right."

"Well, no drama. Let's just go and get this over with already."

Then I knew I was a hypocrite, because what I wanted was for the scene with the little woman to have upset Kath enough to make her change her mind.

In the waiting room, under a hard, bright white, fluorescent light, sat a middle-aged woman with big breasts and a black girl who looked to be our age. There were three faded, gold-framed posters on the walls. One was of a white woman in a graduation cap and gown brandishing a diploma in victory; one of a unibrowed Hispanic woman in a business suit with huge shoulder pads gesturing from behind a desk; and the third of a black woman in overalls and a hard hat grinning and giving a thumbs-up from inside a manhole. A plastic ficus tree with dusty leaves and fake mulch sat in a planter next to the only window, which looked out on a brick wall. Kath went up to the counter, and I sat down in the one empty folding chair next to the girl. Her arms, extended like bars of steel, ended in fists clenched on her knees, and all her veins stood out. I had an unkind thought about her knees pressed together so tightly now and smiled at her to make up for my silent rudeness. She smiled back with nostrils flared, and I could see that she was terrified.

As Kath filled out her forms, a side door opened and a child walked out. I mean she couldn't have been more than twelve or thirteen. A nurse held her elbow and guided her unsteady step over to the middle-aged woman. She stood and hugged the child, who, dazed, did not hug back. She stroked the child's long black hair. *"Pobrecita."*

I tried not to stare.

The woman held the child. "Is finish?" she asked the nurse. "Gone?"

"Yes," the nurse replied. "Gone." And then, "You need us to call you a cab?"

"No, no. Bus."

They left, and the black girl said, "Puerto Rican."

Kath sat down and reached for a magazine on a low center table. "It shouldn't be too long, Grace. You will probably reach back to work by"—she looked at her watch—"eleven-forty-five, twelve."

"Kath I'm not even thinking about leaving. Evie taking him to the park, she'll feed him if I'm not back."

"I cannot stand that *comess* woman. God, she common."

"I can't stand her either, but look how Ule is the one who upped and disappeared." I couldn't believe that we were having this conversation.

The nurse came out again and glanced at her clipboard. "Jacqui Fentson."

The black girl didn't move.

"Come with me, please."

Jacqui Fentson still didn't move, and both Kath and I looked at her. She turned to Kath. "If you're in a hurry, you can go before me, you know."

The nurse turned to Kath, and she looked at me and shrugged.

"I told you I'm not in any rush, Kath."

She picked her bag up off the floor. "Ah shit, Grace, this chair uncomfortable as hell. Let me just get it over with."

"You sure?" I asked. But Kath had already got up and was walking toward the nurse. Jacqui Fentson nodded her approval.

The nurse said, "Why don't you leave your bag with your friend?" And Kath turned back and dumped the big red mess on my lap. "See you in half hour," she said.

I leafed through one of the college catalogs mixed in with the fashion magazines. The office was warm and still. No music played. Nobody came in. It was just Jacqui Fentson and me. She sat there in her robot pose, looking down at the floor. Outside the single window, the wind rose with a hollow *whoop,* and she grabbed my wrist in a vise hold. "Oh, my God, is that it . . . are they doing it?"

"What?" Her hand was freezing cold.

"That noise! Is that . . . the machine? The one they use to—? Oh, my God. What am I doing here?" And Jacqui Fentson released my wrist, picked up her backpack, and ran.

In the end, Kath insisted that I not come home with her, just put her in a car. "You tell me I'm stubborn," I said to her as we both held on to the cab door, I trying to open it and Kath pulling it shut from inside, "but you're the stubborn one. Look, you barely have enough energy to hold on to the door."

"Grace, just let me go alone, okay. Thanks for coming, but I need to go home and sleep. I'll call you when I come back to work."

I let go of the door, and she closed it with so little strength I needed to reopen and slam it again. Kath didn't wave, only slumped against the upholstery and hugged her red bag close as the cabbie drove off.

OF COURSE SUMMER WAS my favorite season. I loved the heat, the humidity, and the hot afternoon sun that was more brutal than anything I had ever felt at home. Ben had traded the sandbox for the sprinklers, and I often took him out again after lunch, when the sun was hottest and the other sitters had retreated to Evie's for cards and soaps and naps. In the days after Kath's abortion, I didn't want to see any of them. I didn't want to deal with Petal's righteousness or Meena's repeated awe that I was pretty even though I was black black, or Marva's silent bruises. I wanted to be home reading in my gallery with my mother washing clothes outside, my father gone to work, and Helen taking a nap. I wanted normal.

Ben looked me in the eyes one morning when I bent to buckle him into his stroller. "Why you so sad, Grace?" he asked.

I almost lied to him, but then I said, "I miss my mommy."

He understood. "Don't worry, Grace. You'll see her when you go home."

And I wondered when that was going to be.

Downstairs in front of Duke's podium, I ran into Evie. "You going park?" she asked.

As if there was anyplace else.

"Wait then," she said, "me will walk over with you."

Duke ignored me and saluted Ben. "Good morning, Mr. Benjamin, sir."

Evie angled the twins' massive double stroller through the single doorway. I loved the wave of warm air after the cold air-conditioning. I followed Evie out to the pavement.

"So me hear your lady not going back to work after she make baby?"

"Maternity leave, Evie."

"Not that me talking about. I hear she not going back at all, at all."

"Where'd you hear that?"

"Oh." Evie pushed the twins back and forth as if she still comforted babies. "Is news I giving you, then?"

They hadn't told me a thing. "Who told you that, Evie?"

She turned and looked at me full-on. Through the grease-clumped hair of her bangs, I saw peaks of ripened pimples on her forehead. "Oh, I not telling no tales on nobody, mama. When you see name call later, nobody can say Evie was involved in so-and-so. I learn my lesson with nigger people long before you was born. Anyhow, long time now me no see the thick, brown-skin girl with one piece of hair like donkey tail you lime with. She get fired for looking too nice?"

"No, Evie." I laughed in spite of how bitchy she was. "Kath's sick."

"And who take she work? The people looking for somebody to mind the baby? She coming back?"

I stared at her for three seconds and pushed on, furious that she didn't ask about Kath. She trotted to keep up with my stride. "Eh, like you want to leave Miriam to go and take that work instead?"

I escaped with Ben to the sprinklers. None of the other sitters ever came into the water, and I didn't mind getting wet with him. I grabbed Ben under the arms and ran him squealing through the spitting whales, and when I saw Bruce looking at us just outside the water's reach, I grabbed him and ran him through too. Petal was nowhere to be seen, but through the rainbow spray I thought I saw Ule's familiar profile. I couldn't believe it. There she was sitting on a bench in the park, pushing a new carriage with her foot and holding a folded newspaper less than an inch away from her eyes. Evie's double-wide was parked in front of the bench, and she and Margaret sat next to Ule, chatting.

I ran over to her and jumped up and down like an idiot, getting water on them all. "Ule!" I squealed as loud as Ben had in the sprinklers. "What you doing here?"

The paper snapped her forehead, and she kicked away the carriage. "But look my crosses. Child, is heart attack you want me to get heart attack and drap dead right here in the people park? Look how you make me heart beat fast. Is where you want me to be?"

"I thought you were gone, Ule."

"Gone where, child?"

"Just gone." I looked over to the two of them sitting on the bench. "Margaret's working for Linda Bloomberg, and Evie said—"

Evie scrambled from the bench and looked at me. "What me say, missy? Come, let me hear what me tell you." The twins looked up at her from their shaded seats.

And then, come to think of it, I realized that Evie hadn't said anything specific. She'd never actually said that Ule had gone. She tapped her foot. "Well, is wait I waiting to hear. You know why you have nothing to say? Is because is lie you lying. Not one thing me tell you. Always playing you so quiet."

Margaret rose too, nylon fabric rustling, and put her hand on Evie's heaving shoulder. "Mind your blood pressure, now." And to me she said, "Grace, is perhaps best if you said no more." She bent to unbuckle Sammy and Caleb. "I cannot abide this heat. It is worse than in Bimshire, not true?"

I wanted to choke her. "Why you wearing a tracksuit if you're so hot, Margaret?"

Ule tsked, and Evie answered for her fellow Bajan. "Is not everybody like to show off their body line to all Tom, Dick, and Harry, you know."

Ule said, "Especially them that don't have body line to show off."

Margaret freed the twins. "Go frolic in the water," she told them. "Evie will soon be with you." They moved away like little old people, and Ule shook her head. "Is a sad sad thing to see little mongoloid children, eh?"

Evie wheeled around with her hands on her hips and bent her face low to meet Ule's. "Don't call them that, you hear. Is Down syndrome them have. Don't you call them no mongoloid."

"But, Evie, you acting like I insult your grand. Is not mongoloid we call them mongoloid in the West Indies?"

"Well, we not in the West Indies now, is we? No need to act ignorant in this here America."

Ule set down her paper and started to rise from the bench. "Who you say you calling ignorant, Evie? Don't make me get off this bench here this God early morning. You best watch your mouf." Her accent thickened, and I wondered if Margaret and I were going to have to part a fight between two grown women.

Evie backed down. "Come, Maggie. I don't have time this morning to sit down in idle hall. All I want is for black people to mind they own business and leave my name out of they *comess*."

They walked off, and I was stunned. I didn't know what had just happened. Ule saw the look on my face. "Sit down," she said to me. I sat next to her. "All me will say is this. You like me own daughter. You think I would up and leave and not tell you say me gone? Not give you a telephone number or a address on a piece of paper for you to come and look for me on a Sunday evening? That sound like me?"

It didn't sound like her at all, and I wondered if I just wasn't very bright. That it was so easy for Evie to fool me. I didn't want to cry, but I couldn't help it. Tears slid down my face, and I pulled in my lower lip. Ule put her arm around my shoulder, and I leaned into her, crying more. Ben paid us no mind as he and Bruce dodged in and out of the mist.

"Come now, Grace. You can't let people get you down. This America is a hard hard place, and sometimes you got to harden yourself to get by. I sure your mother tell you not all skin teef is grin?"

And boy had she. Whenever the *comess* women waved at us sitting in the gallery, or told her that she was lucky to have such good daughters, she said it low and urgent: *remember all skin teeth is not grin.*

"You good now?"

I blew my nose, and Ule swung the carriage around. She reached in and took out a tight single bundle, fat like a caterpillar ready to burst its cocoon.

"Ule, that child too hot. Is ninety degrees out here," I said to her.

"Don't start with your stupidness." She cradled the baby in her arms and pulled the blanket away from its face.

"Okay," I said, "this is a good-looking baby." The tiny pink face was perfect. No blotches or splotches, no cone head, no squashed nose. No marks at all to mar pure beauty. I stared at the baby's face, and then she yawned long and opened bright blue eyes. "Here"—Ule passed her to me— "hold she let me get the bottle. The mother saving she breasts for Miss America."

I couldn't believe how light she was. How whole. I shifted the baby in my arms and looked down at her small, round head, the crescent-moon slices of her closed eyes. And then I started to cry again.

"But what trouble is this." Ule sat back and looked at me. "Child, don't tell me say you making baby, you know. Them likkle and nice, but is one whole heap of work and money it take to raise them right."

I didn't say anything. Ule looked at me for another second and went back to rooting around in the baby's bag.

Later, after Ben was dried and drowsily sipping juice in his carriage, and Ule had agreed to unwrap one layer of the baby's swaddling, the other sitters began to leave the playground for cooler climes. Bruce passed by, and a small Chinese woman with a wide rice-picker's hat held his hand.

"Where Petal, Ule?"

"Long gone like she was never here, child."

Chapter 29

One late June morning Miriam announced that the baby was de
manding fresh strawberries.

Sol snapped his newspaper. "And why, pray tell, didn't Grace
get strawberries at the farmers' market yesterday?"

"Because, male of the species"—there was laughter in her voice—
"yesterday your fetus wanted my mother's meatballs. Today it's strawberries."

Ben smacked his lips. "I love red strawberries, Mommy."

"See? We'll drive up to the country. I'm not doing anything else."

I listened from the kitchen, happy with what I had heard. Driving to
the country to pick strawberries sounded so American. The countryside
would be fresh and clean, a minty green place for picnics with checkered
tablecloths, crustless sandwiches, and tall glasses of cool iced tea.

"Planning to stop by Duck Hollow?" Sol asked.

"If I have the energy, maybe."

"Well, take the keys," he went on. "Maybe a visit will tempt you."

"We'll see."

Miriam was over six months pregnant and so big already she waddled.
"Grace, we're going to the country to pick strawberries. Pack Ben's bag
and make me smoked turkey with honey mustard, jalapeños, and sprouts.
Mmm, lots of jalapeños. Make yourself a sandwich too. But use the
bologna. It should still be good." Her voice seemed to have thickened
with the weight of her pregnancy.

"When are we leaving?" I asked. I wanted to change.

"Soon as you're done with lunch and Ben's ready."

I hurried and, between making lunch and dressing Ben, slipped into my brand-new halter. I'd been waiting for the right day to wear it.

"Come on, mister," I said to Ben as I turned off *Pooh*. "Time to go pick strawberries."

He slid his bottom off his furry chair. "You look very nice, Grace."

"Thank you, Ben." I kissed the top of his head, realizing that he'd just made me really, really happy.

"Grace, can I wear my orange shirt too? Then we match."

"Of course you can. Let's find it."

"Oh, and my choo-choo pants, then I can look like a farmer."

"Okey doke." I found his Wednesday overalls and dressed him on the floor, the two of us making up verses to "Old MacDonald."

Sol appeared in the doorway. "You guys almost ready?"

In fact we were. I pulled Ben up by his arms, and we turned to face his father, who wolf-whistled. "Grace, you look smokin' in that top," he said. He looked at Ben. "Hey, buddy, tell Grace orange is a pretty color."

"I already tell her she look nice, Daddy poopy." He ran to hug his father's legs.

Miriam came up behind him. "Sol's right, Grace. Orange goes well with your black skin. Why did you put Ben in overalls?"

"Because I'm Old MacDonald, Mommy. We going to a farm."

Before she could say anything about our matching colors, I said, "And Ben chose his orange shirt himself. Didn't you, Ben?"

He tugged on his collar. "Look, Mom, me and Grace twins like Caleb and Sammy."

Sol looked at his watch. "Okay, I have to get going. You guys have a good time. Grace"—he raised both eyebrows—"look out for the farm-hands."

"Is everything ready, Grace?" Miriam asked.

It was. "Good," she said, and then added, "You might want to wear a shirt over your top. It can get hot out in the sun."

"She's an island girl, Miriam. I bet you Grace loves the heat."

"I know what kind of girl she is, Sol." Miriam bit her lip. "All I'm saying is that she might want to take a cover-up, just in case."

I didn't want to put a shirt over the top that I'd waited so long to wear, but I didn't want to piss off Miriam either. "I'll get a shirt. Better safe than sorry," I told them. It was something my mother said at least twice a day.

"Hurry up, Grace. We've wasted enough time already this morning," Miriam said.

And again I hurried, even though I knew full well that I hadn't done anything to slow us down.

TACONIC. I LIKED THE sharp edges of that word—Taconic. Ben had fallen asleep, and Miriam, driving I thought a little too fast on the curvy road, talked to me more than she ever had. Mostly she asked questions.

"So, Grace, how come you don't have a boyfriend?"

"I haven't met anyone."

"Don't you go out on the weekend? Clubbing at Limelight and Webster Hall? Palladium?"

I didn't know what those places were. "No. Sometimes I go out with Kathy. But not too much."

"I went out all the time before I got married. I'd come into the city with my brother and we'd dance all night long."

She turned off the air conditioner and rolled down the windows. Before we'd left the house, she'd tied a yellow scarf around her yellow hair. When it was pulled back, you could see her darker roots.

"Miriam?"

"Mmm?"

"Nothing's come for me in the mail?"

"Why would you get mail at our house?"

I supposed I couldn't expect my business to occupy her mind, but I had been thinking about the mail nonstop. "My green card application. I thought something might have come from INS by now."

"Of course." She looked over at me. "You know I've completely forgotten about that." She pushed another button, and the sunroof slid soundlessly back. "Why don't you just get married to an American, Grace? Wouldn't that be much easier?"

We were just done talking about me not having a boyfriend and now she was asking me why I didn't get married? "I don't have an American to marry."

"Yeah, but you could get a man like that." And she snapped her fingers like Bridget had. "A white man, even. Hey"—she glanced away from the road to me—"what about Danny?"

"Danny the doorman?"

"Yeah, Danny. You two should go out."

I thought about Danny and his mouth full of overlapping teeth. I thought about him breathing on me and laughed. "Danny's not my type, Miriam."

"Well, beggars can't be choosers."

I wanted to tell her that I wasn't begging, but instead I watched the trees. Whenever the forest cleared or the car crested a hill, beautiful rolling farmland, laid out in neat squares, stretched forever. This was what I had always thought a farm should look like. My mother's garden was reclaimed jungle land. Her crops were divided not by banked hillocks and ancient stone walls but by tall plantain patches clumped together like old *higue* sisters.

"How long you think it'll take INS to get back to us?" I asked.

Miriam shrugged. "I haven't the faintest idea how that stuff works." She felt around the dashboard and turned on the radio. R.E.M.'s "Losing My Religion." I sang along, feeling hopeful and homesick at the same time. Miriam laughed. "Your voice might actually be worse than mine, Grace."

I didn't doubt her. Helen sang in the village choir; I stacked chairs after their concerts. "Yeah, but this song is beautiful."

"I like it too." Miriam started singing. Our voices together were terrible, but for a moment, speeding up the Taconic, we almost felt like friends.

WE WERE INDEED ON Old MacDonald's farm. The bright red barn had big Xs crossing the opened windows. The farmhouse was set off on a hill and was surrounded by a low, white picket fence. The grassy field was dotted with picnic benches, and while they weren't covered with checkered cloths, the raw, worn wood looked just as authentic as I'd imagined. I don't know who was more excited, Ben or me. He ran ahead, shouting at us to look at everything.

"There's the barn, Mommy. Grace, look, cows! Old MacDonald had a farm. Mooo!"

I had taken the bag from the car but left my shirt on the front seat. The air was warm, and the sun shone silver bright from a cloudless blue canopy. Miriam waddled over to one of the benches. "What kind of farm is this?" I asked as I took out the sandwiches.

"Mostly fruit, I think," she said. "Peaches and strawberries—pick your own type deal. They come down to the market in Union Square, but mostly to advertise and to get city folk to come up."

"But they aren't city folk," I said, referring to a group of women nearby.

Miriam spun around and sneered. "Oh, no. Orthodox."

The Orthodox women sat at many of the benches with lots and lots of children. In a way that my mother would approve of and that so annoyed me, their heads were covered with dull-colored turbans, and even though it was so warm, they wore long-sleeved shirts and gathered skirts that came to the laces on their running shoes.

"Are they Jewish?"

Miriam shaded her eyes. "Ultra. They live in some kind of commune near here." The Orthodox women had brought plenty of food—jars of gefilte fish, boxes of crackers, and bags of bagels. Their children too ran around, beautiful boys with long eyelashes and side curls, and girls in full-length dresses and flyaway plaits. Their Hebrew was punctuated with calls to Avi and Dov and Gitty.

Miriam said, maybe to me but likely to herself, "Two and I'm done."

I was surprised to see that the farmer was a black guy in his early twenties. His denim overalls looked like Ben's, and he wore a plaid shirt and a green bandanna knotted around his neck.

"All right," he called, "are we all ready?" The Orthodox children scampered up some steps into a wagon hitched to a tractor. Their mothers came behind them, and we followed. The farmer, or maybe he was the farmer's son, didn't offer to help any of the women up the steps, but when he saw Miriam in her white short shorts and tented gingham top, he reached for her hand. Ben didn't want his help, but the farmer placed his hand on the small of my bare back to guide me, even though there were only three steps. He touched my back and said "hi" in a low voice. I grinned and sat on the plank next to Miriam.

"Are you comfortable?" I asked her.

"No. What did that guy say to you?"

"Nothing. Hi."

"Okay, just know that you're not up here to make friends, okay? Hold Ben on your lap."

I guided Ben over, and as the farmer came around to the front of the tractor, he gave me a look with raised eyebrows. I ignored him and said to Ben, "Are you ready, mister?"

"Ready, Grace!"

We drove away from the picnic area, and the Orthodox children started singing. Ben stared. Miriam closed her eyes, and I watched the farm roll by. I loved it. I liked that the trees were planted in straight lines, that the lettuce was evenly spaced, that the scarecrows wore hats, that there were bunnies . . .

Miriam opened her eyes and looked at me. And then she laughed.

"What?"

Ben said, "What so funny, Mommy?"

The roar of the tractor made it difficult to hear much, but Miriam sang in her wobbly voice, "*'Gonna pick a bale of cotton, Oh lordy, Gonna pick a bale a day.'* Do you know that song, Grace?"

"Never heard it before."

"Are you sure?" She was still laughing and had one hand steadying her belly. "My dad used to sing it whenever he drove us out of the city in the summertime." She closed her eyes again. "This brings back memories."

When the tractor stopped near a wide shade tree with a bench underneath, the farmer catapulted out of his seat. "Okay, everybody out. Here's how it works. You can eat as many strawberries as your tummies can hold, and fill your bags to the top. We're here for"—he checked his watch—"two hours, and then we head back. Get pickin'!"

"Come, Mommy, we have to get our strawberries," Ben said.

Miriam reached into her handbag and pulled out the sack she had paid for at the barn. "Here, Grace. Try and find ripe ones, big ones. Make sure they're red, the pale ones aren't sweet." She sat down on the bench and took out a fat Danielle Steel novel. I just stared. "What?" she said. "I can't bend over to pick strawberries. Take Ben with you."

Ben said, "Come, Grace."

We walked down the first row, and Miriam called out, "Only ripe ones, remember."

Now, I thought, my mother would enjoy the farm. If she could see me dressed up in my expensive halter and laboring, she would be satisfied.

Ben and I picked berries. At first, we ate more than we put in the bags; the sweet, warm fruit was like fresh-made jam. Around us the Orthodox women picked too, and their children ran up and down the rows with red juice staining their mouths and faces.

After about forty-five minutes, Ben said, "I tired, Grace."

"Me too, mister," I told him. I held up our full sack. "Think we have enough?"

He thought so.

"Hi." Miriam looked up from her book. "Did you guys have a good time?" She pulled out a fat strawberry by the stem. "Oh, this is so good. Good work, Ben."

"Grace pick a lot of strawberries," he said as he crawled into her lap. "Tell Grace good work too, Mommy."

"Good work too, Grace," Miriam said as she ate more berries from the bag.

I was about to sit down on the bench when Miriam, her mouth full, said, "Uh-uh." She took out a second sack and flapped it open. "For Ettie."

How I wanted to say no. How I wanted to tell her that the pregnant Orthodox women seemed to be able to bend over and pick strawberries just fine and that nowhere on the list of my responsibilities did it say farmhand. But I didn't. I couldn't. I took the bag and went back to the rows. Ben didn't come this time. An Orthodox woman bent over in the row next to mine looked at me and smiled. I smiled back at her.

The young farmer had been making his way among the pickers. "Having fun?" he asked, looking down at me.

"Not anymore. This is hard work."

"You telling me."

"So"—I glanced over at Miriam, who was absorbed in her book—"this is your family farm?"

"Are you for real?" He grinned. "I'm from Maryland. This is summer work. I'm a senior at Cornell."

I laughed. "So you're not the farmer's son?"

"Hell no. My dad's a D.C. lawyer. I either had to go caddy at Burning Tree or do this shit this summer. . . . I prefer to not carry other people's loads."

"That makes sense to me."

"So what's your story?" he asked. "Where you from?"

"Caribbean."

"And what, you and your girlfriend drove up to the farm for the day? You missing the old country?"

"She's my boss. I take care of her son."

He looked at me. "For real? So you're the mammy?" He pronounced it different from me.

"No, I'm the babysitter."

He shook his head. "You island people keep setting us back, man. What you doing minding white people's kids? You need to be reading some books, girl."

I took a step back from him, and then another, and then I turned around and walked away fast, crossing over the rows, putting space and strawberries between the two of us as quickly as I could. When I was good and far away, I stooped down again and finished filling up the sack.

On the drive back down, Miriam wanted to know what he'd said to me. "I saw you talking to him."

"He was talking to everyone. I think it's part of his job."

"So, what did he say to you?"

"Nothing, just were we enjoying the farm and were the strawberries sweet."

"He didn't want your number?" She glanced away from the Taconic to me.

"No."

MIRIAM DROVE UP THE rutted road while Ben, tuckered out from his afternoon in the sun, slept peacefully. His red-stained face matched his red hair, and he looked like a boy clown at the end of a party. The car turned in to a dirt driveway with an old wooden sign shaped like a duck, its gray and white feathers weathered and faded. I could make out some letters on its raised wing: DUCK HOLLOW.

Miriam got out. "Stay by the car with Ben," she told me.

She unlocked the side gate and went around the back. The house was big, with windows stretching away from both sides of the entrance for two stories, up to the attic. A dried wreath hung from the front door. The land off to the right was terraced and banked like the farm in miniature, except the squares held no crops. And the flowers all around—marigolds, dahlias, sunflowers, roses—needed to be pruned and weeded.

I walked off a bit, still close to the car. Some oaks on the property I recognized, but none of the immortelles and poui I knew from the forests back home. But there was a willow. I'd never seen one before, but I knew that's what the tree had to be. Long branches hung down to the ground like uncombed hair obscuring a crazy face. Hair that needed to be lovingly brushed back and plaited the way my mother did for Helen and me before we were too old to resist. Under the leaves the air was green, the color of the dark walk to my mother's farm. No matter how hot the day, the forest roof shaded the track and kept you cool until the dry brightness of our fields.

I liked the way the leaves on the willow curled into scrolls, and the way the branches shushed together as the wind blew through. This spot was magic. And then I realized that Dave and Vincent must have thought so too. At the base of the tree's trunk was a small marble heart with the initials V F. "Oh," I said out loud and stepped away from this hallowed ground.

I went back and sat in the car. Ben sighed in his sleep. The leaves of the willow writhed like something alive. Miriam came around the way she had gone, walking slowly, and I could see old Mrs. Forgione stamped on her. She got into the car, took a tissue from her purse, and blew her slender nose hard. She'd been crying.

She hesitated before putting the key in the ignition. I hesitated too. I wanted to reach out to her, to ask if she was all right.

"Miriam, are you—"

"Huh, Grace. Your nice top got stained with strawberry juice. That'll never come out."

I'd seen the drops dotting the front of my halter, plus Ben's small red handprint. Maybe the cleaners downstairs could make the fabric clean again. And even if he couldn't I realized that I wasn't upset. It had been a beautiful day. As Miriam drove away from Duck Hollow I pulled the paperback out of her handbag.

"What page are you on, Miriam?"

Her eyes were red. "It's bent in. Why?"

"I'll read out loud while you drive?" She could only say no.

She looked at me again and shrugged. Then she laughed a little. And I started to read.

Chapter 30

Not two weeks later Dave rang the Bruckners' doorbell. It was early, nine o'clock in the morning. "Hey, Maria full of Grace," he said in an exaggerated Brooklyn accent. "How ya doin'?"

"I'm doin' good," she Brooklyned back. Dave had his arm around her neck as they walked to where I sat on the floor with Ben. He obviously hadn't combed his hair yet, and Miriam tried to fluff the flattened side with her fingers. "What are you doing here this early?"

Ben ran over to Dave. "Hi, *zio,* Grace and I are going to the playground. Want to come with the doggies?"

Dave flipped him onto his back. Miriam covered her eyes. "No, I do not want to go to your baby playground," he told his nephew, "but that's why I'm here." He kept Ben upside down. "Mir, I'm going to Brooklyn to the gardens, and I wanted to see if you wouldn't let Ben and Grace Jones come along."

Dave winked at me, and my heart did a jump. I needed a break from the summertime routine. Lately, I'd been doing what my mother called taking stock and had realized that I was tremendously bored. Being in the towers was far better than being at Sylvia's, but still, day in and out, I minded Ben. This was my job, and the luster of going to Union Square almost every day was beginning to dull. I waited to hear what Miriam would say.

"Do you have a car seat in that truck?" she asked.

"Oh, come on, Miriam. What's going to happen? Grace can sit in the back and hold him if you're scared. Plus"—he looked at his bare wrist—"we'll be there in fifteen minutes. Or have you forgotten the way to Brooklyn? And, got ya, he doesn't use car seats in cabs."

She made a face. "I don't know. I've been trying to keep him out of Brooklyn as much as possible."

"Oh, Sister Maria Forgione"—Dave sounded scandalized—"you are such a hypocrite."

Miriam shook her blond and black hair. "The opposite of a hypocrite, actually. But okay, they can go."

Dave grinned. "How long till you're ready, Grace?"

I was ready now. "Whenever you are. I just need to pack Ben's bag."

He checked the time on the sunflower clock. "Okay, let's meet up in the lobby in fifteen." Twenty minutes later, as we headed downtown in Dave's truck that was meant for hauling garden supplies, he looked over at me. "So, Ms. Jones, how are you going to thank me for making your day?"

I rooted around in Ben's bag for the comb and hairbrush. "I'm going to work on your hedge."

When we got out, Dave said, "Do you know where you are?"

I laughed and opened the back door to get Ben. "Dave, I stay right down the road on weekends."

"You do? Down by the Lubavitchers? Then you go to the garden all the time. And here I was thinking I was giving you a treat."

We crossed the parkway. "You know what," I said as I held Ben on my hip, "I've never been to the gardens."

"Well, good," Dave said. "Or maybe not good that you haven't gone, but good still. I get to take you to one of the most beautiful places in Brooklyn."

The gates revealed a secret world hidden in plain sight, and it was just blocks from Sylvia's apartment. Noisy Eastern Parkway fell away, and suddenly we were in paradise. Ben ran along the paths ahead of us, and I stopped and turned to Dave. "You must be kidding me."

He put both hands on his waist and laughed. "What?"

"How come I didn't know this place existed? Dave, look."

We'd come to the lookout. Spread below us were rows of trees set on trim lawns and a rambling rose garden in full bloom, all bordered with forest trees that kept the Brooklyn I had come to know at bay. Ben ran to us and back, checking out the water fountains and doing cartwheels on the grass—trying to, anyway. Dave, happy to be showing me around, watched and waited patiently as I gaped at every leaf and flower.

"How long has this been here, Dave?"

He shrugged. "A hundred years? From the early nineteen hundreds, at least. Vincent would have known exactly."

"He liked coming here?"

"He used to be a gardener here."

"Oh."

"Okay"—Dave started walking downhill—"let's go down to the back. I need to order magic muck."

The muck turned out to be compost, and since the guys were still turning the heap, Dave ordered some bags to be delivered when the rot was at its peak.

"Want to go sit in the cherry orchard before it gets too hot?" he asked.

While Ben wove in and out of the shady trees with twin boys he had met, I got my comb and brush and knelt behind Dave.

"Okay, I'm going to plait your hair."

He leaned his head back. "I'm game. How are you going to do it?"

"Cane rows."

"You mean cornrows?"

"That's what they call it in America, but I guess on the island slaves planted rows of cane, so we ended up with a different name."

"Huh." Dave looked at me. "That's so very, very plausible, Grace."

"Thank you. Now stop turning around." His curls were not easy to part. "Dave, you need to use conditioner."

He tried to look around again, and I tapped him with the comb. "Ow, Grace. You know, since Vincent died, I don't think I've bought a single grooming product not meant for a dog or a plant."

I decided to go ahead and ask him. "How long ago did he die, Dave? If you don't mind me asking."

"No, no, it's okay. It'll be two years now come December."

December would also make it two years since I had come to America. I thought that, exactly when I had been at the airport and afterward, Dave had been dealing with Vincent dying. "And he was sick?"

Dave took a big inhale. He waited until Ben and the twins ran past and said, "Leukemia."

"Oh, I thought—" I shushed myself before I said it.

"What? Did you think he died of AIDS?"

I nodded because I had thought so, and I had wondered if Dave wasn't also sick.

"Don't worry. Everyone thinks he died of AIDS, but it was cancer. As if it should make a difference. Gone is gone."

"So how come the Forgiones didn't come to see him, then?"

"Because, Grace, it had nothing to do with him being sick. They cut him off because he was gay. They just couldn't deal with that in that family. The only reason they deal with Miriam's conversion is because the old bastard of a father can't stand to lose two children."

He stopped when Ben ran up for a drink, and I had a chance to think about what he'd said. Ben stared at the plaits I'd made in his *zio's* head as he drank the juice and then wandered off again. Dave said, "I am forever making you depressed, Grace Jones."

He made me think. "It's sad, though," I told him.

"So, okay, my turn. Can I ask you something?"

"Sure." He tried to turn, and I swatted him again with the comb.

"Ow. Okay, you don't have to answer it if you don't want to, but I'm curious."

"Now I'm curious too."

"Seriously. How'd you end up in America working for Sol and Miriam? Your folks are still back on the island, right? What, you just got on a plane and came to Brooklyn?"

Funny how simple truth can be. "You know, that's about right." I told him about my aunt and my mother and Daddy and Helen; about leaving home; about the scary flight; and about my cousin not picking me up at JFK.

He turned again. "Wait, no one picked you up?"

I didn't spank him. "Nope."

"And you were how old?"

"Sixteen."

"Jesus, Grace. So what did you do?"

"I took a cab to Brooklyn to a friend's house."

"What do you mean you took a cab? To which friend? What happened?"

"Dave"—I pushed his head forward and started plaiting again—"you sure you want to hear this?"

"Yes, Grace. I do. . . . Tell me the whole story."

The whole story. Kathy knew pieces—Sylvia and Mora too—but I'd never told the entire tale from beginning to end. How could I? It was still a story without an end. I took a breath, made a fresh part the length of Dave's head, and thought back to waiting for my cousin.

"Well, once upon a time . . ."

"Cut it out, Grace. Be straight with me."

I decided not to point out the joke in what he had just said. "Well, okay. I waited for almost three hours, and then a man in a trench coat came up and asked if everything was all right. He had the bluest eyes, and I knew enough to know that men in those kinds of coats are usually trouble, so I told him everything's fine, thank you. Then a taxi driver who turned out to be from Trinidad asked me if I was all right. I told him I was waiting for my cousin, but for hours. He asked me if I didn't have her phone number. You know, the country mook that I was I didn't even think to call. Without me even asking, he gave me a handful of unfamiliar change and showed me where the phones were. Man, I called and called, and the coins kept falling into the return slot. The taxi driver was gone and the trench coat man came back and then I noticed he was wearing a badge. I told him my call wasn't going through, and he said I didn't need to dial the area code. Next try went through, and I got my cousin's answering machine. I left her a message. I left her about five messages. And then I remembered some other telephone numbers I had. My friend Colette had come to America just before me with her family. Her youngest sister, the one who's a little touched in the head, answered, and she yelled to Colette that Gracie was on the phone. I heard Colette say, 'Gracie better not be calling collect, you know.' At first she didn't believe I was at JFK. Then she said hang up let her call her mother at work and to call her back in ten minutes. I called back in seven. Her mother said to take a taxi and come to their house immediately. Don't talk to anyone.

"I went up to a taxi driver and told him I need to go to Rockaway Parkway, please, but I only have this money, and I showed him the traveler's checks my mother had got from the bank in Penal. He put my suitcase in his trunk, locked his car, and took me to a counter in the airport to cash the checks. Then we drove into Brooklyn, the two of us alone in this black car as big as the prime minister's limo. The driver asked me if this was my first time in America. When I told him yes, he looked at his watch and at me in the rearview. 'Make some Bajan friends,' he said. 'Bajans won't steer you wrong. Trinis like to party too much.' I said 'yes,' but nothing else because I didn't want to talk. I wanted to see America.

"He charged me fifty dollars but took only forty-five saying that the five dollars off was a welcome-to–New York discount. Colette opened the door before I could ring the bell, and the first thing she did was pick a wild licorice leaf out of my hair and say, 'You bring the bush with you, girl.'

"Dave?"

"Uh-huh?"

"You're very quiet. You still listening?"

"Go on, Grace Jones. I'm listening."

"Upstairs, I kept calling my cousin, and finally at around four-thirty she answered. Turns out she couldn't get the time off from the bank to pick me up and another sister was supposed to meet me—unfortunately, she is something called a crackhead. I was to take another taxi, a cab she called it, and come over to her house. I was so relieved. I finally looked around Colette's tiny apartment. She lived with her mother, her mother's boyfriend, two sisters, and a child aunt. The second bedroom had two double-decker beds and not much space for anything else. Fat chairs covered with plastic stuffed the living room to the walls, and the whole place seemed like a dolly house. My suitcase had to stay out in the hallway.

"So, finally, finally I got to my cousin's apartment, which you know is just down here on Bedford. It's early evening of a long day. I'm in a daze. This morning I was in the village and now I have no idea where I am. She has a nice two-bedroom apartment, but it's just my cousin and her son and now me. We can all fit here nicely, I thought. He was playing Nintendo Duck Hunt, and together we shot and killed ducks flying on-screen. She went out to get Chinese for dinner. Delicious pork-fried rice and sweet and sour chicken, food you only ate back home if you went to some fancy function. I gave her the presents my mother sent and took a few things out of my suitcase. We talked, and then I started falling asleep on the couch, so she showed me where I am to stay, the top bunk in her son's room.

"The next morning my cousin came into the room and asked what my plans were. Well—and I was a little shy in front of this, after all, stranger—show me what you usually make your son for lunch, maybe the shop you use, and, oh, where his school is of course. The things I need to know to help you mind him, right? And maybe tomorrow take me to register for high school. She made this face I recognize, and I think we really are cousins in truth, but then she says, 'I told my mother not to get me mixed up in her business. You can't stay here with me. I need my privacy, and my son needs his space. I did my part. I got you off the island, but I can't have no sixteen-year-old girl living in my house, and you looking like that.'

"I wanted to say, 'Can we call your mother, my aunt, and see what she says? And how do I look?' Also I want to tell her, 'This wasn't the plan,' but I don't say anything. She told me I could stay for a couple of days, but no more than that. Then she made her son a peanut butter and jelly sandwich and took him to school herself."

"Grace," Ben piped up. "I could have a peanut butter and jelly sandwich?"

"Only if you give me the magic word!"

"Pleeeeeeeeeeeeeeeeease!" Sandwich in hand, Ben ran off. Dave turned to me and smiled.

"At least I ran up her phone bill," I said, laughing.

"First I rang the woman on the hill and told her to get my mother. That involved waiting for a taxi to pass, sending a message up the Quarry Road, and then waiting for my mother to come back. I told her I would call back at noon. Then I rang Colette, who was gone to school, but her mother, Hyacinth, was home, so I thanked her for yesterday and told her my today problem. 'Talk to your cousin again tonight,' she says, 'then call back.'

"At noon I call my mother, and she sounds so genuinely happy to hear my voice, I will myself not to cry. I tell her that my cousin won't keep me, and we end up arguing on the phone. My mother of course wants me to get on the next plane and come back. Change my flight and come home. I tell her let me at least stay out the duration of my ticket. Let me at least spend a little holiday. I'm sure Colette's mother will keep me for three weeks. My mother is hysterical, and I hang up the phone. I stay inside all day, find Channel Two and watch *The Young and the Restless*, eat nasty cold Chinese for lunch because I don't know how to operate the microwave, then the food upsets my belly and I break the flush toilet. When she comes in that evening with her son, my cousin hasn't changed her mind.

"I call Hyacinth again, take a cab over to their house, where the first thing she tells me is that I can't stay there for long, which is obvious because their place is a rabbit hole already filled with people, but I may stay for the three-week duration of my ticket if I'm going home when my time is up. So I lied and said of course I'll go home, at least I got to see America and snow. The second thing she says is that taxi ride from the airport shouldn't have been more than twenty dollars. When Colette offers to make drawer space, Hyacinth says it'll be easier if I just take things out of my suitcase as I need them.

"Still, they were all so nice to me. I did all the housework during the days, and on Christmas morning I even had a gift under their tree, a white cardigan two sizes too big. Then the Indian woman next door, Seema, she's from the island too, said she needed someone to hold her job in Jersey the week between Christmas and New Year's while she tried out something new. Everyone agreed that I should do it because I'd make one hundred and fifty dollars. That, together with my traveler's checks, should give me enough money to go shopping before I go back home. So I went to Highland Park, New Jersey, with Seema, who on the bus told me she'd say I was eighteen, but if her boss lady Mora ever found out my real age, she'd say I lied to her too.

"As I was fixing my suitcase to leave, Colette asked me to plait her hair like I used to back in the village. While I'm plaiting she says to me that I shouldn't worry. I had come to America before Jesus was ready for me to come, and that, for as long as she'd known me, I had always been in a hurry to do things before Jesus was ready for me to do them. Look how long it had taken for her to come and stay with her mother. Just go back home and wait, and Jesus would let me know when the time was right."

Telling everything took a long time, and Dave didn't interrupt. Finally, I tightened up the last plait, liking the way the thin black braids contrasted against his pale scalp. Ben had long before fallen asleep on Dave's lap, and I tapped Dave with the comb. "Hey, rasta, you awake?"

He turned to stare at me, his mouth open, and I laughed when I saw his hair from the front. He was dead serious though. "Grace, my God. I had no idea—"

But I cut him off. "Of course you didn't. I don't tell people as soon as I meet them: Hello. I was abandoned at the airport and then my cousin kicked me out." I laughed again. "The Lord works in mysterious ways. Sometimes I think it was all for the better that she told me to leave, you know?"

Dave gave me a crazy look. "No. I don't know that at all. But how did you manage? What did you do? How old were you? Sixteen? And all alone in New York. That cabbie could have decided—Let me not even think that. But do you know how many people, especially young girls, just disappear in New York City?" He made a face and repeated my cousin's line the morning she'd told me I needed to leave. "And you looking like that. Grace, do you know how lucky you are?"

I had yet to feel lucky.

"You know something, Grace? You remind me of Vincent."

This came as a surprise. "How?"

"He wasn't scared of anything. Not his father or the thugs he grew up around. And such an optimist. To hear him tell it, everything was always going to be all right." Dave paused. "It's good to not know fear," he said, almost to himself. "So, Grace Jones. Now you're in America, but what are your plans? I mean your long-term plans."

The time had come to leave Eden, and I thought over Dave's words as I put Ben's bag together, wondering if maybe I shouldn't be scared. "Sol and Miriam are sponsoring me. I'll go to school. Live, I guess." I didn't know how else to put it.

He stopped on the path. "No going back home?"

I kept walking. "Nothing to go back home for."

"And this sponsorship business with Sol and Miriam, how long will that take?"

"Donkey years. I've heard eight, ten. A long time."

He lay Ben in the back of the truck without a seat belt and didn't answer until he sat behind the wheel. "But, Grace, this means that you have to stay with Sol and Miriam for all this time. What if they move, if Miriam starts, hah, starts acting crazy? What will you do then?"

"Dave, it's not like I have a choice."

"Come on, Grace, there's always a choice. How old are you now, seventeen?"

"I'm eighteen."

"Eighteen. Look at that. You're young, pretty, and one of the smartest people I know. Think about what you're saying. Do you really want to work for Sol and Miriam until you're almost thirty?"

Did I really want to work for Sol and Miriam until I was almost thirty? It was a stupid question, and it made me furious. Dave didn't understand. But then, he lived at the top of the world. I didn't expect him to.

"Now you're mad at me," he said. "Don't be, I'm just trying to help you think of options. Grace, who knows where Sol and Miriam will be in ten years? In even one year?"

He pulled into the tower's driveway, and I jumped out and got Ben. Dave came and stood next to me. "Grace, please listen."

But I didn't want to listen. To him or to anyone else. Duke was doing his best to see us through the glass. "I'll see you later, okay, Dave? Give the purple anthuriums a little water tomorrow." He left the car in the driveway and walked behind me to the front door, but I wouldn't turn around. In the elevator I found that I didn't want to cry. I was just mad and had the bitter taste of pretzels and grape soda choking my throat.

Chapter 31

I stayed mad at Dave, but in truth I was more annoyed at myself. I felt like I was a spinning top in mud. I didn't know what I was doing or what I wanted or where anything was leading. And to make matters worse, Kath, who was all I had ever had in America, was talking about going home.

Fridays before I went to Sylvia's, I stopped at Kath's room. She'd quit her job and was spending her time lying on her unmade bed undoing the rhinestone patterns she had dazzled into almost every piece of clothing she owned. At first she had wanted me to take her job. But I wouldn't.

"Grace, don't be stupid. It's twice the money you make. Leave them." Her hair, uncombed for weeks, was almost dreaded down around her shoulders.

"Yeah, Kath, but it's live out. I'd have to come home to Sylvia's every evening. When was the last time you saw her apartment? Place is a mad-house with all the construction. Where are your combs?"

She waved a lock of her hair at me. "Dumb-dumb, you wouldn't have to stay at Sylvia's anymore because you'd be able to afford your own place. It's three seventy-five a week they pay; you could probably get four hundred."

The big money I could earn at Kath's job made me pause. In two months, I could have enough saved to send for my father. I could get a room like the one Kath had for less than a hundred dollars a week, and I'd never have to see Sol and Miriam again. I'd miss Ben, but I'd probably see him in the park every day. And, if I felt like it ever again, I'd be able to visit Dave in the evenings after work. But I couldn't leave.

"I can't do it, Kath."

"Grace, why?"

Had she really forgotten? I couldn't tell anymore with Kath. The weight she'd lost after the abortion hadn't come back. Her skin was gray and her lips cracked, as if now, in July, a winter wind blew just for her.

"My papers, Kath. You know they're doing the sponsorship. I can't leave now. Hey"—I rushed on before she could answer—"what about you? When are you and that guy getting married?"

"Please"—Kath's voice was scornful—"I'm not doing that anymore."

She hadn't told me this. "You're not?"

She shook her head slowly. "Nope. The license expired after thirty days, anyhow. I forget all about that, Grace."

"But, Kath, so what are you going to do?"

And that was the first time I'd heard her say it. "I'm ready to go home, Grace."

"Home?"

"Ow, Grace, don't pull."

"Sorry. But what are you talking about? You can't go back to the island."

"Give me one good reason why not."

Because if you left I'd be alone in the world.

"What would Donovan say?"

"Come on, Grace. I said a good reason. And besides, he'd be relieved if I left here. He's only still around because he feels guilty for what happened." Kath twisted to look at me, and her hardened face made me miss my old friend. "Well, don't you want to know why he feels guilty?"

"Why?"

"Because he ruined my fucking life, that's why." And then she hung her head and cried, her whole body shaking as she sobbed for everything lost.

Later we ordered from Gloria's. As I inhaled a plate of rice and oxtails, I watched Kath take apart a chicken roti without actually eating more than a few curried *channa*. She fussed with the food as if she intended to eat, but in the end she had three piles on her place, roti scraps, shredded chicken, and potato and *channa*.

"So how long you been thinking about this, Kath?" I couldn't believe she was serious.

She shrugged. "Oh, I don't know. It was always in the back of my mind."

"From before Court Street?" Neither of us ever spoke of the abortion by name.

Kath picked up a piece of chicken. "My father has been trying to get me to come home for a year now, Grace."

"Oh, Lord, he thinking about running again?" The big man in South Trinidad had twice run for mayor of our borough.

"And, we're opening up a new store."

"But, Kath, how long now you're here?" I knew exactly, remembered Mora handing me the phone and, expecting my mother on the line, hearing Kath instead, telling me she was in Brooklyn. "You know if you go home you won't be able to come back for ages, right?"

She ate the tiniest triangle of roti. "Not necessarily."

"Oh, yeah, once you've overstayed, that's it. You'll get stamped 'undesirable' on your way out. We're in the same boat, sister."

I expected her to laugh, but she didn't. "Grace, my visa never expired."

"Now who's the dummy? B-twos are only valid for six months, Kath."

"Who said I had a B-two?" She studied a chunk of curried potato. "Daddy got me a student's visa, Grace. You know he knows Tom, Dick, and Harry." She shrugged and set down the potato. "Nope, I won't get stamped, and, when I get home, I'll tell them not to date my passport and everything'll be fine."

I stared up at Kath with my mouth open. "So you can go home and come back when you like?"

"If I want. Daddy, you know."

But I hadn't known; we weren't in the same boat at all. "So you really going to do this? You're going back for real?"

She started folding up the sides of her paper plate, imprisoning the remains of her meal. "Well, we'll see, Grace." She smiled her old smile for the first time in a long time. "I gave someone an ultimatum, and if they want me to stay, then everything will be fine and my poor daddy might never get to be mayor."

Chapter 32

As much as I waited all week for Fridays to come to get paid and to leave Sol and Miriam's apartment, the reality was that coming home to Brooklyn offered me no respite. Sylvia's apartment was wrecked. Before, I could come in and, after a few cosmetic changes, a quick sweep of the meat rug, the breakfront straightened, and everything else crammed into the hallway closet, I'd be able to relax. Now, relaxation was impossible. Jacob's Russians had torn the apartment apart. What had started out as a cover-up job had turned into a full redo after the city inspector's report decreed Sylvia's dwelling a lead trap.

A toxic confetti of chipped paint blanketed everything. Micky and Derek spent as much time as possible outside. During the long summer days, they played on the parkway's sidewalk from when camp ended, at five, until their exhausted bodies demanded bedtime at ten. Sometimes they took Dame out with them, but more often Sylvia left him with the old Jamaican woman next door. Still, when he was home, he had unfettered access to the paint he so loved to eat.

When I told this to Sylvia, she got mad at me. "So what it is you want me to do, Grace? Look at this place. Watch how we living like bums. You get to live like a lord with them white people in the city. You don't spend the week here with we."

The apartment was a hot den. Because the grates had been removed, the windows were supposed to remain closed, and the trapped heat only swirled thickly when disturbed by the standing fan. The weathermen had been predicting a summer storm to come and wash it all away, but rain clouds showed no sign of gathering. Sylvia reclined on the couch in a thin red negligee with Dame in only a diaper flopped against her sweaty bosom. I lifted a piece of paint from the side of his mouth. "So call the city and complain, Sylvia."

"Grace, you don't know how this city does operate. Is not when I want them to come"—she settled herself, and her belly shifted, sliding Dame a few inches forward—"they does show up without even telling you they coming."

I had nothing else to say.

Sylvia burped from deep within. "At least the work getting done. This is only for a time. By the time they finish, them boy father will be home and things will go back to normal around here."

It had been weeks since I last saw Bo, and I had, of course, never got back the twenty dollars I'd lent to him. "Sylvia, when last you see Bo?"

"Ages now, mama. He wouldn't stay around here so to see them Russian and them doing work he should be doing."

"He by Dodo?"

"Nah. Now you see it warm warm outside, he and Nello and them does camp in the park."

So Bo hadn't been given the gutting job Jacob had promised him back in the spring. At least camping out in the park sounded like a fun thing to do. I had this picture of Bo and Nello and the other men he hung out with living in tents with a roaring campfire, singing songs and swapping jokes under the stars as they drank bottles of rum and played all fours until early dawn.

Sylvia fanned the still air in front of her with her palm. "Lord, but this heat is killing me. I have half a mind to open them damn window, you know. Take Dame, Grace."

I leaned over and peeled him away from Sylvia's belly, damp with her or his sweat. He was three now and still couldn't form any words. The city had assigned a speech therapist to come to the apartment, but Sylvia said not until the workmen were done. She didn't want strangers to see her house like this. She had so many plans for after the renovations were finished. Her husband would be well enough to come home; she would lose the weight; finally, Dame would start his therapy. Everything would be just fine once the work was done and she could get her life in order.

"You doing anything in the morning, Grace?" she asked.

I didn't have any plans besides calling my mother at two. "No, why?" Usually her agency didn't send her out on Saturday jobs.

"Stay here with them children for me. I want to run down Pitkin before the big rain come for some curtain I put on layaway for when you see this place done."

"SO HOW'S THE BABY doing?" Cassandra Neil glanced at quiet Dame. "He started speech therapy?"

Sylvia was right. Those city people didn't give you any warning.

"Um, you're going to have to ask my cousin when she's back. Did she know you were coming?" I was sure she didn't.

"Okay, okay. I was just asking."

She was very professional in her assessment. I sat on the couch with Micky and Derek on either side and Dame on my lap while she went from room to room, placing her meter against the walls and the radiators and the window grates propped against the baseboards. The children were very quiet, and I gave them each a candy. She finished and stood in front of us. "When's your cousin coming back?"

I looked past her to see the time on the VCR clock. "She should be back any minute now."

"Good, I need to wait for her."

There was no place to offer her to sit, even the box over the radiator by the window was gone. I got off the couch and perched Dame on my hip. "Sit down," I offered. She said thanks and sat, and both Micky and Derek got up and disappeared into the bedroom.

"So"—Cassandra pulled one leg up under her—"you register for fall yet? Hunter you said, right?"

"Not yet." Dame was liquid in my arms.

"Well, I brought something for you." She leaned forward and dug into her back pocket.

"For me?"

She handed me a card with two phone numbers written on it. "The top one is for the main admission office, and the second one is for Hunter's direct admission. You should give them a call."

"Thanks." I slid the card into my back pocket. "How did you know I'd be here?"

"Oh, I just had a feeling."

Then we heard a key in the front door, and Sylvia came in. Micky and

Derek flew out of the bedroom and down the corridor, and I heard her say, "Where? In my living room? Now?" She walked in carrying two shopping bags, her hairline beaded with sweat. "Miss Neil, I too too shame for you to come and see my place looking like this."

Cassandra got up. "Oh, Mrs. John, don't mind. It's not you, it's the landlord. Come in and sit down. Hah, I'm telling you to sit in your own house. But sit, sit."

Sylvia sat next to me and reached for Dame. "Grace, but you didn't even offer the lady a glass of water self to drink. Where your manners, man?"

"No, no," Cassandra said. "Grace did. I didn't want anything. I was just waiting for you to come home."

"Get up, Grace, let the lady sit down."

I moved to the windowsill, but Cassandra did not sit down.

"Mrs. John," she said, "you can't stay in this apartment with your children while this work is going on." Sylvia started to speak, and Cassandra put up her hand. "No, you can't. Your landlord has to find you other accommodations or pay for you and your family to stay in a hotel. He has thirty days to do that, and there can be no more construction in the apartment until you and your children are resettled."

That word made me think of Haitian refugees.

"But what is this I hearing? Miss Lady"—Sylvia had forgot Cassandra Neil's name—"I can't leave my house."

Micky started to cry, and Derek said, "We moving, Mammy? But how my daddy will find us when he come home?"

Sylvia looked around her house, and if she saw what I saw, she must have known that Cassandra Neil was right. "Well, they say what don't meet you does pass you. But look how trouble come in my house today, nah."

"Don't think of it as trouble, Mrs. John." Cassandra sat down next to Sylvia. "If you're out of the apartment, the workers can get the job done much faster than if you're here with the children."

Sylvia shook her head. "You don't know Jacob."

"I do know Mr. Kaplan, very well in fact. He'll get to work."

I was listening and thinking only about myself. If Sylvia and the children had to move, I might not be able to go with them. Where would I go on the weekends? I couldn't bear the thought of living with Sol and Miriam full-time.

The thunderclap was so loud it stirred Dame from his deep, quiet place, and he howled. Micky and Derek ran to their mother, and Cassandra Neil said, "Wow." Lightning flashed silver bright, and another boom of thunder made Micky fling her arms around her mother's neck.

"Stop behaving so stupid," Sylvia said, but she rubbed Micky's arm with one hand and patted Dame with the other. "Is just some rain to finally cool down this heat. Weatherman say this morning rain going to come."

Cassandra Neil got up to leave. "Wait until the rain pass, Miss Neil. This kind of weather could give you ammonia, yes," Sylvia told her.

Cassandra smiled. "You sound just like my mother, Mrs. John."

"Then your mother is a smart woman."

"PLENTY RAIN FALLING HERE too," my mother said when the lady on the hill passed her the phone, "but is rainy season, so what else to expect?"

"You leave Helen and Daddy sleeping?"

"How you know?"

I knew because, back home, the sound of a hard rain drumming on the galvanized roof was a country lullaby to the sweetest sleep.

"So how everybody doing, Mammy?" I wanted to hear her voice. My carpeted nook was now storage space for Jacob's workers, and I curled in a corner of the couch in the warm glow from the tatty maiden lamp. Sylvia and the children had gone to nap away the summer storm, and I had the living room to myself.

"Everybody good, you know. Same thing as usual." I didn't expect her to say more than this. "How you going?"

"Ah, I good," I answered, but she knew me too well.

"What happen, Gracie? Something wrong? You and Sylvia quarrel?"

"No, no, is not that."

"So what it is, then?"

Sylvia will have to move just now, and I can't go with them. And the money I work for is not enough to rent a place and continue saving for Daddy's foot, not to mention start saving to pay for school. And, I can't leave Sol and Miriam because they're doing my sponsorship. And, Kathy's talking about coming home. And, I miss you and Daddy and Helen. And, I don't like the rain in America.

"Oh, Mammy, is nothing. Rain here just different from home is all."

She was quiet for a while, then said, "Huh, rain might be different, but you is still the same, Gracie."

"I suppose," I mumbled, more for me than for her.

"What you mean you suppose? You're still the same Gracie who start to read when she was four, who always come out first in class, who tell Mr. Parris you not calling him Mister unless he call you Madam—"

I laughed. "I did that? How much years I had?"

My mother laughed too. "You playing you can't remember? Not even five. From then on he called you Madam whenever he pass. You know they say when he was traveling on he sickbed, he laugh and say, 'The child tell me to call she madam, *oui*,' right before he give up the spirit?"

I hadn't even known he had died.

"And is not you who pick up and decide to go America?"

"Well, you had to let me go. Is not like I just walk out the house."

"You think I could have stop you, Gracie?"

This was new to me, because although my mother and I had always clashed, she had also almost always won our battles. Even in the ones she did lose, she still triumphed by virtue of being the mother whose word and will had dominion over mine. Our house had not been a one man, one vote kind of place, and Helen and I were forever plotting bloodless coups to get our way.

"Nothing I could have say or do was making you stay on this island, Gracie. I know that for sure."

So long I'd had to wait to hear this from my mother, and all I wanted to do was go home to her and take a long sleep to the sound of the falling rain. I couldn't even begin to acknowledge what she was actually saying to me, so instead I asked again after my father.

"Daddy good, I tell you. The sugar okay and the blood pressure not too high. The other day he even went alone to clinic for a checkup and everything looking good."

"He traveled alone? Why you or Helen didn't go with him?"

"That is what I trying to tell you," my mother said, "everything over here going good. You just take care of yourself and not to worry about us."

She convinced me, but I still wouldn't let her get off the phone. Not until she had answered my questions about my na, and Rhonda, and our dogs and the plants and trees growing around our house and in the big garden. Finally, when I was filled with the sound of her and home, I told her I would talk to her next time.

After, I got out the card with the numbers Cassandra Neil had given me. Of course the admissions office at the college was closed on Saturday, but the main office in the city was open, and I requested a catalog and all the information they could send to me. I didn't know what was going to happen at Sylvia's apartment, so I gave the encouraging woman on the phone Miriam's address in the city.

SUNDAY NIGHT WHEN I got in, Danny jumped off his little pedestal and landed in my path with a sharp *clap* from the taps on his repaired shoes.

"Hey, Gracie Mansion, I've got a question for you." His pointed finger-tip touched my chest.

"What, Danny?" I didn't want to talk to him or to anyone else. I had too much on my mind.

"What are you doing after you get off from work this Friday?"

"What?"

"What you doing Friday? You wanna go get something to eat or go to the park or something?"

I looked more closely at Danny, hearing that he was asking me out. Skinny, with the stupid captain's hat on his too small head, his plucked-chicken neck stretching up from the wrinkled collar of his unpressed shirt, narrow, sloping shoulders, bad-fitting uniform, unpolished shoes, back up to the nasty teeth. I looked at him and willed Brent instead, sexy, sad eyes and goatee, that body I wanted to hold me, that smell I wanted to inhale. I shook my head. "I can't, Danny."

"Hey, why not?" He sucked spit through his snout. "Maybe another day after work, I could come by if I'm off, or next Friday?"

What was the non-Kathy way out of this? The way that didn't involve a head thrown back with a wail of laughter, a fly swat of the hand and "Oh, please"?

"Thanks for asking me, Danny, but I can't. I'll see you later, okay." I tried to walk past him, but he sidestepped and blocked me.

"Yeah, but hey, why, Grace? You seeing somebody?"

He smelled like milk one day past good.

"I know you're not seeing the big boss man upstairs because you can't give it to him the way he likes it, if you know what I mean." He thrust his bony hips, and I stepped back. "But hey, ha-ha, butt, maybe you're giving it to the other boss man, the redheaded one? Is that why you won't go out with me, Grace? You and Mr. B getting it on?"

I walked past him without answering. I was my mother's child after all, and we didn't waste our time entertaining village trash.

Chapter 33

I heard voices before I rang the Bruckners' bell. Sol's and Miriam's and others, loud laughter and silverware against plates. It was Nancy who opened the door.

"Grace, darling, long time no see. How are you?"

"Hi, Nancy. Good, thanks." She leaned and kissed me somewhere between my cheek and my lips, managing to hit and miss both at the same time.

She'd been drinking. I walked down the long hall behind her and came to the dining table under the sunflower clock. Sol sat next to Miriam massaging the bare, swollen foot she had propped in his lap; Susannah looked beautiful and deathly pale in a white cotton top that showed off her skinny arms and sharp clavicles. Michael looked tired. Dave's hair was a fuzzy mess, still in the cane rows.

Nancy put her hand on my back and presented me to the table. "Amazing Grace is here."

I said hello to everyone and hi to Dave, whom I hadn't seen since our trip two weeks earlier. He winked at me and smiled. "Are you coming up this week?"

"Maybe."

"Oh, come on up, Grace."

"Okay, maybe Wednesday."

"I'll expect you on Wednesday, then."

"Hey, Grace-before-meals," Sol said, "have some wine with us."

"No thanks, Sol."

"Oh, come on, Grace." Nancy picked up a bottle and started to pour red wine into one of Miriam's fancy gold-rimmed goblets. "We're having a soiree."

"Don't force her, Nancy," Miriam said. "Grace is shy."

"Well, okay, if you're shy, here." Nancy handed me the glass poured to the brim. "Go have it in your room, but you are having some wine tonight, because we are celebrating."

I took the offered glass, told Dave I'd see him later, and went into my room. I could hear them all out there, laughing and talking, Susannah at times piercing through the rest. I sipped some of the wine Nancy had poured. It was much drier than Canei, but not unpleasant once I swallowed.

Chairs scraped back from the dining table, and Susannah's shrill voice said, "Now? You're going to go up and look at plants now, in the middle of the night? You men are ridiculous. Michael, plants?"

"Come on, Suzy," Nancy said, "you know what kind of plant they're going to look at. Green trees, wacky tobacky. Dave always had the best stuff. Roll me one for the road, Sol."

Miriam said, "Nancy."

And Nancy laughed. "Hey, I'm an artist, and anything that will conjure the muse is welcome."

"Muse my ass," Susannah said.

"But you have no ass, darling," Nancy replied, and they all laughed. I drained my glass and listened. More wine was being poured.

"Oh, Nancy," Susannah said, "don't you dare pour more wine for Miriam."

"How many times do I have to tell you that it's only during the first trimester you're not supposed to have alcohol," Nancy told her. "The organs are all formed already. I was premed, remember? One glass of red after a full meal isn't going to hurt the baby. In fact, the French think it will 'elp zee baby. Here, Miriam."

"Bullshit that's her first glass. When she's born with flippers, you'll say I told you so."

"Suzy!" both Miriam and Nancy called.

"What? I'm just saying. Pour me another glass, darling."

"Come, come," Nancy said, "another toast, now that the males of the species have gone. To Miriam, about to join the ranks of the idle rich. Here's to time, money, and help."

They all laughed, and their glasses clanked off each other.

"Grace!" Miriam called me. I had hoped I wouldn't have to go out until they were all gone. "Yes, Miriam?"

"Do me a favor, darling." She had never called me darling before. "Put on a pot of Sol's coffee and then start clearing this mess, will you?" She turned to her sisters-in-law. "You guys want gelato? The real deal from Luigi's in Carroll Gardens. Full cream and heavenly."

Susannah patted her nonexistent stomach. "I'm so full I cannot eat another bite of air. I can drink, but no gelato for me."

"Nancy?"

Nancy looked at me while she nodded yes to Miriam.

"Bring it, Grace, and the glass clover bowls from the top shelf," Miriam said. "Be careful."

I took some dishes with me into the kitchen, put on the coffee, and came back with the ice cream, leaving Miriam's DON'T TOUCH! label. And, even though Susannah had said she didn't want any, three of the green, leaf-shaped bowls. "You have the most beautiful arms," Nancy said as I set a bowl in front of her. "Can I feel your muscles?"

Without waiting for me to answer, she groped my upper arm. "Like marble. Suzy, feel Grace's arms."

Susannah set down her glass and felt my right arm. "Wow." She flexed her own right bicep. "Do you lift, Grace? I can't tell you how much I had to curl to get this little bugger to pop. How'd you do that?"

I set down the last bowl in front of her, the one she didn't want. "Climbing."

"Ah," she said, "rocks."

I laughed. "Not rocks, trees. I grew up in the country."

Miriam sniggered, and I took another load of dishes to the dishwasher. Suzy's voice was lower but still shrill. "I really don't know how you do it, Miriam."

"Do what?" Miriam snorted.

"Have such a smokin' nanny working for you. You've seen our Theresa—face looks like the rocky mountain in Peru she climbed down from. Perfect for me, not for Michael."

Nancy laughed. "Susannah Bruckner, you are so uncharitable."

"Only where no charity is due, darling. What, Miriam, you think Sol can't see? Michael totally checked her ass out when she walked by.

Remember that maid's outfit she wore at Pesach? Pure fetish. I don't care what Aunt Ettie says, there's no way I would hire her." I held my breath.

"Sol's not into black women," Miriam said.

Both Susannah and Nancy said at the exact same moment, "Alana Monet."

"Who?" Miriam asked.

"Suzy, are you trying to get my little brother in hot water?" Nancy asked.

"Not me," Susannah said. "I just want some more red wine and maybe the world's tiniest scoop of gelato in the lower-left quadrant of my lucky clover."

"Have the hazelnut," Nancy said. "Divine."

"Okay, so maybe two tiny scoops, because I want to try the pistachio too."

"Pig."

"What? You're eating from the tub."

Nancy and Susannah bantered on, and, by either wine or design, neither answered Miriam's query or my curiosity about Alana Monet.

Later I heard Miriam's raised voice, and I realized then that in the five months I had worked for them I had never once heard her and Sol quarrel. They'd bickered, but I'd never heard them have a proper row. Miriam's growling anger rumbled through the walls. Sol's voice was a lower, steady murmur. Then I heard her cry.

Chapter 34

"What'd you kill in my absence?"

"On the contrary, I'll have you know that I propagated several colocasia." A long, skinny pot held a row of variegated, heart-shaped leaves. Dasheen-bush cousin, my mother would call them. I tugged gently on one of the stems, feeling resistance as the baby tubers held tightly to the soil. "Not only that—" Dave pointed to the papaya and the Jesus Christ arms that branched out just below the vase.

"Yay, Dave. Look. I told you so."

"You did indeed. Now we have to see the flowers."

"O ye of little faith."

He laughed. "No, my faith in you is solid, Grace. It's the rest of mankind I'm not too sure about. Just don't come anywhere near me with shears, okay?"

His deck was glorious on a summer evening. The forest in the sky was in full bloom, and unless you parted the trees and looked down on the busy city far below, it was easy to imagine island isolation.

I tucked a waxy, white frangipani behind my ear. "I like that it stays light for so long in New York. On the island, the sun sets at six, and then it's like you trip and fall into night."

He laughed again.

"What's so funny about that?"

"It's not funny, it's just the way you said it."

"Well, how'd I say it?"

"Like poetry, Grace."

It was good to be upstairs again. Over the last few days, Miriam had ridden me hard. Any time I didn't spend with Ben at the park was spent indoors working. Her lists had grown longer, and I had cleaned out kitchen and bathroom cabinets, scrubbed top shelves and floorboards, and begun sorting Ben's used things in anticipation of the new baby. Yesterday, Ule had explained to me that Miriam was experiencing the nesting instinct, and I said I thought that mother birds took pride in building their own nests.

I worked with Dave. The colocasia wasn't the only plant that needed separating. The warm weather, the humidity, and the occasional summer shower had come together to create rain forest conditions, and the plants in the sky garden had done well and multiplied. We potted baby alpinias, trimmed runaway zebrina, and watered everything. Tucked along the farthest wall, I found the dropped fruit of a lucky seed tree. "Hey, I didn't know you had a lucky seed," I said to Dave. "Helen and I used to play jacks with these outside my mother's church. Let me show you." I threw the seeds onto the worktable to start the game.

Dave gave me the look I associated with benne and hibiscus toothbrushes. "Lucky seeds, Grace? You played with these?"

"Uh-huh, go ahead and destroy another part of my childhood."

"You're lucky you *survived* your childhood." He pointed to a bin, but I refused to drop in the diamond-shaped nuggets. "Try oleander, Grace. Poison."

"Oh, come on, lucky seeds are poisonous?"

"Those things can trigger a fatal heart attack in a grown man. The whole tree is toxic."

"Are you serious? Then why are you growing it?"

"The flowers are pretty, plus I don't have a crazy daughter trying to play jacks with poison, do I?" Dave pointed to the bin again, and this time I dropped in the seeds, liking the *plonk-plonk* sound they made when they hit the bottom.

His stand-in children, Brutus and Cesar, were miserable in the heat and moved from the shady spots only to lumber over to the many water bowls scattered around the deck for their convenience.

"They need trimming too, Dave." I pointed my shears at a melancholy dog.

"I know, poor boys, but they've had their cut already and need to fill out for the cold weather. Looks like we might still be in New York."

"What do you mean? You had plans to be somewhere else?"

He pulled off his leather work gloves. "Let's take a rest, okay?"

We washed up at the deep outdoor trough. He used the opener attachment on the penknife I'd got him to open our beers. It was sweet to sit on the lounges and look up at the ten city stars, to hear the distant hum of the nighttime traffic far far below.

"So answer me, Dave. Where you going?"

"Back to Old Town, maybe. Someplace where it's always warm."

That I could understand because, even in late July, I thought with dread that it would turn cold again.

"What about you?"

"What do you mean, what about me?"

He cocked his head. "I don't want you to disappear again for two weeks."

"I will not disappear, plus, it's not like you didn't know where to find me."

"So then, what about you? What are you going to do?"

I faced him on the lounger. "Well, maybe I'll take a class at Hunter in the fall." I shrugged, but saying it out loud made it sound so possible. That I could be on my way.

Dave sat up and straddled his lounge. "Grace, that's a brilliant idea. Hunter's a good school." He reached his beer to knock cheers. "What do you think you want to study?"

"Plantology."

"What?"

"Botany, Dave. Something to do with plants. I don't know. Maybe I could design gardens, work outside." I shrugged.

Dave was nodding. "That is so solid, Grace. Wow."

"You think so?"

"Oh yeah. You're good with people, and you healed my papaya. Grace?"

"Yeah?"

"This could really be something."

We knocked our beers together again, and I relaxed into my seat to look up at the twinkling stars. The longer I looked up, the more I saw.

BEN TWIRLED A STRAND of spaghetti on his Pooh fork. "You going home, Grace?"

"I am. I'm getting on the choo-choo train and taking a ride into Brooklyn."

"Wow, Grace. Ya-ya took me on the choo-choo train."

It was the first time in months he'd said anything about Ya-ya.

"Was it fun on the train?"

He nodded, then covered his ears. "But it was too loud. . . . Hi, Mama!"

"Hi, big boy." To me Miriam just said "Grace—" and placed a large manila envelope on the table. My heart did a little flip. I tried not to smile too broadly, because I knew that finally INS had replied to my application. It wasn't going to be a green card, but it was something.

"What's this, Grace?"

Miriam was not smiling. I spun the envelope around and saw that it wasn't from INS at all but from Hunter College.

"Oh"—the disappointment in my voice was clear even to my ears—"I thought it was something to do with my papers."

Miriam pulled out a dining chair and sat spread-legged across from me. Her white maternity shorts were very short, and her now fat thighs filled their width.

"Your what papers?"

"The sponsorship papers. I thought something might have come by now."

"Oh, that." She spun the envelope around to face her again. "But what is this?"

"I called up the college to get a catalog."

"And why did you have them send it to our address?"

"Just to be sure that I got it."

"Yes, but you don't live here, and you shouldn't get personal mail here."

I didn't know what to say.

"So you're going to school? You're leaving? When were you planning on telling us? After the baby came?"

Ben, seeing that his mother was upset, threw down his Pooh fork, and it clattered off its matching plate. "I don't want Grace to go, Mommy."

I understood now why she seemed so upset. "Oh, Miriam, no," I said and shook my head. "I'm not leaving. I'm thinking about taking night classes." I ran my hand over Ben's curls. "I'm not going anywhere, mister."

"You promise, Grace?"

I handed him the fork. "Promise."

Then Miriam said, "Night classes when?"

I pulled the envelope over to me again. I could feel the heavy catalog inside. "I have to look at the schedule, but probably evenings after work. Hunter's not far."

"You should have talked to Sol or me before you did this."

I hadn't done anything, just called for a catalog.

"Because this isn't going to work." She went to the kitchen and came back with the list she had given me on the day of my first interview. Since then the paper had been bayoneted to the fridge with a chicken magnet. After the first few weeks, once I had got the rhythm of all I had to do, I never bothered to look at it.

"What does that say?" She pointed to almost the end of the list.

"What?"

She shook the piece of paper. "Number twenty-four, Grace."

I read out loud: "Tend to Ben at night if he gets up." In the five months I had been at the towers, Ben had never once awakened during the night.

"You can't do it," Miriam said, "unless of course you want to go on Friday or Saturday night. Those are your nights to do as you please. But from Sunday through Thursday night, you're needed here. I'm not paying you to go to school, or to read, or to run around New York City. You're full-time live-in, and I need to have access to you at night. Midtown isn't upstairs. Do you understand?"

And Ben, who had been listening to his mother, said, "You understand, Grace?"

Miriam turned to him and laughed. She put her hand under her big belly and cradled it as she laughed. "Oh, baby," she said.

Ben, happy that he could amuse his mother so, said it again, and Miriam laughed even harder. After a bit, she sobered up.

"Okay, Grace?"

"Okay."

She got up and took some bills from the pocket of her maternity shorts. "Here you go. The receipts in the money cup were off by three ninety-four, so there's a hundred and ninety-six dollars here."

. . .

KATHY WAGGED HER FINGER at me. "I warned you about these people, Grace. Once you see they start that sponsorship for you, it's over. Now she feels she owns you."

I wanted to disagree with her, but how could I?

"And talking about sponsorship, what she say about that? Anything come yet?"

"Not that she's told me about."

Kath sat on the pouf. I lay on her quilted bedspread. "Grace, you have to ask her. Maybe something come already and she isn't saying anything. You suppose to at least get a letter saying you've filed, right? Something."

My head hurt, and I wondered if Miriam would do that. Get something that important for me in the mail and not say anything.

"Anyhow," Kath went on, "if it was me, I'd already dig up in every drawer to see what I couldn't find. You too good for your own good."

"Don't say that, Kathy."

She spun on the pouf. "I am saying it. Time to start acting as if you really planning on staying in this country."

I sat up and looked at her. "And how is that, Kath?"

She clenched her hands into two tight fists. "With some balls, Grace."

Her spunk was coming back, but this was bullshit. "So what about you then, hypocrite?" I pointed my palm at her. "How you been acting lately?"

"Don't you worry about me, darling." She reached for the ponytail, but her hair was down. "I've already made up my mind. I'm not staying in this country."

"So you're really going to do it. You're really going to go back to live at home with your mother and father?"

"Well, what so wrong with that, Grace? It's not like . . ." She stopped.

"It's not like what, Kath?"

"Nothing, Grace."

"No, please, tell me. What's it not like?"

Kath stretched out her legs and crossed her left ankle over the right. She put her elbows onto her Formica dressing table and arched her back. Her hair dipped down. "Well, I'll just say that I'll have it easy, is all. Can I say that without pissing you off?"

She didn't piss me off at all. What she said was fact. She was rich at home, and there she could live like the young white girls who lived at the towers, the ones who talked about boyfriends and college and nightclubs. Never about work or money.

"See, now you're pissed. Grace, don't be mad. After"—she paused— "after, you know, I don't know. I just want to go home."

I got off the bed and started searching her upside-down room. "What you looking for?" she asked.

"Comb. At least you could go home looking decent, right?"

"SO WHAT YOU KNOW, Sylvia?" We were busy bagging up her existence on Eastern Parkway. I never would have thought it possible that the apartment could have looked more dilapidated than before, but here it was, finally not fit to be inhabited by humans. Micky and Derek had been banished to Dodo's. Dame remained with his mother, and Sylvia had stopped taking assignments from her agency to try to get out of the building as soon as possible. Of course, every weekend when I got in, the packing looked stalled at exactly where I had left off the previous Sunday night, but Sylvia just claimed that the more she did, the more there was to do.

"Not a damn thing. You ever see more? Jacob really playing the ass in truth. I suppose to be moving in two weeks, and up to now he not telling me where I going." She sized up a dress that Micky might have worn three summers ago and flung it into one of her piles. "As long as he keep me on the number three line, I tell him, everything good. But enough already, man."

I was getting worried. There was noplace I could rent for sixty-five dollars a week, the most I figured I could spend out of my two-hundred-dollar pay and still be able to save something. At least noplace I wanted to live. Kath had told me not to worry, that I could stay with her, rent free, until I found a place, but her little hot room could barely hold her.

Sylvia read my mind. "So what you planning on doing, Miss Grace? You going to stay seven days with them white people? You know you could always go and stay with Dodo, right. She would be glad for the extra fifty dollars."

"Are you crazy? Me and Dodo in the same house?"

"Is only two days, one and a half when you count church time. I bet you anything she'd keep you. You know she can't make children, right?"

I actually hadn't known that and thought she was just too sour for anyone to like.

Sylvia shook her head. "She have fryballs."

"What?"

She rubbed somewhere beneath her navel. "In she womb. Fryballs. Anyhow, Grace, I been meaning to tell you."

"What?"

"Your mother."

My heart seized. "What?"

"No, is nothing. Just remember to tell she not to write you here for a while."

That made it real, that after next weekend, I was going to have to find someplace else to go. I was about to tell Sylvia about Kath's offer when the doorbell buzzed.

"But who the ass is this ringing my bell on a Saturday morning?" she asked without making any effort to rise. "I bet you is the lady from the city again. Miss How-she-name."

It wasn't Cassandra Neil. It was Bo, and he stank. He looked like a vagrant. His skin was grimy and dull and his hair kinky and dusty. His clothes were filthy, and he smelled rank, all at once like unwashed body, rotting dirt, and stale beer.

"But look who it is"—he grinned, showing mossy teeth—"my almost wife." And the stench of his breath pushed me away from the door. I hurried down the corridor before he tried to do something crazy like give me a hug.

"Jesus Christ, look at you, Bo," Sylvia said. "Before you even try to talk, go straight in that bathroom and bathe yourself. Christ, man. You looking like one of them black American bum on the subway."

Bo grinned again, and he looked fearsome. "You have something clean for me to wear?"

Sylvia stretched over to one of her piles and tossed him some clothes. "Don't come out until the water run clear, and throw away any washrag you use, you hear me," she ordered him. "Grace"—she used one of Derek's jerseys to fan under her nose—"bar or no bar, open up that window let some fresh air come in here. God didn't mean for the living to smell so, man."

Even though Dame was asleep on the couch, I only cracked the window. After about half an hour, Bo came out in a much too large Hawaiian print shirt and a too tight pair of jeans shorts. Sylvia sang:

Jean and Dinah,
Rosita and Clementina,
Round the corner posin',
Bet your life is something they sellin'

and we both cracked up.

"What you give me to wear, girl?" Bo laughed too.

"Is my shirt and one of them boy father old pants."

"You have anything to eat?"

"You know where the kitchen is. Go and see what you find."

He came back with a mountain of rice and peas and turkey wing and what looked like a caramel-flavored snow cone.

"Bo, where you get shave ice?"

"I scrape inside the deep freeze."

Sylvia shook her head and held up another old dress of Micky's. "You go ahead. You don't know that is snow poison?"

Dame woke up, and Bo offered him a lick. Sylvia threw the dress at him. "Jacob doing he best to try and kill my child. I don't need you to finish off the devil work."

"So"—Bo took a big bite of fridge frost and pancake syrup—"what really going on here in truth?"

Sylvia filled him in, and he salted her entire speech with curses. "Jacob really better don't let me catch him outside after dark."

"What to do, Bo? At least the city making him fix up this place."

"But watch the place around you, Sylvia. Not even dog supposed to live like this in this here America. You think Jacob would ever give one of them Jew family down the road a place like this to live? Not even them illegal Russian living like this. Is only nigger people they feel like they could treat so."

"Everybody does do for they own, Bo."

"You talking stupidness, Sylvia. Every month you give Jacob good good money to live here. You talking like you asking him to do you a favor. And what about your child? Dame can't even say boo."

She touched Dame's head. "Anyhow, Bo, don't act too righteous. You self did know this place have lead and you didn't say nothing."

My stomach tightened, and I glanced from Sylvia to Bo.

"What you talking about? What I did know?"

Sylvia said, "Not you self who tell Jacob the paint in here making my child a mongoloid? How long now you know that? You never tell me nothing."

I didn't look up again, just kept folding smaller and smaller the tattered kitchen tablecloth until the bunched fabric was board stiff and I could bend it no further.

"Who tell you that, Sylvia, Jacob? And you believe him? You think I would know something like that and not tell you anything? You and them children is my own blood."

"Blood? Money mean more than blood in this America, yes."

"So who you believe, Sylvia, me or Jacob? What other lie he tell you?"

"Up to now I tell you is Jacob tell me anything?"

I didn't dare move in case one of them noticed me sitting there.

Sylvia said, "The good Lord don't hold no grudge and me neither. This place fixing, Dame will get he treatment, and my love coming home soon. Let we just forget about it."

Bo didn't look as if he wanted to forget about it, but he turned to me and asked, "And where you planning on going when Sylvia move, Miss Grace?"

Sylvia said, "Is the same thing we was talking about before you come. I tell she to go and stay by Dodo."

Sometimes Bo came through. "Sylvia, you mad or what? Grace and Dodo living together? Two fowl cock can't live in one coop, girl."

"See, Sylvia, even Bo know that," I put in.

Then Bo said, "Grace, let me hold a twenty, please?"

I noticed he didn't ask to borrow the money. "Till when?"

"I still owe you the twenty from before. This time I want a gift."

"When is your birthday?"

"Okay, okay, you give me ten and ten from what you give Sylvia. Ten each."

I looked at Sylvia to see if she was okay with this arrangement. She turned down her mouth and shrugged.

"Hold on." I high-stepped around the rubble on the floor and closed the bedroom door behind me. I had just over $500. I took $20 for Bo, $40 instead for Sylvia. Now $440. Back in the living room, I gave them each their money.

Bo said, "The vault in the back. You still saving up for we thing?"

"I can't marry a man who living in the park, Bo."

He tucked the money into his tight shorts. "You will remember me as the one that get away."

To her credit, Sylvia laughed, "Heh-hey," and said, "Bo, go quick before you kill me here this Saturday morning."

Chapter 35

Miriam put her fingers to her lips, taking time to close the door soundlessly. "You should let us know if you plan on coming in early, Grace. Anyhow," she said, "just try to be quiet. I only just got Ben to go down and Sol's resting. He had an accident."

"What happened?"

"Cut his hand. Lost quite a bit of blood."

"Oh."

"Please keep Ben quiet in the morning, okay, out of our room. I've got errands, and Sol needs to get some rest."

It wasn't even eight yet. I went up to Dave's, but he wasn't there. Not a sound from Brute and Cesar either. There was nothing to do. I didn't want to go in and turn on the television in case the sound disturbed Sol. I wasn't hungry enough to make something to eat. The evening outside was still warm and light. I took the elevator back down and was surprised to see old Paul still behind the desk. "Working a double, Paul?"

"What, Grace?"

I said a little louder, "Doubling up tonight?"

"No, no. Waiting for the Duke to come in and relieve me. Danny Boy called in tonight." He looked at his watch. "Better come soon. I've got a dance to go to."

I wasn't sure if he was joking.

"Okay, then . . ."

I headed off to the square and sat down on a bench far away from the playground, where I didn't need to be until the morning. I could see the shops across the road, the entrance to the subway, and the steps leading down to the paved area where kids on skateboards practiced their moves in the dying daylight.

That Miriam didn't want me to take classes on the nights I worked was nothing too major. I'd just take something on Friday night or during the day Saturday. More important, I needed to figure out where I was going to be staying in two weeks.

The subway exhaled a batch of riders, and I watched them come up, get their bearings, and move on. A blond girl ran up, and before her feet touched the top step, she hopped on her board and pushed off toward the guys on the ramps. She crossed a familiar profile, and I pulled back to see Evie standing with the double carriage a few feet from the entrance. I wondered if she ever went home. Evie raised her hand to greet someone coming up the stairs.

Duke.

He walked over and gave Evie's lifted cheek a brief kiss. She slowly circled him, straightening his high collar, dusting his yellow-fringed epaulets, and brushing flecks off his coat. Satisfied, she came back to the carriage, and they walked off together toward the towers.

"Wow," I said out loud, and the woman sitting on the next bench turned to look at me. I had no idea that Duke and Evie were, what? Were they married? Ule had never said a word, but then she prided herself on not gossiping. I said "wow" again, and the woman got up and walked away. I laughed and spread my arms along the back of my bench, wondering what else I might see if I stayed out late enough.

BEN WAS ANXIOUS TO see his mother.

"Maybe she'll come in and see us before she leaves."

"Grace, my daddy hand hurt."

"It is?" I couldn't bring myself to ask him questions about his parents. "Oh no."

"We were playing in the grass and Daddy and Dave were trying to cut down the big tree and Daddy cut his hand."

"Uh-oh, I hope he's all better now."

"He my daddy, Grace. He very strong, you know."

"I know."

"Can we go and see Mommy now?"

I could hear Miriam readying herself out there. "Okay, mister, I think Daddy is still resting. But you have to let me carry you into the living room, okay?" He stretched up his arms to be lifted. "And be vewwy vewwy quiet," I said in my best Elmer Fudd impersonation.

Miriam was dressed in the flowery tent I'd ironed on Friday evening, her white short shorts, and open-toed sandals. Ben leaned toward her. Now in the eighth month of her pregnancy, she was huge around her middle and wasn't able to carry him for more than a minute. Instead of taking him, she put both fists on her fat waist and crossed one foot behind the other. "What did I tell you last night, Grace?"

I felt stupid pointing out that Sol was not in the living room.

"I specifically told you to keep him in his room." She slung Ben low on her hips. "How's my big boy this morning?"

"Hi, Mommy. Can I come with you?"

"How do you know I'm going somewhere?" And to me she said, "What, you can't even follow simple directions now?"

"I know," Ben said. "Can I come?"

"Not this time. But, Ben, why don't you and Grace go for pizza pie today?"

"Yay, Grace! Pizza pie." He wiggled for her to put him down, and as soon as his feet touched ground, he started hopping about, chanting, "Pizza, pizza, pizza."

Miriam turned to me and, glaring, pressed her finger to her lips. Then Sol came out of their bedroom, shirtless in navy striped boxers. He held up a fatly bandaged left hand like a king crab's *gundy*.

"Daddy." Ben ran straight to his father, who managed to catch and lift him midsprint. I saw Sol grimace.

Miriam blew wet hair off her face. "Grace, this is exactly what I wanted to avoid. Sol, what are you doing?"

"Mir, I'm not straining my hand at all. Hey, buddy." He kissed Ben on the lips.

"Wow, Dad, look your hand."

Sol rotated his hand like the waving queen of England.

"Hey, Grace, did Mir tell you what happened?"

His chest was muscular, with a sprinkling of curly red hair in the middle.

Miriam answered for me. "No, I didn't get a chance to tell her last night. But, Sol, you really need to go lie down. The doctor said."

He cut her off. "I feel fine, Mir. You got me to stay home today, but I'm not going to spend the whole day in bed. Especially if you're not in it with me."

Her blush started just above her bosom and crept all the way up to her hairline.

"Can you throw a ball, Dad?" Ben asked.

"I can't throw a ball, but I can throw a boy." Sol moved closer to the armchair and plopped Ben into the soft cushions.

Miriam picked up her bag, "Okay, I can't watch this. I'll be back this afternoon. We'll talk tonight, Grace. Just try your best to keep"—she pointed her chin in Ben's direction—"away from this one as much as possible, please. Sol, go back to bed." She left, and Sol sprawled a little indecently on the floral couch. Ben slid off the armchair and scampered over to him.

"So what happened?" I asked Sol.

"I forgot I was born on the Upper East Side."

"What?"

"We went up to Dave's country house for the weekend, and I was helping him dig up this huge root from the backyard and I almost chopped off my thumb."

"Daddy had a hax, Grace."

"You cut your finger with an ax? How?" I couldn't understand the physics.

Sol laughed. "No. We'd busted up the stump with the ax already and were using these hand trowels to dig at it and I was clearing with my other hand and—" He made a stabbing motion, and I felt the slice.

"Ow."

"You're telling me. The doctor said I was lucky I didn't lose my entire thumb. But the painkillers cure all."

"Hey, Dad, do you want to come have pizza pie with me and Grace?"

"That sounds like fun, bud, but Daddy has to go back to bed or else Mommy might be mad when she gets home." He rolled his head against the back of the couch toward me. "Did you make coffee, Grace?"

"Not yet."

"Good, put on a fresh pot, will you?"

While the coffee brewed, I settled Ben in with a Pooh video and lay on the carpeted floor next to his chair. Maybe Miriam was going to fire me tonight, and that would be about perfect, right now. No place to live during the week or on weekends. The tape was halfway through when I heard their shower going. Ten minutes after that, Sol called me.

"Daddy want you, Grace," Ben informed me. He didn't look away from the Hundred Acre Wood.

Sol stood at the foot of their bed in an unbuttoned dress shirt and different boxers. A necktie dangled from the *gundy*. "Hey, I need some help."

I was a good ten feet away from him. "You're going to work?"

"Just for an hour, two tops. I'll be back before Mir gets home, so this is between us, okay?"

Wet, his hair was darker, more like copper.

"Do you know how to tie a tie?"

"Yes."

"Good, help me with the buttons, and then the tie."

Up close, he smelled fresh, like water and soap. I did the buttons quickly, having no choice but to look up as I got to his chest and then his neck. He stood with his arms up like a cornered bandit. After flicking the collar, I said, "Tie, please," and slid the silky fabric from the bandaged claw.

The job that I did flawlessly for Derek on countless mornings in Brooklyn was impossible to get right now.

"Christ," I said in frustration.

Sol laughed. I could feel his Adam's apple vibrate. "Just take your time, Grace."

I looked up and laughed too.

"Have I told you," he said, "that you look a lot like someone I used to know?"

I concentrated on tying the tie right this time. I measured out the two sides, pulled the thicker end almost down to his waist, and smoothed the fabric. I felt him against me but didn't move away. Maybe Miriam was going to fire me tonight. I fiddled with the tie some more and used my thumb to dimple the fabric just under the knot. The bristly hairs on his bare legs rubbed against my thighs. I was done with the tie, but still I ran my hand down the length of the silk, pressing the material against his body. I was giving him time.

I didn't lean into or away from him, only stood there with my hands hanging down. He was kissing me, and I was kissing him back. And it felt good. The elbow above his wounded hand nudged me to him, and I remembered Brent in the backseat of his car an age ago. What if Miriam did fire me tonight? Kathy would do it, and Bridget had done it. He cupped his able hand around my waist, and just when I decided to touch him, Ben called out—

"Grace," he shouted. "The tape end."

I jumped away from Sol.

"Grace, wait. Go put him in the crib. Close the door. Ah, fuck."

I moved toward the door and said, "It's done."

"What?" The king crab *gundy* was up again.

"Your coffee," I said. "It's done."

"I KNEW YOU HAD it in you," Kath said when I told her what almost happened.

"I am royally screwed."

"So very very close," she said.

"Please be serious. Plus, I think she's planning on firing me tonight, anyway. Jesus Christ."

"Then you should have gone ahead and fucked him for fucking him sakes, Grace."

"Why did I call you?"

"Why'd you call me? Let me tell you why you called me, because I'm the only one who'll tell you like it is. You know what?"

"I think so, but what's your what?"

"I think you're going to get fired tonight. She's been building it up for you. *I'm not paying you to go to school, go pick my strawberries? Can't you even follow simple directions now?* Give me a fucking break, Grace. Massa day done."

That was the campaign slogan of her father—he who had descended from indentured servants—the year it looked like the East Indian minority was going to take political power on the island. I laughed. "Shit, Kath."

"Tell me about it," she said. "You know what I would do now if I were you?"

"What would you do, Kath?"

"I'd tear up that frigging place to see what I could find."

"What? Why?"

"You heard me. That's all I'm saying."

.   .   .

I DIDN'T KNOW WHERE to start. There was nothing in the bedside tables and nothing beneath the layers of clothes in the dresser drawers. The
boxes on the top closet shelves held sweaters and long underwear, and
Miriam's smaller summer clothes left unpacked during her pregnancy.
The shoe boxes held shoes. All the way in the back of her walk-in closet
was a fat fabric garment bag. I unzipped the front expecting to see
Miriam's wedding dress and instead saw her black fur coat. I'd always
wanted to try it on.

I lifted the coat off the padded hanger and saw that it cloaked a large
brown shopping bag. I felt sheaves of paper and envelopes. I draped the
coat over my shoulders, surprised such a big, shaggy thing was so light,
then I took the bag off the hanger and sat on the raffia rug. There were
lots of greeting cards from Miriam's Brooklyn family. Happy Easter,
Merry Christmas, Happy Birthday, all addressed to Maria. I flipped through
them the way Evie fanned the cards during a pause in our all fours games.
And there were letters too. One fell out of a card, and I opened it to figure
out where it belonged. "Dear Solomon," it began in Miriam's familiar
looping script.

> Who knows, this might be the last letter I write to you. Whether
> it is or isn't depends on your response, but I had to write and let you
> know that I'll respect your decision, regardless. This is not how I
> pictured our relationship ending, me pregnant and contemplating
> not being and you being put in this god-awful position. Forgive me.
> You have to believe me when I tell you that this was an accident. I
> know what your mom is saying. I know what they want you to do.
> In the end, I can't tell you what choice to make, and I'll say it again:
> I'll respect your decision.
> Do know that I love you.
> Your Maria

Maria. Miriam . . . What Ettie must have put her through. And then to
have suffered one of the nightmares my mother regularly dreamed for
Helen and me, a baby born less than nine months after a wedding. "Jesus."
The letter had fallen from a white card embossed "For My Love." Inside

was a picture of a Miriam I barely recognized. Her hands were on her skinny waist, and she was laughing into the camera at something hilarious. Curly black hair framed her face and fell about shoulders. Her nose was different too—same as her father's and siblings' in Brooklyn. She looked young and beautiful and happy. I tucked it and the letter back in and, after running down the hall to check the door, continued going through the big brown bag.

"Inspector's Report." The address listed was unknown to me until I scanned down further. "Also known as Duck Hollow" in brackets. Under the report were several mortgage approval letters on bank stationery. From Citibank, Chemical, Apple, Merchants. "What the—?" My body was heating up in the fur, and I shrugged the coat off into a luscious black pool around my hips. Then I knew. Miriam and Sol were buying Dave's house in the country. It made sense. Dave had said that, when Vincent was alive, Sol and Miriam were always there. And she was crying at the house after our trip to the farm. I wondered just how much money Sol had, that they could afford to buy a weekend house, but when I saw the listing I understood.

SPACIOUS TWO-BEDROOM APARTMENT WITH SEPARATE MAID'S ROOM. TWO FULL BATHS. SWEEPING DOWNTOWN AND UNION SQUARE VIEWS. CENTRAL AIR. TWENTY-FOUR-HOUR LIVERIED CONCIERGE. HEALTH CLUB, HEATED OLYMPIC-SIZE POOL, AND DRY CLEANERS. MANHATTAN AMENITIES FOR UPSCALE, URBAN LIVING. SAT–SUN SHOWINGS ONLY.

"Holy moly." I closed the folder and put both my hands into the warm folds of the fur. And then I saw it. The manila envelope I had given to Miriam months ago with all the sponsorship forms filled out and my passport photos signed on the back and my money. "Oh, God." I reached for the envelope, half hoping that it was empty. That she had transferred everything to another envelope and kept this one for reference, but it was full and still unsealed. I tilted it over onto the floor in front of the fur. It was all there. My seven twenties and one ten fanned out, and both photos fell facedown.

It was 10:34. Twenty minutes had passed since I sat down, and everything had changed. Except of course nothing had. All this time I'd been waiting and asking and scanning the piles of mail not a damn thing had been going on. Now I didn't know what to do. I couldn't confront Miriam about this because then she'd know that I'd been digging around and would fire me on the spot. But what if she did fire me tonight? I decided that, if she let me go, I'd ask for my money. In the meanwhile, I had to see Dave.

He answered the door this time. "Hey, Grace. What a great surprise. I love it when you come up in the daytime. And look who's with you. Hello, Benjamin Bruckner. Come on in, guys." Brutus and Cesar had already found refuge from the sun in the short morning shadows, and Ben made off to pet them.

"You want coffee?" Dave asked me.

I shook my head, and Dave asked Ben, "How's Daddy this morning?"

"His hand is hurt, but my daddy strong, *zio*."

"He is," Dave said, and then to me he mouthed, "Oh, please. Did they tell you what happened yesterday?" he asked. I nodded, and Dave said, "City slickers." He hoisted a sack of the gorgeous compost delivered from the botanic garden onto the table. "So what's going on with you, Grace Jones?"

"Dave, how come you didn't tell me Sol and Miriam are buying your house?"

The penknife I'd given him slit the threaded edge of the burlap, and the rich fertilizer spilled out, dank and woodsy sweet. "Miriam told you? Finally."

So it was true then.

"Oh, Grace, I wanted to tell you so many times."

"So why didn't you tell me something?"

"You don't understand. I couldn't. Miriam specifically told me not to mention it to you, or to the doormen. She outright asked me to not say anything."

"But, Dave, we're friends."

"I know we're friends"—he stuck the opened knife in the bag— "and I tried to drop you hints."

"When'd you drop me hints?"

"In Brooklyn, that time in the garden when you told me about coming to New York. Remember? I asked you what you'd do if Sol and Miriam ever moved?"

"That was a hint? Just last week I was telling you about going to school, and you said it was a great idea. Solid, you said. Bullshit, Dave."

"But it *is* solid. Grace, please. You're so upset. Just listen to what I'm trying to tell you."

But I couldn't care less about what he had to say. "Ah, forget you." Sylvia had said it to Bo over the weekend, everybody looked out for their own. And I was not his own.

I WASN'T FIRED THAT night after all. When Ben and I came in from the playground that evening, Sol and Miriam's bedroom door was closed. I fed Ben his dinner, gave him a nice long bath, and then took him into his room. After a while I heard Sol and Miriam's shower running, and later, both their voices in the living room. Then they came in. Miriam's hair was still wet and she had changed from her morning outfit into a white, strapless maternity dress. Her breasts were huge, and I saw little red hickey welts all over her neck. Sol stood behind her and she cocooned into him.

"Okay, Grace," she said, "we're going out, so you're on tonight."

"Okay."

"Where you going, Mommy?"

"Daddy is taking me dancing."

"Wow, that sounds like fun," he said and slid off his chair and danced a jig.

I looked past Miriam to Sol, and he winked at me.

"Have fun," I said.

After Ben fell asleep, I poured a glass of their red wine and went to my room to think. Then I had another glass and thought some more and I came up with nothing.

MIRIAM WAS STANDING AT the foot of my bed. "Grace."

"What?"

"Telephone. It really is too late to have your friends calling you here."

I thought so too. "Hello?" I said into the receiver.

"Grace?"

"Helen?" And all the blood in my body pooled in my stomach. "Oh, God, oh, God."

"He back in hospital, Grace. They want to cut the other foot."

"What? When?"

"Dr. Silverton say soon, maybe by Sunday."

"What? This Sunday? Helen, what going on? I thought he was getting better."

"Mammy didn't want to worry you."

"Jesus Christ."

"You know how she is, Grace."

"Okay, so you tell me. What happening?"

"You know how the general hospital does operate. Quick, quick to cut. If we could get him to Cumberland, maybe they could do something."

"Well, he should be in Cumberland, then."

"You know how much money that going to cost? Plenty."

"Mammy know you calling me?"

"No. I just stopped by the lady on the hill coming from hospital. Was my turn today."

It was so late for her to be traveling alone.

"Okay, listen, come back by the lady on the hill tomorrow. Come for noon."

"You have the money?"

"Just come tomorrow, okay. Don't say nothing."

"Grace?"

"What?"

"He was talking about you tonight."

"Yeah, what he say?"

"You want to know?"

"What he say?"

"That he too too glad you not here to see him like this."

"Oh, Hel."

I COUNTED THE MONEY three times to be sure. Two hundred dollars was missing. Late as it was, I called Sylvia.

"Sylvia, the money was there on Saturday when I gave Bo the twenty dollars."

"What I could do?" Her voice rose. "You think I take your money?"

I didn't think so at all. But Micky and Derek had come to the house for a while on Sunday when Dodo had gone to church. "Just ask Micky—"

Sylvia cut me off. "What you saying in truth? You think my children take your money?"

"Sylvia, I have to send that money home."

"You don't think I have enough problem in my life right now? Now you come from where you come from to accuse my children?" She was screaming at me. "You don't see Dodo was right in truth. I should have leave you right on Eastern Parkway where I find you."

"Sylvia . . ."

"I don't want to hear it, Miss Grace, just come and get your thing before I put them on the side of the road. And find somewhere else to stay from this weekend."

She hung up and I was stunned, but I knew I wasn't crazy. My money was gone. I rang Kath. "Don't worry," she said after I'd told her what was going on.

"Don't worry? Kath, my fucking life caving in."

"No, it's not, Grace." She yawned. "Let me call Daddy. Call me back in the morning, early."

WHEN I SAW MY swollen face and puffy eyes in the mirror, I laughed. "Black Chinee for real," I said to my reflection. Cold water didn't do much, and by the time I finally came out of the bathroom, Miriam was waiting for me in the kitchen.

"We have to talk, Grace."

This was good, because I needed to talk to her too.

"You have to respect our home. You don't live here, you work here. I think you've been forgetting that lately. Sunday night I asked you to keep Ben away from Sol, and you did the exact opposite. You're getting personal mail here now. You're drinking our wine. And now your friends feel like they can call you up in the middle of the night?"

Sol came out of their room and stood in the hallway behind me.

Miriam went on. "Do you know what time I finally went back to sleep after you got off the phone last night? I didn't—I knew you kept calling friend after friend."

"Mir."

"No, Sol, this is not acceptable."

It was my turn to talk. "Miriam, I need the money I gave you to file my papers."

"What?"

"When I gave you the immigration forms, I gave you a hundred and fifty dollars. My sister called me last night. Our father's sick, and I need to send them money."

Sol moved into the kitchen and stood next to his wife. "Is everything okay, Grace?"

I didn't want to, but I started to cry, because I had the feeling that everything was not okay.

"How do you know—"

But Sol cut her off. "Not now, Mir. Give Grace the money. Grace"—he looked me in the eyes—"is there anything we can do to help you out? Anything at all?"

I tried to dry my eyes, but the stupid tears wouldn't stop flowing. "No, Sol, thanks. Just let me have the money. I have to go call my friend."

Miriam said, "Grace, I didn't know."

I nodded and moved past them to ring Kathy.

Chapter 36

I had taken this drive in reverse a lifetime ago. I had come in the cold, and Kath was leaving at summer's peak. Leaving hot for hot. Kath and I talked nonstop as if nothing had changed. I guess for her it hadn't. But I was two Graces, because inside I was numb. How could I be going to the airport but not going home? How could I let Kath get on a plane when I was the one with the dying father? Because I had no doubt he was going to die soon.

Every fifteen minutes or so, Kath remembered how come she was leaving and that I couldn't go and she quieted down for a while. But then she remembered that she was going home, Grace, home. And her daddy was going to let her manage the new store. I didn't want to take that away from her, her happy return. I was all mixed up. I wanted to stay in America, but I wanted to go home too. Just for a while to see my father. But I couldn't because my daddy didn't know every Tom, Dick, and Harry.

"Kath?"

"Um?"

"Nothing."

"No, what, Grace?"

And I said nothing again, because how could I tell her that I wanted to switch places with her and that she should give me her ticket and her passport and I should get on the plane and she should drive back to Brooklyn with Brent?

"You remember I told you that Dave's boyfriend died from AIDS?"

"What? Vaguely."

"Well, he had cancer. And, go and see Daddy when you get home, okay. Tell him you used to see me all the time, and that I'm settled."

"Oh, Gracie, you don't have to tell me to do that."

Brent squeezed the back of my neck. Kath had refused to see Donovan her final night in the city. "No fucking way, Grace," she'd said to me. "Never again. None of that baggage coming home with me. I'm shedding the shit I picked up in this city."

She had also shed her hair. That morning when I got to her room, now my room, and Kath opened the door, I screamed. Shivani came running down the stairs to see what was wrong.

"Do you like it?" Kath, in a short khaki skirt and matching jacket, turned slowly around. She had a slanted bob just like Ettie Bruckner's. It didn't flatter her new, desiccated frame.

"Oh, Kath," was all I could say.

It was Shivani who spoke up. "What you gone and do that for? Look how you had all that nice nice *coco-'pañol* hair and you gone and chop it off. Watch how you spoil yourself, girl."

Kath only laughed. "Go back upstairs, Shivani."

Shivani splayed her fingers at her own neck and looked worried. "You know, I did never give you back that pack of maxi pad you lend me that time."

I looked at Kath, but she laughed again. "Don't worry about it, Shivani. I forget about that long time now."

Kath and I moved into the room. It looked exactly the same. The white, quilted spread on the bed, her frilly curtains tied with white ribbons hanging in the window, her tubes and tubs of makeup on her dresser. "Kath, where's your luggage?" I had expected a row of suitcases, hastily packed and bulging, but instead she pointed to one carry-on bag on the floor.

"That's all?" I opened the closet door, and the closet was bare. "What happened to your clothes?" I asked, astonished.

"I threw them all out, Grace. I told you I wasn't taking any load, and I didn't want to leave baggage for you either. Everything I need in that one bag."

That bag was the size of one of her larger pocketbooks.

"Anyhow, remember idiot-boy paid rent until the end of September, so don't let that crook Bajan try to jack you. Brent call already to say he on his way."

I closed the closet door. "Brent called?"

"Yeah." Kath nodded, and her newly short hair snapped like shutting blinds in front of her face. "I didn't tell you he driving me to the airport? He'll bring you back too."

I hadn't seen Brent since the night of Kath's birthday. And now, as we drove closer to the airport, with the planes flying low and gigantic, he and I didn't talk to each other much. Kath jumped out when we arrived at the terminal, and I got out with her.

Brent leaned over. "Me soon come, yeah. Make me find a park."

Kath tucked her bob behind her ear. "No, B, just wait a minute."

She turned to me. "Grace, don't bother to come in with me. Is not like home anyhow. Once I check in, I gone."

"So what, you want us to leave you here on the curb?"

"Look how you turn American already, saying *curb*."

She was stalling. "Come on, Kath, I'm not letting you go in alone."

She hoisted her bag and looked more like a flight attendant than like a passenger. "You've never let me go alone, Grace. Is just, I have to do this." I kind of understood what she was saying, but still. "Go, Grace. Go back to the room and have some fun, finally." She winked and smiled at me, showing her wide-spaced teeth. "I'll see your dad soon."

We hugged, everything we'd been through pressed tight between us. Kath turned and walked through the revolving doors. They swept her in, and I didn't see her again.

IT WAS STILL MORNING when we got back to Kathy's block. It still looked the same. Children squealed as they ran in and out of the spray from the fire hydrant. Teenage boys in baggy shorts and white undershirts hung around waiting for the day to pass. West Indian women carried grocery bags from Bravo or vegetables from the Korean market. Brent stopped in front of Kathy's building. I didn't hesitate. "Coming up?" I asked him.

We climbed the four flights, and once inside, Brent was so big in that small space.

"Go ahead, sit on the bed," I told him.

The sounds of Brooklyn's summer came up, kids, cars, water, all accompanied by the nonstop Puerto Rican anthem, *Nen-neh-neh, nen-neh-neh*. The room was warm.

Brent patted the quilt. "Come sit with me."

Somewhere in this world my daddy was dying, and all I had left of him was some spilled dirt in the bottom of my bag. I knew what was about to happen between Brent and me, but I couldn't stop thinking about my father. I closed my eyes, and the tears landed on my bare legs. Brent wiped away the drops with his thumb, searing me.

"Darkie, watch me," he said.

He held my chin with his fingertips and guided my head to face him. I wouldn't open my eyes.

"Watch me," he said again, and I took a deep breath and looked at his beautiful face so close to mine. He lifted his eyebrows and I smiled and then he laughed and said, "Good. Things gone be all right, you know. You can't believe it now, but mark what me say, yeah. You especially gone be all right. Come." He leaned over and, instead of my lips, kissed the corner of my eye. "You want feel likkle better?"

I nodded.

"All right then." He kissed me on the mouth, and my body flared hot and liquid. Heat rose up from my chest and flushed my face, and I was sure he could feel the warmth coming off me. I tried to pull back, but instead he crushed me to him and murmured, "Uh-uh."

"Wait, Brent," I said, and he stopped kissing me at once. "Wait."

I slid off his lap and stood between his opened legs. I unbuttoned my shirt and then kicked off my slippers and stepped out of my shorts. I undid the banana clip holding my hair off my neck. I unhooked my brassiere, then stepped out of my panties and straightened up. I wanted him to see all of me.

Brent made a noise. He knelt in front of me, burying his face just under my navel. He kissed me lower, and to steady myself I held on to the back of his head. His breath was hot on my legs. His hands clasped low around my waist, holding me.

"Come," he said.

I sat on the bed's edge and watched him take off his shirt and lower his jeans; then he came back to me and we lay down together. His hands were cool and hot. Cool on my breasts and hot on my hips and scorching between my legs. I liked that he could fold me up in his bear body, that he could almost consume me. I liked his full weight pressing me into the bed, that he kept whispering "Darkie" in my ear, and how slick his back felt when I wrapped my arms around him, pulling him into me. I liked the pain, and when he tried to pull away after I winced, I wrapped my legs around him too.

We slept for a long time afterward, and I smiled, drowsy, and thought what a roundabout way to finally experience the luxury of lying in on a summer's weekday. Later, I watched him get dressed, and when he was ready to go, he came back to the bed and kissed me. "So, me can stop by tomorrow after work?"

Tomorrow was Saturday. "And Sunday, too."

After he left, I stayed in the bed. Lying on my stomach, I could feel my heartbeat thudding into the quilt and blood pulsing through my neck and elbows. I was truly alone in America, and I didn't mind at all. In fact, I was thirsty. I went to grab a glass from Kath's cupboard to go to the house's communal kitchen. I opened the door and laughed when I saw her BeDazzler. Right next to it, bulging like pirate's booty, were two bags of recovered gems waiting for their rightful owner.

WHEN I'D LEFT WORK Thursday, no one had said anything about the next week. So here it was Sunday night, and I was back at the towers.

"It's Princess Grace and her pretty face," Danny said. I made up my mind then and there to ignore him. Either he'd stop being a pest or he wouldn't, but I couldn't be bothered.

Sol opened the door. His thick brown bandage had been replaced with a much smaller white one. Last week's fat *gundy* was now a pair of pincers. There was no hug tonight. "Mir had a rough weekend," he said. "Sit down for a second."

I sat on the edge of the armchair, the one that had sucked me in on the day of my interview, the day he had told me that I reminded him of someone.

"How's your hand?"

Sol sat too. "So much better. I can even move my thumb a little bit now. How's your father?"

I bit my lower lip. "He's in a different hospital, but it looks like they're

going to have to amputate his other leg anyhow. This is the island, you
know." I was sure he didn't know.

"Again, if there's anything we can do, you just let us know," he said.

I wondered if Sol even understood what his words meant, that they
were an offer of help. What they could have done was filed my immigration papers, or told me they were moving, or not paid me forty dollars
less for taking last Friday off. I was so tempted to tell him these little
things that they could have done, or to ask him what specifically he was
offering to do, but all I said was "Thanks, Mr. Bruckner."

"Anyhow, Mir and I talked, and she's fine. She's sorry, you know. She
had no idea that it was your sister on the phone. We didn't even know
that your father was an amputee, Grace." He exercised the thumb a little
and reached for the remote control to unmute the baseball. "You gonna
go see Dave tonight?"

There was no awkwardness on his part. Sol acted like nothing had
happened, and, after the weekend with Brent, I realized that nothing had.
His game was already on. "I'm tired from this weekend too," I told him.
"I'm going to bed."

MIRIAM CAME OUT OF her room looking ready to deliver. Her hair
was unwashed, her bare feet red and swollen. Her pregnant belly was
huge. She held a tall glass of iced water in one hand and massaged under
her robe with the other.

"Morning, Miriam. How are you feeling?" I said.

She gestured with the glass and grimaced. I grabbed Ben before he
could dash to her.

"Grace and I going playground, Mommy."

"You are?" She had no oomph in her voice. "Good. Give me Rabbit,
and I'll snuggle up with him until you get back." I set Ben down, and he
handed his mother the toy. I was waiting, waiting to hear if she would
ask how I'd known about the unfiled forms, or that the money had still
been there, tucked away with their important papers. But she didn't say
a word.

On our way to the park, Ben twisted in his carriage. "Grace, your daddy
only has one foot?"

I wondered who he'd heard that from. "He does."

He nodded. "Wow, that's a big cut. Your daddy strong, Grace?"

I made bodybuilder arms. "Very strong."

"How does he walk around?"

"He hops like a bunny rabbit, or a froggy." I bit my lip hard, remembering my father coming to the living room without his crutches on the night I left home, and how hard he had breathed after going the short distance.

"Really, Grace? Can he hop for a long time?"

"Uh-huh, for hours."

Ben hopped over the sprinklers. Soon, Sammy and Caleb and Bruce and all the other kids were hopping in and out of the sunlit spray. I sat on the bench next to Ule and Meena. Evie stood by the swings talking with Margaret and Marva. After that morning in the park, we had spoken to each other only when the children played together. She and Ule were through. Now she came over. "So how everything go?" She had watched Benjamin on Friday, and my forty dollars had gone to her.

"Good, Evie. Thanks for asking."

But this was Evie. "So they cut the other foot?"

"Chut, man," Ule chided without saying her name.

"What? Is only ask me asking."

"Not yet. They still waiting to see how things go."

Marva shook her head, the bruise on her temple barely visible. "Me, mama? Me don't trust West Indian doctor to come cut my toenail, far less come for cut foot. When you see I go Montserrat, is nearly the whole pharmacy I does take, *oui*."

"Is the same thing I was thinking," Evie said, "and Bimshire ain't no backwater island like where you come from, Marva."

I laughed and Ule and the rest too, like we used to before. Marva wasn't too sure what we were cracking up about, and she looked around at us. Gradually, as the morning temperature rose and the humidity started to smother, they left, but I stayed on the bench with Ule. When it was just the two of us sitting there, Ule said, "Skin teef. She and that one waistband Duke, the two of them aiming to dominate domestic work. That woman is a *mapepire*." She opened her bag and pulled out a few pieces of paper. One by one she brought them very close to her eyes.

"You want me to see something for you, Ule?" I asked her.

"Why? Something wrong with my eye?"

"Not at all, I just offering."

"Good"—she handed me a piece of paper—"what that say?"

I laughed and took it. Her full name, her address in Brooklyn, and her telephone number were written in a very neat penmanship. "Me didn't want talk me business in front all Tom, Nancy, and Harry. Tomorrow is the last day I on this work, and then I gone Kennedycut for six weeks."

"Tomorrow? Connecticut? I thought you only worked in the city, Ule."

"And is who tell you that?"

No one had. I'd just assumed.

"With baby nurse work, you go where it have babies, my child. In truf, I did think Miriam was going to hire me for this one coming, but maybe Miss Evie already get one friend for her."

"I think they'll be gone by the time the baby born."

"Miriam tell you they moving?"

For sure Ule'd disapprove if I told her that I went digging through their papers. "I saw their apartment listed for sale," I said.

"Well, but you never know. They could be getting another place maybe right in this same building. They gone need more space, you know."

"No, they're buying Dave's house upstate."

"Aha. And what it is you going to do? You going with them?"

My shoulders felt too heavy to shrug. Over the weekend, whenever Brent hadn't been in my bed, it was all I had thought about. Maybe up until a week ago I might have considered going with them. But now I could not go. "No."

Ule squeezed my shoulders. "Good. You have to try your own luck. You can't take nobody else life and make it your own. Petal used to talk all that God and prayers talk, but you have to have plenty common sense too. Good good."

I didn't want to ask Ule if she thought I had common sense, because seriously, sometimes I really thought I didn't have a drop. Kathy was sharp. Bridget, razor. And me, I was just floating by on a breeze, pure luck and chance.

Chapter 37

We were winding down the day. Ben had just chosen his perennial favorite book, *Pish Posh,* and the newer *Alexander and the Terrible, Horrible, No Good, Very Bad Day.* "Bed or lap?" I asked him.

"Lap please, Grace."

"How about I sit on your lap for a change?"

He laughed. "Grace, I'm a little boy. You would break me."

"Okay," I said and gathered him onto me.

"Wait, Grace." He scooted off for Rabbit.

"Ready?"

He climbed up, smelling deliciously of baby shampoo. "*Pish Posh* first, please."

"Since you asked so nicely."

Sol and Miriam were at the movies. Now in the final stretch of her pregnancy and despite her discomfort, she was determined to go out as often as possible before she was *saddled with two.* Her words. I liked them being gone. I had Ben to myself and could relax.

The phone rang.

"One minute, mister." I passed him *Pish Posh.* "Show Rabbit the pictures."

"Hello?"

"Grace? Is that you, Grace? Grace . . . is you, Grace?"

"Micky?"

"Yes, Grace. Is me. Grace . . ." She sounded spitty and garbled.

"Micky, slow down. Take the fingers out your mouth."

"Grace . . . my brother. My bro-bro-ther," she stammered.

"Okay, Micky. Did Derek do something? You want to put Derek on the phone?"

"No, Grace. My b-r-oth-er . . ." She was hysterical. "Grace, is Dame."

"My brother what? Micky, breathe. Slow, slow." She took great sobbing gulps of air and then cried hard again. "Micky? Can you hear me? Tell me what happen. Where Mammy? Where Sylvia?"

"She, she, she went to the hospital, Grace."

"Hospital?" This wasn't good. Had something happened at the G Building?

"Grace, can you come? Can you come now, Grace?"

"Micky, I can come in a little while, okay? But first you have to tell me what happened. Take your time."

"Grace"—the word twisted—"is Dame . . ." She began wailing again. "Dame fell."

"Okay. Dame fell off the couch, off the crib? What?" I didn't want to lose my patience with her, but I needed to know what was going on. "Micky," I said a little too sharply, but I couldn't help it. She was scaring me. "Stop. Tell me what is going on."

I heard her snotty inhale and then, "Grace, Dame fell out the window."

And that feeling again, all the blood in my body pooling in my stomach and leaving the rest of me cold.

"Who home with you and Derek? Where Auntie Dodo?"

"Uncle Bo. And Nello. We moving. Auntie Dodo in church. The police." She wasn't making much sense. "Grace, I'm scared."

"Okay. Hang up. I'm coming."

Sweet Ben was showing Rabbit the kooky pictures. "Come on, buddy," I told him, "we have to go."

"Go where, Grace? Can I bring my book?"

I took *Pish Posh* away. "It's just for a little while, Ben. Leave your book."

"Can I bring Rabbit?"

I was only taking him down to Evie's. "Okay, Rabbit can come." I scooped him up. "Let's go."

I had fifteen dollars and change, about enough to take a cab one way. I took the week's twenty from the money cup and started to write a note—*Ben with Evie*—but I heard the elevator ding and ran out of the apartment.

Evie came to the door in housecoat and slippers, tightening her curler. "What you want this hour of the night?"

"Evie, I have to run Brooklyn now. Sol and Miriam not home. Watch Ben for me please till they come?"

She sized me up. "What big emergency you have so?"

"Evie, it *is* an emergency . . ." But I couldn't get the words out, I couldn't explain. "I'm in a hurry, please?" I held Ben over to her, but she turned down her lips and shook her head.

"No, my hands full right now. Caleb and Sammy have cold and fever."

"Come on, Evie. This is an emergency. Just put him on the couch, please. I have to go now."

Evie smiled. "Now you upset, me could hear the Trinidadian in your voice."

"What?"

Ben craned out of my arms to catch a glimpse of the twins. "Can I have a sleepover with Caleb and Sammy, Grace?" he asked.

Evie reached out and touched his hair. "Not tonight, bad boy." She smiled a little. "Why you don't run go ask your best friend Ule?" This was bullshit. "Or maybe the friend she give the work can watch him for you?"

We rode up to Dave's. No answer. "Oh, come on," I said as I slapped my palm against the door until it hurt, and Ben too banged and called to the dogs. "I don't think *Zio* home, Grace."

"I think you're right, buddy." I thought about the numbers on the refrigerator. I could go back and call Ettie or Nancy. But then I'd have to wait around for one of them to show up, or ride all the way uptown. I had to get to Brooklyn *now*.

"Hey, Ben, want to ride a taxi at night?"

Duke was hanging up the intercom. He tipped his hat. "You in a hurry, Miss Trinidad."

"Duke," I said. "Do me a favor?"

He looked up from his bifocals. "Yes?"

"It's so so important. I have to go to—"

"You want *me* to do *you* a favor?"

"Duke, please, this is serious. Tell Mr. and Mrs. Bruckner I have a family emergency. Ben is with me, and we'll be back soon, okay, Duke?" I didn't wait for him to answer. I couldn't. I just ran out the door.

"Ben, we need to find a taxi," I said. "Want to help me hail?" I wriggled my hand in the air to show him how.

"Here he comes, Grace." Ben clutched Rabbit and shot his other hand in the air.

"Good. But we need one with the light on. See the light on the top?"

"Okay, Grace." He tried to hail the next one, but it was full as well.

"Okay. How 'bout I try to get the cab and you keep a lookout for Mommy and Daddy?"

C'mon, cab, I pleaded into the night. And *c'mon, Sol and Miriam. Please. Please. Please.*

A cab stopped to let someone off, and I tumbled Ben into the backseat before the driver even knew we were there.

I slammed the door shut, relieved. "Eastern Parkway, please. Between Nostrand and New York."

The driver shook his head. "I don't go Brooklyn."

"What?"

"No go Brooklyn."

"You have to go Brooklyn. I'm not getting out of this car." He switched off the ignition. "Are you for fucking real?" I demanded. I didn't have the time for this. "Oh, for fuck's sakes."

"That's a bad word, Grace."

"Get out my cab."

I grabbed Ben, wanting to curse the driver more. Instead, I left his back door wide open. We'd already walked away when he got out and flung Rabbit the distance between us. "Grace," Ben screamed and hugged his buddy tight.

Without really thinking, I ran down the station steps and into the subway. It was screeching loud and especially hot, but the train we wanted was already on the track. Finally something working out my way. No one noticed or cared that Ben was in his shortie pj's and barefoot. He sat facing me, with his legs splayed and Rabbit held to his chest.

"Wow, Grace, this train is loud," he said.

"It sure is. Do this." I showed him how to clamp his hands over his ears.

He wedged Rabbit between us and covered his ears. I hugged him to me. I knew that Sol and Miriam were going to be furious. In fact, they were going to fire me as soon as I got back to the apartment. I nuzzled

Ben's red hair as the train sped through the tunnels. The conductor made an announcement just past Franklin: "Due to police activity, this number three train will be bypassing Nostrand Avenue, Kingston Avenue. The next station stop on this local train will be Utica."

People fretted, and I said, "Oh, for fuck's sakes."

"You said a very bad word, Grace," Ben told me.

The woman sitting next to me laughed. "Aye, so 'im feisty with 'im fire hair."

At Utica the trains were doing the express route in reverse. "Okay, Ben," I said—he was heavy to haul up the stairs—"we have to walk. This is an adventure."

"A venture!" he repeated. "Let's go, Grace."

After one block we got in a livery cab, and the driver said eight dollars for the six-block ride.

"You mad or you crazy?" I asked him. "Between New York and Nostrand I say. Just down the road."

"You see what going on down there." He pointed toward New York Avenue. "Is real bacchanal out here tonight. Seven dollars, come." I cut my eyes to let him know I knew he was ripping me off, but I had to get to Sylvia's. Our four-minute ride took twenty.

Brooklyn was on fire.

"What's going on?"

The cabbie had rolled up all the windows, locked the doors, and turned on the air-conditioning. Something was happening. Everyone was angry and shouting and running toward Union. People were crossing Eastern Parkway against the lights, cutting through the mostly stalled traffic, forcing the moving cars to stop. The Hasidim were out in full force too.

"Look, Grace." Ben pointed to the groups of Hasidic men in their black suits and white shirts. "They look like penguins."

And they did kind of. Agitated penguins. Then about twelve black boys charged one penguin colony, and the whole crowd went down. I covered Ben's eyes. "Jesus Christ, what is going on?" It looked like the end of the world, as if the messiah had come and was very very angry.

A police car was parked in front of Sylvia's building. The elevator was out of order. I ran up all five flights carrying Ben and saw two of Sylvia's neighbors and an officer outside her door.

"Somebody, please, tell me what is going on."

"Uh, uh, uh"—the Jamaican lady who watched Dame sometimes held her housecoat closed—"is a damn shame."

"And who are you?" the officer asked.

For a second I didn't know exactly who I was. "I'm a cousin. Where's Sylvia?"

Micky ran out into the hallway. "Grace." Her hair was wild, she was wild. "My brother dead, Grace." The officer let me in, but there was no in to go. The front closet had come tumbling down along with everything else in the apartment. Another officer stood by the opened window. A Chinese man with a pen behind his ear and a camera around his neck was also in the living room. His latex gloves were almost the same color as his skin. Micky and Derek now stood next to me, a little shy of Ben, who was watching everything with wide eyes.

"Aunty Dodo and Bo not here yet?"

"And you are?" the second officer wanted to know.

"A cousin. Can somebody please tell me what happened?"

"Dame fell out the window, Grace," Derek whispered. I had never seen him this calm. "My brother dead."

"The baby's dead?" I asked both the officer and the Chinese man. Neither answered. Micky started to cry.

"And whose baby is this?" the officer wanted to know. Ben had been quiet the whole time, clinging to me like a monkey.

"I mind him. I'm his babysitter." With the three kids on me, I needed to sit. I picked up a pile of clothes to clear a place. There was so much stuff on the couch.

"Please, no touching anything, ma'am," the Chinese man said.

"Look"—I let the pile fall away from my hand—"is just clothes. The landlord been fixing the lead paint."

He took a spiral notebook from his jeans and the pen from behind his ear. "And who is the landlord?"

"Jacob something or other. You have to ask my cousin."

The policeman's radio squawked, and the one in the hallway echoed its call. That officer came in. "Sounds like it's heating up bad down there. We're gonna have to go soon. You almost done, Ting?"

Ting started snapping again. Their radios didn't stop, and I made out "All units respond, all units respond, all units in nonemergency situations respond."

Loud knocking startled us all. "This is my sister's house," Dodo shouted. "Let me come in, do you hear me?" She ran down the hall ahead of Bo, took in the wrecked space, the officer, the Chinese man, the opened window, and started screaming. Micky started to cry, and then Ben began to whimper.

The officer came over to Dodo, his blue eyes warm. "Ma'am. Ma'am, please. You're upsetting the children. Please, ma'am."

"Oh, God, you mean the baby dead, in truth. Bo? Bo?"

Bo lit a cigarette, and the orange flare reflected on his sweaty face. "I done tell you what happen, Dodo. That mother-ass Jacob have plenty blood on he hand." He leaned against the entryway in a dirty undershirt, three-quarter jeans, and sneakers without laces. "Grace, who child is that?"

"The little boy. But I have to go back. Bo, what happen?"

Barely, he raised his chin at the officer. Dodo calmed and asked if the children needed to stay for any reason.

The officer looked over at Ting, who shrugged. "No, they can go."

"Come, Micky and Derek. Come, let's go. This place is hell."

"Grace, we could come with you?"

Dodo wrenched Micky's arm. "I say come on. Grace have to go."

We tried to hustle out, impossible in the madhouse the apartment had become. The space in the corridor was tight. You had to turn sideways and rub the roach-streaked wall to get by. Micky stopped, and the parade halted behind her. She bent and tugged at something from deep under the pile.

"Micky, move it. Let's go," Dodo ordered.

She ignored her aunt and kept pulling. She tugged some more, freeing what remained of Hannah Speiser's wings.

"I could keep this, Grace?"

I hugged Ben and nodded.

THE WARM AND SMOKY summer's night was sparking. Dodo took Micky and Derek away. I needed to get back with Ben and too late realized that I should have called Sol and Miriam from upstairs. Crowds were moving deeper into Crown Heights, and I wondered for the third time what was going on. The late light was starting to fade, but in front of all the solemn buildings on Eastern Parkway, groups were gathered and restless. Bo pulled me aside from the others on Sylvia's stoop.

"Hear what go on. Me and Nello come to help Sylvia, scene? Girl, we move so much box and it was so hot up in that place, jackass Nello open the damn window. I didn't see and Sylvia didn't see. The place didn't even feel no different. After about fifteen minutes, Sylvia say, 'But where Dame?' Me didn't pay she no mind, until maybe about five minutes later she say, 'Bo, but where Dame gone in truth?' Then we start to look around, and, girl, is me first who notice the blasted window open and you know how Dame like to sit down on that windowsill and when I look out I see him bend up on all the rubbish outside. I bawl."

I wiped my tears, and, for the first time since we got to Sylvia's, Ben spoke. "Don't cry, Grace."

I rubbed his slim back. "And where Nello?"

Bo lifted his chin to Miss Florence's dark stoop. "He there." He dropped his voice even lower. "But don't worry. We going down the road. Jacob not getting away so easy with this."

"And Sylvia, Bo?"

"Grace, I thought that girl was going to dead here tonight. If you see how she fly down them steps, bawling. She bawl so until the ambulance come, and she was still bawling when they drive away."

"Oh, God." I had to ask him because I still wasn't sure. "And Dame dead, Bo? Really and truly dead?"

He ground the cigarette butt out. "Dead dead."

I DIDN'T KNOW HOW long it took to get a livery cab back into the city.

Ben fell asleep in my arms, and I realized that we didn't have Rabbit. I felt around, and once I was certain he wasn't there, I was sure he was gone forever.

The cabbie, who looked exactly like Ali at the newsstand, watched me through the rearview. "You helping them out, eh. Getting him out of Brooklyn for your friends?"

I didn't answer. We were driving over the bridge, I didn't know which one, and there again was the nighttime city before me. It was still beautiful. Still dazzling and alive. But crazy. Real crazy.

Danny picked up the intercom before the door had even closed behind us. "They're coming up now, Mr. Bruckner." He hung up and said, "Princess Grace is in trouble tonight."

Sol was standing outside the elevator. A police officer stood beside him. He snatched Ben out of my arms, waking him. "How dare you, Grace? How fucking dare you?"

The officer said, "Sir, please," and Sol loped down the hall with his son. The officer followed. Everyone was inside: Big Ben and Ettie, Nancy, Susannah and Michael, Dave, and Duke. Miriam was laid out on the couch while Evie massaged her bare feet. The television was tuned to Channel Five, and the caption under the live reporter read, "Riots in Crown Heights."

"You see, Miriam." Evie used her thumbs to apply pressure to Miriam's instep. "What me tell you? He here all safe and sound."

"Oh, my baby," Miriam sobbed. "Come, come to Mommy."

Ben was now fully awake. "Big Ben," he said, "Grace took me on the choo-choo train! And, Big Ben, we saw all the people. And the fire and the penguin people."

"You saw penguin people?" Big Ben asked.

"Uh-huh, and the baby fell out the window, and she put on the wings, and Grace said a bad word."

I was fucked.

"Wow." Big Ben worked his old hands into Ben's curls. Everyone watched. "You had quite an adventure."

"That's what Grace said."

In the pause, the officer's radio squawked, and I jumped.

"Is everything okay, Grace?" It was Dave.

Miriam sat up, and Evie, moving as quickly as she did at the park sometimes, slid to the floor and kept massaging. "Is *Grace* all right? Dave, you fuckin' kidding me?"

"That's a bad word, Mommy," Ben said.

"Okay," the officer said, "so what do we want to do here? Do you want us to take her down?" And I realized he meant me.

"Yes, take her down," Miriam said. "She kidnapped my son."

"Miriam, stay calm," Ettie said.

"Grace, what were you thinking?" Nancy asked.

"And on this night of all nights," Susannah said. "I have never understood anyone from Brooklyn."

"What happened, Grace?" Dave asked.

"There was an accident in Brooklyn, and I had to go. Sol and Miriam, I'm so sorry."

"And she stole our money," Miriam said.

"I borrowed the money. I used it—" I started to explain how I had sent all my money home for my father, and that I had every intention of giving them back their twenty when they paid me, but I was so tired and little Dame was dead. Dead dead. I started to cry.

"Watch the crocodile tears," Evie said.

"Okay, Grace," Sol said, "just leave. Tonight, okay. We trusted you with our son."

I looked at him, and he stopped.

"So you pressing charges?" The officer wanted to be sure.

"Thank you so much for coming," Ettie said. "The family will handle this."

The cops left, and so did Susannah and Michael. I went to my small space, and Miriam came in with me.

"Do you mind if I look in your bag?"

I watched her dump my jeans and shirts, my halter, onto the bed, as she fingered the secret pockets and netted pouches. "Fine." She dropped the empty bag on the bed. "We'll keep the twenty dollars you made today—right? Forty minus the twenty you *borrowed*—until the phone bill comes. If there's anything we owe you, I'll send you a check."

"I don't have a checking account."

"Then take it to a check-cashing place, Grace."

Ettie, Big Ben, and Nancy were gone when I came out. I didn't see Sol and Ben. Duke and Evie sat together on the floral couch, and Dave sat under the sunflower clock. It was just after eleven.

I walked past Miriam's menagerie for the final time. Dave came out with me. "Grace, I am so sorry. Sol came upstairs frantic and I came down with him. Is everything okay? Are you okay?"

I shook my head.

"Look, do you have somewhere to go? You know what . . . Fuck it." He grabbed Sylvia's bag out of my hand and held my elbow. "I'm abducting you. You're staying upstairs tonight."

I didn't argue. How could I? I had no fight left in me. I just followed him to the penthouse where I spent a sad, fitful night. I rose early—I didn't exactly wake up because I didn't exactly sleep. Neither Brutus nor Cesar barked when I left. Dave was still asleep.

"Ahhhh," Danny said as I walked by. "Ladies and gentlemen, Princess Grace has left the building."

Afterward

The headlines were filled with news of the West Indian boy who had been accidentally killed in Crown Heights, about the neighborhood that burned bright for three days as angry black people attacked angry Jews who attacked them right back. But not a word about Dame. Sweet Dame.

I needed to get another job, put another ad in the *Irish Echo,* find another little boy to mind, or maybe a little girl. But I couldn't bear to think about all that, about money and papers and school.

Not yet.

Instead, I lived off Kath. After she'd gone I found that she'd left me $200 under the BeDazzler. Plus she had already paid the rent for a month. Thank you, Kath. Brent had tried to give me money but there was just no way I could take cash from him. Not after what we were doing. He came over often, sometimes in the middle of the day and sometimes late at night, and although I never turned him away, I knew there wasn't ever going to be anything more between us. I didn't ask about his life and we didn't talk about the future, and when he wrote down his beeper number, I threw the piece of paper outside Kath's window.

I went often to the botanic gardens, in the opposite direction on the parkway from Sylvia and the unrest. During the hot hot days there was hardly ever anyone there, and I read under the willows and watched the guys pack compost into the soil around plants my mother grew at home and Dave grew in the sky. When I was homesick for both I went into the humid tropical greenhouse to marvel at the tall papayas and the sugary sapodillas and mangoes fruiting in the middle of Brooklyn.

One evening after I'd left the gardens and was walking toward Kath's room, I thought I heard a bell like the one Leader Elson used to call his Sunday flock at my mother's church. I looked across the street and saw under the yellow and blue bodega awning a lone woman in a long white dress and a tall white head tie, walking in circles and ringing her bell. No one paid her any mind except to avoid her. "The end coming for all of them," she said. "All of them going to burn and who don't burn gone turn into a pillar of salt to salt the coming seas." It was Petal. I looked around for someone to share this with, but of course there was no one. "This America is a wicked, nasty place," Petal continued. "Remember thy father's land and keep thyself pure."

Someone from a window above shouted, "Then shut the fuck up and go back to yo father's land."

Something about Petal scared me. She had worked in the towers and limed with us in the playground and in the Zollers' apartment, and now here she was resurrected as mad as mad can be taking her crazy message to the highways and byways. It was time to make a plan.

Two weeks after the riots, and the Sunday before the big West Indian Labor Day parade—the deadline I had given myself to start getting it together—Kathy's buzzer rang. I didn't answer it because I wasn't expecting Brent, but it rang again and I heard Shivani's footsteps tripping down the hall. A minute later I opened my door to see not only Dave, but Brutus and Cesar.

"Dave! What you doing here? How did you find me? Shivani, this is my friend Dave."

Shivani said, "He hair nice, eh? Thick and curly curly."

I laughed and we hugged. "Come on in, but you're gonna have to leave the boys in the hall. There's no room for them in here."

He looped their leashes around the cold pipe and came in. "Hey, Grace, let me ask you something?"

I pointed for him to sit on Kathy's pouf and got two beers out of the fridge that I always had to walk all the way to Ali's to buy without ID. "What?"

He grabbed a fistful of his fro. "Do I have fucked-up hair?"

I laughed. "What? Your hair is fine, Dave."

"I don't know. The kids downstairs all ran over to pet the dogs and one little girl with these tiny braids asked me how'd my hair get to be like theirs. The *dogs'* hair, Grace."

I knew exactly which little girl had asked him that. "Okay, your hair is a bit high. But how did you find me here? What are you doing here?"

We knocked cheers like old times and Dave took a drink. "Solid detective work. I got a phone bill from Sol and Miriam and called the number you called on the island. A woman answered the phone and said she had to get a message to your mom. Then your sister, who sounds exactly like you, answered when I called back the next day and she gave me your friend Kathy's number. I called Kathy and she told me you were staying in her place in Brooklyn. And voilà, here you are!"

"You're crazy, Dave," I said. But I was so happy to see him. "And Ben's fine, right?"

"Of course he's fine. Riding the subway never killed anyone, except, you know, if they fell on the tracks or got shot or something. Miriam's from Carroll Gardens, for chrissakes."

"Still though, he's their baby."

Dave looked at me. "Grace, you know I couldn't tell you they were buying the house, right? I gave them my word and I couldn't go back on that. But I am sorry."

"Dave, it's okay. It doesn't make a difference now anyhow. How's the garden? Is the frangipani still flowering?"

"Better than that." He pulled something out of his pocket. "Check this out."

"Hey." I looked at the big green emerald nestled in his palm. "Is that a baby papaya? Dave, yay, but why did you pick it?"

"'Course I didn't pick it, it fell off. But yeah, the two new branches are loaded with fruit. You did it, Grace. But that's why I'm here."

"To show me the fruit?"

"To offer you a job. I'm going back to Key West and I need someone to keep the place going. You interested?"

Of course I was interested. "But what about Sol and Miriam? I couldn't live in the towers and—"

"Don't worry about that," Dave said. "They've closed on the house. You won't be running into them unless you take a detour to Duck Hollow."

I couldn't believe my luck. "Really, Dave?" I asked. "Minding plants instead of . . . you know. Oh my God, yes!"

"Good, I was hoping you'd say that. You get to live in the guest quarters and take care of the plants, but you'll have the run of the apartment. You can practice your plantology as you go along."

"When do you want me to start?"

"How soon can you?"

There was nothing keeping me in Brooklyn. Sylvia was lost to me. Micky, Derek, Bo—they were gone and I didn't know where.

"Let me call Shivani and pack up a few things."

I was ready in less than an hour. Shivani kept asking if I didn't want this or that, but it was all stuff left over from Kath and of no value to me. She opened up a cupboard and saw Kath's BeDazzler. "Here, this you have to take. This is a spensive thing."

"You take it," I told her. "Use it to decorate your saris."

"Huh, you wouldn't catch me dead in one of them thing."

"Be good, okay?"

"Okay. Don't forget me, you hear?" I hugged her and we left.

CROWN HEIGHTS LOOKED EXACTLY the same in spite of the recent ugliness. I felt sorry for the big old trees on Eastern Parkway that their job was to divide north/south traffic, and not to be majestic in a forest someplace.

"Dave, stop."

He braked too suddenly and the driver behind us pounded his horn.

"Some more warning, please, Grace."

But I wasn't listening to him. We were about to go past Sylvia's building, and next door at Miss Florence's house I saw the old Russian workman on a ladder and Mutt or Jeff carrying a pigtail bucket of something to throw in a Dumpster parked out front. Jacob was standing in the yard with his hands on his waist under his black jacket looking up at his man Mikhail. Next to him, dressed identically, a boy about Dame's age stacked a red brick tower.

"You want to say bye to someone?"

I looked for a little while longer, but didn't see anyone I really knew.

Acknowledgments

My husband, Grey Thornberry, who never once doubted. Who read when there was only one paragraph written, and praised it. Who supported me, and supports me still. I love you, Star.

I am also honored to thank the following friends:

Nancy Willard, who six years past my graduation told me she'd be interested in reading anything I'd written since Vassar.

My agent, Jean Naggar, who named *Minding Ben* so aptly. Jean, thank you for seeing what my pages could become.

Brenda Copeland, my editor, who with both hands on her waist, tilted her head, sized up the manuscript, and said, "Let me show you what you've got here, Missy."

Susan M.S. Brown, who saw typos I had been staring at for nine years.

Catherine Hoskyns and Sol Picciotto for their quiet refuge in Leamington Spa and their lasting friendship.

Thuy Linh Tu, John Morely, and Melissa F. Zeiger, who each read the manuscript when, with a flourish, I thought it was done.

Sandra Hanson for taking me back how many times, and counting? Cecilia Macheski for being everlasting. Daniel Lynch for encouragement so early on.

The Hunter College Fall 2009 Workshop Class, with Peter Carey at the helm.

Gretchen Gerzina, my mentor from that first class.

Robert DeMaria, because of you, I always get the Swift and Pope questions on *Jeopardy!* Susan Davis for being a champion. I miss you, Ms. Imbrie.

Susan Bethel and Marian Alfonso; every girl needs at least two Kathys.

And Rhonda, my oldest friend in the world (please watch out for jep nest when yuh tiefing people plum).

Nancy Ney and David Rockwell (and Joey!), on whom the Bruckners are not based.

Sally White, this could have gone in a whole other direction, couldn't it?

Trevor Wilkins for finding that tune.

Helen Dekker and Mase-Mase, you guys are exactly what I asked BJ for.

And to go back to the beginning: Pansy Crawford and her family; Sharon Huggins and her family; Lora Speiser and her family.